By Lloyd Kaufman

with Jordan Young and Regina Katz

BearManor Media

2017

Pests
© 2017 Lloyd Kaufman
with Jordan Young and Regina Katz

For information, address:

BearManor Media
P. O. Box 71426
Albany, GA 31708

bearmanormedia.com

Typesetting and layout by John Teehan

Published in the USA by BearManor Media

ISBN—978-1-62933-186-7

Dedicated to my incredible wife Amanda,
for always believing in me; Christina Foxley,
who gave me hope and a chance, and anyone else
that says yes to independent artists.

"YOU TRASHY CUNT!"

She threw a punch square in the jaw of the older, bigger girl. She didn't see it coming. The bigger girl in the pink t-shirt punched the small girl with braided, beaded hair and a white hoodie, in the nose. Without giving her any time to react, she ripped out the smaller girl's tightly knit braids.

"OHHHH, SHIT!"

Three little boys were outside watching the entire thing. They were laughing, pointing, and one was filming them with his iPhone. This was all happening in front of the 7-11 in the Seven Hills strip mall by a church. How fucking perfect is that? It was these three kids flipping out, me keeping a healthy distance, and two tween girls beating the shit out of each other. We were all standing by the free weekly newspaper bins to the far right of the entrance, witnessing this gruesome fight. The cashier reached for the phone. He was the only one who was actually concerned. His eyes were glued on the fight. The cashier was probably calling the cops; who would show up an hour and a half after, survey the situation and say, "Well, there's nothing we can do here." Best and brightest my ass. After hanging up the phone, the cashier shuffled around to the front, locked the door, and ran back behind the counter.

Cars pulled into the lot, then immediately turned back around. I saw one of the drivers mouth "what the fuck" mid U-turn. The girl in white punched the other one in the stomach. While the older girl in pink leaned in to the hit, the little girl did a Chun-Li type of leg sweep, and the bigger girl toppled over. This was absurd, they looked no more than 13, and this was the most devastating fight I've ever seen. Who learns how to fight like this at her age? The girl in pink was down, and the other girl kept kicking her in the stomach and chest.

All I wanted was a coke, and to go home and sleep. Now I have this shit in the way. Stunned, the boys stopped filming. They weren't as boisterous as before, they were scared. Something was seriously wrong here. This huge girl on the ground was coughing up a lot of blood.

"That's what you get for calling me trashy you stupid ho! Mind yo' shit!" This huge girl on the ground couldn't catch her breath.

"What the fuck?"

"This is what you get you big assed nigga! What you fuckin' get!"

The small girl in the white jacket then paused, and looked like she had an idea. She smirked and moved the girl from the sidewalk entryway to the curb. Fuck. I've seen *American History X (1998)* one too many times to witness a curbstomp right in front of my face. I took a deep breath and rushed towards the girl in the now blood-stained white hoodie. Someone had to do something here, and no one else is stepping in to help. I grabbed her arm right as she was raising her leg. She looked back at me with the eyes of someone who was ready to kill with no remorse.

"Listen, you are not about to curb stomp this girl, okay?"

She looked at me with all of the hate that she could muster.

"Who the hell do you think you're touching, white boy, and what the fuck is a curb stomp? I was gonna just leave her in the curb and kick her to make sure she don't mess with me again."

Without being able to respond, I heard a bellowing from the entrance of the convenience store.

"What you doin' to my sister?"

I turned around and saw four huge teenagers. It was some menacing, overgrown linebacker looking dude and his friends. This guy's a monster. With this new group of guys heading towards me, the kids laughing and filming ran like hell.

"I'm helping your sister from what could have been a huge mistake."

He looked at me without blinking. This guy was waiting for me to make one wrong move.

"This could have gotten a lot worse if I didn't step in." He shoved me away from his sister.

"Get your hands off of her. She can take care of herself."

He shot a concerned look at her.

"Who do you think you are anyway? A hero or some shit? With your faggot jumpsuit, you look like some burnout bitch that still hasn't got his dick wet."

Fuck. I forgot what I was wearing. I had on my white, Larson & Sons exterminating uniform with brown scuffs on the elbows and knees. I tried to make a joke of it to calm him down.

"My work clothes—heh—I forgot." He cut me off.

"Did you hear that attitude? My work clothes." He repeated in a mocking voice. His friends got riled up.

"Oooh!"

He stood there with a sneer and folded his arms slowly. He exuded confidence in all the ways I wish I could.

"You know what man, I think we all deserve an apology. Give me whatever cash you have, and we're good, alright?"

"O-ok." I stuttered and shook as I reached into my pocket. I took out my swiss army knife to reach down to my wallet.

He stepped closer to me.

"You thinking about stabbing me, faggot?"

"No, I needed to take out my swiss army knife to reach my wallet!

He cut me off again and pushed my chest. "We only want one thing from you, your money and your cell phone."

He paused.

"Okay, we want two things from you."

"Two things!" One of his jackass friends echoed like any other dumb fucking lackey with no personality; just like that waste of space of Tony fucking Roberts."

"Take whatever you want, just leave me alone."

"Hear that, boys?" My Dikembe Mutmbo sized antagonist looked down at me and smirked. I pictured him waving that monstrously huge finger and shaking his head no.

"We'll leave you alone right after we're done with you. Lyssa, go inside and get a drink. I'll be back in a bit."

He grabbed me by the collar.

"Smile when you walk with me! We gotta put on a good show for the public."

One of his friends dragged me up the block, turned on Biscay and took me across the street to the dried up field of weeds. This was where dumbass neighborhood kids routinely shoot off fireworks and burnt land without a care in the world. The only light around us during this time of night was a street lamp facing the other direction about 50 feet away. It was slightly flickering. This was in a secluded field behind a fenced off housing development at eleven at night. Fuck.

Circling around me, they huddled around a duffle bag. One pulled out a glass bottle, one had a bat, one guy was punching his palm and gritting his teeth at me, the first guy had a knife. This looked like the fight scene from *Blackboard Jungle (1955)*, without the letter jackets and Sidney Poitier.

"Lucky for you, we brought our toys."

He smiled and took a swipe. I sucked in my chest and backed up. The blade grazed my uniform.

"Why are you doing this? I'll give you what you want, just leave me alone."

"Shut the hell up, faggot! It's none of your fucking business, alright? I didn't think you were gonna be the guy to pull a knife on me, so now I gotta show you who's boss."

I looked to my left and saw xeriscaped rocks around the perimeter of the field. If I broke through, I could grab one bigger stone and get in at least one good hit or two. I might have a chance of survival. Everything was still for a brief second. I was getting distracted, I needed a plan.

Logically, it'd be best to throw a punch at the alpha male. If I asserted dominance over him, the others might back down in fear and scamper away. They were chomping at the bit to kill me. There was no way out. I punched him in the stomach with my left, then crossed with my right. He fell hard. Where the fuck did that come from? I've never fought before.

"Wrong move asshole!"

One of them screamed. They surrounded me. A barrage of fists hit me from every direction. I closed my eyes and swung to no avail. The guy with the bat went straight for my calf and knocked out my prosthetic. They couldn't believe it. Everyone was wide eyed and mouth agape. It seemed like this was happening in slow motion. You could see the prosthetic from the calf down twisting and turning up in the air, the joint glinted as it spun. It was almost beautiful for a thousandth of a second. Then, one of the lackeys kicked me with steel toed boots in the rib. I was immediately brought back to reality. One of them had a hand over his mouth, as if I told him his parents were getting a divorce.

"Holy fuckin' shit, bro. You knocked his leg off!"

I couldn't resist what I said next, even though I immediately regretted it. I smirked and pushed myself up from the ground, standing as best as I could with one leg.

"Where's the blood then, you idiot? I'm a transstadial amputee dumbass. Do you know what that means?"

I emphasized that last sentence heavily, probably not a good idea on my part.

"Of course, you fucktards don't know what that means!"

One guy picked it up, smiled, and looked back at me.

"That means that we just got a new toy to use on you." He quickly flipped it, caught the socket, and pistol-whipped me with my own fucking foot.

I'm not too sure what felt worse; the feel of the titanium foot coming across my face, the fact that I could see a couple of teeth knocked out, or how stupid I felt for gloating not even a minute before this happened. In retrospect –if this weren't me—this would have been pretty funny to witness.

Another lackey broke the bottle and proceeded to carve it into my ribs. I felt the tearing of my sinewy muscle. The alpha screamed at the rest of them.

"Hold up!"

He held his clenched, bloodied fist in the air.

"It's my turn to have some fun." He walked closer to me.

"You think this guy's a faggot?"

"Yeah, he's a faggot. What the hell else would he be?"

"This guy, with the dumbass backpack? Yeah, that's a safe bet."

I didn't look at any of them. I choked down the blood in my mouth.

I was panting heavily.

"It's my sprayer. F-for work. I'm an exterminator."

"Yeah? Well, you about to get exterminated, bitch!" One of them said. I tried to push myself up, but I felt one of the put a heel in my back and stomp me down.

"Since you like it up the ass so much, how about we have a little fun?"

The alpha gave a nod to his friend, who picked up the sprayer pack and looked confused.

"Pull down his pants!"

One of the guys grimaced and undid my belt.

"What the fuck are you doing?"

"We're gonna give you a little taste of your own medicine. Spread that ass."

"Whatever man, you are gonna OWE me for this one." He said, pulling down my pants and exposing my pale ass to the world.

I screamed raspily, trying to catch my breath.

"Take my fucking money and leave!"

"Why would we do that? We're just starting to enjoy you." One of them said while holding the sprayer and twirling the handle in his fingers.

Two of the guys pulled apart my butt as far as they could.

"What the fuck is this?" I felt a chill of fear down my spine, and my entire body clenched up.

"Ugh, man! *sniff* What the fuck man?! Yo, Antoine, I'm not doin' this no more if this dude shits himself. That's disgusting!"

Oh great. I'm the guy who shits himself when he's afraid. I'm no better than a fucking house cat.

Antoine looked furious.

"Really, Marcus? Did I tell you that you could use my name? Because of that, you'll keep spreadin' that nasty ass of his. Listen bro, spread his cheeks, jam that fucking sprayer up his ass and pull the trigger and you're done, okay?"

Without any hesitation, one of them jammed it straight up my ass. It felt like I was melting inside. Tears were streaming down my face. I've never felt pain like that before.

"Tie it down so we don't have to look at his ass."

I will never forget the stench of my rectum burning.

"You know what? This is mean. We've gone too far. Why don't we do something nice for him?"

The guys looked confused. He moved closer up to my face, unzipped his pants and whipped his dick out.

"Why don't you go ahead? I'll let you suck it off."

I didn't have any dignity left, but I was not about to do that.

"No. I'd rather be dead."

Wrong answer apparently, I got kicked hard in the ribs. Who the fuck was still wearing steel toed boots? I thought that shit was out of style long ago. Blood spilled down my chin. He picked up the knife again and walked over to me with his dick out.

"That could be arranged, motherfucker! Do you understand me?"

He put the knife up to my throat. When I felt blade against my throat, I started to bawl. The last thing I remembered was him shoving his dick in my mouth. I had a nozzle in my ass, a dick in my mouth, and the icing on the cake was the refreshing knob of a bat to the back of my head.

That was the last moment of agony I had to endure.

SITTING DOWN in the loveseat, she pulled down his pants and whipped out his 10 inch cock and licked her lips.

"Fuck yeah!"

She squealed.

"Where do you think you're going?"

She looked at him with a pouty; make-up caked face while the second black guy turned around, smirked and strutted over to her. He smiled, walked closer to the whore, and whipped out his dick. She smiled, and sprawled herself across the loveseat. She grabbed the second guy's cock, pulled him over by it, spit on his dick and started jerking him off with her hand while the first black guy at the other end of the seat let some spit drop down onto his massive cock, rubbed it up and down, and impaled her pussy without hesitation. He slammed her balls deep with his first pump. She screamed in agony. The second black guy was pushing his cock down her throat. She was gagging; tears were streaming down her face.

The second black guy reached down to slap her tits and pinch her nipples. His hand moved down her breasts, past her pierced belly button, past her four leaf clover tattoos and her short, thin, bright red bush and started to rub her clit while the other black guy fucked her like a hammer. Suddenly, he knelt down and separated her butt and started licking her asshole while jerking himself off. The second black guy stopped gagging her slowly, and started to skullfuck her while pulling her hair. The first black guy, after fingering her gently slid his huge hard cock into her wet, tight asshole. She screamed. The second black guy pulled out of her mouth slapped her across the face and walked in front of the loveseat to fuck this girl, while the other guy spread out her asshole and fucked her harder and harder. He picked up the girl with his dick still inside her ass, sat down on the loveseat, and the other guy forced his dick in her pussy. Her eyes rolled into the back of her head.

As soon as I started to spasm and cum, my Grandma's face came on the screen through the messenger app.

"Have a great day, Philip! Your bubbie loves you!"

This was without question, the saddest orgasm ever. I grimaced in disgust. Thanks for ruining my shit, Grandma. Even all the way across the country, you still can make me miserable. She's not even typing that, it's her fucking helper. Damn that woman.

It's weird, I never used to be into hardcore porn before, but my taste has changed over time. It can't be all softcore with big titted lesbians.

Before I felt too sorry for myself, I took off Melissa, the love of my life. She was the sock I always came into and personally hand washed. I reached under my bed and pulled out the Lysol and unraveled the huffsock. It was very important that I never confused the two. By this point, I was immune to it except for the added chlordane. Once, I added more chlordane than normal and gave myself jaundice. Shit got weird for two weeks. Luckily, no one put those pieces together.

Back in the early 2000s I smoked a lot of weed and watched *Waking Life* (2001). That was the extent of my drug use. I realize now that everyone watched it under the influence of something; maybe that was the point. A couple months after that, I saw *Gummo* (1997). Sure, Harmony Korine made me not want to emulate those kids with all the desaturated colors and unflattering angles he shot them with, but I felt like it was a visualization of how I felt every day. After that I started to use contact cement. I quickly got bored of that and started to experiment with any inhalant that I could find around the house--that wouldn't directly kill me. I sampled until I found the best high I can get.

I got into huffing to avoid all of the garbage around me. A friend of a friend that went by Panda was telling me about it, and offered to give me a call the next time he had some. I started with whippets, but then I went off and experimented with a lot of other things. It felt good to finally be free and not give a shit.

I took the huffsock to my face and shot in two sprays of my mix. Instantly, I felt my eyes dilate. It was like in *Requiem for a Dream* (2000). When I huffed, all the fog around me lifted. I interpreted everything clearly. It was an overwhelming amount of focus and my outlook on life radically changed. It made my mind race, but my body slowed down. I took this time to reflect on stuff I didn't want to think about otherwise.

What am I going to do tonight? This should be a night I go out and do something, not like those other bullshit nights where I say I'm going out. It's going to happen. I'm going to go out to, uh; where do people go out, a coffee shop? That might be fun. Do people meet people at libraries? People meet people anywhere, what am I even talking about? Fuck, who meets people at a library? How lame is that shit? Well, whatever, who cares if it's lame? It's what I want. I'm going to give it a shot. Libraries are the places where I think I can meet a person more like me; reserved, shy, and inhibited. Do I want to meet a person like me, or do I want to meet a person radically different than me? Opposites attract after all right? Right? Stay focused and follow through.

Starting tonight I'll go to the library. I'll meet some people, talk to them, and pick out something. Shit, what type of book should I get when I'm there? Which section should I hang out in? Which is the one section with the girls that will be hot, smart, and a little socially maladjusted? Is that even the kind of girl I want? A girl like me, or do I want a girl that challenges and pushes me? Should I look in philosophy, or, the cultural studies section? I could look in contemporary fiction for a new, complex interpretation of an Antihero. Yeah, that sounds good. Dammit Phil! It's not about the book it's about the book to find the girl in the section.

I'd love to find a girl looking through the film section; it's the only section I ever want to be in. Maybe we will have one of those grabbing the books at the same moment kind of thing and it will be Eisenstein's *Film Forum*, and we could talk for days about his editing theories. Or, I'll casually bring up Dziga Vertov and how he brought those arguments to life in *Man with a Movie Camera* (1929). Then we can go out and watch it together, and, fuck. *Fuck me; I'm getting ahead of myself. What happened to stay focus and follow through? Heh. I'm talking about focusing while getting distracted by a book that expounds on focusing. That's fucking ridiculous. Wait. Fuck. What time is it? Steve is gonna be pissed. He's always pissed and disappointed. Shit. I have a monster headache. I'll grab some Maxalt first.*

I looked down at my phone; it was still paused at the threesome I was watching. *That actress is fucking hot, wonder what else she's in?* I searched her name, Cherry O'Toole, and found some more videos she's done. Before I knew it, I started jacking off for the third time that day: it was 8:30 in the morning. I didn't cum this last time. I knew I needed to start my day. *So much for staying focused.*

I know that huffing has its side effects; like absent-mindedness, brain damage, and death. I've seen *Love Liza* (2002), I can't completely escape my life, nor do I want to. I'm looking for a better way to experience it and this is the lens that I have chosen to view it through.

Dad wouldn't have been proud. It doesn't matter. It's been a little over two and a half years, and since he died I wasn't feeling any better. They kept telling me I'd bounce back. I didn't.

When the settlement came through it wasn't nearly enough for Mom to put me in college; it barely covered legal fees. I thought it would be best to continue the family business. That's what he would have wanted. I had the grades to get into a decent college, but I don't even think it's worth it anymore with student loans as high as they are and the number of available jobs for post-grads being lower than ever. There are a lot of success stories of people who got out of this town, but not me. Not yet, at least. I have to help keep my mom afloat until I move out at least. Business hasn't been good enough to help her pay down the bills, and save up enough for a deposit on a place in a more central location to the work.

I hate it here, the sleepy suburb of Aurora, Colorado; tree-lined streets and mountains to the west and all that. Beyond the beautiful scenery you still had to deal with jackasses; the only difference was, were they rich or poor? The figurative class divide becomes even more literal with the intersection of Park Meadows mall. There is a clearly identifiable poor and rich entrance. One side has the finest couches, fireplaces and marble; while the other side has the Radioshack that's been broken into four times, perpetually changing graffiti on the outside along with a smattering of gutterpunks with Leftover Crack shirts (and a surely manufactured dirty appearance). In spite of their grimy, hole-riddled clothes and skinny dog they brought around to get sympathy money; they always had the newest iPhone. Those trust-fund hippie pseudo-grungy fucks drive me crazy. Boulder is their home base, but some of those scraggly twats make it down here occasionally.

Surrounding Park Meadows, there is a section of four-room family homes in a fixer-upper neighborhood with minor fire damage to most properties. I set my watch to the weekly meth lab explosions. It'd be hilarious if the Craigslist ads for these properties accurately reflected them.

> For Sale: 3.5 Bed 2 bath house in a neighborhood with the highest dropout rate and the lowest performing school districts in the country. Off Street parking to make sure your car will get broken into. Former owner may have hosted Meth Lab. If you're looking for a restoration project, here it is! Doors battered down due to FBI raid, minor damage. Call Vinny to make an appointment. $450,000 OBO.

I need to get moving. I had 20 minutes to get to a house an hour away.

"I'll lie to them about I-25 being really backed up. It's rush hour after all."

I said aloud.

Why did I sound so fucking corny? Why am I even talking right now?

I finally got up, dressed, and headed to the garage. I got into mom's 1999 Tercel and turned the keys. Her classic rock station started blasting. I grimaced and turned it down, but kept it on to drown out the normal traffic noise. A lot of people place the value of music in the resolving harmonies, but when I was more into music, I was a lot more invested in the dissonance. Without the dissonance, the resolving chords are not poignant. The noise I loved in music was quickly replaced with the power of visual dissonance. I'll never forget watching Ingmar Bergman's *Persona* (1966) and getting completely absorbed in the first five minutes. I must have watched that sequence six or seven times in immediate repetition. Those non-sequitur quick cuts were spellbinding.

I'll never be able to tell you the meaning of those shots, and I can never express to anyone how happy that makes me.

In life there aren't always answers, and that's just something that we need to accept. The difference between all these art forms was that music could help you understand emotions and moments where language failed; words and compelling narratives can satiate wanderlust and the desire for knowledge in general; and with film, well, film is the only art form that doesn't have to be held accountable for its actions. It can leave you with no answers whatsoever, and that's perfectly acceptable.

Every day that I crossed Alameda, I went from the "well off" side of the street to the shithole side of the street. You know how they always warn you about the wrong side of the street? Well that's wrong, it doesn't really matter where you are; people are garbage everywhere.

I've seen quite a bit of horrific shit at people's homes. It doesn't matter where they ended up on the socio-economic ladder. Unlike the Mac loving zombies that work at a computer repair store, if I see porn, I don't have to report it. I can choose what I want to do. It's a different response every time. 75% of the time I ignore it. 25% of the time I look through it. However, if I ever came across a serial killer's underground sex dungeon/buffet table, I would probably do something; I just don't know what. Why do I go on people's computers? Well, why fucking not?

By the time I got there, Uncle Steve was leaning against his van looking impatient. The logo still read Larson & Son. Seeing that logo, kicked my ass everytime. He nodded at the canister of Chlordane at his feet.

"I know you were running low from last session."

"Thanks, Uncle Steve, sorry I'm late. There was more traffic than I expected on I-25. I shouldn't have taken it."

"Boy, if you weren't my nephew, I would've fired you by now."

I rolled my eyes.

"Okay, I get it. I'm sorry." I grabbed the canister and took a step towards the house. I quickly turned around.

"Oh, before I go, what's the call for today? "

"Spiders, termites, and box elders."

"Cool. Are you sticking around?"

He sighed, "Phil, you know I only show up here because you aren't fully licensed yet. Just take the damn test. Please?"

"I'll work on it, Uncle Steve, I promise." *I'll do it when you change the name of the company, you inconsiderate asshole.*

"Is it a money thing? I could lend you some cash if you want."

He gave me a concerned look. That same concerned look that I get from most people. They care or whatever, but I'm sick of seeing that shit. He grimaced and looked as if he were about to spout platitudes.

"It's frustrating to me, Phil. You have so much untapped potential."

There it was. The elephant in the room that Uncle Phil always called out. This was the crux of all the arguments I had with anyone in my family. Everyone forgets that it's my potential. I can choose to use it or not. It's not anyone's to discuss.

Steve shifted uncomfortably.

"I don't have time for this whole thing again. I need to go. I'm heading up to Blackhawk today with Beth!" He said with a huge smile. He expected me to be impressed by this, but I couldn't give less of a shit where he went with that bitch. He looked exactly like any other skeezy old guy going to Blackhawk; the Reno of Colorado.

"If you need anything, well, I'll have bad reception up there. I'll try to call you back when I can."

"Alright, Uncle Steve. Have fun, and tell Beth I said hi and that I miss her!"

That lie lingered in my mouth like halitosis. It was bad and I knew it.

"Will do, buddy. See ya!"

I fucking hate Beth. She is completely see through and nothing about her is genuine. Uncle Steve met his glorified arm candy and year and a half ago. Both of them have been through the ringer of divorce, and have no plans on remarrying.

I walked up in the driveway and assessed the house. Beige, aluminum sided, brick walkway to the door, grass perfectly trimmed, it was the type of house that you would see in any commercial for the newest antidepressant on the market, with a rising sun in the background and inoffensive acoustic music throughout. My instructions for this house were to spray the "problem areas"; the living room, the basement, and the perimeter. A typical job for a typical house. The one cool thing about this job was searching around other people's houses.

On the inside, it was nothing but colors that bled together and inoffensive corporate art that looked like a sad Rothko rip-off. In the living room bookcase, on the second shelf up from the floor, there was a centerpiece portrait of a waspy family with 2.5 kids that were straight out of a Sears catalog. Nothing about this was genuine. The dad with slick, combed hair wearing the dark blue and white striped polo shirt; the mom with the excruciatingly botoxed face, pearly whites, and cropped blonde hair; the son wearing a sports jersey, for his little league where he was praised an inappropriate amount for his athletic prowess—that annoying, perfect little fuck- and the little girl with her cutesy gapped-tooth smile and pink shirt.

I decided at this point, I needed to give them names lame enough to match their photos. They looked like they were the model family in whatever bullshit-peddling, multi-cam sitcom that was likely to die after 2 weeks on whatever network this fall. Anyway, for the names of our Nielsen bait of a family; for the dad, the easy answer is Mark. Mark is a solid boring-ass, middle of the road name. The wife needed a Christian friendly name. She was one of those women that had her life turned around when she found God less than a decade ago, Emily. My best guess for their kid's names is the something annoyingly modern, Clayton and Kaylee.

I looked around the living room for any termite damage. I checked the corners, and the windows up top. Nothing. As a precaution, I sprayed by the doors leading outside. I can't believe this call is for box elders. These bugs are harmless and disease free. Sure, they have a mild stench, but that's it. I went outside and saw a couple of box elder bugs by the fence. If you need to kill some boxelder bugs, stabilize them with laundry detergent, and get out your vacuum. This isn't as torturous a method as salt on a snail, but it is a way put them in a state of paralysis. They are pretty slow creatures regardless, but if you have any trouble disposing of them, this is the best way to do it. I found a vacuum in the cupboard in the kitchen and took care of them. It's also important that you throw the bag away so they don't continue to stink up the place.

I could patch up the hole in the kitchen—the reason they were getting inside in the first place- but I'll leave that to the other pseudo-professionals. I hate vacuuming and cleaning shit in general, so it's pretty ironic that most of the time I get paid to do it for a living.

I took off my sprayer and put it on the floor. I looked to see if there were any other signs of bugs. I got my mini flashlight and shined it under the couch. I saw a shoebox. I put my gloves on and pulled it out. Easing off the cover, It was a dusty shoebox full of old Polaroids. All of these photos were of Emily on the kitchen table getting gangbanged by four guys while the husband was in a chair behind the train of men fucking his wife, jacking off and licking his lips, while wearing a cockring. After seeing this, why not investigate more? Emily was fucking hot.

In the living room there were a couple bookcases and a TV. I browsed the bookshelf, like I always did in people's homes. You can learn a lot about a person by seeing what they're reading. As I scanned the shelves, I noticed that there were a lot of the topical, and of the moment books. None of them had any longevity. John Waters got it right when he said "If you go home with somebody, and they don't have books, don't fuck them!" To no surprise, it looks like Emily's attempting to be preoccupied with Oprah's books, and a Mark looks like a boring uninspired prick. That explains how he prefers watching his wife get plowed as opposed to doing the plowing.

The kitchen was nothing to write home about. I explored the cabinets and only saw white dishes, black mugs, and clear glasses. Although I did find a pretty choice liquor cabinet.

Is that Green Label Johnny Walker? Nice!

I poured myself a very tall glass on the rocks. I took a step over to the fridge to use the automatic ice maker. The whiskey splashed up out of the glass and on my uniform. Why was it set to shaved ice? Who the fuck even invented that? I need a billion dollar dumbass idea like that to get me out of this hell.

I topped off my glass and sat down at the kitchen table. *I wonder if every family's kitchen encounters were as awkward as my own.* I looked down at the corner of the kitchen door and saw one more box elder. This was already shriveled up and dead. Out of all the bugs I kill, the box elders are collateral damage. People would rather have an exterminator be a "one and done" type of scenario. They normally give me a list of bugs they want me to remove. Box elders are the last to be mentioned; an afterthought, an annoyance. The customers never need them killed, but it's always requested. I feel bad for these bugs. I'm sure I'd be an afterthought as well. These are the only bugs that deserve my mercy. I kill them humanely. Only them. Fuck those other bugs; they don't mean shit.

Picking up the bottle and the shoebox, I went to the kid's rooms. *Did I just have two full glasses of whiskey? Who cares. What else do I have to do today anyway? I'll just make some coffee before I head home.* I took a swig from the bottle and moved on. Upstairs on the left, I found Clayton's room and went inside. This was the trophy kid. Literally, he had shelves of them: karate, soccer, spelling bees, and little league. I hate this kid and I haven't even met him. He is one of those "everything is easy" pre-alpha male little bastards. I'm sure Mark calls him sport. I shudder thinking about it. Regardless, his room is way too clean for a kid Clayton's age. There is no way bugs can be in here, so I figure, why bother? Actually, looking around a bit more, it looked like Uncle Joey's room from *Full House*. Wait a second, what does that say about Uncle Joey?

The next room was Kaylee's. Exactly how I imagined it, bright pink, and slathered with One Direction posters. This was a tween girl's room with all the accoutrements, complete with *Twilight* books and other relics of an earlier version of Kaylee as well. I dove on the twin bed and took another shot from the bottle. I took out the photo of Emily and checked it out again, she was everything I wanted. Obviously, she's adventurous. She was a sexy blonde with a great body, full of confidence and life. I got a semi-hard and started to rub myself. "PIIIIIIIII-KAAA-CHUUUUUUUU".

What the fuck?

I looked to where the sound came from and there was a bright yellow Pokémon clock right above a Sleepover puppy staring right at me. It was a dead-on, instant boner killer of a stare. The Sleepover puppy realized how much of a sick fuck I am.

I did the only obvious thing to do in this scenario. I took the shoebox, placed it on Kaylee's bed, pocketed my favorites, discarded the rest and put the box underneath her bed. I took one last, sweet swig of whiskey, and put the bottle there as well. I smiled and thought about how much fun that conversation would be. Kaylee seriously needs to reconsider how her room looks if she ever wants to get laid. I'm sure she's getting trained to be a waspy solipsist just like her bitch of a mother.

One thing I liked about this job is the power trip I get when killing bugs. It was analogous to playing *Grand Theft Auto*. I didn't care about the missions. My job was about killing the highest amount of bugs in the shortest amount of time in the most inhumane way possible. I loved finding nests and obliterating them. Every house was a new level with different limitations and challenges.

The main part of a job is sealing the perimeter and making sure nothing escapes. This is exactly as boring as it sounds. Spraying the windows, doors, and walls. The first part of my attack depends on what I was told to kill first. Cockroaches are normally in more humid spots like bathrooms and kitchens. How can you not sympathize with them, when all they really want is warmth and food? These sons of bitches don't make it easy on you to kill them either. They hide during the day, and can stay alive for 3 months without food. They are very similar to us, aside from the longevity and universal hatred. Plus, we don't make the best crunching noise when we are stepped on; they do.

I sprayed around the exposed pipes and down the spouts. It's overkill to do both, but, then again in *Grand Theft Auto*, my favorite part of the game is getting into a car with a hooker, having sex with her for "points", driving the car off a dock with her still in it, and rolling out at the last possible second.

For spiders, they find great hiding place like the cracks and holes in the walls. A really quick fix for those holes is a little wood screw with some paint on it. If they are hiding in there, you get a nice, satisfying, crunch if you shove in your filler fast enough. Unfortunately, most of the time they burrow pretty deep into these walls. It did happen once though, and it felt amazing. I didn't see any holes in Mark's room, but maybe they were in some other spots in the house.

I retraced my steps through Clayton's and Kaylee's rooms looking for these holes. I found a mini nest of spiders in Kaylee's closet. These were a lot of fun to kill, it's not nearly as gratifying as it appeared in the scene from *Arachnophobia* (1990) when Jeff Daniels burns that huge nest, but it still feels pretty good. I reached for my spray gun and slowly got up to the height of the nest. I pulled out the flashlight with my other hand, and gently pressed on the trigger while I shine a light on them. I do this because it's hilarious to see their last moments. They writhe in agony, shrivel, and immediately tense up as if it were the visualization of a death rattle. They call those post-mortal convulsions. *Huh, that is a great metal band name.* I'm getting chills down my spine from the joy I get from killing these little monsters. The most life affirming thing you can do is watch something die.

* * *

I DECIDE I should spray around Kaylee's window, but do a half assed job. That way, they can smell that I've been working so they wouldn't question it. The reason they called me here was for termites, found in wooden basements or attics. Normally, those are my last stops before I trace the exterior.

I walked down to the basement, imaging my next kill. With termites, I have to imagine their death. As soon as I head down to the damp, unfinished basement, I can see the bites on the studs that hold the insulation. The basement was empty aside from one uncovered mattress on the floor. *Weird. Did I just enter a sex dungeon?* There is no frame, no blankets, and no pillows. There was only one mattress with some huge tears and stains. Why would anyone have that? I wander over to the boxes to see what else this place was hiding. Old clothes, toys, baby stuff; pretty disappointing. There was a box up against the side of the wall next to the leaky water heater which was lopsided.

"What's in the box?" I imagined Brad Pitt screaming. *Man, I should watch that movie again, it's been awhile.*

Hesitating, I walked over to that box and chills ran down my spine. That wasn't a fucking box. That was a mound of termites. How do you neglect a house so much, that you don't even realize a fucking mound of termites? I've seen general laziness and in some cases hoarders, but this was a first.

Unbelievable. We're in Colorado. This whole god damn state is in a drought, but your leaky water heater in the basement has enough moisture in the room for a mound to develop? As I looked closer, I realized there was a fist-sized hole between the crack in the cement panels that lead to dirt. That's an impressive amount of neglect.

Getting closer to the floor, I saw all the workers in a row leading to the stairs, stripping them for nourishment. You can tell that they're workers because the only other ones that venture outside of the mound are the soldiers. I'm looking at a micro-scale commute. We aren't that different from these bugs. They have workers, soldiers who sacrifice everything, the queen, and the bugs trying to fuck the queen. Humanity has soldiers, workers, lovers and leaders too; we just think we are less vulgar than insects.

Like our frontline equipped with semi-automatics, the soldiers on this concrete slab next to me have huge red pincers for attacking. Normally, they are incognito, and wouldn't appear in the middle of the day in a conspicuous place waiting to attack. Their inflamed and engorged head is an easy tell. They look like an aggravated retro video game boss after you attack them. Weirdly, these warriors can't even feed themselves. Workers have to break down the food for them. That's how strong their sense of community is. In addition to giving a homeless person your food, you'd be cutting it up into little tiny squares while counting the number of times they chew each morsel to make sure they don't choke. What a bizarre world that would be.

What was I doing? Oh, right.

I took out some carbamate acid from my utility belt, and doused the mound. I walked back upstairs, looked in the drawer underneath the liquor cabinet and found a matchbook. I went back downstairs and the mound had sprawled out horizontally on the floor. This was reminiscent of that devastating crane shot in *Gone with the Wind* (*1939*), with all of the dead and wounded soldiers. I put on my gloves and walked up to the collapsed mound. I made sure to spray directly in the center of it. Most were already dead, but to be sure, I took a match in my left hand lit it and threw it in. I sprayed one last time to catch the flame, then I watched the fuckers burn. This was a very gratifying kill; a quick and heartless mass genocide. I imagined thousands of barely audible screams. I smiled with relief and pride. Flames can be very soothing and cleansing.

I was proud of this beautiful purging of innocent termites. Mission accomplished. Uncle Steve would kill me if he knew how much time I wasted with this massive overkill. I swept up the mess and thought about throwing it away. I looked down at the ash and realized they wouldn't notice if I cleaned it or not. They didn't notice the mound after all. I figured; eh, why bother?

While driving back home, I realized that I passed all of my former schools along the way. Every drive I had, I realized how little progress I made with my dreams. I pulled over and looked at the school for a second. My high school sat on the top of a hill. At the base of that hill was my middle school. A couple blocks down from that, still in my eyesight bit furthest away was my elementary. These buildings looked more along the lines of prisons or community centers as opposed to the idealism and hope they should represent. Weren't schools at one point and time supposed look like they commanded respect? These schools did not fall under that category.

I was a hyper kid desperately seeking attention that shied away from it when it was received. In retrospect, I was the kid that would always ask questions about everything, even if I didn't care to hear what the answer was. Everything was a puzzle that I almost deciphered, but never comprehended. I hated thinking about how annoying I used to be.

Equidistant between the two properties was my middle school. This was the place where I was ostracized and alienated the most. I was an outcast, specifically because I was a half-heartedly practicing Jewish kid surrounded by a bunch of Mormon people. By no means was I a zealot. I practiced because that was what my parents wanted. Hell, I still don't even know the fundamentals of Judaism. What happens when we die if we don't believe in heaven or hell?

I can't concretely say if it was my choice to be ostracized or not. Was I angry at the situation itself, or only my perceived injustice of it? This place helped me become the miserly fuck that I am today.

At the top of the hill was my high school. Here, I outgrew giving a shit, and gave in to sweet, sweet apathy. My freshman year was full of optimism and all that new start bull that we tell ourselves. I made a small amount of friends, only to realize they were using me.

I worked two jobs to save for school trips and to start a college fund. There was multiple times where my parents would let my friends over to my place before I got home. After coming home tired as hell at 11:45, mom out of town, dad out with his friends, I would walk in and see that my place was trashed. In addition to property damage that I would have to pay, couples I never met before had sex in my bed and left. It turned into everyone's private fuck palace. This was infuriating considering I was a virgin with zero prospects. Mom was a woman that liked distractions. If people came to the door asking to come in, she would routinely let them in, pour them a drink and assumed that I wanted to see them, that was never the case.

It's funny how I always thought that I would be at my happiest when I was free of high school. Now I've grown to be even more isolated and the few friends I had got out of this fuckhole of a city long ago. I grimaced, and then got back in the car.

I pulled in my driveway and saw an ad posted on a telephone pole by my neighbor's lawn. Normally, it was a lost cat that I'd inadvertently killed while I was spraying. The cat would be hiding underneath the deck, or deep in the kitchen cabinets, four out of five times these cats would turn up dead within a week of my spraying. This ad was different.

Do you feel alone? Are you tired of being left out? Are you experiencing high anxiety and use drugs recreationally? Well head on down to the basement of Olin Hall at the University of Colorado, and sign up for a medical experiment!! After this study has commenced; not only will you finally feel comfortable with yourself, but we will pay you six hundred dollars! Call Dr. Thompson on Thursday, the fifth, and take control of your life!

This is the same kind of universal appeal that is repeated ad nauseum on all of late night infomercials—are you having trouble getting to sleep at night?

This one, however, struck a chord with me. I could use a change of mindset, maybe it would help get me out of here. That's two days from now. I don't have any appointments. I can do that! I can get $600!

I grabbed the tear-away phone number and felt a stabbing pain. I had a splinter. I tried pulling it out with my fingernails. That didn't work. I took out my house keys and dug in to my hand to fish it out. I ended up deeply cutting my palm. Blood started to fill into the newly opened wound. I wiped it on my uniform and put the ad in my pocket.

There are some people in life that think about what's next. I'm always in the moment. The problem is, I get completely overwhelmed with what I can and should be doing. I'm sick of not accomplishing anything. Maybe if I did one of those daily checklist things, I could see what I did each day and feel better. Then again, jacking off 5 times and huffing three times each day are not exactly checklist worthy. I'm overdue for a change and that experiment might be the answer. I opened the door. My mom was directly behind it. I jumped back.

"Jesus, Mom, you scared the hell out of me!"

She stared at me, dead eyed.

"Clean your room or I'm going to make you do your own damn laundry."

She scowled at me again. I smiled exceedingly hard, and sarcastically.

"Love you too, mom. Going to my room now!"

I didn't even entertain her shit anymore. I ran downstairs and dove into my bed. I don't know what triggered it, but my mind drifted off to when I was watching a documentary at my friend Dan's house about The Beatles. It finally got to their experimental phase with *The White Album*, and in the background played George Harrison's first sitar experiment, "Within You Without You." I paused it.

"So Dan, if you ended up a grungy addict after doing drugs, but you would create something amazing, would you still do it?"

He concentrated and scratched his chin.

"You know, Phil, being a famous artist would probably be as cool depicted, if not better, but you have to think about if it would be all worth it in the end. Are you going to be remembered as the amazing artist like George Harrison, or are you gonna be remembered as the dude who forced a girl to have sex with a shark? There is always going to be unforeseen consequences. Could I be the next Hemingway, or would I be remembered as a bitter, out of touch old man? Or even worse, if I got into meth, would I be remembered as methhead Dan?"

I remember laughing for a good ten minutes after that. Unfortunately for him that nickname stuck. *When was that? Three, four years ago now?*

I tried to shake the memory off and looked around the walls in my room. This was place where I could relax and ignore everything. When Mom brought laundry to my room, she attempted to make me decorate it. She left notes saying, "Can you make it look like someone lives here? That would be a welcome change." I put all of my equipment away, and sat on my bed and went online, I wanted to see if there was anyone on that would talk. I checked my *Second Life* account, Tumblr, Facebook, and there were no notifications or messages. Nothing. I then decided to head on the message boards and movie blogs. Oh shit.

George Fucking Lucas, the last stand out for major independently owned franchises—not good ones in his most recent work—just sold Lucasfilm to Disney? That's a shame.

What the hell happened to integrity? Something needs to be done about this megastudio system. There are unique visions of movies out there, and unfortunately, they all get churned out and amalgamated for broad audience that devours garbage with the same tropes and scenarios that Joseph Campbell painstakingly documented.

* * *

I HEARD Methhead Dan honk outside; I smiled knowing that wherever the night took us, we'd have a good time. I jumped out of my bed, ran upstairs and shut the door to the basement. My mom was on the couch watching TV as usual.

"See ya, mom."

"Okay, tell Dan I said hello."

"Will do. Later!"

I ran out the door. As I was illuminated by his headlights, Dan honked again. I knew he saw me; he was just fucking with me. I jumped at how loud it was. I flipped him off as I walked over to his passenger side.

"Sup bitch? Did you poop yourself a little when I honked at you?" He laughed.

"Very mature as usual, Dan. One day, that won't be funny."

"Fortunately, that hasn't happened yet."

I rolled my eyes and smirked. He was right and I knew it. Methhead Dan got annoyingly cocky sometimes, but generally, he was a good dude.

"Come on, Phil, you know I'm kidding."

He turned up the radio to a deafening level. I think its Notorious B.I.G. He started nodding and rapping along. He's still fucking with me. As soon as he pulls out of the driveway, he turns it down, adjusts himself in the seat, and looks at me with a very serious face.

"Hello, Phil. How are you this lovely evening? It's a beautifully starry night, don't you think so?"

"How 'bout you shut up and drive, Dan. You sure you aren't drunk already?"

"Not yet, man. Let's go get started on that!"

Dan changed the station. He put on some over the top 80s cock-rock station that we both like and we drive with windows down while enjoying the breeze. I respected Dan, no matter how off the walls weird he was. He's the guy who's willing to do anything to make people laugh.

"So what's the plan for tonight, Methhead?"

"Well, I was thinking of going to Wings and Things, and then there are a couple of parties we could go to. Or, if you aren't feeling that, we could chill out at my place."

"Okay, cool, man, sounds good."

"To which one?"

"Oh. Right, an answer would help, wouldn't it? Well, let's go out and we'll see how we feel."

"Cool man, sounds good."

I smiled at him, turn away, and roll my eyes. I'm never in the party mood. Dan was my connection to a lot of these people that I otherwise don't give two shits about. He always guilts me into going. Any party experience I've ever had is exactly the same. Small talk with some assholes I haven't seen for a while for the first 30 minutes. Followed by me drinking alone and trying to fit myself into conversations with those same people for the next hour or so, then convincing Dan to leave the party. Sometimes it's longer when he is desperately hitting on a girl, which never works out.

We pulled into the Wings and Things parking lot and saw Kacey standing outside smoking. She flicks her cigarette on the ground, then stomps it out. She smiles and runs over to us. I loved that smile.

"I was wondering when I'd see you two next!"

She walked towards us motioning for a hug.

Kacey was a very slender brunette with a smile that you don't forget. It's genuine, yet full of secrets. Fun to flirt with and impossible to understand, Dan and I jokingly called her the Kobayashi Maru. Like the test that made Captain Kirk of the U.S.S. Enterprise so legendary, Kacey was a no-win situation. You could never figure her out. Is she telling the truth, or is she captivating you with one of her million lies? The world may never know. Also like the test, few people have figured out a loophole that I can't even begin to fathom.

In addition to being friendly with us, she was able to get us some drinks before we were legal. That was a win-win situation; I'd hit on her, and Dan would score some booze. Conveniently, after we both got a buzz, I gained confidence and Dan would assign himself to wingman duties. We were a team that worked well together. Dan walked over to her first.

"What's up, Kac?"

I followed up meekly with a wave.

"Hey, Kacey. Good to see you." She looked at me and laughed.

"You're not getting away from me that easy!" She reached over, hugged me and kissed my cheek. *What was I thinking? Hello Kacey, Good to see you? Is this a job interview? What am I saying?* I tried to have some semblance of calm, cool, and collected. That clearly was not working. She was comfortably leaning up against the rugged brick wall, to the best of her abilities. *Another great metaphor for the type of person that she is.*

"So what's up, guys? Joining my section tonight?"

"That's the plan," Dan said enthusiastically.

Maybe he had a thing for her too? Son of a bitch.

"Okay, I'll be inside in a bit. Tell Tina, the new hostess, that we're friends and she'll sit you with me." Kacey then mumbled something, but we could hear her say "bitch" between her otherwise incoherent ramblings.

"Alright, we'll see you in a sec."

"See you soon, Kacey. Sorry to bother you on your break." She looked confused.

"You weren't interrupting anything! I'll see you in a bit."

Kacey walked away to light up another cigarette. Dan whispered to me, "Nice."

"Fuck you Dan."

We walked into the restaurant, and were greeted by a blonde and a frighteningly tan girl with a huge smile and a Tina name tag.

"Hey, welcome to Wings and Things. How can I help you to-day?"

She didn't seem like a bitch at all. Dan and I looked at each other. He clenched his fist and whispered.

"Kobayashi."

"Party of two, for Kobayashi?"

Starry eyed Tina was totally oblivious. I snorted and laughed.

"Not quite. We're actually friends of Kacey. Could we sit in her section?"

"Okay, great!" Tina says, still smiling.

"Right this way. Isn't Kacey the greatest? She's so sweet!"

"She's, uh, She's something alright." Dan says rolling his eyes.

"She'll be with you in a bit."

Tina walked us down the main aisle to our table, smiling and making eye contact with us the whole way. She wasn't doing that server thing where she was flirting with everyone. Tina seemed genuinely nice.

"Okay guys, here you are. Is this table alright?"

"This is great, Tina, you've been more than accommodating, thank you." Dan responded, cordially.

"Of course, any friend of Kacey is a friend of mine! Enjoy your meal and nice meeting you!" She walked away and waved. I gave Dan a confused look.

"What the hell was that? She seems like the exact opposite of what Kacey said." Dan looked perplexed.

"Yeah. I don't know. Maybe we didn't understand that there was a comma in Kacey's sentence. Also, who was the bitch?"

Dan smirked it me.

"It always has been, and always will be you."

That night was so vivid to me.

I woke up with crippling pain under bright fluorescent lights with a song in my head.

⋆ ⋆ ⋆

"**WHAT** seemed like dreams are really nightmares
What seemed like fiction's really real
When my brain won't take in what my eyes say they've seen
Then we've surely reached the end"

Who is that again? Is that? yeah, I think that's the Stiff Little Fingers.

I haven't listened to that in, five years. Ever since, wait, where the hell am I? I smelled an antiseptic, abrasively clean scent. It had no distinct smell. Fuck. What is this, a hospital?

The room was the typical light blue and beige with the designless large beige tiled floor.

"Jesus, he's finally awake! Doctor, get in here. Stay right here young man, don't move a muscle!" *This poor fucking kid.*

"Wh—what did you say?" The nurse looked a little annoyed, and overemphasized her words. "I said, do not move, a muscle, the doctor will be right in!" *I hope that was slow enough for him to understand me.*

I nodded in agreement. I didn't see her lips move, but I recognized her voice again. *Maybe I'm hearing things? What the hell am I on? My body feels weighed down, like i'm under 500 lbs of pressure.*

The doctor arrived in the room.

Okay deep breath, how am I even going to tell this kid what's going on with him? We've never seen anything like this.

My eyes focused in. I heard what he said, but I was sure his lips weren't moving while he said it. *Is there someone else in this room with me?*

"First off, do you know who you are? What's your name?"

"Phil Larson."

"Ok, good. Who's the president?"

"Barack Obama."

"Well Phil, you sound okay, thankfully. They really did a number on you didn't they? How are you feeling?"

"Alright, a little sore actually."

Aaron, be honest with him, there's no shame in that.

Where was this other voice coming from?

"Doctor, I'm sorry, I didn't catch your name. What was it?"

"Oh! Terribly sorry about that, I didn't introduce myself, my name is Aaron Faeber. Phil, I'll be honest with you, you came in barely alive and we have never seen anyone with your symptoms before. Frankly, it's a miracle you're here. I wanted to check with you and see what's the last thing you remember?"

I was enraged at the mere mention of it. I clenched my fist and my eyes were welling up with tears.

"That, that kid, and, what he did to my mouth."

This poor fucking kid.

"Well, they weren't quite done with you yet. After that, they beat your head in pretty good with a bat and a rock they found. We had to do extensive, reconstructive, experimental surgery." He cleared his throat and shifted in his seat.

Come out with it, man. You aren't doing him any favors by stalling.

"What I'm trying to say is that physically, you are fine. We had to bring in a specialist, Dr. Thompson, to operate. He used some methods I wouldn't have; but you appear to be in great shape. Also, it's best to refer to specialists in, well, unique cases such as yours."

I cut him off.

"So how bad am I, doctor?"

"Well, the damage done was mainly only skin deep, but with all this restructuring that happened to your skull and brain, we don't know what to expect from you mentally. Additionally,"

Here comes the hard part.

"Wait, what was the last thing that you said?"

My god, the signs of damage are already showing.

"The last thing I said was, we don't know what to expect from you mentally. Let me be honest with you Phil: the reconstruction, and all the exposure from the gas that was coursing through your body, left you in an extremely unique position that we haven't really seen before. To be perfectly clear with you, your brain might be capable of things that you previously weren't, and similarly, you might be incapable to do things you previously could do. We have no idea."

It's a hard pill to swallow, but I think I did okay telling him that. Let's see what he says.

"What's, what the hell is that?"

"Are you hearing any other voices? It's you and me in here, isn't it? Will I need some pills or something?"

Dr. Faeber's eyebrows raised curiously.

"No. No pills, just take it easy. There is another patient behind the dividing curtain. Why? What did you hear?"

"I don't know something about a pill and a swallowing? Don't worry about it." The doctor looked concerned.

He's still coming off of heavy medication, the poor kid is hearing things.

"Well Phil, you are coming down from some pretty heavy medication so I wouldn't worry about it yet. Why don't you try to get some more rest?

"That sounds like a good idea, doctor, I think I will."

That went a lot better than I thought. Although, it seemed like he preemptively knew what I was going to say. Ha! That'll be the day. Well, on to lunch I guess.

I turned my head to follow him out of the room. As soon as my head turned to a 45 degree angle, I felt extremely sharp pain.

Not going to be doing that again anytime soon, shit that hurt!

One that made me immediately wince and grit my teeth. I'm thinking I shouldn't do that. *What the fuck was that all about? It was like I was hearing his thoughts or something?*

"Nurse! Nu-u-rse!" I yelled. "I have a question!"

"Yes?"

"Is the doctor still available? I thought of another question to ask him."

"Oh. I'm sorry dear, I believe he stepped out to lunch, is there anything I can help you with?"

Holy, fucking, shit. This is really happening; I can read people's minds now?

Phylum

THIS WAS a life changing moment. I was just another number to them, as I stood here sweating furiously in my tux.

"We will now see anyone with the last name beginning with L through O. Once again, if your last name starts with an L or an O, they are ready to see you now."

There was five of us that stood up, instruments in hand. The one towards the O side of the line was pretty cute. A brunette with a nose ring and an asymmetrical haircut. But what punk girl that plays the clarinet? Punks normally play bass or percussion. We all were nervous, but I was a walking disaster. The last thing that this girl would want to see.

Okay Phil, drop the bullshit at the door and go in that room with confidence. I know I can do this, I've been to group auditions before, and I've gotten into regional orchestras without problem, this is just another audition; even if it is for your dream school.

I walked in confidently and assembled myself in line. There were three professors at the table at the base of the auditorium, all tweed wearing; exactly what you would assume a music professor to look like.

"Recite your names."

I couldn't be bothered to learn the other's kids names, except the cute punkish girl's name was Marissa.

"Phil."

I mumbled that off almost unintelligibly, but I think they got the point. One of the professors adjusted his tiny glasses.

"Okay, now let's all start with scales. We all want to make sure that you know your key signatures. Jason, let's start with you. Play us an B major scale."

Jason took a breath and started to play, he was adding vibrato on to everything and elongating the scales for added emphasis. *This jerk is showing off for no reason. I couldn't believe he was trying to be a diva during a fucking scale. Calm down man, save that for your audition at least. In addition to that, he was still pitchy! How do you botch that?*

"Thank you, Jason. Well done."

Well done?

"Phil, play an A minor scale, if you would be so kind."

I took a breath and adjusted my reed. I was going to present them with a standard quarter note, eighth note scale, without any bells or whistles or anything.

I started to play, and I kept it at a slow tempo, making sure I think through, and sink the landing of each note. During my second to last note I got cut off.

"That will be enough, you may leave."

"What?" I said incredulously. "How did you let that guy finish?"

One of the more paunchy professors stood up.

"Because although his presentation was uncommon, he didn't cut short one of his notes by an entire thirty-second note. That will be all."

"Sir, I'm sorry. As you can imagine I'm very nervous, can I at least play my audition piece?"

As I was saying this a vein on his neck watching twitching.

"No. First off, I don't need to see what you can do. I already know that the youth orchestra I conduct has a better sense of timing than you do. Secondly, you can go home right now, and practice for eight hours a day for a year. Then, you can come back and try again. Don't waste all of our time with your unworthy audition. Good day."

I shot Marissa a quick look, and she returned a look of disgust at me.

"That son of a bitch!"

* * *

I SCREAMED as I woke up to my audition piece in the overhead sound system of the University of Denver hospital room. Anytime I heard Stravinsky it made me furious. They had it coming through their shitty, internal tin can speaker sound system. This is why I don't listen to music in general anymore. That moment was the last nail in the coffin for my self-esteem.

The nurse was jostled by my screams.

Fucking kid nearly gave me a heart attack!

She grabbed on to the chair she was sleeping in, I could see her nails digging into the armrests.

"Listen kid, you have to get out of here, we let you sleep in today, but on all accounts you are ready to be discharged."

She threw the clothes at the foot of my bed.

"I'll leave now, but you need to get up and go."

I fought off my heavy eyelids, but I was clearly weighed down by the drugs and moving at a snail's pace.

"Is, uh, is someone here to take me home?"

The nurse shot a quick look at the ground. *She didn't even want to look at me and tell me face to face.*

"Sorry, kid. There is a bus off of Colorado on the other side of I-25; get home safe okay?"

She walked out of the room and shut the door. I begrudgingly stumbled out of the room and after an elevator trip down two flights to collect myself. I ended up in the main courtyard of the University where that fateful day my confidence died a couple years back. The discharge orders were clear, stay away from any type of drug use or toxic chemicals. They were clear about any potential "adverse" effects that were unknown given my condition.

"No exterminating for two weeks at least!"

It's a damn shame that I will absolutely ignore that order. I have my bills in addition to mom's to worry about so I really can't afford to not work. I started trudging through the campus, making my way to the bus stop. Then I thought, maybe with my new found abilities, I should go visit my favorite teacher.

I walked toward the imposing concrete building with the jazz figures etched on the side. They were supposed to look like musicians, but ended up looking like the Kokopelli figures in my quirky Aunt Cindy's apartment. Chills came down my spine as soon as I stood before the doorway of the building. It was a foreboding, castle looking structure. I took a deep breath and walked in. The secretary's eyes jumped out of her head when she saw the blood stained—and god knows what else stained—jumpsuit.

Ugh, who is this creepy guy and what does he want?

"Can I help you with something?"

I could hear her voice trembling with fear. I look like I have been through complete hell and back.

"Oh, sorry, I'm fresh from studio art class where we were recreating Pollock pieces. I'm looking for Professor Sampson. My—uh—family wanted to make a donation to the Centennial Philharmonic Youth Orchestra."

Yeah, that'll work.

She still looked at me like I was trash, but at least she picked up the phone. "Hi Dr. Samson, I have someone here to see you who wants to make a donation to the philharmonic." She shot a look at me.

"What's your name?"

"Oh, sorry, it's Phil Larson."

"His name is Phil Larson. Mmhm. Okay, sounds good."

"Dr. Sampson will see you now. Up the stairs, second door on the left."

"Thanks."

Alright, I'm heading up to see this son of a bitch that set me down this spiraling k-hole of depression. I'll finally be able to tell him off.

Sure, it is pathetic that I needed to psych myself up, but normally I'm not the angry type. I'm the let it eat-away-inside type of person.

I opened up Dr. Samson's door and was surprised to see a young blond boy in there, just finishing up a private lesson.

"Excellent lesson today, Clayton, glad to see you took my suggestions to heart!" Dr. Sampson squeezed and rubbed into Clayton's right shoulder.

He said that he wouldn't touch me anymore. I didn't like that camping trip and he knows it.

Clayton looked extremely uncomfortable and didn't even bother to pack up his instrument as he quickly got out of the room.

"Bye, Dr. Sampson!" Clayton's eyes widened in fear as he ran past me.

"Don't you just love kids? I've been a director of the CPYO for ten years, and every year I am blown away by them."

What a horrifying double entendre.

"Anyway, Ms. Macmillan was saying that your family wanted to make a donation to the CPYO? To what do we owe the pleasure, Mr. Larson, was it?"

"I, uh, yes. Mr. Phil Larson. My family has admired your work for a long time."

"Oh! Well, I'm flattered. Please sit down Mr. Larson."

As I sat down in his office across from him he sized me up. *A little older and chunkier than what I usually like. Too bad.*

Was he just eye fucking me?

"What happened to your shirt?"

I forgot how ridiculous I looked.

"Oh, right. Fresh from art class, my apologies."

"Ah! Good to see students being so involved in their passions that they completely disregard everything else."

He sat back at the desk, interlocked his hands and started rubbing his thumbs.

"How do you know my work then?"

Dr. Sampson smiled at me and rubbed his stubbly beard. He was either very curious, or mildly curious and mildly attracted.

"Well Dr. Sampson, we have encountered each other previously. I'm not entirely sure if you remember me or not. But we first met about three years ago, at an audition. Do you remember anything yet, you smug self-righteous fuck?"

He stood back up in an attempt to exert power, in a very old man cliché he started wagging his finger at me.

"Now hold on a damn second!" He raised his voice and change the pace of his finger was for emphasis; almost as if he were conducting his own body language.

"Who do you think you are, coming into my office and talking to me like that?"

He went on an egotistical rant that I'm sure would have annoyed me and only further prove how much of a dickhole he is. Instead of listening to him, though, my eyes were wandering across his office. It was a fairly predictable, mahogany furnitured pompous office that you would see at any school. Around his desk he had a smaller collection of older instruments that are mounted for display. It looked like some cheap ass hall of instruments at the Met, except a lot less captivating.

"Are you even listening to me young man?"

Oh, so he treats everyone like children, not just actual children.

He looked at me again with an intense focus.

Is he one of my students that I spent extra time with, could he be one of my special students that I don't recognize?

I stood back up to him in defiance and my voice became raspy with anger, I couldn't hold back how I felt.

"So, just to be clear Dr. Sampson, you don't remember telling someone that they should drop everything and practice for a year for eight hours a day?"

Dr. Sampson looked bemused for a short time, but then it changed to completely disinterested.

Oh, it's this again?

"Why don't you losers just give up and leave me alone? Did you ever think that maybe, just *maybe* you weren't meant to play an instrument?"

I couldn't believe what he was saying.

"You mean you've said that before?"

"Kid, I say that to everyone I don't want in my program."

"What the hell kind of person are you to do that? You ruined me, you fucking sociopath!" How could one person, not acknowledge this horrific type of behavior? This man is initiating lifelong inadequacies, and he doesn't even give a shit?

"Listen, Phil, don't put that all on me, you were involved too. In case you forgot you were the one that screwed up your audition. Not me."

He looked agitated and took a moment to regain composure. I on the other hand, started to tear up and shake in anger like a whiny little bitch. Dr. Sampson got up from his chair and walked over to me slowly and methodically. He grabbed a shoulder of mine and wiped a tear from my cheek.

"Listen Phil, I think I know something that would make you feel a lot better."

His hand ran down my back.

He is cute when he gets vulnerable, he reminds me of the CPYO kids. A little different, but, good enough I suppose.

What could make me feel better at all right now? Then it hit me all at once. *Oh my god. Claytons horrified face, camping trip, he called me cute. This guy is a fucking pederast!*

I pushed him away with all my strength. "Stay the hell away from me, you sick bastard!"

I grabbed the mounted piccolo from his desk stand.

"These piccolos aren't the only thing you like blowing, is it, you twisted fuck!?"

I have never been this angry and disgusted in my life.

I swung the piccolo as hard as I could and it hit him square in the jaw. It felt extremely vindicating, I saw him spit blood out of his mouth as he fell. He was on the ground. Something needed to be done about this poor excuse of a man, and I was the lucky bastard to do it. With each hit I levied, I screamed at him with everything I could muster. This felt right. It feels like something I've seen and lived a thousand times before.

"Who do you think you are?"

I snarled. I was wailing on him with this dumbass "antique" of his, that I'm sure he valued more than any of the lives he's ruined.

This felt great for me; not so much for him. I concentrated on his ribs only because I knew how much it would hurt him later. I've lived through that agony and now he will. My arms were sore and dead tired. I couldn't stop though. It felt too good. I was lashing him in the same way I'm sure he's lashed dozens of kid's faces with his flaccid dick.

I threw the piccolo at his face and grabbed the nearby wiry music stand, folded it up and started whipping him across the chest. Then I pried his mouth open. I pushed his gums gently apart, then I forced it through the flesh and the tips of it were protruding through his cheeks.

"Here is what's going to happen. I'm going to keep beating the shit out of your flabby disgusting self, and you're going to not tell anyone. I know about what you did to those kids, and I know what you did to me and I'm not letting you get away with either of these things anymore."

He looked at me with a sadistic twinkle in his eye.

"You really think you can get away with this?" he said in an exasperated manner. The blood pooled up in his mouth and outlined every tooth. Dark red spit bubbles were forming in his mouth and they were popping up at me.

"When I take your laptop out of here, with all the details of whatever child porn ring that you run, you bet your ass I'll get away with it."

That's when the door opened, and the secretary screamed.

*   *   *

THE SECRETARY swung the door open and gasped. She was understandably horrified.

I got up slowly and tried to calm her down. My hands raised slowly and I started to put them above my head as if I was innocent. I was definitely not innocent.

"Listen, Dr. Samson…"

"Got what he deserved?" She finished my sentence for me. She smirked in slow motion.

"Exactly."

We smiled at each other and she left the room. I got down on the floor and moved within an inch of his face.

"See, Dr. Samson? No one is one your side here. We are done here."

I spit on his face before I pushed myself back up and walked towards the door.

Fucking punk thinks he can just get away with this!

I quickly turned around, smiled, and rubbed my chin.

"Oh yeah! Thanks for reminding me!"

I went over to his desk and grabbed the Macbook.

"If you say anything, to anyone at all I'm turning this over to the cops! Who knows what kind of horrific shit they will find on here."

I slammed it down, and started to whistle as I walked away. I gave the secretary a snap and a point and she waved goodbye. As I walked back out of the campus to the bus stop, I felt like the meme of Leonardo DiCaprio walking through the campus.

After about five minutes, the bus pulled up and I threw the $1.75 in the coin collector and sat down next to a beautiful girl.

"Uh, excuse you," the girl said with a judgmental look on her face.

"Huh?"

I looked down and realized I was sitting on the edges of her jacket.

"Oh, sorry, I didn't see that."

I moved. The girl kept shifting in her seat, trying over and over again to get comfortable. There was another bus rider that was reading the entertainment section of *The Denver Post*.

The headline was a jaw-dropping "Disney buying Lucasfilm for $4.05 billion; to make new *Star Wars* trilogy."

God dammit. Is nothing sacred anymore? Are there really no more independent artists or arbiters? I guess everyone does have a price. Being an artist *did* used to mean something at a certain point and time, but now it all falls down to whatever the oligarchs and media elite decide to force down the masses collective throat. Is this really any artist's only end game?

I can't believe how uncomfortable this is!

She continued to shift her butt in the seat. This girl was interrupting my rage; which was extremely enraging. What is she bitching about now?

I'm never letting Johnny do that again. I don't care how drunk he gets me. I totally know why people don't have anal sex now.

I started cracking up. I knew the girl was staring at me in confusion, but I didn't care. I was laughing so hard tears were coming down my face.

"Next stop, Alameda."

The bus driver mumbled into the mic. I brought myself together enough to stand up. As the bus driver pulled up to my stop, I finally took a break from laughing and wiped the tears away from my eyes. I looked at the cute girl, and held my aching ribs from the laughter and the pain was seeping back in after the drugs.

"Next time, use some lube!"

I threw my head back with laughter. The beautiful girl's face turned beet red. She pulled the strings on her hoodie to tried to hide As I got off the bus, I was still wiping the tears from my eyes from laughing so hard. At that exact moment, I had realized the gravity of the situation I was about to step into: I can go home and now hear what the hell my mom was thinking. I stood on the front lawn thinking about all the possible scenarios that were about to take place. Which could happen?

Could it be the unrealistically optimistic scenario? Could I go home and finally have an actual connection with her? Maybe I could uncover an important aspect of who she is and we could finally step away from all the miscommunication we've had and realize how much we love each other!

Hold on, maybe if my life was a fucking soap opera. After that scene, we could then cut to a commercial for a new erectile dysfunction pill on the market. There's no fucking way that would happen. *Cut the shit, Phil.*

Or would it be more likely, only slightly optimistic? Maybe we start talking, and she would have a very telling thought. I could move closer in to play like I'm interested in the conversation, and from that point on we could make the first steps of a great relationship afterwards.

Ugh. Are you even listening to yourself? In what world would that happen? Get your head out of your ass Larson! Heh. Coach Kilgore used to always say that. Man where is that dickhead now? Probably still teaching middle school gym and being a prick; that's where. My mind is racing. I need to calm the hell down and see how it goes.

Remember, you're not clairvoyant, you can somehow read people's minds. Nothing new or exciting will happen, nothing will change. You will deal with it.

In any other interaction with her; we would talk for three to five minutes, then I would inevitably get extremely annoyed and we'd start yelling until one of us decided to walk away. As I opened the door this time, I knew it would be different. This is especially true considering she wasn't even home. Wait a second. Come to think of it, when the hell was the last time I saw her? How the hell long was I even at the hospital? I should've probably figured that out before I left the place. Did she even visit me?

As soon as I walked up to the property line, I noticed that the door was slightly ajar.

Fuck. If there is someone breaking into my house right now, I do not think I can survive another encounter like this.

I walked around the place looking for any sign of her; a note, her keys, anything.

What the hell was she up to anyway?

My stomach growled and I realized I haven't had real food in a day or so. Come to think of it, I've only had saline solution in the hospital. That would explain how weak I felt. I walked into the kitchen and peeked into the fridge. There were only condiments. I could have had a mayo and ketchup sandwich with thousand island dressing and stale bread, but as appealing as that sounds I think I need some actual food. I opened every cabinet I could until I finally grabbed some crackers, and settled on some water to drink. I munched on a couple of those and chugged water and left the glass on the counter. I decided to give up looking for her and head to my room.

As I opened the door and walked down the stairs, I started to hear my creaking bed.

Dammit, who did she let in here while I was gone? She's up to her old fucking tricks again. I thought she learned from our last fight to not randomly just let my friends in the house.

Even before I peeked my head around the corner, I could start to hear some random squeals, moans, and other sex noises.

"Just like that, baby."

"Uhn! Fuck! That's so fucking good, I love that fucking cock! It's so big!"

I peeked my head around the corner to see one of the moments that I can never unsee. My mom, getting fucked doggystyle by Kyle, a biker with a humongous pot belly, handle bar mustache and a Danny McBride style gericurl/mullet, sweating all over *my fucking bed*. Her sagging, wrinkled tits and stretchmark ridden arms were all over my headboard and pillow that I use every night. She was biting her lip white with pleasure and pain. Also, I never thought of it before, but why wouldn't a man like Kyle have pierced nipples?

Did he really have to keep is bandana around his head?

Kyle looked up suddenly and locked eyes with me.

"Shit, what's this fucking kid doing here?"

*   *   *

MOM SCREAMED, grabbed the covers and shielded herself.

"You weren't supposed to be released until 7pm tonight!"

What the fuck happens now?

I've seen a lot of weird porn that starts this way.

I laughed at her, looked back incredulously, and completely disregarded Kyle's horrifying thought.

"Oh, I'm sorry, am I inconveniencing you? What a shame."

I laid on the sarcasm as thick as I could.

How could she be offended here? She's fucking our horrifying neighbor Kyle, I had to take the bus home from the hospital, and she is the one that's upset?

"Whatever Mom, you can finish up with Kyle and I'll be upstairs. I'm just grabbing my laptop and walking away. Hell, go for another round while you're at it."

Mom rolled her eyes, and Kyle looked at her with an intuitive, "Let's get back to it" type of look, and sure enough I hear:

"Well Cheryl," he said, "we should finish, so why fuckin not?"

I headed upstairs in disgust and popped open the laptop while I stretched out on the couch in the living room. I jumped on to my email to see what I missed in the world, and all it consisted of was one day sales from Macy's email blasts and coupons from some of our vendors. *I feel like there is one of those one day sales every fucking week. Stupid ass Macy's.*

At the very instance that I let out an audible sigh- confirming my sinking suspicions that no one really gave a shit—Uncle Steve sent me a pop up chat on Gmail.

"Holy shit, man! You're back! How are you feeling?"

"Hey, Steve. Yeah, I'm back. Sore as hell and tired, but I'm better."

"Good, Good! So, what are you up to tomorrow?"

"Well, nothing yet I guess. I can't really head back to work yet, Doctor's orders. Sorry."

"I thought that was the case, I wanted to see if you wanted to grab some lunch tomorrow?"

"Oh. Yeah sure, that sounds great!"

"Great! Well rest up, and I'll see ya at noon! We have some work stuff to talk about, but not a lot."

"Okay, Uncle Steve. Sounds good and I will see you then!"

Steve Larson has left the chat.

I already assumed we had work stuff to talk about, but what does that even mean? Something sounds weird about that.

I was just about to get completely absorbed in the rabbit hole of infotainment sites that I normally read, when mom and Kyle came back upstairs.

I really wanted to finish, but next time I'll make it worth it to him. You fucked up good Cheryl, how the hell are you gonna tell Phil about the move now?

As usual, there was never good news with mom. It was always rip the carpet out from under you kind of news. Everything was a big deal to her—big or small. They kissed a little more, presumably played grab ass, though I didn't bother to look, and they finally said their goodbyes. Mom tried to primp herself to look as proper as should could, then sat herself down on the couch right next to me.

"What do you want, Mom?"

"Really, Phil?"

She always knew exactly what to say to upset me the most, with the least amount of words.

"Yeah, really. Mom, did you even come visit me at all in the hospital?"

She began shifting uncomfortably.

"Well, the first day I tried."

"The reality of this is, I don't have any idea how long I was even there, what the hell happened, or wait a sec, where the fuck is my car?"

"Well Phil, before you decided to be an asshole, I did visit you a bit on the second day. But it hurt too much to look at you like that. So, Kyle suggested that we take a weekend trip to Garden of the Gods to try to relax. We were still on track to pick you up tonight. There's no reason for you to be this upset with me. You just happened to get off early."

Yeah, like Kyle didn't this time?

I wanted to say that, but, that would just be way too weird to talk about with my mom. I tried to breathe and calm myself down, I could understand that perspective. She did at least come in for a visit. No one could be blamed for the horrible timing, or the image of her saggy, overly pointy tits hanging over my bed frame while she was getting pounded. Ugh.

"Oh, and regarding your car, well, It's at the impound. I've already worked it out with Steve that he will take you whenever you are ready."

"Okay. Fine."

We both shot each other a look and knew that we were holding back what we really wanted to say.

"Is that it, Mom? I still feel like you have something you maybe want to tell me?"

Crap. He can see right through me.

"Well Phil, over the course of this weekend, Kyle and I decided it would be best that I move in with him!"

She immediately covered up how nervous she was with a huge fake smile.

I didn't buy it. I snapped back at her with squinted eyes.

"Mom, how long have you been with Kyle?"

"Well, only a couple months. But you don't understand Steve, a little while after dad died, and before Kyle got completely separated, we've always had feelings for each other."

This felt pathetic. This was like every recycled bullshit fucking dialogue that you hear in any adultery subplot that was half-assed at best. There is probably a supercut online somewhere of overly dramatic actors saying, "You just don't understand." I'm sure it already has thousands of views too. This was just another overly saccharine weepy movie of the 1950s that.. wait a second. I think I'm currently living the plot from *All That Heaven Allows (1955)*. Maybe I am Ned Scott in this case, *"The only Kyle I know is the neighbor!"* Is mom wearing any colors that she normally wouldn't wear?

I should really watch that again soon, what a beautiful movie.

"Why do I even bother talking to you when you don't listen? What did I just say?"

"Uh, you just said that you've always had feelings for each other, right?"

"Damn it Phil! I said I'm moving by the end of the week, and I told that you better have saved up on money; because I can only help for a couple months or so max. Don't worry about the impound, I talked Steve into helping out with the costs for that."

Shit. How will I be able to pull this off? Can I even afford something like the mortgage? What is that even? Wait, I'm getting ahead of myself.

"Hold on. Mom, why are you even moving at the end of the week?"

She didn't have to think about it for more than a second.

"Because I want to start being happy, and I think I finally have the opportunity."

That's when I got up and walked away. Those words would linger for a while:

"I might finally have the opportunity to be happy."

What the fuck has the past 22 years of my life been then, aside from a burden to my mother? This was unbelievable. That phrase might be the last memory I have of living with her. Who the hell does she think she is? I haven't been the world's best son, but I'm damn sure I wasn't the worst.

I turned back to see her holding her head in shame.

Maybe that was a little too much. I should have thought that out a little more. But, he should understand that I've been trapped with him for four years! After his dad died, I haven't been able to move on. Forget it, he wouldn't ever to be able to understand that.

She shot a look at me, and then a faint smile that I took as a tacit apology. Her love isn't completely lost for me, but maybe this would be best for her. I headed downstairs to the only place I could truly be happy; my room, alone. I flopped on to the bed and passed out.

I woke up about twenty minutes before noon, just enough time to have a cup of coffee before I headed out. If I didn't have it within an hour of being awake, I would normally get the headaches. I felt truly pathetic getting these. Out of all the possible withdrawal to get, caffeine is the saddest of them. I tossed in the single-serving coffee cup into the machine and stared it down with extremely heavy eyelids and a glare. I grabbed my phone and scanned the main page on Reddit. More upsetting shit. That's really all that is out there. We are in a truly amazing age of connectivity and the only thing we can do is continue to spread extremely pessimistic headlines coupled with snarky; disruptive comments. I would say about one out of every hundred headlines give me faith in humanity, whereas the others continue to push me further and further away. Especially if it is in Florida.

I sipped on the coffee that I was currently white-knuckling and was finally able to relax after my first swallow. At that exact moment, Steve sent a text saying his was five minutes away. I still felt like hell, and a shower would have helped, but I'll do that later I guess. I poured the rest of my coffee into a travel mug, and grabbed my shoes in front of the basement door. I decided to head outside and wait for him. Maybe the air would help me feel better. I grabbed my keys, headed outside and sat on the first step down from the door. I stared at the opposite side of the cul de sac I was on, which was at the corner of South Pine and South Pine. This kind of bizarre construct felt like a time and place completely disconnected from reality. In fact, the more I thought about it, the more I likened it this ornately embellished street corner to the "reality" we experienced in *Synecdoche, NY* (2008). Maybe all of these struggles I faced on a day to day basis were actually the product of an old, annoyed man named Caden, who can't even poop without a struggle.

As my mind continued to wander down the serpentine road, I saw the bulky, and broken wellbeing of the Larson & Sons company van, a Chevy Astrovan of the early 90s with a new engine and a disregarded everything else. Steve pulled up curbside.

"Hey there, Phil! Am I just waking you up?"

"Morning, Steve! Sort of, I guess. Just thinking."

"Well, okay then, what are ya thinking about?"

I couldn't help but laugh.

"To be honest, I'm thinking about if we actually exist, or if we only exist within the mind of a cancer ridden playwright."

Without missing a beat, Steve shot back with, "Ah, just thinking about some weird movie I've never heard of?"

"You got it. Anyway, what's up, where are we going? "

"Well, I figure it's been awhile since we went to the Lazy Armadillo. You okay with that?"

"Sure thing, Uncle Steve, sounds good."

Steve shyly smiled as he drove. I always felt as if he was someone I had to pull information from. He wasn't a big casual talker. That's fine considering I'm still waking my ass up by nursing this coffee. He did look really nervous, he had a horrible poker face. Whenever he was nervous he was always scratching an itch behind his neck that I'm sure didn't exist. From what I can tell, he was itching that one spot raw.

Appropriately, Steve was listening to country music as we drove to the restaurant. It fit him well, and he'd always been a fan, but I never could connect with it. I didn't want to, but I don't think I could if I did try.

"So uh, how ya feeling, buddy?"

"I'm okay, just really sore. I'm not feeling weighed down by the drugs anymore though, so that's good."

Rather than dance around the topic, I thought it would be best to address it upfront with him.

"Uncle Steve, the doctor said I absolutely could not work for the rest of the week. Is that okay? I'm so sorry but, could you cover for me?"

"Of course, Phil! What kind of uncle or co-owner of this business would I be if I didn't cover for you?"

This will be the last time I do it anyway, so what the hell do I care?

Steve then smiled at me, lying through his teeth. But what was he talking about?

"Oh shit! Phil, I forgot to ask you, you aren't on any weird dietary restrictions or nothing from the doctor, are you? Or, will you need help getting around? I'm sorry man, I really should have thought all this through before assuming where we can go and what we could do and all that."

I had to laugh at Steve's nervousness.

"No, I have no restrictions or any physical thing like that. The doctor just specifically told me to keep away from the toxins for a little bit."

"Oh, okay. Good. Just want to be sure you know?"

After a few more uncomfortable silences, we finally pulled into the restaurant of the parking lot. He actually got out of the car and opened the door for me.

"Steve, this isn't our first date, so you don't have to do anything like that; thank you, though."

My sarcasm was clearly disarming for him, but he fake laughed it off with another nervous chuckle.

"Oh, right. Sorry Phil, just want to make sure you are okay."

He clearly wasn't listening, seeing as he held the restaurant door open for me as well. He was definitely nervous about something. We walked into the restaurant and were greeted immediately.

"Hello, welcome to the Lazy Armadillo. Is it just the two of you? Wait a second, are you Phil Larson?"

The host was around my age, and looked vaguely familiar, but I couldn't quite remember him.

"Yes, I'm sorry, who are you?"

Of course he doesn't remember me. Who would considering how shy I was back then.

"Hey Phil! It's me Brad, Brad Whitlock from high school? We had band together, and I played the trumpet."

It finally clicked for me, Brad looked a lot different from the extremely nervous pimply faced kid that I remember. He was always nice, but an extremely shy and sad kid. It looked like he went in the total opposite direction after school, he carried himself with poise and confidence now.

"Oh wow, Brad! How are you doing man? Good to see you, sorry I'm horrible with faces and names."

"No worries, man. It's going well for me, working here in the days and going to night school for some HVAC certification. It's pretty good, man."

Like a jerk, Steve decided that this would be a good time to loudly and uncomfortably clear his throat. Brad obviously picked up on this.

Good ol' classy Steve. I love him and all, but that was pretty shitty. Dude can be a huge jerk when he wants to be.

"Sorry to tie you two up, let me get you a table. Phil, I'd love to hang out with you and catch up sometime."

"Yeah, that sounds real cool man, I'd like that too!"

Brad walked us over to the table. I'm not really sure why he would, considering this place was empty. While he walked us over I gave Uncle Steve the stinkeye.

"Your waiter will be with you shortly."

"Thanks Brad, we'll talk soon."

Steve sat down, and immediately folded in his elbows and rested his chin on his clasped hands. He looked and acted like an irritable, spoiled child. One with the moms from Highlands Ranch who made sure their little douchebag was the best dressed in whatever bullshit function they attended. Steve started itching again, and I continued to grow more and more annoyed with him by the second.

I lashed out at him for acting like an asshole.

"Okay Steve, cut the shit. What's going on here? What do you need to tell me?"

Just come out with it man.

"Fine. No need to be rude, Phil. The fact of it is, I talked with Beth, we have been together for a while now. We decided to move to Pueblo together at the end of the month. The business is in your hands entirely now, and you can make it or break it. You can do anything you damn well please with it."

Steve let out a huge breath. I now understand why he was so nervous about this.

"So listen Phil, I need you go get the Pest Control Business Certification. Only after that, can I transfer the business to you. Until you get that, you cannot run it on your own."

Fuck. Steve wanted me to now fully commit to this idea for life. I wasn't ready for this.

"Hey, Brad!"

I yelled and desperately signaled.

"Is it too early to get a drink?

I knew exactly what I wanted.

"Could I get a michelada? Extra hot sauce?"

Brad smiled. "Start the day off with a strong one. I like that. Sure man, no problem."

"Thanks man, good to see you."

Brad walked away, I heard one last thought.

That poor fucking guy, I'll hope he'll be... His thought faded away.

Maybe there is a certain radius where I can hear people's thoughts or something?

I really should've seen this coming but I didn't. I always thought Uncle Steve was a sincere, great guy. He wasn't a "lucky at love" type of guy, and he's been with her for a bit now. Come to think of it, been three and a half years. He could see my dissatisfaction with this, it was probably pretty obvious. Even though I can read people's minds, I have no way of knowing when or how my face contorts in regards to pleasure or anguish. Clearly, it was a not happy look.

Steve kept yammering on and on about something. Probably about how happy he was with Beth, but I didn't care. All I heard was that endless ringing. I can tell his lips were moving, but I heard nothing that he was saying, and I didn't care enough to attempt to lip read. It was like that tinnitus effect in *Saving Private Ryan* (1998), obviously without the wartime carnage and bomb-induced hearing loss. This very simply, was me blacking out what I did not want to hear.

"Phil, I'm sorry to be stern here, but you knew this was coming! Eventually we already discussed that when you were ready, you'd take over your father's business, and sorry if I've pulled the rug out from under you or whatever, but you are ready! I don't care if you were unprepared. Maybe someone needs to light a fire under your ass. Maybe that person is me."

I could feel my grimace and acceptance. He understood. I didn't even have to say anything. In what felt like perfect timing, Brad brought over the drink.

"Here ya, go man, I got you a strong and spicy michelada."

Just ask him, it's not a big deal.

"Hey Phil, before I go, I wanted to let you know that there was a party at uh, do you remember Kaitlin? She might be there and I think it'd be cool if you came along. There might be some more familiar faces and a good time. What do you think man?

I was surprised at how forward this dude was, I haven't seen him since I graduated, and I don't remember talking to him that much when we were in school. Nonetheless, it would be pretty cool to pop in to a random place and see how the dynamic can shift when I can read their thoughts. *Why was I even thinking this long about it?* Steve's thoughts crept into my mind.

Is this guy picking up my nephew? Is this really happening right in front of my face?

I had that same thought for a half a second, but remembered that Brad was a guy who always had a girlfriend in school, so immediately cast that thought aside.

"You know what? I think I'll take you up on that, that does sound like a nice relief. "

"Oh, okay great. So, I get off of work at 7, the party is over in Arvada, and starts at 8. Do you want to meet back here and I'll drive us over?

"Okay, sounds good, I'll see you then."

"Cool Phil, it'll be a good time."

"Well that guy seems cool, had a class with him or something?"

Steve looked uneasy about what just happened. *Did it really look like he was hitting on me?*

"He was more like a friend of a friend. A good dude, we never hung out. Should be a cool time tonight."

"Well I'm excited for ya, it'll be good to get out of your own head a bit."

He paused for a second and raised his eyebrows; that was his classic good idea look.

"You know what? I'll give you a ride back here later. I don't want you driving around yet. Can you do three little things for me?"

"Okay, I'll bite I guess. What are your three little things?"

I hate when he's gets condescending like that, he pulls that shit all the time when he thinks he is being funny. His face matched his annoyed thoughts. He perked up and starting counting along with his fingers as he dictated to me.

"Alright Phil, three things: number one, you don't do any of that drinking and driving and stuff, stay over somewhere; number two, you schedule to take that test; and number three you tell me what the hell that ridiculous drink is and what's in it."

I laughed a very welcome laugh. He cut that tension with perfect timing. I'm glad he finished with that, he got so tense and serious with the second statement that he was giving me the stern look and finger point like one of my many disappointed middle school teachers. Uncle Steve was only sometimes serious, but when he was, it was very shocking and very disarming.

Still smiling, I pointed at my drink.

"You've never heard of this before?"

"No, and it looks like a girl drink, if you want a beer, get a beer, don't put it in a red dress or whatever the shit you did to it."

I chuckled and snorted.

"You're ridiculous, you know that?"

He smiled back.

"So what the hell is it then?"

"A michelada is a beer with tequila, hot sauce, and Worcestershire sauce."

"Ugh, does it taste as awful as it sounds?"

"No man, I really like these. D'you want to try some?"

"No, I'm okay thanks."

"Whatever Steve, you're missing out on an adventure in your mouth."

"Sounds like an adventure to some grimy, crappy version of Tijuana. I'm good, thanks."

After what felt like way too long, the waiter finally arrived

"How can I help you today?"

Steve barely let him finish his sentence, and immediately comes out with, "I'll have two tacos al carbon with rice and beans, and a orange soda."

Steve did not try to mimic the proper accents, so it sounded like he ordered the element.

"We have orange flavored Jarritos, is that okay?"

"Uh, yeah sure, I'll have that."

"And, I guess I'll get a steak burrito with guacamole and a cup for water."

Steve and I resorted to checking out cell phones for a little bit, and then before we knew it the food was right in front of us. No point in continuing this dead horse of a conversation I guess. So, why not ignore it like we do every other uncomfortable thing?

My food took a bit longer to come to the table than Steve's. He delicately laid out the unfolded napkin on his lap, and took a fork and knife to mix up the tacos and rice and beans until it was one disgusting looking hodgepodge of elements on his plate.

When my food finally arrives, I immediately hunch over and starting shoveling it all down my throat. I am not too sure where it came from, but I have always seen food as fuel, and not much else. I can't remember the last time I truly enjoyed, and relished a meal.

Well, when the hell was the last time I enjoyed anything that much?

Steve and I could not be more opposite when we eat. Steve methodically chews and breaks down every microfiber of the components of his meal whereas I am literally shoveling food in with my hands. Napkins be damned, I have pants, and I'll use them!

"Whoa, Phil. I didn't know you were that hungry! Damn! You look like a female praying mantis feasting on her former lover."

I responded mid chew.

Chup-chup-chup. "Praying mantis, I don't see a lot of those. I'd like to though."

I probably look horrifying right now. Directly below my hunched over face, there is a pyramid of taco droppings. I'm not doing anything about the guacamole around my mouth and on my cheeks. Who am I kidding? It's probably even on my shirt.

I probably look a little like a praying mantis eating its mate after sex.

Steve's disgust showed on his face, but he was thinking it as well. *God, it's like this kid never even got socialized.*

After the burrito was done, I licked my lips and sucked at my fingers. I then heard the familiar buzzing and default ringtone of Uncle Steve's work phone.

"Who the fuck is this? I'm supposed to be off today!"

* * *

"HELLO, this is Steve?"

His eyes lit up, "Ma'am, I am so so sorry. I had a meeting go on a little later than expected."

One of the not so great aspects of being in a smaller businesses is the always expected, dire need to fulfill, excellent customer service. Which is a constant, inescapable part of the job. Steve hung up the phone and looked at me.

"Phil, I am so so sorry."

"What's going on?"

I responded complacently, accepting my pre-determined fate of being dragged in to this nonsense.

"We have a follow up to do. 35 minutes ago. I completely forgot about it. I'm so sorry, Phil."

"Hold on. What's with this we? You were right here not five minutes ago when I told you I needed to be away from these chemicals for at least the remainder of the week. Or was I talking to myself?"

I had no qualms with being snarky, Steve pulled this shit on me all the time. He was an extremely disorganized man, which is the exact opposite of what you want in a small business owner.

"I'm gonna need your help, Phil, this was a bigger property. I know I told you that we would relax and you didn't have to worry about going to work; but the reality is, we have a business to run."

I felt like an annoying little kid. "I know, I know, fine. Whatever."

"We gotta run then. Uh, I'm sorry to ask, Phil, but do you have any cash?"

I stared him down.

"Are you serious? I don't even have a fucking wallet. Everything I had got stolen when those kids beat me up!"

"Oh. Okay, I'll pay card. It'll take longer. Sorry, I forgot. After this little thing is over, I'm buying you a wallet and slipping you a crisp twenty to restart everything for ya. Would you like that?"

I rolled my eyes.

Do I look like I'm fucking twelve or something? Will he get me a Yu-Gi-Oh wallet? Christ, man.

"Sure, Uncle Steve, whatever, let's go and get this over with okay?"

"Okay, sounds good, give me one second, and we'll go. I swear this will be quick!"

He ran over to the cash register, pulled out his wallet, fumbled with it, and finally gave a card to the cashier. Steve then motioned me over with his head. I grew more annoyed. At that moment, Brad came back and tugged at my arm.

"Just come back here at about seven and I'll give you a ride. Then you can just either crash at my place, or I'll give you a ride back; whichever."

"Alright, sounds good man, let me get your number."

As Brad dictated, I put it into my phone. I had an embarrassingly small number of contacts in my phone. Either it was family, vendors for business, or repeat customers. That was about it. I still had some old friends in there as well, but I don't talk to them anymore. Steve waved me over to the car. I begrudgingly followed him. I shouted back to Brad.

"See you later tonight man, I'm looking forward to it!"

"Okay, see you then, I am too!"

Now back to reality of an annoyed Steve taking me on the job again. Am I in any state to work and be around all of those chemicals? I guess we will have to see. We walk out to the parking lot, and before we get in the car he asked me to dive in to facing those chemicals head on.

"Would you mind setting up a new batch of nozzles for the Cyper? I ordered you some new ones when they couldn't recover the old one after the accident. It'll be deducted from your paycheck next week."

My eyes lit up with rage, and before I could freak out at him he responded.

"Just kidding, Phil. Lighten up man, jeez."

Okay, looks like someone is not in the mood for joking. I didn't know I needed to be so delicate around him.

"I was serious about building up the sprayers though. Would you mind doing that in the back while I'm driving?"

"Fine, sure."

I got out of the car and begrudgingly went to the back of the van. I opened the door and went over to the accessory section of the shelves in the back. *At least Steve keeps the van organized, even if outside of work his life is a clusterfuck.* He was a complete disaster, four times divorced with a gambling addiction and what I can imagine is a hell of a lot of baggage.

I tore open the bag of extendable wands and started to unscrew the nozzles on the bottles. This should be a process that is relatively quick. These are the most horrible of the chemicals we work with, but there's no chemical that we have in the back that is non-toxic. It's a matter of exposure and tolerance. In the exact same way that Mosquitos were tolerant to DDT, I was now like a super mosquito; tolerant to quite a bit of the toxic chemicals we use. I unscrewed the caps of the gallon Cyper jugs and screwed on the extendable wands.

"You finished yet?"

I heard him shout from the distance.

"Only the Cyper, right? They're done."

"Great, bring one to me and come in if ya like."

I walked it over to him, but I wasn't feeling like doing this today. I was light-headed in general and just wanted to relax.

"I think I'm gonna stay in the car if that's cool with you Uncle Steve. I need to take it easy for a bit."

"Shit, Phil, I should have told you to stay in the car. What am I thinking? You're fresh from the hospital, of course you can stay in the van."

He dug in his pockets and pulled out the keys for me.

"Make sure you keep the AC on and that you're comfortable, okay?"

"Okay, cool."

"Heh, still making jokes I see. That's good."

I chuckled and rolled my eyes when I realized what I did.

I got in the front, turned on the air conditioning and the modern rock station. I didn't want to listen to it, but I needed some static noise. If I'm ever in a place that's too quiet I get uncomfortable; fast. I started checking out some film review sites. If I love a movie, or a director, I tend to devour everything about them. No detail is too inconsequential for me to be aware of existing. There are a couple people whose films always leave me wanting more, I think those are the best films. For contemporaries, David Fincher, Rian Johnson, Shane Carruth, Ridley Scott, Coen Brothers, Terry Gilliam, all leave me filled with wonder after their movies. For classics it's Bergman, Ozu, Kieslowski, Powell and Pressburger, Fassbender, Herzog, De Sica, Varda, and Svankmeijer. It always astonishes me that as much as I have seen their movies, I can read something new about them every time that I never would have noticed before.

Unfortunately, I have to sift through about 80% of the bullshit puff pieces that don't do anything in regards to rewarding the audience and are only there to bolster the content and clickbait of whatever site is pushing for pageviews that day. However, there are some standouts.

All this reading was giving me a pounding headache. I tried to ignore it, but then started searching the glove compartment for any medicine. Nothing. Maybe I'll try to take a nap for a bit, my eyelids are getting really heavy after all.

* * *

I WAS ALREADY feeling it. Dizzy, lightheaded and a little tired, this was nothing new; but it was always surprising when and how this happened.

The more drinks Methhead Dan and I had around her, the more of a horrendous flirt I was. Normally, I was always the shy one when it comes to flirting, but the fact of the matter is, with her, I always felt more confident. Especially with drinking, Dan grew more reckless and I grew more carefree. After our 4th round and 2nd shot, Kaycee came up to us with a look of concern.

As the restaurant cleared out, Kaycee looked at us from across the room rolling her eyes. She hurried over to the table and smiled sweetly.

"Okay, assholes. You're way too drunk to drive, so I'm taking you to my place. You are leaving your car here. That's the end of it. I'm not going to argue about it."

Dan shrugged and said, "Yeah, fuck my car anyway right?"

Kaycee snapped back at him, "I've seen you talk about your precious car before, you probably do want to fuck it. The point is it's not happening tonight."

Kaycee grabbed our arms and got a knowing nod from her manager who smiled and waved goodbye.

"Thanks for taking care of me, Kaycee. I'll see you in two days!"

"See ya, Sam!"

Dan and I both slurred.

"Bye Sam!"

After we got outside Kaycee let go of our arms and turned to face us.

"You're lucky I love you two idiots and that I have a party tonight at my place. Otherwise, you wouldn't be getting such hospitality from me."

Dan shouted at her.

"Love you too, Kaycee! Woo!"

Kaycee smiled sinisterly, it was a smile that all at once said shut the fuck up before I regret my decision. Or at least, that was my impression of it. We got in to Kaycee's pristine Accord. It was clean on the outside but full of trash and completely unkempt on the inside. If I wasn't as hot for Kaycee as I actually was, I would have realized that her car was an apt metaphor for her persona. The surface impression can be very deceiving at times.

Dan and I pushed aside the notebooks, textbooks, fast-food wrappers and makeup kits to find the actual fabric to sit on. This was difficult enough without actually having to search for the seatbelts. Kaycee turned on her cd player, which started blasting Siouxsie and the Banshees, something you never want to be blasted, and then we had about a 10 minute drive back to her place. Dan was in the back giving her shit about her music, so she decided to turn it up and fade it all to the back of the car. Thankfully, I was in the front with her.

"So what's up with the party tonight, is it a just for the hell of it party, or is there a reason for it?"

Without missing a beat, Kaycee gave me a very stilted response.

"My friend Alannah got into grad school, and we decided to host a thing for her at my place."

"Oh, cool! Which program did she get into?"

"Uh, veterinary science? I forgot what specific field, but she is going to CSU in the fall."

"Huh. Good for her."

I vaguely remember her friend Alannah; much like Kaycee, there was an air of mystery with all of her friends. Everyone I met was very nice, but they were all forgettable stereotypical cool kids. The people you wanted to hang out with but you don't know exactly why, or how to go about it. They were all overly confident and determined to spread the gospel of what they were into; regardless if you wanted to listen to them or not. The only thing I ever did at Kaycee's parties was float around and have extremely superficial conversations about very profound topics. It was all conversation that scratched the surface, it never went anywhere beyond that, which always made me wonder who was truly genuine, or who was into these topics for the fad appeal.

"Alright, here we are, let me know if you don't know anyone's name or something."

In a moment of sobering elegance, Methhead Dan produced a 50 dollar bill out of nowhere.

"Kaycee, before we go in, I insist you take this, this should cover for Phil and me tonight, for whatever else we drink; or if you got a keg or food for Alannah."

Kaycee looked genuinely surprised.

"Oh, thank you so much Dan! That's so nice!"

"It's the least I could do."

He proceeded to be a raging, judgmental asshole for the rest of the night, dissecting her friend's pseudo-intellectual conversations. I loved that son of a bitch like a brother; this only further validated my feelings for him.

As I walked around the party, I was a stereotypical wallflower. I made the rounds to people I only vaguely remember and care about even less. It's almost as if I were completely robotic at these events. I scan for a topic I can discuss, jump in with whatever little discourse I am capable of, then I retreat to another group for the same thing. While I'm talking, the only thing on my mind is what type of drink to get next and to see if anyone wants anything. *Why am I acting as a bartender right now? Is it because I was extremely uncomfortable, or is it because I naturally feel subservient to all these ridiculously pretentious people and don't know how else to function with them?*

I imagine if I was looking at a diagram of where I've traveled so far in this party that if someone traced the path it would be an infinity loop with the furthest points of the loop being at the liquor cabinet in the living room and the fridge. Finally, I see a break in the repetition; Kaycee is stepping outside for her just drunk enough cigarette. She's not a regular smoker, but sometimes when she is drinking she is. She nods me over and we head to the porch.

She's given me this look multiple times, this is the, "I want to smoke and bitch about something that's happening right in front of us" look. I knew it well. I'm not too sure what she sees me as, a brother or a really good nonsexual being of a friend. Either way it sucked. I was extremely attracted to this gorgeous girl, but again I knew she was the Kobayashi Maru, so I always resigned myself with an *eh, why bother?* type of approach with her.

As soon as I met her outside, rather than fumble around her pockets for a loosey, she immediately grabbed me, pulled me closer and drunkenly fumbled around with her tongue in my mouth. What the shit is this? I've seen her drunk before, a lot more drunk than this, but here she was, in exactly where I wanted her.

We continued to make out. Is this really happening? My mind was racing at the possibilities of what could happen next for us. We've been friends for so long that this had to work out; right? I wrapped my hand around her and pulled her close to me. I took a chance and slid my hand down her pants and grabbed her butt, because well; there's no because needed. Of course I grabbed her butt. You would have done the same thing in my position, don't judge me.

Kaycee smiled and indicated she was into it. I made out with her a little more, then she very quickly pulled away.

"I'm sorry. I, I can't. What the fuck am I doing??"

She looked distraught.

"Kaycee?"

Before I got a chance to apologize she ran her fingers through her hair, opened the door, then slammed it behind her; leaving me dumbfounded on the porch.

Did I do something wrong? She's done this dozens of times with other people, and I was probably the closest one to her at this party, so what the hell just happened? I stood there, perplexed, leaning against the railing that leads to the stoop, rewinding the situation in my head.

Did I do something wrong, why did this happen now? Why tonight?

* * *

"PHIL!"

It sounded like I heard this through an audio filter; it was muffled and heavy on the bass.

Man, how drunk was I?

I fought against my heavy eyelids and gauged my surroundings. *I'm in the front seat of the van? Where did the party go?*

"Phil! Are you okay? Wake up!"

Uncle Steve reached through the cracked open window and jostled me up.

"You've been out for hours, Phil! The appointment took a lot longer than I thought and, oh god, what's that smell?"

I deeply inhaled and couldn't recognize any stand out, dominant scent. Uncle Steve stood by me, grimaced, and immediately covered his nose and mouth with his hand.

"You really don't smell anything?"

This fucking kid is an idiot.

I looked at him and tried to shake off the overwhelming groggy feeling I had.

"I don't know what you are talking about, Uncle Steve." I inhaled again. "Just, could you please calm down?"

At least I knew that I was upsetting him, I haven't seen it a lot, but I recognized his rage.

"Well gee, Phil, let's think about this for half a second. What were you fiddling around with in the back of the van before I went inside?"

"Oh shit. The Cyper."

There it is. Took him long enough.

"The fucking Cyper nozzle wasn't screwed on tight enough and now it's leaking through."

"That would explain why I feel this way."

"Phil, first off, you could have died if the window wasn't cracked open. Secondly, you know how expensive that shit is and how much we have to order!"

I hung my head. I know he gets upset when I unleash my "I screwed up and I'm sorry face." It's not unlike an ashamed puppy dog, knowing he shouldn't have pissed on the carpet.

"Unbelievable Phil, you really didn't notice? I guess I have to watch you like you were a fucking infant now. How old are you again? How can I trust you to run a business after I leave when I can't even trust you to do the most basic upkeep things correctly? I mean, shit; this is the stuff that the part-timers or interns would do. Come on Phil! This isn't something a co-owner should be doing!"

Steve has never talked to me this way, so I decided to fight back and defend myself.

"Good! You know that I don't want this fucking hand-off pity job anyway. Who cares? Dad only ever started this business because he didn't have any talent in anything else!"

"Oh, so you think you're so different and better than him? What exactly is your amazing talent that will land you a high-power high paying job?"

Where is all this hostility from Steve coming from?

Before I could respond he cut me off.

"Yeah, I thought so. You're in the exact same boat he was in, except our dad didn't give us shit. You at least have a business that he built from scratch and handed off to you, you ungrateful little asshole."

If only he knew of the powers I have. He makes a good point though, what the fuck can I do with this? I definitely could use this to have the upper hand in a lot of situations but how so, and in what capacity?

This fucking kid is eating away at my patience. I have to pay for it; I know he can't afford it.

"Steve, if all of this is about money I'll fucking pay for it. It's really not that expensive."

"I know it's not but it's the principal man. If you can't learn to not be wasteful now, then you never will!"

I rolled my eyes.

"Okay, Steve, I got it."

I know I'll hate this. After he moves I'll bail on this company and really get started. But in what?

He finally walked away to put his supplies in the back.

If this kid bails on this company, then all that his dad sacrificed for him would be for nothing. I can't let that happen, can I?

His thoughts continued to trail off, but I got interrupted by my phone buzzing in my pocket. The caller ID didn't register.

"Hello?"

I always sounded extremely skeptical when I picked up the phone to an unknown number.

"Hey Phil, this is Brad! What's up man, where are you?"

"Uh, what do you mean?"

"Phil, it's a quarter to seven. Did you still want to hang out tonight. Are you feeling up to it?"

"Oh damn! I didn't know it was that late! Sure man, uh, where are you?"

"Well I'm just about done with my shift. Do you want to come back here and I can just drive you over?"

"Okay, yeah man, sounds good."

"Alright, I'll see you in a bit."

"Cool, later Brad. See ya."

I can't believe it's so late! I was asleep for that long? Jesus Christ that can't be good.

Steve sat down up front and turned on the ignition.

"So what's up, Phil, where are we going?"

"Could you take me back to the Armadillo? I'll meet up with Brad and go from there."

Steve nodded and remained silent.

If it's a lost cause to try to teach him these things, then it's a lost cause I guess. I'll be in Pueblo and not thinking about this crap anyway. Maybe I should just write it off entirely.

I knew he was upset, but it didn't matter to me. He was right, Should I try to calm him down, even if it is a total lie? He would eventually figure out that I had other plans; even if I didn't. Wait a sec. My eyes just lit up with an epiphany.

Tonight will be a great way to gauge if I can really utilize my powers to persuade people. I'm suddenly a lot more excited by the prospect of heading to this party.

I felt like a stereotypical evil old man, twiddling my thumbs and hatching a dastardly plan. All I needed was to be bald and have a cat in my lap.

What the fuck is on this kid's mind? I would love to be that far away from it all, all the time.

Without me knowing we had arrived, he parked right in front of the restaurant.

"Alright Phil, don't be an idiot tonight. Be safe out there! Smart decisions!"

"Okay Steve, I'll see ya later!"

Fuck him. I'll do what I want tonight.

* * *

AS I STEPPED out of the van, Brad simultaneously stepped out of the restaurant.

Perfect timing, how did he do that?

"Well, are you ready?"

Still feeling light headed, I could only express myself with a shrug.

I finally mustered up the strength to *actually* communicate.

"As ready as I'll ever be."

I thought about it for half a second, he lead the way to his car, and then a question popped into my mind.

"Wait. Will I know anyone else there?"

"Uh, maybe. I invited some people, but I'm not too sure who will show up."

"Alright, we'll see I guess."

"Okay, here we are. Hop in."

He pressed the unlock button on his key to his car. I didn't know the pristine Chevy Nova in the parking lot was his! I'm sure I had a dumbfounded look on my face.

"My dad's a big, big car guy, I tried to help him with it a bit, but I never really got my head wrapped around it. He does the upkeep, and well, I show it off."

It was a car that's had to have major upkeep done.

"This is yours? Shit dude, that's awesome! Are you sure you didn't steal that from the set of *Death Proof* (2007)?"

He laughed it off as we stepped in. He revved up and we were on our way, he probably did that just to intimidate me.

"I really like Tarantino. He seems like he has so much fun on screen, you know? Are you a film guy, Phil?"

"Yeah, I've always loved it. I didn't think I'd want to do anything with it, seeing as how crazy it is to make a living off in that industry. You have to be really good at what you do. "

Brad looked confused.

"I know what you mean, but didn't you think by choosing a music program, that would be a lot more competitive and unrealistic to make a living in, as opposed to film?"

Shit. That was a really good point. What was my dumbass thinking?

"Yeah. I guess you're right, and I really should have thought about the whole picture of it. What the hell was I thinking?"

Brad shrugged it off.

"It's all good, man. I'm a huge hypocrite. I'm going to school for performing arts now as well as working at the restaurant. Don't worry about it, just find what you love then do it."

He started to smirk.

"Did, uh, did you ever go to one of the film festivals in this state? Starz, Aspen, Telluride, any of those?"

I sighed.

"I wish, man. I just haven't had the time or resources yet. As soon as I do though, I would do it in a heartbeat."

"Okay, so what are you doing on Monday?"

"Uh, working I think."

Tomorrow was difficult to think about much less three days ahead. Regardless, everything was going to change with Steve moving away.

Hold up, with Steve out of the way, I'll be a business owner. I can make my own fucking hours!

Before Brad could respond I cut him off.

"Actually, I'm not too sure yet. I might be able to get some time off. Why, what's going on?"

Brad rolled his eyes at me.

"Telluride, dude. Let's go!"

"Well, I don't think I can afford it right now, in addition to slower work, I'm anticipating some high hospital bills coming soon. Thanks, though."

"Don't worry about it, man. I'll make sure you get in, no charge. Plus, you don't have to tell me why you were in the hospital, but I'm pretty sure you can use a brief vacation."

"How the hell are you going to do that?" I responded as incredulously sounding as I possibly could. Just then, I felt like a co-host on an a talk show, baiting him with lines.

"Phil, my Uncle is one of the highest paying angel donors to the festival! My family goes every year and we'd love to invite you. I know you'll hit it off with them really well. I insist! Especially with all the crap you've recently gone through, man. We'd love to have you."

"Holy shit, that sounds amazing!"

My mind instantly ran off with the possibilities associated with this.

Who would be there? What premieres could I attend? Should I ask any questions? Shit, I should ask some really great, insightful questions. Am I capable of even doing that? No, that sounds like it would be pretentious of me to do that. Maybe, I could even have a one on one time with some directors, or actors I really love? God, I could, I could change everything with this, I might even be comfortable in my own skin, surrounding myself in people that all have a deep love of movies. I could make something of myself.

"I don't really know what to say, this sounds incredible. Thank you so much for the offer, Brad, that's so nice of you!"

Brad just laughed it off. He had a Dave Franco type of relaxed personality and he didn't know how to respond with how seriously I appreciated this.

"Don't get all weird on me, man; it's not a big deal at all. If I can offer this to you, then why wouldn't I?"

I'm floored by Brad's kindness. I was normally ignored with the exception of Dan and Kaycee, so why is this happening now?

Before I knew it, Brad pulled into a driveway into his apparently huge house in Highlands Ranch.

Who are these people that are so well off?

"Here we are, man. Looks like some people have already been let in."

I wonder what kind of Can't Hardly Wait (1998) *type of scenario I'm walking into right now?*

* * *

BRAD OPENED the door for me and it looked a lot more low-key of an atmosphere than I expected. There were people casually drinking, lounging on the couch having conversations with some minor background music.

Alright, hopefully this guy isn't too weird. Hopefully he won't turn out to be so cool that Brad steals all of your friends away. Wait, why would you even think that? Come on Phil, get it together, and be confident, that's all you'll need to do to be swimming in it.

That's all that girls like? Hmm. What an opportunity to test that out. I have the upper hand as it is, but if I fake my confidence, this could get real interesting, real fast. Let's see what happens.

"Hey everyone, this is Phil, he's an old friend from school. Phil, from left to right, this is Kaitlin, John, Sam, Aly, Em, Stan, Kathleen, Ed, Rita, and the Chach."

Everyone did a half-assed waive and went back to their conversations. Rita and the Chach sounded like an amazing buddy cop show from the 1970's. I eventually at some point and time have to meet, and be friends with (or at least make fun of) The Chach. I wandered over to the crowd and even though there was a steady hum of noise. I could still hear all of their thoughts at a mile a minute.

I can't believe Rita showed up tonight, what a fucking bitch.

Aly is lookinn cuuuuuuuute tonight!

God, why do I keep coming to these things? How long have I been here? Can I go home yet?

Who is this asshole?

Is it too early, and would it be too weird for me to bring out the cocaine? I think a hit will help me relax.

Look at this jackass. Who does he think he is?

I need another drink, this is booo-ring!

I don't know who was thinking what, but it would be tougher to focus on one person. I made my way into the living room then as a gesture I offered to grab everyone a drink or a refill of something. A lot of people politely declined, but there were a couple people that barked their orders.

"Jack and Coke. Actually, make me a double."

"I'll take a beer."

"Um, I don't know what I want. I'll head in there with you."

This last comment came from Kaitlin, I think? She was one of the few that didn't look like as much of a stoner as everyone else. She had shoulder length dark brown hair, green eyes, a smile that would make you weak at the knees and a septum piercing. She looked like she was put together enough, but at the same time, it was like she was trying to look like one of those kids that begged outside of the Lightrail stations for money. I didn't really consider myself a guy that had a type of girl that I was usually interested, but I immediately recognized her as this type. This party might turn out to be not a total waste of my time after all. She came up to me and reintroduced herself.

"Hey, it's Phil, right? I'm Kaitlin, good to meet you."

He looks kind of familiar, he's pretty cute too! Little mousey and weak though. Why does he look so miserable?

"Good to meet you too, Kaitlin, is it cool if I call you Kate?"

"Yeah," she smiled again. "I'd prefer it actually."

We walked to the fridge and I threw open the door.

"What can I grab you?"

I think he'll judge me if I go for something too strong, so I'll grab some wine.

I interjected and took advantage of the opportunity, because, who the hell wouldn't?

"Did you want some white wine?"

"Sure, that sounds like exactly what I want. Thanks!"

"Makes sense. I can read minds after all."

How the hell did I come up with that line? She'll probably think I'm weird. Or, maybe she'll think I'm really confident. Is that from a movie or something? Did I really make that up?

I realized I've been looking in the fridge not doing anything. I felt like I was frozen in this moment until she reacted. She looked at me, and then eventually, after an agonizing eyebrow raising reaction, she started to crack up. This felt like an eternity of a wait, but it wasn't. Thank god.

"That's hilarious!"

I smiled and exhaled in relief. I could finally start moving again. I grabbed the wine, and the coke. *Wait, who asked for that?* I wasn't even paying attention. I closed the fridge, and looked at Kate, who was still doubled-over laughing and wiping a tear away from my "not as corny as I thought" pick up line. She looked back at me and pointed.

"Nothing for you?"

"I'm gonna wait it out a bit and see how I feel. I had a drink earlier that didn't agree with me too well."

I had an opportunity for easy sympathy here. Should I take it, or let it slide? Who am I kidding, of course I'm gonna take it.

"Well," *Remember your dramatic pauses, Drag this out for more sympathy points.*

"It's not a big deal or anything. I'm finally out of the hospital. I want to take it kind of easy. I mean, they didn't say I couldn't do anything specifically, but just in case, I'll play it safe."

She raised her hand to her mouth.

"Oh my god, I'm so sorry to hear that! What happened? Or, you know, if you don't want to talk about it, that's fine too."

This was kind of a cheap trick and I knew it. Play up the sympathy and reap the benefits, but you know what? Fuck it. I got nothing to lose. I'll roll with it, and punch it up as much as I can.

"I'm sorry. I'm not really comfortable talking about it yet, but maybe later. Let's talk about better things; tell me a little about you. You know, you do look a little familiar. Which high school did you go to?"

We were taking our sweet time in the kitchen, while I was very slowly making that one person's drink.

"I went to Smokey Road County School. How about you?"

"Oh, well, I went to Grand Hill. We were rivals! I'm so glad we don't have to deal with that rivalry bullshit anymore."

What's he talking about? It's worse than it was before?

"I'm in school now at CSU, and the rivalries are alive and well up there. I'm pretty sick of it though. Where do you go to college?"

Hmm. How to handle this one? Would she think less of me If I told her I wasn't in school and had no plans to go? She probably wouldn't be too impressed if I told her that I was an exterminator, or that it was my dad's business that I'm begrudgingly inheriting.

I finished the double jack and coke, and poured myself another.

Wasn't this for someone else? Oh well, fuck it.

I poured her another glass of wine, all the while remaining silent and thinking through my options. I'm probably about getting to that threshold of uncomfortable, and I need to say something sooner than later or I'll be weirding her out.

I finally blurted out.

"I'm taking some time off right now, working and figuring out what field I want to study in. It's all so overwhelming you know?" Before giving her the option of a response, I interjected again, "Let's head back to the party before we stick out too much."

Let's see how this works out.

I handed her the glass of wine. She sipped it enthusiastically.

"Okay, sounds good. I want to hear more of this later though!"

He seems so confident and put together, why did it take me so long to meet this guy? Why was he in the hospital? I hope it wasn't something too serious.

I smiled at back at her, and gestured to her that we should head back in the room. Maybe I've thought about this relationship thing way too much. Maybe all it amounts to is a higher stakes game of cat and mouse.

The rest of the party was okay. I made sure to keep eye contact with Kate, who did the same with me. I'm not so sure of what my next move will be or when, but I feel like nothing else matters and I am waiting for that to happen. I watched from afar for about an hour plus three drinks.

Shit. There goes taking it easy I guess.

Everyone else was having whatever boring conversation came up, and the Chach, expectedly, only threw in over the top hyperbolic exclamations for the sole reason of making everyone else laugh.

How. Fucking. Interesting. I really wanted to like this guy, but never mind. God. That's a mean thought. I think I'm the epitome of antisocial. When the hell did that happen?

I remember why I hated going to things like this. With the rare exception of meeting someone and tried to get laid or something, I always felt basically like a revolving door. Conversations start, I jump in where I deem fit, then I quickly get the hell out of there if I don't get immediately included. I never successfully adjusted to the party dynamic Frankly, I have yet to really try that hard at any of these things. I was never outright dismissive or condescending at these kinds of parties, but then again no one was forthcoming enough to invite me into the conversation.

Maybe I have extremely closed body language?

I looked down at myself, to see how I was standing. Sure enough, I had my arms crossed and I was tapping my feet like I was trapped in a mandatory business meeting.

Oh, well there you go. That might be why.

I immediately readjusted my position. Also, I still heard all of their thoughts. I didn't give a shit about any of them. I mean, why bother talking to people that I didn't give a shit about?

"You look like you're trying too hard to look comfortable."

I heard someone whisper into my ear over my right shoulder. I actually jumped at this, and felt an arm grab me and heard some giggling. I caught a quick glimpse of Kate's hair over my right shoulder before she moved into my peripherals.

Well, there goes trying to be masculine and confident.

"Did I seriously scare you? Calm down, Phil!" Her breath reeked of booze and smoke. Even worse, she was smoking cloves.

"I wasn't scared."

I think I'm actually going to own up to it this time, instead of trying to be dismissive and confident.

"Fine, you scared me. And as it turns out, I'm a little drunk. It's not that difficult to scare a drunk. Don't be too proud"

"Oh really?"

Where did this sassy side of him come from?

I finally realized she was hitting on me. *What card should I play now?* Before I could make what probably would have been the wrong move, she cut me off.

"So, what kind of a drunk are you? Are you a fun drunk, a sad drunk, or an adventurous drunk?"

Without thinking or showing any signs of weakness, I confidently responded.

"It depends what I end up drinking and who I'm around."

She grabbed my arm and dragged me back into the kitchen.

"I guess what you're saying is, depending on the next shot I pour you, it would determine the outcome of your night, right?"

"I guess so."

I took a change in my normal response to a woman I'm interested in for tonight. I attempted the terse, distanced, "Hemingway" approach as I called it; my version of it was a little less misogynistic, and more ambiguous and confident.

Kate smiled at me, still dragging me towards the liquor table.

"Well, let's determine your destiny."

Hmm, what shots could I make him do that would get him to make out with me?

"What do we have here anyway?"

She played around with some of the bottles of the table full of booze.

"We have tequila, some whiskey, some bourbon, vodka, or gin."

Please god, do not let it be tequila. I am not accountable for my actions on that stuff.

I think he likes his whiskey or bourbon, but let's get him some tequila. I'd bet he is pretty fun on that stuff.

Fuck.

I immediately faked a smile.

"So what are you gonna pour for me?"

"Oh, I'm pouring now too, am I? I thought I was picking out some booze, but I guess I could pour you some. Let's go with some tequila!"

"Okay, sounds good. I'll warn you now, I apologize for nothing. It's tequila for Christ-sake."

"I think you'll be fine."

She poured what looked to be a very hefty shot, it could have easily been a double. She poured herself one (a bit shy of a single), as well.

"Alright Kate, what are we drinking for?"

She looked cute as she thought about it, but cute in an overly exaggerated "I don't know kind of look" with a finger on her chin and everything.

"Seeing as you are still recovering, let's drink to your health and happiness."

I was honestly surprised and a flattered by this. This was a very nice gesture by a beautiful girl, who is clearly interested in me. Things are turning around and looking up. This might work out to be okay after all. I smiled at her.

"Okay, let's drink to that."

We clinked our glasses, and I swallowed an instantly regrettable shot. My entire face scrunched up as a reaction to the painfully cheap tequila.

"Ugh god, where's the lime??"

I needed at least lime or something to chase how bitter that was. I heard an "mmffh!" and looked to my right and Kate had the lime facing out, holding it in her mouth.

Part of me, the former, nervous me that couldn't read minds. In this situation would have meekly asked, are you sure about this? But the meek me was something that I was sick and tired of being. Also, so far, the overly confident me has hit it out of the park judging by the fact that this girl I met not even an hour ago I smiled and kissed her, and bit the lime and kissed her harder. I wanted it to be a quick thing so I pulled my head back. She pulled me right back, spit out the lime on the floor, and kissed me again. Kate started to bite my lip this time as well. Kate then put her hand on my chest and pushed me away. She pushed my chest hard. It actually hurt, but, I had no intention of showing it. Remember, I'm playing the role of the confident, cool, guy.

"Hold on. I have a better idea. Let's go upstairs. "

"Okay."

Opposite the living room side of the kitchen, there was a stairwell. She pulled me up those stairs by the collar. I liked having a girl in charge. Was this really it? If it was so easy to get laid in this scenario, why was it so difficult before? Sure, I had a huge upper-hand with being able to read minds, but there was not a lot of heavy lifting that I really needed to do in order to make this work out. This was so much easier than I could have imagined. All I actually did take advantage of, was the cues I got from her mind. Previously, I would have to second guess what the preferred action, or response to an action would be. This was unbelievable.

Am I really doing this right now? He's so cute, and I'm really drunk. His ass better have a condom on him. Ed and Stan will hate me for this, but fuck them, I haven't got laid in a while either and I am long done with both of them. That was only a one night thing.

I decided to quickly forget her last thought. As I was being pulled through the corridor to whatever room she decided to settle on, thankfully, it was so dark she could not see the concerned face I was making. *This girl can't be that much older than me, and she's already had a threesome. What the hell kind of life was I living?*

Kate finally picked the room down the hall and pushed me into the bed.

I wish he'd kiss me hard then pull my hair, it's so fucking hot when guys take control and tell you what they want.

Well, damn, did I crack open an instruction book with this power too? Thank god!

Class

"WHAT THE FUCK!"

She screamed and immediately pushed me away. As I tasted a salty substance and realized that it was Kate's blood. She was applying pressure to the wound and yelling at me through her hand.

"Whut tuh hull iw wong wif you?"

"I'm so sorry, let me see if I can get you a tissue or something."

I look around the room, nothing in sight to seep up the blood sanitarily, so I took off my shirt and gave it to heard to help slow the blood flow.

She threw it back at me.

"Juth futhing go!"

There was a lot of blood. I grabbed my shirt. I was dumbfounded, how could I not notice this?

"Is there anything I can do for you? Let me go to the bathroom and I'll grab some toilet paper or something."

"GUH!"

"Are you sure?"

She screamed as if she was a preteen girl. *Wait a second.*

"Hold on, wait a sec, how old are you?"

"Whut ah u tuking about?"

She swallowed down some blood and responded.

"I'm thtithfeen!"

It felt like a punch to the stomach.

"What the fuck is wrong with you? Were you planning on telling me that at some point?!" I was screaming at her now.

"You lying bitch!"

She spit her blood out on the floor next the bed. In spite of that, it was still overflowing from her mouth.

"Not that it matters, but I didn't lie to you."

"Then what the hell was CSU about? Where did that bullshit come from?"

"That's not bullshit, you idiot. I'm at CSU for the summer for an accelerated English program."

I rubbed my forehead, the way I always do when I'm stressed out. I took a very deep, three second breath.

"Alright. I need to get the fuck outta here, and I don't ever want to see your crazy ass again." Fucking gutterpunk. Go take a shower and stop listening to the Misfits. It's embarrassing. Also, when you say to someone you like it rough and want to bleed, then how about you be prepared for the consequences!"

I turned away and opened the door.

She swallowed more blood down.

"Or don't bite my tongue you crazy fu—"

The door slam cut her off, man that felt good. What the hell is wrong with people? I did exactly what she asked. How else would I have made her bleed?

I made my way downstairs and found Brad. I nodded at him to come over to me.

"Where the hell did you disappear?"

"We need to go. Now."

He shot me an annoyed look.

"But, Phil."

"Now. I'll tell you later, I'm sorry."

Is this guy serious? What the fuck?

I looked around, the room was staring at us.

"Hey guys, nice to meet you, but I just had an emergency at home. I need to go, my aunt's in the hospital."

The flood of pseudo-concerned voices came in.

"Oh well, great to meet you feel better!"

Damn poor kid, hope his aunt's alright.

"Sorry man, we'll see you later though, right?"

What was his name again? Ah fuck it, I probably won't see him anyway.

"See ya, man."

"Shit, hope everything's okay."

That sucks, he seemed okay.

"Fuck. Sorry 'bout that."

Hopefully we'll see him later.

"Damn, dude, sorry"

Wait a sec, where the fuck is Kate? Mom's gonna be pissed if she's too hungover for chores tomorrow.

That last one was the Chach. *Is Kate his? Fuck. That's totally his little sister.*

He looked back at me one more time.

"All good, man. We'll smoke up later!"

"Sure, Chach... Sure."

Well, fuck me.

"Alright, see ya."

I grab Brad by the shoulder and pull him outside. He seems like a pretty mild mannered dude, but I can tell I upset him.

"That was pretty damn rude, but I'm sorry to hear about your Aunt, dude. Which hospital is she at? Do you want me to drive you there?"

"Huh?"

What the hell was he talking about? I finally remembered my lie. He turned the ignition and stared at me.

"So which hospital do you need to go to?"

"Shit man, I was lying, sorry. It just got really weird in there with that Kate chick."

He look horrified.

"Oh god. Did you two fuck or something? She's like 12 dude."

"Twelve?"

I snapped at him.

"Sorry, man. We didn't do that. But, almost."

"Oh man, yeah she's weird as hell, man, I should have told you. And she's actually 14, my bad."

"Jesus, man. I feel like I can't breathe!"

"Heh. Yeah, she's real weird. Ever since she started meth man, that stuff definitely fucks with you."

"Wait, seriously?"

"Yeah, it's bad man."

I had nothing to say. The more I thought about it, the more I realized it was true: fucked up teeth, really skinny, extremely laid back and really pale. Was I really that dumb? I knew I was into the punk type of girl, but I'd rather not fetishize meth addicts. I thought I'd be more aware of that after all of the driving I've done in Wyoming, where they have the huge "Before and After Meth" billboards that were so terrifying. I could have sworn that shit was burned into my mind, for better and for worse.

I snapped out of my digression and realized that we were still in the driveway.

"Shit man, I just realized you have no idea where to take me, do you? I'm sorry."

"Yeah, I was wondering when you'd realize we were still here."

"Well, let's go in the Mountain View direction, you know where that school is, right?"

"Yeah, I know where that is. No problem."

He finally pulled out of the driveway. Shit, is he cool to drive? I know I had quite a bit to drink, but hearing that I almost had sex with a fourteen year old sobered me the fuck up.

"You cool to drive, Brad?"

* * *

BRAD ROLLED his eyes.

"Come on, man, do you really doubt me right now? If I wasn't okay to be driving, then why would I be driving?"

He doesn't need to know about my last two DUI's. I'm a changed man.

"Alright, well never mind then. Anyway, moving forward from the bukkake of bad decisions tonight that I made. I'm looking forward to Telluride man! Who did you see that you really loved? "

He exploded with laughter, but then his expression changed into doubt.

"Bukkake of bad decisions, huh? You, uh, you know you used that wrong, right?"

"Did I, Brad? Did I?"

"You're ridiculous, man. I like that. By the way, regarding my family. They're a little stuffy, but feel free to let jokes fly like that amongst ourselves. They only really care how they are perceived in public."

"Oh, so they're like every upper middle class family in the country then? Got it."

Thankfully, Brad still chuckled at that. As it turns out, that wasn't too dickish.

"I guess, but, they're pretty chill. Don't worry about it. Anyway, I didn't answer your question yet. This is a while ago, but when *Burn After Reading* (2008) came out, Joel and Ethan were in Telluride promoting it. Someone much smarter than me drew a parallel between that movie and *Barton Fink* (1991); one of my favorites. It turns out that John Turturro was in the audience, and joined them on stage for an impromptu q&a about how they work with their cast and how hands on they are! It was awesome!"

I was awestruck by hearing this. That's absolutely one of my favorite movies. I felt very much in the same boat as that character. He is perpetually stuck in his own mind; unable to comprehend real world struggles in his skull shaped lofty tower of a hotel room. *Maybe in retrospect that was heavy handed? I don't know, either way I fucking loved it.*

"So, what was the question, man? I can't think of any parallels between the two."

"Shit, man. I have no idea. I'm not good at that deep thinking shit. I just like the movies, ya know? It was just some nerd question about the framing of certain scenes and blah blah nerd shit."

"Oh. got it."

Is this the cruel truth of the festival crowd? The people that love film theory and all that, don't go to these things and the only people that do are the nepotistic silver spoon fucks that don't even care, or; the disheartened, former idealistic creators that are just beaten down film critics with press passes? Ugh. I'm a lot less excited now.

How do I use this to my advantage? They are always saying that this is the industry of "know somebody who knows somebody," but how do I get out of my own mind enough to enjoy myself, and have enough confidence to market myself?

I truly shuddered at the thought of this. Sure, there are entire industries based on the simple premise of figuratively selling yourself to sell whatever the product or service is, but it takes a certain kind of person to do that. The only thing I can think of regarding that kind of persona is that dumbass *Tommy Boy* (1995) quote about how he could "Sell a ketchup popsicle to a woman in white gloves."

But how the hell do I gain that confidence overnight? Maybe I should just do a bunch of coke and dive into being a sleazy, rubbing elbow types of person. I don't want that, but maybe that's something I have to adjust to being.

I had to pry to be certain that Brad was not this type of person.

"So, uh, what's a stand out part to you? Why did you say it's one of your favorite movies?"

He looked at me, and without hesitation cried out: "The life of the mind man! That shit is great, his performance is amazing!"

Well, okay, I'll give him that. I can't argue with it but, there is so much more to that movie. Oh shit, am I one of those hugely analytical overzealous "everything matters" type of film fan? It's just a fucking movie bro. Don't make your life revolve around it. There's too much cocaine and pussy to not enjoy everything, and be stuck drooling over nerdy shit like this.

Brad interrupted my train of thought.

"Okay, where do I go from here?"

"Right, sorry man, I was totally distracted. Next two blocks take a left, and follow that winding road down until you hit a cul de sac, and I'm the corner of the cul de sac of South Pine and South Pine."

"South Pine and South Pine?"

Once again, no one ever believed me that I was stuck in the "corner" of both two streets. Come to think of it, It did feel like less of a place to live, then a temporary spot in a perpetual motion machine, but that is what life is I guess.

"Yup, true story, my friend."

Brad snickered and carried on.

"Well, would you fucking believe that? Give me your number and I'll give you a call once I talk to the fam and we figure out the times we are leaving and everything."

"Sounds good, man, it's 720-111-1112."

"Man, that's fuckin' easy."

As we pulled into the long road and saw the cul de sac take shape, Brad and I both noticed a moving truck obscuring the view of my house.

"So, this is your place? With the moving truck? What the hell is happening, man?"

* * *

"**WAIT, WHAT** the hell is this, are you moving somewhere?"

He is showing a lot of concern for someone who I would still consider an accomplice.

"No Brad. Just my mom."

I reassured him the best I could, but he did seem extremely concerned about this.

"She's packing up, and eventually, I will have to move out. For now she is moving in with some dude. It gets a little complicated man, call me later. Thanks again for the ride, Brad!"

Shit, that sounds crazy. I'm not looking forward hearing more about that mess.

Brad waved goodbye, but before he headed out, I made sure and yelled in his direction.

"Don't worry, man, we are still on for Telluride! I'll see you on Monday!"

With the window rolled down, Brad stuck his arm out and waved it at me as he pulled away. He kind of looked like a dumbass biker signaling to cut through the traffic. I took a deep breathe, rolled up my sleeves and headed inside.

The house was in complete disarray. Everything was already either packed up neatly, or left in multiple obvious "discard" piles throughout the house. It was all packed up in mismatched, used food boxes and it smelt like the bottom of a dumpster behind a grocery store. *How could she do this to me? Mom knows she is all I have.* This isn't completely unlike her. She always flirted with spontaneity, it was never completely detrimental to us, or her health directly, but you could tell there were only a couple razor thin wires tethering her to the world we both knew.

Walking through the living room, I was surprised by the things Mom did not want to take with her. To a certain extent, I understood why she would leave the painted fish that I made her out of paper mache in the third grade, but then again, all the photos and frames were in the exact same spot. Then it all hit me at once as I looked at the long forgotten family portrait. This was where Dad had his arms wrapped around her, and they had the completely over the top surprised look as they both poured over her pregnant belly. I was there too, completely oblivious to that situation. I was smiling at the photographer, who just out of the right side of the frame had a bike horn that he was squeezing. I was completely enthralled and too distracted to be paying attention to my parents in any regard.

Looking at it now I felt guilty. Not much has changed apparently. I'm still a space cadet with my head way too high in the clouds to be rooted to all of the problems that my mom was facing. For instance, I had no idea then, that we were in dire financial times. I can't speak to her situation now, but I'm sure it's not that much better; she's always been conservative in that regard. I took some steps away from the photo and stopped thinking about what could have been, what was meant to be, or anything like that. I decided I needed to actually get some fucking sleep.

This was it. With her leaving and Uncle Steve moving to Pueblo; anything is possible for me. I can completely reinvent myself. Fuck this city, this state, Larson & Son, it doesn't have to be anything except a memory. This could be turning over a completely new leaf for me! It doesn't matter who I've been, it's who or what I am capable of becoming.

I took a second, realized I was being too blindly optimistic, and decided that I needed to be grounded back in reality. So, I decided to head to downstairs, pull up my pitiful bank account information and wallow in shit for a while, and jack off to some pitiful cuckold porn—in keeping with the theme of degradation. Sometimes, it was rewarding to feel like shit. Is that just me?

After that was done, I wanted to check out the Telluride Film Festival programming.

I wonder if Brad is in any special tiers of membership that would get him access to some of the after parties, or after—after parties?

It saddened me to flip through the 75 page program, only to see that 60 of the pages were ads. Then again, why would I be surprised to see that? These are all fledging films, in dire need of sponsorships and angel investors. Instantaneously, I remembered that this will be an extremely sleazy scenario of hobnobbing and rubbing elbows type of affair with soulless, self-promoting creators trying to sell out.

Sure, there are the all too familiar avenues of crowdfunding films (regardless of how disingenuous these sound), that's one way to hold on to artistic integrity. But ultimately, does everyone end up selling out? Can independent artists truly survive in this industry without compromising their visions? There are the widely publicized fall outs of creators and studios, but how many of these directors or artists quietly shut their mouths, swallow their pride and succumb to the fistfuls of dollars in order to make their somewhat compromised film?

I'm getting caught up again. *Who the hell is in the festival?* Let's get to the meat and bones of this and stop getting sidetracked in my passions.

As I was white-knuckling my mouse, scrolling through what the festival consisted of, I was surprised by the diversity of their films. A lot of unique voices, with a small smattering of majors masquerading as independent films. It looks like it will be some really interesting films, and I would love to go to all of them but that is completely unrealistic.

Okay, let's see, we have some: Nicholas Winding Refn, Rian Johnson, Tim Heidecker, Shane Carruth, Duncan Jones, Wim Wenders. James Franco has a sit down with, Harry Dean Stanton? What the hell is that? Hmm. That sounds like a hard pass to me.

I spent probably an hour or so pouring over the possibilities of how I can map out my time of where to be, with whom and why. I was ecstatic. How the hell would be the best way to handle all of this? I felt completely overloaded. I hit my bed hard, and stared off into unfinished wood ceilings.

"Fuck."

I didn't even think about how to handle an encounter with someone famous. What should I do? Obviously they want to be treated as normal; but I'd imagine, out of all the scenarios where they can be praised and pointed out, a film festival is not uncommon to them. Then again, it's probably not expected either—at least I hope.

So if I come across a director I love, what the hell do I do?

Just be yourself.

My gut was telling me this and to a certain extent, it did ring true. However, my intuition has always failed me. *Who or what, should I present myself as? A nervous burn out who loves movies? Well, that hasn't worked out so well for the duration of my life. A confident, film fan with a nonchalant approach? No, that wouldn't make any sense. That's probably like every other film school douchebag that lurks around these festivals.*

Who the hell should I be? How should I present myself? I've been asking myself that since I was born.

There are no answers. Would there ever be? Probably not.

Alright, it's well beyond the time that I shut my mind up. If I didn't have booze or any other supplements to do that, I generally just drowned it out with dumbass mind quieting TV, which was practically all of that.

Somehow, I got in the habit of watching those stupid reality food shows. I'm a big fan of people screaming at each other and trashing shitty bars and restaurants. Big fan. It took me about 45 minutes to really escape from my own thoughts and be able to escape.

Until then, I am left with the refrain: *Who the hell should I be?* Over and over and fucking over again until my mind shuts up.

In all seriousness though; who the hell should I be? What would be my defining move? Or do I have any uniquely defining characteristics?

Who the hell should I be?

* * *

I WOKE UP with a mission today. In order to restart myself for this film festival, I needed to change a couple things to come across as a drastically different person. Namely, I don't want to continue to look or feel like shit, and a great way to do that is a haircut and some new clothes.

I rushed out of the house this morning and headed over to pick up some breakfast and get a haircut. After that, I'd come back, shower, and not scratch my neck like a cokehead for the remainder of the day. Then I'd go do some shopping. Fortunately, the Supercuts was really close by and it was dirt cheap. No need to pay for a ludicrously expensive salon when the only two haircut options for me were short or long.

I drove up the block from the cul de sac and two long, winding roads ahead of me was the shopping center. I first went into Peet's to grab a coffee and a blueberry muffin. Good enough way to start the day right? As I was impatiently waiting in line—everything done before my first cup is impatient- I turned around to look at the rest of the stores in the distance of these huge parking lots. Why did it look like I was the only one out today? Where the hell is everyone? Is it really that early on a Saturday morning?

What's this guy's problem? He looks way too fucking uppity for 8am. Ew. He smells horrible. Why can't you meet a cute guy in line once and have him fall for you like it does in all of those dumb movies? Yeah right Chrissy, that's bullshit and you know it.

Oh great, I'm the smelly weirdo now. Awesome. That's exactly what I want to completely rid myself of being. With the right clothes, haircut, and approach; I could easily be the cute guy. But, I still wouldn't want to be with Chrissy or whoever the hell this girl is; she looks like she's trying way too hard.

After hearing a couple more of Chrissy's problems and unshakable hopelessness, I got my breakfast and headed outside. There was a really nice spot at the tail end of this strip mall/shopping center that was slightly off the road. There, you could sit down and a tree framed perspective of the housing development in the valley, and the rockies off in the horizon. I loved it. I wanted to make sure I didn't take it for granted.

Seeing as I had some time to kill, I decided to try and relax for a bit. I never could successfully truly relax, but dammit; I'll always try. As I walked further away from the Peet's, I noticed a homeless looking addict holding up some ineligible cardboard sign behind the coffee shop, probably hoping for some dumpster diving finds later.

I walked into the small, lush, wooded area by the opening of a larger gated community. I sat down against a tree thought about how I wanted to come across for this festival.

Did I want to be a typical film student/intellectual type that Brad apparently loathed? Or, did I want to be someone over the top artsy, like those stereotypical art jackasses in the fucking sitcoms that would appear at galleries and poetry readings? Should I be one of those beret wearing sad bastards?

I took a sip and nestled myself against the tree.

Damn. This coffee is exactly how I like it. Well played, Peet's.

My mind started to race with the exponential amount of these options, but I stopped myself before I fell into a rabbit hole of thoughts.

Why did I want to be completely different, and why haven't I been able to be happy with myself how I am? I didn't really hate myself. Do I?

At that moment, I heard another voice entered my mind.

This guy can only limp away! Man this couldn't get anymore like fish in a barrel.

He approached me very quietly and carefully. Even without the ability to read minds I would be extremely skeptical of this dude.

Fuck, it was the addict looking guy.

"Hey man, can I borrow your phone? Mine died and my car broke down by Gun Valley road."

Upon first glance, it could be assumed that he was telling the truth, he looked like he was dirty and tired as hell not homeless per se, just, ragged. Maybe he was roughed up by his dealer. God damn crystal meth, it really does some damage.

I played coy and cool.

"Damn, dude, I'm sorry, I left that at home."

Shit, well… maybe he has some cash and he's still worth beating up.

"Ok, well, no worries, man, I think I saw a payphone up the way a bit. Do you have any quarters, or any change?"

This guy was persistent. With every sentence he moved closer and closer to me. Alright, I don't think I should be that cool to him.

"I don't have any change either, man. Could you just back up? You're weirding me out."

He put his hands up in the air.

"Alright, man, alright. I can take a hint it's good. "

Holy shit, look at his leg! That's gotta be worth some coin. Looks titanium or something.

Sitting down stretched out against the tree, he finally was close enough to see my prosthetic.

Why can't I shake this asshole?

He leaned down to get a closer look at my leg.

"Whoa, man! What happened to you? Sorry for staring, I just, I haven't seen an amputee in person before."

"It was a car accident, could you leave me the hell alone now?"

With an extremely creepy smirk, he reached in his pocket and pulled out a butterfly knife.

Was this supposed to be threatening?

"Can't do that, man, I'm going to need to take a closer look."

He inched closer and closer to me all while failing to look increasingly menacing. He looked ridiculous. At that moment, I got an idea in my head to get out of this situation, unlike one I ever had. It was a combination of bolstered confidence from the previous night and ingenuity.

"All you want to do is check out my prosthetic?"

He looked disarmed by this.

"Well, yeah, I'm going to take it, pawn it off, and get some easy cash. There's nothing you can do about it either."

I shrugged and played dumb.

"I mean, if that's all you want, then sure."

I took off my shoe, removed the socket and rested my leg up against the tree for balance. I proffered my prosthetic to him with arms wide open.

What the hell is this guy doing right now?

* * *

AS I PUSHED away from the tree trunk, I grabbed my prosthetic by the ankle and shoved it against his throat with enough force to push him to the ground. I was in control. I pushed my leg lightly against his throat.

In an extremely brief, and fleeting moment, I had a flashback to my rape. It was more like a flash frame however. I saw the alpha's disgusting smile, right before he decided to whip it out. My jaw got sore thinking about it, and I quickly shook it off. I made the decision that I would never let myself get in that scenario again. I will never be taken advantage of in that regard; from now on, I'll be in complete control. I instantly regained composure and intensely focused in on what I was doing. And more specifically, what I was capable of doing. I'm the master of my own destiny right now. I wasn't about to let this piece of shit get one over on me, even if he was not nearly as threatening as the other guys.

"Give me one fucking reason not to kill you, asshole. I've had enough shit in my life to see right through the petty garbage you were trying on me."

Fuck. Why did I have to try to rob this crazy asshole on my comedown? The chick I robbed earlier didn't put up a fight and this dude looked like even more of a lame duck. Maybe that was a shitty batch. I didn't feel that last hit of Flacca for nearly as long.

Holy shit, this dude was on Flacca? What the hell did I just get myself into?

I was nervous in a way I've never felt before but at the same time, I finally was in the position of the higher ground. This is the first time in my life I've felt nothing but pure testosterone flowing through me. I made sure to not let my nerves get the better of me, and I stayed in total control, knowing what I should and shouldn't do in this scenario. I knew I shouldn't let this guy thrash around much, seeing as that could lead me to touching him and leaving fingerprints. If I only held onto my prosthetic, the only thing they would see is a blunt force to the throat. Thankfully, titanium has a very high tolerance for abuse, with an extremely low corrosion rate. It wouldn't oxidize, or in this case, leave any shards of any sort.

His eyes were finally open, a rare sight for junkie trash like this guy. He developed this slick, knowing smile.

This guy has no idea who he's dealing with. He doesn't how many pricks I've killed for less.

He spit in my face and tried to stab me in the neck, but only ended up grazing my throat with the blade.

I knew what needed to be done. I kneed him in the balls with my good leg to distract him, while I pushed down with all the force I could on his Adam's apple with my prosthetic. That was when I heard the clinking of the knife dropped on a nearby rock.

Shit! How did I get myself into this?? I'm way too young to go like this.

Well, fuck me. Not only do I have to kill this guy, but I also have to hear his dying thoughts? I have to hear his sad bastard life montage? I've already seen Midnight Cowboy. *I know how these junkies die. Alone and derelict. I don't want to hear this shit again.*

I focused intently on the sounds of his gurgles. I really tried to wrap my head around every aspect of them.

From the faint and staccato "ech" style of coughs, to the longer drawn out gurgle sounding "urughhk"s. I was completely fascinated by the range, intonation, and pitch of the natural sounds your body made when you were dying. It was like an extremely personal performance.

Additionally, the more I thought about this, the less I heard his pathetic dying wishes about how he wanted to fuck his junkie side-piece one more time, or how he wanted to maybe once not be a disappointment to his entire family that probably already gave up on him and never told him they loved him or some shit like that. The more you humanize something, the harder it is to get rid of it—like naming a cow that's already meant for slaughter. You just shouldn't do it.

Wincing in pain and panicking, and his face quickly turned beet red. His Adam's apple wriggled out of the weight and force of the prosthetic. For the first time, I was in charge. And it felt really fucking good.

His limbs were flailing in all directions, sometimes hitting me, but it was all so weak that it didn't really bother me. I started to hear his gargling, desperate hopes for airflow. I pushed down harder and recapitulated my hands so they were on the ends of my prosthetic to give me more force. He kept making these disgusting sounds the more and more I pushed down. It felt like time slowed down. His eyes were getting more bugged out, he started to drool, and then finally, his struggling stopped. His body went completely limp under mine, and I felt an extreme relief. There it was. The death rattle.

Hearing that last gasp for life was not something I took lightly. I'm not a spiritual person, but I firmly believed that noise was the escape of the soul. I think that's a Native American thing, or that's something that I have appropriated as a Native American thing, because I have been told that in multiple viewings of *Wayne's World* (1992).

Sure, I had an ounce of pity for this person, but I had to also consider that he put himself in this situation. His choices have lead him to this moment, and my choices would do the same. I haven't been proud of everything I've done, however, I could shape myself going forward in any way I could.

Maybe the Phil of Aurora was a pathetic victim with no real sense of agency, but the Phil of Telluride would be one who is completely determined and eager to take on any challenge that life throws at him. I got out of my own head and looked at the body before me. There it is, I've actually killed someone. There was always that scene in those movies where after the protagonist kills, and looks at his hands and his palms in disbelief. We get it, this is done to show how they couldn't believe what they are capable of, and how their life has come to this moment. It's a very important aspect in the development of blah blah blah.

Those scenes drove me crazy. They were unrealistic and trite. Should I be looking at my prosthetic in disbelief of what I've become?

Killing someone is easy, especially if you can focus away from hearing thoughts. Now, the body on the other hand. What do I do with that? Fortunately, we are in a fairly well covered area. I need to pick up his knife, which could have some blood, or other trace DNA on it, give a check over on the body, and then just head out. I still had a pretty busy day ahead for myself. I pocketed the knife and inspected the body.

Look at this pathetic kid. I won't ever go into the really hardcore drug scene, that could easily destroy me, or anyone. Let's see, I didn't see any swollen wrists. I didn't grab them in the brief struggle we did have. I only kneed him in the balls and destroyed his throat.

I think we are good here.

I was in the unique position where I had to walk away with the murder weapon. That is definitely in my favor. I took a couple steps away, and then rushed back over to check the body. This nervous tick was exactly as if I was making sure all your lights and appliances were off before you left your house for the day. I peeked over again, and sure enough it was still fine.

So where do I go from here, do I go about living my life as usual, or do I go completely downhill and along all the wrong paths? I know I needed to avoid confrontation going forward, but I can't let myself be the victim anymore. I walked away from this crime scene with the same swagger as Verbal Kint in *The Usual Suspects* (1995). This was brief though, considering I knew to not be an idiot, and have a better poker face than that.

I shook that off and carried on with my plan. Get some new clothes, a haircut, pack, and go forward into this festival with a newly found confidence that would help me in a myriad of ways. I needed to consider that I haven't changed for better or for worse with my actions as of yet. Killing in self-defense is what a lot of people have done. So, I haven't changed, but I have certainly grown for the better.

Now to go forward and live.

I still needed to figure out what the hell was happening with my mom, the house, and everything else, before I did the complete kiss off and moved on.

For the most part, it was the rest of a normal day. I shopped, got a presentable haircut, and went home. Who says you immediately go through seismic shift after you kill someone?

I fucking wish that I could earnestly say that. I'm a disheveled mess right now and I can barely keep my head on straight. Is this where my descent to madness starts? It sure as hell feels like it. This would be that moment in Vertigo *(1958) where it does an extreme close up and zoom into Jimmy Stewart's forehead.*

In actuality, I was sweating through my clothes, with a Parkinson's like shake, looking even more pale than usual and on the verge of throwing up. But fortunately, I could sell it as one really terrible hangover. Who would be able to tell the difference anyway? The methheads in my area were a common sight, and looked dead anyway. In this nicer shopping center, I clearly stood out. I needed to get my ass back home and showered.

Am I okay to drive? I'm nothing but nerves and anxiety.

I took a couple of very deep breaths, and drew them out as long as I possibly could; then headed home without any issues. It was a very quick drive after all.

As I pulled up in the driveway, I knew I would have to face my mom for the last time in god only knows how long. She could be the only person that notices how I'm acting differently than a mere hangover.

You got this, Phil. This is cake.

Looks like it'll be Mom and Kyle, just riding off into the sunset together.

I found her at what remained of our kitchen, she was smoking in her robe looking completely disheveled while her entire world for the past 25 years was being dismantled around her. She looked like she didn't even care.

Ok, just keep it cool, everything is fine.

She was shaking and awkward as hell too, but why? What did she have to worry about? She looked like Allison Janey in one of her deadbeat roles, like Dot in the *Ice Storm* (1993) but on Quaaludes and *just* after a key party. She straightened up her posture as soon as she saw me.

"Hey, Phil. Nice hair cut!"

She feigned interest in me, then got down to business as usual.

"What are you doing here?"

I was astounded by how little she seemed to give a shit about everything that was happening.

"What am I doing here? I'm still trying to recover from the hospital, while you are dismantling the only place I ever felt comfortable. Why are you doing this?"

As much anger as I had in speaking to her about this, her response was completely devoid of any and all emotion.

"Well, if you were listening earlier this week when I told you, you might remember that we are moving out. You also might remember that we could only afford to pay for this place for a couple of months for you while you sort out what you want to do. But surprise, surprise, you didn't listen. Again."

How could she be so blunt about this? She was acting very weird, a little twitchy even. I thought I'd be direct with her to see if she was anything. I never have known her to be a drug user, but her energy was screaming as if she was coming back down from something.

"Mom, are you okay? Are you and Kyle, *using* anything?"

She looked appalled at the question. Her eyes widened immediately after that, she looked to be guilty of something,

"Mom? Hello? What's going on you didn't respond? Are you, are you shooting up with Kyle or something?"

Her whole body twitched this time. At that moment, Kyle waltzed into the room with nothing but a towel on. Kyle had a little bit of a lean and mean biker look. Not those, older, fatter over the hill bikers, but the ones who were right before heading up that last hill of giving a fuck about what they look like. He did have one bad ass salt and pepper handlebar mustache, so that was in his favor at least.

He looked awkward at first, and then warmed up to me.

"Phil! Hey, buddy! How've ya been?"

Kyle looked at her with a forced smile.

With my forced smile, I lied through my coffee stained teeth. "It's going great Kyle, how are you?"

"Good, man! Good to see you. Man, you are taking this well! This is going great! Sorry if your mom sprung news of the move on ya. I heard you took that a little tough. We've been talking about this for a little while, and it'll be good for us. Ya know?"

Mom twitched again, it was starting to bug me. It wasn't a facial twitch, or a nervous tick, which I've seen her do before; it was a full body twitch. I couldn't take it anymore and asked them both point blank.

"Kyle, could you do me a favor? I know you two probably just hooked up or whatever, you both are nearly naked after all, but are you two using drugs or something? Why the hell is mom twitching like that?"

It was at this beautiful moment that it all became clear. The house got so quiet, I could hear ever so faintly, the hum of the vibrator in my mom's room. Her eyes shifted towards disdain, and focused them towards Kyle, who started to massage her shoulders and smile.

I shuddered as soon as I heard this, and found a way to tune it out to the best of my abilities. Again, I decided to focus on the tones of her voice, as opposed to the subject matter of her ridiculously horrifying conversation. Maybe mom and Kyle watched that piece of shit James Franco documentary about *Kink* (2013) and decided to take some of those ideas literally. Either way, I don't know if I could ever truly look her in the eye again.

Kyle started talking as well, who knows, or cares, about what. He had a much more bassy *hummmm* to his voice that cancelled out the vibration. His tone was lower, but he spoke in the parlance of an old roadie; almost like Sebastian Bach. I could never take him seriously. He sounded more like a post-college bro than a man to me.

I finally shook it off and tuned back into the conversation. Thankfully, they have moved on to their future plans, which was of exactly no concern to me. But Jesus, about fucking time they changed the subject.

"Well, kid, what do ya think?"

Without knowing what the hell he was talking about, I responded perhaps over enthusiastically.

"Yeah, sounds great, count me in!"

He looked surprised at my response.

"Okay, so just to reiterate, you have a month and a half to find a place to live before we cut you off of rent, utilities, and put the house on the market. This sounds great to you?"

I carried on the illusion for the hell of it. They already made their decision after all, what say did I have in it?

"Yeah, I'm excited! I get to look for my own place, and really get started to pave my own path in the world out there."

I ran that last part by in my head. *Pave my own path? What kind of ridiculous, trite crap is that? What Disney Channel bullshit movie did I rehash that tired cliché from?*

Mom looked thrilled.

"Phil, I'm so happy to hear that you feel that way, this is just the kind of optimism I'd always hope you'd have!"

Kyle looked pleasantly surprised too.

"That's great, kid! It looks like you got yourself a good one, Linda."

Mom started sniffling.

"I always have. I just sometimes forget."

The tenderness of the moment quickly fleeted when I heard the muffled screams of I'm assuming a duct-taped third person in the bedroom. Kyle's shit-eating grin widened. My stomach got weak and I clutched it quickly. I could feel the bile bursting up through my throat. Kyle chimed in with a fact that I couldn't care less about.

"Man, in my hangover days a shower beer would clear that one right up!"

I felt myself getting extremely pale.

"I got to go mom, I think I'm going to be sick. "

With that, I ran downstairs and nudged past my bathroom door to immediately throw up in the bathroom. My nerves and the whole awkwardness in general finally got to me.

Yup, this is a very promising, brand new start for me.

* * *

MONDAY ARRIVED quicker than expected. The rest of the weekend consisted of trying to relax as much as possible all while being completely anxiety riddled. I was paralyzed by my fear of what could happen next. After you kill someone, can you go back to an unassuming normal life? The body of that drifter was found, the local news reported it as self-defense, but they were still investigating the matter.

At 8 a.m. I woke up and started to pack, I brought out some slacks and button downs I bought over the weekend, in addition to some casual bullshit graphic T's and jeans. This is no Cannes after all, so aside from some potential after parties. Who really cares?

My only real concern about this upcoming road trip is meeting Brad's potentially stuffy, upper crusty family. First off, how would I relate to them? I can't fathom that any of them really give a shit about film or its cultural impact, but you never know. The last thing I want to do is have nothing but a long weekend with bourgeois waspy assholes that are treating this film fest not as a cultural touchstone of our time, but a happy jaunt in Telluride to flaunt their money and treat it like yet another high society elbow-rubbing elitist affair.

Then again, maybe I should be more worried about how I interact with them. Can I maintain a happy, well-adjusted facade? Maybe I should read their thoughts and merely be a mindless "yes" man to them. The rich are surrounded by people like that right?

According to Brad's last text, he would pick me up at 11:00 with his family. It was 11:15, and I of course was still packing. I wasn't completely unprepared, but I was mostly unprepared (as usual). Then I heard this first *Beeeeeep* of his car. It was long, inconsiderate, and extremely impersonal. I really hope I was ready to deal with whom and whatever I was walking into by encroaching on this family trip. I threw the last of my toiletries and clothes in my bag and ran upstairs.

Before I ran out of the now, almost completely barren first floor, I legitimately checked how I looked in the mirror.

Why does this matter so much to me now? I've never given a shit about first impressions. Maybe this will be a lesson in why I should have always cared. You have to remember about all the potential opportunities you could have just because of your interactions with the right people during this time.

One last straightening of the hair and I was out. I faced the door, locked it, and turned around to by far the nicest car that has ever been in my driveway, a brand new black Cadillac Escalade. Was this seriously happening right now?

Well, if they have to travel, may as well be comfortable and travel in style, I guess.

It was as if I looked from bottom to top of this gawking, ridiculous car in slow motion; stunned by its mass alone. I felt like Charles Foster Kane in Xanadu, completely dwarfed by the cavernous monstrosity in front of me. Brad rolled down the window on my side.

"Hey man! You ready for this trip? Let's fucking do this."

With that, he kicked open the door, and the foot lift jutted out from underneath the car in an motorized, streamlined fashion; then locked itself into place before I stepped up on it to enter the car. I have never seen something as ridiculous as I am witnessing right now. This was a completely unnecessary luxury.

"Brad, honey, don't talk to your friend like that!"

The shrill, demeaning tone coming out of the Stepford-esque woman in the front seat continued, but I thankfully stopped paying attention.

"You must be Phil! It's a pleasure to meet you and my, you look so nice! I'm Jeannie, you can call me Jean. This is my husband Samuel, he prefers to be called Sam, and this is my daughter Lindsay. If she really likes you, she'll let you call her Linds!"

Lindsay followed that with an eye-roll.

"Shut up mom, geez."

I thought it was very curious that by introducing people in the way she did, a la Vanna White turning around letters, she drew some visual parallels with the type of women they are: trophies. That could be an unfair judgement, but first impressions matter. Their thoughts were bursting out of my heads and overlapping, but I discerned quite a bit from them. After deciphering them all, I think I finally understood them. I didn't know how to comprehend to everything I just heard, or what would be the best way to do it.

One at a time, Phil, just think about each thing you heard and you will be able to place their thoughts correctly.

Jean looked exactly like the trophy wife she was. Brunette with highlights, obvious, unapologetic, plastic surgery, to sum up; fake. Everything about her seemed disingenuous.

He seems like such a nice boy, cute too, but a little chunky. Maybe his personality will make up for it.

Sam struck me as a less quirky and a lot more boring version of Michael Sheen. He looked as square as you can possibly imagine. Khakis, blue button down shirt with a dark blazer that reeked of self-importance. He looked like one of the many clients I had that would "try me out" and then never call me back. Sam was the one that probably thought, *that kid is a sharp dresser! Maybe he'll have a good influence on Brad, that lazy ungrateful little prick.*

Dad had this idea for a "satisfaction guarantee" promotion that killed a lot of clientele for us. A lot of the times people wouldn't listen to us, so after we would do a spray, we would tell them they should expect a lot of dead bugs as the spray seeped in the property and started working. Sam looked like the type of guy that would still freak out and complain even after the fact. He looks like the type of guy that will fight to preserve every single cent he has, regardless of how many millions he had. Dad was always weak when it came to people screaming at him. he always folded after about 15 minutes of arguing. He was not a strong man by any means.

Linds was an atypical girl. She was in the same vein of the girls I normally found myself attracted to, but she was different. She was more of a waif, and less of a junkie. She had the frame of an early American Apparel model. Sort of heroin chic without the heroin. She was blond, wore extremely little make up, and looked more casual than the done up GWAR girls or even the *shudder* *Social D* fans that I normally enjoyed being around.

After unraveling that mess of thoughts, her thought was the one that surprised me the most:

Where does my gross little brother keep finding these guys? He's okay, but I bet if I give him a piece of me, he wouldn't be one of those ungrateful fucks... He would rather die trying to get me off than not try at all. I could shove his face in my pussy for days and he'd be so thankful for it. Hmm.

Should I respond to Sam first, and hopefully win the favor of the entire family by reinforcing his assumptions of how I presented myself? Or, should I immediately fuck Lindsay right there in the car and not stop. I can tell you which I wanted to do the most, but thought that I shouldn't piss off the rest of the family for a first impression. Before I drifted away into staring at Lindsay, I decided to respond to everyone.

"Hello, so good to meet you all, thank you so much for having me!"

Brad couldn't stop laughing at me, and merely reiterated his thoughts to me.

Phil looks really good, but does he know that he just dressed up for a six and a half hour car ride? Hopefully his dumb-ass won't get too uncomfortable.

"Dude, this is a six hour car ride! Go get comfortable, man. Don't be ridiculous and wear this stuff, go back in a change real quick!"

Sam looked at me, and raised his eyebrows.

"You make a good point, Brad. Phil, make sure you bring that outfit with you, but go change into something a little more tolerable for this ride. We'll wait for you."

After introducing me, Jean's face was buried in her phone the entire time. But suddenly, she gasped and popped her head up right as I was turning away from the car.

"Oh my god! Did you all hear about this dead drifter that was found right outside of the Greenwood Village housing development! The police have no leads or suspects! Thank god we decided to move into a better neighborhood!"

I turned away and yelled back to them.

"Be right back! Don't go without me!"

Fuck fuck fuck fuck fuck. Take some deep breaths, there is no way they would suspect you, remember to just breathe and relax. They said they have no leads! Don't forget that.

*   *   *

I WAS LEFT there on the porch, cold and shaking. That was where he found me.

"Shit, dude, you don't look good. Ugh, show me where you puked and I'll help clean it up."

I lashed back at him quickly.

"Fuck you, Dan, I didn't puke. I just, I'm kind of in shock I think."

"Oh really?"

He sounded genuinely concerned but he reeked of booze, and he was mumbling.

"Wha-what happened man? You look pale like shit, man."

Great, he was starting to slur his sentences too.

"It doesn't matter what happened, you're too drunk to understand me anyway."

"Whatever dude, I'm gonna head over to that corner store and coffee up."

"That's a horrible idea but whatever asshole."

Coffee normally does help him, but still he really shouldn't drive. I've been worrying about his drinking for a while. Sure, this was a party and everyone was expected to drink and have fun, but when all of your free time is spent drinking, and you're doing it by yourself, it very quickly becomes clear to everyone else what was going on.

At times, I've been known to be a hypocrite, and I drink too, but he was a special, arrogant blowhard when he drank. It comes to a point where no one can rationalize with him and he won't bother to listen to you at all. In spite of all that though, I am fresh from a sea change of a moment with Kaycee.

So what the hell happens now? Do I just ignore everything and move on? Do I try to call her and talk through this with her? Or do I play cool and ignore her from here on out? Also, why am I shaking so much.

"You look pale. Really pale, man. What *hiccup* happened?"

"Dan, please go inside and get some coffee, and don't put any Bailey's or Molly's or anything else in it. Okay?"

"Whatever, man."

If at one point, I ever had confidence it's gone now. This was the only time I had really put myself out there and look where it got me. Rather than be the mopey asshole the rest of the night, I need to go back in there and man the hell up. Being a whiny bitch on the porch does nothing for no one.

I'll go back in, make some rounds, try to flirt with some other girls and ignore what the hell just happened. Then when fucking methhead sobers up, I'll just leave.

I cracked my knuckles and went back inside.

You know what, this could be fun. I should flirt with the girl that would piss off Kaycee the most. Hmm, would that be her friend Elana, or Christine?

I walked inside with full bravado; there was no real reason to, but then again what the hell else did I have to lose? I scoped out what was going on where in the party. To my left, there were a couple dudes talking to Elana and some other people I haven't met. They were sitting there, completely oblivious to the horror story that is that blue couch. Kaycee's roommate Rachel has told me horror stories of that fucking thing.

She has told me stories of multiple lines of coke being done on that couch, in addition to the almost foursome that she walked in on one night after Kaycee's heroin dealer brought two of the most disgusting kicked out of the trailer park and into the rehab center women she has ever seen. Rachel was interesting because she could tell this story in a very off the cuff matter, in a very casual sense. Essentially, she turned on the lights in the living room after Kaycee had some friends over and passed out. When she did, Rachel shrieked when she discovered two of the most pockmarked, rail thin, toothless junkie women licking the coke dealer's erect—yet misshapen and uncircumcised—three inch dick, in a way that can only be described as their last hopeless action for a really good hit. As it turns out, it was exactly that. I remember asking her why she called it a foursome when in fact there were only three of them.

"Well, it was almost a foursome, because standing on the side of the couch closest to the door facing my direction was the fiancée/coke addict of one of the horrific women, being cuckolded, and jerking off almost into my face. The jizz fell in slow motion, and landed right before my feet."

The way she described it was almost operatic in the amounts of drama and deception she was experiencing. It was like that extremely graphic and totally unsettling, like a Shohei Imamura film.

Something tells me, I should stay as far away from that couch as I possibly could. I decided to look into the kitchen, where people always hang out, even though it is the tiniest space in the apartment. Tonight was apparently the exception to the rule. Somehow, Kaycee and Rachel had a huge kitchen; the biggest I've seen in fact. As I turned the corner of the living room to enter it, I realized the lights were off. I turned them on, and in an instant, I got yelled at and heard a shriek.

"Get out of here, man!"

There were two people in the far end of the kitchen, opposite of my entrance, leaning against the fridge. I looked at the fear in their faces, and slowly backed away and turned off the light, when I realized that this guy was fingering some girl against the fridge.

Sure, I walked away from it and turned out the lights, but I was completely awe-struck by that. I didn't know if I should be angry at the lack or respect of where they were and what they were doing; or, if I should be impressed and their ludicrously brazen action. I thought that I should tell Kaycee or Rachel, but I decided against it. That would mean I'd have to talk to either of them, which I really didn't want to do.

I quickly walked away from the kitchen and thought I would check out who, or what was going on in Rachel's bedroom. People often broke off from the party to get even more fucked up here. Sure enough, I creaked open the door being as conspicuous as possible, and saw that they were all in a circle sharing a bong listening to my favorite band, the Germs. I fucking hated Darby's voice. This was also the worst getting high music imaginable.

I thought about joining the circle and taking a hit. I could completely use one right now, but at that moment, it felt like I was watching something extremely sad unfold right before my eyes. No one was having a good time here, maybe that's because at the time, I didn't know I was hanging out in a junkie playhouse. Either way, I felt that I wanted to be far, far away from all this.

"Hey, man, shit or get off the pot, what the hell do you want to do?"

I was too lost in my own thoughts to realize that they were holding it, waiting for me to take a turn.

"I'm good man, thanks."

I walked out and closed the door behind me. I felt scuzzy. In this moment at this house, I felt completely disgusting. More than I ever have before.

I imagined for a brief moment, that they were all colonizing and someone eventually would need to get them to scatter. They were like a nest of cockroaches, carrying nothing but disease and whatever trash they could get their hands on. Thankfully, Dan showed up with a small coffee in his hands for me.

"Alright, man, let's get the hell out of here. We're done with this place tonight."

Methhead was still slurring his words, but I think maybe after we sit through this coffee—away from here—we would both be in a better position to drive home. I followed his lead outside, not saying goodbye to anyone else, and he started to stumble back to the car.

"Do you think that's a good idea?"

I said this to him as I grabbed his arm.

"Come on, man, don't do this. Let's finish our coffee at the corner shop and then we will head on back, okay?"

Dan shot back at me immediately.

"Don't fucking touch me!"

I heard it again.

"Don't fucking touch me!!"

* * *

IT GOT LOUDER and higher pitched this time, and I woke up in a mild sweat.

"Don't fucking touch me like that! Phil, get off of me man, this is getting weird!"

"What?"

I wiped the drool from my mouth, and shook my head to wake myself up.

"What happened?"

Brad looked at me in disgust.

"You were fucking, rubbing up on me while you were sleeping, man, it was weird. Listen, we're at a gas station, and we still have three hours to go. Let me get you some coffee, man."

Christ, that was weird. I didn't think Phil was interested in me that way.

Aside from some awkward lulls in addition to me falling asleep and apparently grinding on a dude; the road trip was for the most part boring. Everyone was killing time just playing whatever stupid game that their Facebook friends told them to play, and no one was really talking. That's fine, I didn't expect a big, kumbaya type of family bullshit, but I did expect to at least make general small talk and conversation where I could.

Brad and Linds had their headphones in, and Jean was for the most part talking on the phone. Sam was keeping a steady eye on the road, but he had a notification bar inside of his dash that was synced to his phone, which he was completely preoccupied with.

His eyes veered back and forth between the two fervently.

When is Lou going to call? That bastard better not be up to any surprises during this trip. He said it would be a good time in the office to get away from it all.

At about half way to the Telluride, we ended up in Gunnison to gas up and grab some food. Gunnison was a town that looked like a retro version of what Pearl street in Boulder used to be, if they didn't pour money into it. There was a population that was double my high school's class at around five thousand. Although my high school class probably had a concentration in pregnant girls, as opposed to, what I'm assuming are a very wholesome people in this town.

I didn't understand towns like this. People were driving and walking around with huge, dumbass smiles on their faces. *Who does that?* Was this indicative of some local cult that kept everyone from realizing how messed up the world can be? Or, perhaps, was

Gunnison far enough away from everything else that they didn't receive any news whatsoever. Do these people have cell phones, or laptops? Who knows, and who cares. The only thing I do know for sure is that in towns like these, I was skeptical, and extremely annoyed. In addition to the standard smattering of fast food garbage, there were distinct restaurants which were embraced by the locals.

While I was distracted, we parked the car to fill up, and Sam noticed my curmudgeonly attitude.

"You feeling alright there, Phil?"

"I guess so. I just for the life of me cannot, and will not understand how people in general can be blindly happy."

Jean, without being prompted, decided to chime in.

"It's because the people in this stupid little hick town don't know any better. It's like they—" she didn't finish her thought, and was distracted by a notification.

"Oh my god, Lauren Conrad just tweeted she would be at Telluride in support of a friend's new film!"

Lauren Conrad? Isn't Jean a little old to be following up on life advice from a vapid, late twenty year old? Who the hell cares what she thinks?

Linds just shot me a look and silently chuckled. I guess she could tell that I was confused and partially disgusted over that person. Sam played along like he gave a damn, and Brad was in his own world. Sam looked straight at me with a smile.

"Hey Phil, let's head outside and get those legs stretched. I think you can use it."

I was surprised, but intrigued by this.

"Sure. Sounds good, Sam."

I opened the door and headed out with him. Before I could get a chance to read his thoughts or get any kind of an idea of what this conversation would be, he dove in.

"Man oh man, am I excited for this trip!"

He looked at me with an ear to ear, unwavering smile. I decided to play along.

"Yeah, me too! Thank you so much again for taking me with you! I wanted to see what your schedule would be like? Did you have any specific screenings, or interviews you guys wanted to attend? I had written up a schedule that, well, I was planning on giving to you or whomever was planning this eventually."

"Whoa, buddy! Slow down! Hmm, I guess Brad didn't talk to you about what we do at this festival, did he?"

I was embarrassed, and perplexed.

"Sorry, I tend to go overboard when I get talking about film. It's one of very few things in this world that I get completely excited and passionate about."

"It's okay. Yeah, we can tell how excited you get, calm down. So listen, our approach to these festivals is probably very different than anyone else's."

"Alright."

Where the hell is Sam going with this?

"So Phil, I don't think Brad told you any of this, but I'm an entertainment lawyer. My partners and I go to festivals like this, to look at upcoming talent and determine if we should pursue anyone that would like our representation. We have one guy, Adam, who goes to all the screeners that are of new talent, *not yet exposed to the downsides of this industry,*" he said this all while winking, "and he determines who we should go talk to."

I was stuck trying to process all of this.

"Okay, so, if you have one guy that goes to see the screeners, what do you do while he is there? Do you go see anything you want?"

He looked at me appalled, while putting the pump back in the holster. He rubbed his hands together as if they just were washed, and turned around to reach for the window scraper.

"God no, why would I do that? This probably sounds crazy to you, but I'm not much of a film guy at all."

His brows furled and he shot Brad an angry look.

"Brad really didn't tell you any of this?"

He looked at me again while attempting to smile it off.

"This must be so confusing for you right now. I'm sorry Phil. Let me try to clarify this again for you. In spite of us going to a film festival, none of us are really that into film. Jean goes to the spas, and checks out as many resorts as she can, while Linds tries to flirt with whichever star she sees and is the most popular right now, and

Brad, well; Brad just kind of loafs around and tries to rub elbows with people. I swear, ever since that boy saw *Entourage*, he really thinks he can be the next uhh… What's the short one who wears a hat?"

After only seeing one episode of that bro-fantasy show, I unfortunately knew exactly who he was talking about.

I meekly offered the answer to him.

"Uh, do you mean Turtle?"

"That's the one! The next Turtle!"

The next Turtle? That's the single most depressing sentence I have heard in my life.

I smiled coyly, and mainly to appease him. But I couldn't shake the realization I just had. Of this family's annual vacation to a film festival, *I,* as a guest, am the only one who likes films? What the hell is going on here?

*   *   *

AFTER THE REST of quiet and awkward car ride, we finally got to the Hotel Telluride. It was a slightly foreboding place. It reeked of old school class; which I had none of, and the sheer amount of wood (or faux wood), would have been a termite's wet dream.

There is an extremely small part of me that wondered about what it would have been like to scale up *Larson & Son* into a commercial business. For the most part, we dealt with residential and some public places, but the scale of a place like this would have been an amazing addition to the portfolio of clients.

I said this was a part of me, didn't I? The other part of me thought *what the hell was I thinking? And did I just seriously think about the word portfolio in a business sense?* I must have had a knee-jerk reaction of my disgust, because Brad immediately checked in on me.

"Everything okay, man? I know it was kind of a brutal ride up here, but do you smell something weird or something? Are you alright? Do you not like this place?"

I was a little dumbfounded by his response, but then I finally mustered up a response.

"Yeah. Yeah. Everything is good Brad, I just had a weird thought; there's nothing wrong with anything here. It's gorgeous."

My gut reaction was wow, we are really staying here? But I have learned time and time again, that my gut reaction is normally wrong. Instead of being completely awestruck, which would have been easy to do, I opted to have an above it all type of approach. Unfortunately, this was the same approach as the rest of the Whitlock's. They were so far up their own asses, that they barely acknowledged me at all. Jean's thoughts throughout the lobby were completely overwhelming, and devastatingly petty.

Sam better have got the room with the view that I love. I wonder if they still have the same staff that helped me with my clothes up to the room as last time? It looks like they finally got over all the remodeling they were doing. What a shame, it looks more drab and dark then before. It looks like a failed rustic appearance as opposed to a warm and inviting one. If only they took my suggestions on the last comment card I wrote, they really could have done something with this place. Then again, if Sam ever let me finish my degree in interior design I would have been a completely different woman. But no, he insists that I don't need to worry about things like that. But dammit, I could have been something! I always had an eye for these things.

They continued on, but I didn't have the patience to listen in on all of her repressed dreams and hopes. It's sort of sad, but then again, I thought about the comment card. Who the hell would actually write interior design recommendations on a comment card left in the room? Better yet, who the hell would take that seriously? The rest of the Whitlock's were dragging themselves through the lobby, while Sam begrudgingly waited in line to check in.

These check-ins get worse and worse every year, maybe this place has finally become too big for its scope. Oh well. Adam keeps saying it's a great resource to find new, and gullible talent so, I guess we'll keep coming here.

Gullible talent? What the hell did he mean? Is he an ambulance chaser type of entertainment lawyer? Does such a thing even exist?

Brad was in his own world as well, only thinking about himself, as I was starting to notice more and more.

So if James Franco is here, maybe Dave can't be too far away? I wonder if he remembers me? He must, right? We went to a couple after parties and got completely fucked up. He was out of his mind at a certain point in the night, but he has to remember me.

I noticed a nod from Linds, directed at me, I walked over to her.

"Hey, uh, Phil, was it? Do you mind if you watch my bags while I head to the bathroom?"

I didn't necessarily expect a riveting conversation from her, so I accepted her offer.

"Okay, sure could you do the same for me when you get back?"

"Yeah, totally."

She pushed her stuff up against the wall closest to me and started to walk away. Something was different with her. Either I couldn't get a read on her thoughts, or, she legitimately was not having them. She was the typical non-committal type of girl that I've seen in dozens of places before; but something was, well, *off* with her. Like Brad, I was in my own head as well. I was thinking about all of the screenings I could watch, and what types of questions I should ask in the Q&A.

Should I just play it by ear? Or should I come in prepared and ask something about the ongoing themes and leitmotifs in their work? Well, I probably can only ask those kind of questions if those type of things continue to present themselves in their new films. They probably don't want to talk about their old work. Maybe there will be surprise guest like Brad was talking about, which would open the door to ask old, lingering questions I still have on their works. Hold on, would I even have the opportunity to ask these questions, or is it all pre-arranged, pre-screened and do they only allow people with sufficient press credentials to ask them?

Before long, I was too wrapped up in my own mind to notice Linds coming back from the bathroom and her standing right next to me. She tapped my shoulder and I shook in fear not expecting her. She laughed this off and gave me a coy smile.

"You okay there? I didn't mean to scare you, sorry. What were you thinking about?"

I attempted to laugh it off as well and tried to play it cool.

"I was just daydreaming." I paused, and then elaborated.

"This is my first time coming to one of these things, and I have a lot I want to see and do. I'm here with some of my heroes, and I would love to have any and every interaction with them I can, but I don't exactly know how to handle myself around someone I envy so much without losing my shit."

I paused and thought maybe I should attempt to learn from her experience.

"How have you managed it?"

She put about a half second of thought into it before she answered. I think she was intentionally trying to play up her naiveté and cuteness. When she did think about it, Linds tapped her finger on her chin and looked up.

Is she one of those girls that sells herself short intentionally to appear more cutesy? People like that are the worst.

"Well, I would treat them like you would treat anyone else. In my experience, they don't like being put up on pedestals all the time. Talk to them calmly and casually. It's completely fine to ask them questions as well. But, if and when you do, don't lead them with any overly mushy I love your work, or, oh my god you're amazing! Keep your cool and treat them like you would want to be treated you know?"

Her candid response took me completely by surprise. She clearly did put a lot of thought into this, and was well composed during the entire time. Maybe I've misjudged her? I didn't think to look past her obviously Coachella-fueled style choices and I should have done exactly what she said. I should have treated her like anyone else.

I should approach everyone going forward exactly like that too. Part of this trip was me changing how I appeared to other people and, hopefully, by that alone, I wouldn't feel like a cynical piece of shit all the time. Who would have known that it came from a mousy looking, post-EDC fest, kind of messy looking girl.

There I go again, assuming things. This was a habit I really needed to kill.

"I like you, Phil. I can tell that you're a thinker. It is pretty obvious when you daydream all the time, but still, I like you. I'm sure you have a lot to think about regarding who you want to see, and how you want to approach this entire experience for yourself. That's really cool man. I wish I could go to something like this with a fresh set of eyes again. I admit, I'm pretty jaded from the multiple times I've been here, but you are going to have a great time."

"Okay! Kids, Phil, Jean! We have our penthouse, let's head on up!"

Sam yelled this message through the lobby. Announcing it to everyone like he was clearly trying to show off his room. Linds got really close to me and whispered.

"Hey Phil, regarding your schedule, keep some time open so we can fuck. Either tomorrow or the following day afternoon is best for me. Let me know what works."

* * *

I **IMMEDIATELY** stood up and applauded. I was blown away by what I just had seen. I've never heard of this director before, but I couldn't wait to see what he would create next.

What a staggering statement on masculinity in classical vesus contemporary settings! What an amazing soundtrack, which by itself spoke volumes of character development and overall outlook on the twisted circumstances this protagonist faced. I was smiling from ear to ear clapping, but then other attendees thoughts entered my mind.

Standing already? Where does he think he is, Cannes or Sundance? He looks like one of those over eager, starry-eyed undergrads who thinks that film can change the world. What an idiot.

Hmm. This was interesting, but does this deserve a short article unto itself? We will see how the rest of the fest goes, but more than likely it will end up in the "rising star" section. I don't know, I found it really derivative and Franklin hammered the point home. We get it man, masculinity is nurture, not nature.

Ugh, another one of these types. We all saw Pulp Fiction *(1994) okay? This is 25 years later, try to say something new with your work instead of reiterating old themes. When is my next meeting again with my agent?*

I quickly looked around and saw that I was the only one standing. I immediately sat down and tried to not look embarrassed.

"Thank you! Thank you so much!"

The director stood up in front of the room, and started talking about the development process and his previous shorts and other accomplishments. Jeff Franklin, was clearly not a modest man. For his first time at a film festival, he dressed like Bono and was already accustomed to people basking in (what he perceived as) his awesome presence. He stood there with a leather jacket and denim on, and he was completely out of place; even more so than how I felt. All he was doing currently was regurgitating the bio he had already listed in the festival credits for his work.

Smugly, he started bullet-pointing his accomplishments and how he got to where he was. He was already parading around on stage with a Brett Ratner type of jerky, condescending, yet commanding persona. I felt bad for him, but still respected what he did. When he asked the crowd for questions, I made a conscious effort not to appear too eager to ask, but I knew exactly what I was going to say to him.

I laid in wait and let some stereotypical hungry for knowledge film students ask the first questions. They were sort of predictable as well.

"What type of camera did you use to shoot this, and what was your relationship like with the cinematographer?"

Jeff chuckled, and responded very coldly and matter of fact. He intentionally gave a closed answer, maybe because he didn't want to talk about it further.

"I shot this on a Red Epic, with a Zeiss CP2 lens. And I don't know if you saw the credits kid, but I directed, shot, and wrote the whole thing. The only person I had to get along with was me. Well, and the actors. Okay. Next question!"

What a shitty guy. All this kid wanted to know essentially, was how to emulate him, and Jeff treated him like garbage.

"Why did you decide to shoot on Red? This is a pretty lo-fi production."

"Well, that's exactly right. I wanted to capture the lo-fi atmosphere as clearly as I could. Sure, I could have used even 35mm to capture a raw feel to it or whatever, but I got a great deal on the Red's seeing as my dad knew the founders from some older acquisitions he had done."

So essentially, he shot it on Red because he got a deal? That hi-res footage didn't do any favors for the film's look overall.

I was a lot less inclined to ask my question now, but nonetheless, I needed to know. I really saw a bit of amazing work in that film, and regardless of who this prick is, I want to know how it came to be. I stood up with confidence and asked my question.

"Hi Jeff, first off, congratulations on your accomplishment."

He immediately responded to that with a surprisingly sincere: "Thanks man."

"Well, I wanted to ask about your film's soundtrack. I was genuinely surprised by your control of the situation, and how the idealized masculine icon that we all have come to know from John Ford, John Wayne, James Dean, and other classics like that, was deconstructed so simply yet profoundly. My question is, did you have your actor's listen to the soundtrack beforehand to get them in the mood of what the emotional state of the scene was, or, more specifically, how did you work in such a masterfully crafted soundtrack? I was very impressed at the contrast of emotional state you showed the audience, and how that conflicted with the non-diegetic soundtrack you used."

Jeff's first response was to incredulously look at me.

Maybe I was too wordy, or, too specific with my question. I should have just been clear and concise. I've never been good at either of those things. Dammit, I really need to learn when and how to edit myself and filter my thoughts down to the essence before I make myself sound like an idiot yet again.

Finally, he responded.

"Whoa, man. You film students think up the most wild shit. Uh, well, I intentionally didn't give my actors too much direction in any of these scenes, because I trust them. Like how you should trust your actors in a film if you ever get a chance at directing one. But in regards to the soundtrack, well kid; we got to the point of not having money. My girlfriend's brother is in a band, so they just did us a favor."

He continued on, but I grew less and less interested and more repulsed as time went on.

"I really wish I could keep up all the illusory fantasies and whatever daydreams you concocted about this production, but more often than not, it just boils down to the money. I didn't have this grand master plan to do anything like what I think you were talking about, I just knew I needed a soundtrack. The magic that you guys see in film is rarely part of what intentionally goes into the movie, it's what you think about it after. The meanings that you take away from film, are all present in your own mind. It doesn't matter what *I say* about it, it's a combination of the audience and the critics themselves. My work could have an entirely different meaning I was trying to convey but it doesn't matter. You know what I'm talking about? Anyway, next question. "

I felt like an idiot. Does it really not matter what the director's statement is anymore? Or should I even believe in this asshole? Why would he intentionally demystify something like this for anyone? Isn't he proud of his creation?

Sullenly, I sat back down in my chair and listened to the rest of this idiot's speech while anxiously checking my cell phone to see where I'd meet the Whitlocks for lunch. We agreed that we would all go our separate way during the day time, and reunite during meals. I thought that would be best, considering I was still trying to develop steady footing with all of them aside from Brad. Lindsey's command of us hooking up during the festival was looming at the back of my mind during this entire screening as well. Of course I wanted to have sex with her, she was really hot and seemed pretty cool too, but I couldn't help but wonder, *why me?* Was I a pawn to her in all this? Or was she remotely interested in me to some regard?

The next question was from a schlubby, morbidly obese stereotype of a film critic.

"Hi Jeff, thanks for hosting this discussion and congrats again on a great movie. My question to you is what was the first moment you realized you wanted to pursue a career in film, and did that same feeling come back to you at all during this filming process?"

"Thanks for asking, man. Well, let me tell ya little secret. I didn't initially want to go into film. As you all know from my bio, and my earlier introduction, I went to school for finance with a marketing minor. Truth be told, I've always been kind of a movie fan, but I'm not nearly as diehard of a fan as some of you are. After a couple internships at bigger financial firms, I ended up meeting people who were investing in art and film, and it seemed like something I would enjoy doing. Honestly, the artistic capabilities of film are not currently possible without a lot of investors and a lot of money pushing your work to the top. Hell, this is why I'm here at this festival. The more eyes on it I have, the more investment potential I have."

Is this all it really boils down to? We have some egomaniac daddy's boy preaching to us on stage about why we should worship his movie, when the only thing he is interested in is the cash cow potential of this? Where the hell did Canudo's idea of the seventh art go? Is this all really just about a business man with wanderlust? Does anyone here really care about film as a viable, and captivating art form? Everyone's thoughts reek of self-involvement.

Order

I **LEFT** that screening enraged.

Is there anyone here that actually cares about, or has studied film at all?

I turned my phone back on, because unlike some people who were literally tweeting and Instagramming their reactions, I still like to completely get absorbed in a film. It's the ultimate escapist fantasy, but I feel like people forget to let themselves really escape. After my phone loaded for 10 seconds, I saw that I had a text from Sam.

"We all decided to have a late lunch, but I arranged for you to meet up and talk about film with Adam, his insight will really help your appreciation of the festival circuit overall. Head down to The Peaks Great Room Deck and he will meet you there."

Okay, this might be really good for me; this Adam guy might be good to have in my back pocket. If what Sam said was right, then maybe I can be able to really communicate with him about my respect for film and my concerns overall. And who knows what could happen if I play this right?

I looked at the crudely drawn map of the town in relation to the festival, and realized that The Peaks were very close to Werner Herzog Theater. Some part of me realized that I should be approaching this meeting as an interview. Who knew if there were opportunities to be had; but I truly believe everything happens for a reason. Who knew exactly where this would lead?

I wandered around as any other tourist would, fiercely clutching the map, while looking up all the time. I knew how dumb I looked, but at the same time, I knew I needed to appreciate how beautiful my surroundings were. I generally walk around with my head down looking below me at all the concrete-paved, discarded gum and dog poop strewn sidewalks, but maybe if I looked up and out instead of down and in front I could be a little happier overall? I knew I was desperate, but it didn't matter. I wanted to try.

I finally arrived at the intimidatingly classy resort, wearing my Macy's one day sale button down that I got on clearance and some khaki's. I felt like an idiot, but at least I was an idiot who sort of played the part. I asked a concierge, also named Sam where the great room was, and he lazily pointed behind me to a sign that read:

Great Room—>

I attempted to smile politely and walk away, but I made sure that prick knew that I was being facetious. I looked around in the floor-to-ceiling windows to realize that the Great Room was an understatement. This room was incredible. It had views of the whole town, the festival itself, and the golf course where ninety percent of the crusty white old attendees (and the Whitlocks, I could safely assume), would eventually play.

I was completely awestruck with my mouth agape and then I heard a thought come from behind me.

I think that's the kid I'm supposed to meet.

I straightened up, and collected myself.

"Hey, are you Phil?"

This guy looked strikingly like Zachary Quinto, except taller and more built.

"Yeah, you must be Adam. Pleasure to meet you."

I shook his hand, and made sure to give him a firm handshake. I felt completely out of place, but I may as well continue with the confident facade.

"Good to meet you too, I'm seated already over there. What could I get you to drink?"

He motioned to the side of the room right against the windowed walls, or, what exactly do you call them?

"Uh, I'll just go with whatever you're drinking."

"Sounds good. Please take a set over there."

Seems like a good kid, I hate doing these things. Sam always wants me to shape them up and take all of the hope and optimism out of these kids I talk to. Sure it's good for business to prepare them I guess, but it's a motherfucker to take away all the hopes and dreams away from these people.

There was a certain point when someone was walking away when I couldn't hear what they were thinking anymore. I needed to know that exact distance by heart, but it's not something I've cared to really test yet. Then again, how the hell do I do that inconspicuously?

Anyway, it sounds like Adam is used to this kind of a role. Sam has had him speak these young idealists and try to see who can deal with it the best. This was a test that I wasn't aware I was being put through until right now.

Let's see how I can play this out and impress this dude. Thankfully, he has no idea how much of an upper-hand I have.

Adam came back with two beers in hand and sat down, just looking at me for a bit in a judging manner. I immediately said thanked him and instantaneously sipped the beer. Sure, I was parched, but really I was planning out my next move. I had an idea to lead the conversation. I think he was attempting to plan his next move as well.

I swelled up with confidence and sat back into the chair to relax.

"So Adam, tell me about yourself. How did you get into this industry, and what did you pursue in school?"

He looked a little surprised, but mostly entertained. He chuckled and thought the following:

Who does this kid think he is? I'll play ball for a little bit, I guess.

"Hmm, well, I was always fascinated by the film industry. Sometimes a little more than the final products of the film itself; you know, all the usual stuff. Glamour, intrigue, suspense, it's such a bizarre and fascinating industry that I knew I had to be involved in it."

I spouted out the first thing that came to my mind.

"So what, you watched *The Player* (1992) and *State and Main* (2000), and wanted to be a part of that industry? You wanted to be a background player to the stars? Well, I would say I'm surprised, but I'm not."

I cringed when I heard that last part, I knew how condescending that sounded but it just rolled off my tongue. I immediately regretted what I said, but it was too late; the damage was already done.

Maybe a little less harsh next time dumbass. Don't blow this.

I was freaking out in my mind, but I attempted to stay calm and keep my composure. Adam smirked, and thankfully, it sounded like I didn't piss him off too much. In fact, he started cracking up.

"Well, check you out, man! Am I that transparent?" He paused to finish laughing and took a breath. "If you must know, it wasn't either of those, it was Truffaut's *La Nuit Americannes* (1973), but they all revolve around that basic idea so yeah, you're right."

"Wow. I wish I could say you're wrong here, but that is not the case. In short, yeah, I love movies, but I found myself more interested in the business side of film that the creative/productive aspects of it; I still appreciate film, but I've found a path in this industry that suits my skills best."

I challenged him on this, thinking he would continue to be impressed.

"So you're a scout, taking an extremely passive interest in the thing you love the most, as opposed to being in front of, or immediately behind the camera or in the production at all?"

Adam smile quickly changed into a look of consternation.

"You're so young, you really have no idea how this business works, do you? You can love all of the avant-garde auteurs you want, but ultimately *kid,* in this industry pioneers perish and settlers strive."

I was offended by that statement for two reasons. First off, the way he underscored the word kid with such disdain made me think that he still wishes he could have my naive idealism about this industry. I think Adam secretly really hates what he does, because the people he loves, he can't help at all. He may even be doing things to hurt who he loves, because ultimately it makes *better business sense* or whatever hackneyed bullshit he wants to believe in order to be able to sleep at night.

Secondly, I was offended because I'm pretty sure this motherfucker just paraphrased (and ultimately botched) a quote that *Daymond John* said on *Shark Tank* to discourage someone.

Wow, man, really? Great idol to have, well, maybe that's not entirely untrue. That dude started something by himself too, and I kind of like Shark Tank. Regardless, I'm getting distracted.

"Okay, so, you're saying that the filmmakers and people you love you can't really invest in? Is that right? So, how do you make your decisions of filmmakers that you want to represent?"

Adam started to smile again, and took another sip of the beer he had.

That reminds me, I should ask him exactly what it was, because this was really fucking good.

"Well, that question gets a little more difficult, but I'm glad you asked. Before I dive into that, I like you. You remind me of how brash and defiant I was to people that I didn't understand, before I got into this aspect of my career. Essentially what happens—"

My phone made its message indicator noise, which is embarrassingly reminiscent of a theme from the *Legend of Zelda* video games.

I tried to laugh it off and be polite while I saw who it was.

"I'm so sorry, normally I don't get a lot of texts, give me one sec and I'll shut my phone off."

I saw that it was an unknown number. With my curiosity piqued, I opened the text message and saw that it was a naked picture of Lindsay, and it was a POV as if she was sitting on my face. I could see everything.

"Holy shit!"

"Are you okay?"

He blurted out, clearly, I had a visible tell and no poker face.

I was completely shocked and totally intrigued by Lindsey's picture, she was drop dead gorgeous after all, and what the fuck was she doing by texting me naked pictures? I didn't know what to do next, and stumbled to get the message off of the screen in fears that maybe Adam would see it. I barely even noticed that there was a message in addition to the picture.

See you at 4pm in my room.

I checked the corner of my screen and realized it was 3:15 now. I finally put my phone away in my pocket, and realized I never responded to Adam's question.

"Uh, yeah, my fucking phone company threatened a shut off and I *paid* the bill. I just, I have to go call them, but let's finish what we started first."

Adam looked like he didn't buy it, but continued to entertain the discussion that we were having.

"Anyway, what I was trying to say was that all the people in this industry that you love; will never be as profitable as the people who rather than do something to change the game, *exploit* the game."

I was skeptical to what he was saying, but still extremely distracted by that picture. She looked fucking gorgeous. Perfect boobs, an awesome body, a slight, but distinguishable landing strip, with the hottest "come hither" look that I have ever seen. She was on her bed, with her fists clenching the sheets. Almost like an exploited Terry Richardson model in a non-herpes having way. That at least was attractive to me I guess.

Adam continued on.

"For instance, J.J. Abrams, you as well as I know that he's not the guy who first utilized lens flare, but he throws it around all of his movies as if it's his unique signature. Do you know who invented it?"

I thought about it, and I loathed his use and abuse of that technique. It was interesting at one point and time, but now it's tired and cliched.

"Uh, I think I remember—"

"Of course you don't know! The innovators always fade out into obscurity."

"So what I've decided to do is check out as many innovative films as I can at whatever obscure festivals I go to, then I make note of the techniques I have not seen before, and I put them on the back burner. Then, whenever, I see them again, that's who I pursue."

Adam's answer disheartened me.

So you've made a career based off of finding people that have stolen techniques from a myriad of sources, and decide that they are worthy? That's pretty fucking disgusting.

I focused in, and made sure to show my disgust in his answer with my response.

"So, you are pretty much a leech that's late to the carrion?"

"Interesting phrasing, Phil. I guess you can sort of say that, but you sound like a fucking robot. Also, I'm an extremely *well-paid* leech, I'll have you know. "

I felt suddenly embarrassed.

"Oh I mean, sorry. I did some exterminating, so my jargon can become pretty technical at times. Also, sorry for being a dick, but it's the first thing that popped into my mind. I don't think you're a leech, you just have leech like traits. Again, that's a byproduct of my former industry."

Adam was thankfully, understanding and forgiving.

"It's alright, man, I get it. I don't really love it, but that's unfortunately the truth of it. My point being, there is infinitely more potential to profit from the people that are not developing amazing techniques." He paused, and put his finger to his mouth, and then re-summarized his position on my initial assessment.

"Think of it this way, wouldn't you want to be on the team of a guy like Michael Bay, or would you rather be along the trajectory of a person like Orson Welles?"

I thought about the seemingly, unending successes of Michael Bay, and then begrudgingly thought of the descent of Orson Welles. Those damn pea commercials, and Unicron. What a shitty way to go.

"Those pea commercials."

Adam was clearly saddened with my response.

"That's really all he could do left to make money at the end of his days. Regardless, the point I'm trying to make to you is that it sucks, but on my side of this industry you want to be on the winning team. Sad but true."

I started feeling bad at this notion, but then remembered that I have a girl that wants to fuck me within the hour! Suddenly, I stopped giving a shit and regained my confidence. I got out of that pit of self-loathing that Adam dug for me, and shook it off.

"I completely see what you're saying. It makes sense. I can see your perspective."

"Really?"

He responded completely surprised.

"Because, well, normally at this point in the conversation the other person gets infuriated with what I'm doing and goes on to do nothing but chastise me. But, you understand my perspective? Huh. Tell you what, Phil, what are you doing tomorrow for the festival? Did you have any schedule or something? "

"Uh, I wanted to go to one screening and one panel later in the night, but that was it. Why what's up?"

Adam smiled confidently.

"Come to a premiere with me. I'd love to see how you react to a movie, and if you would want to pursue one person I had in mind."

"Okay, cool man, that sounds good to me."

"Alright great. I'll arrange it with Sam and we'll see if we can get you backstage as well."

"Really? That would be awesome man, thank you so so much!"

"No problem, kid. It'll be fun."

Adam stopped and looked at his watch.

"Shit, man, I got carried away with time, I have another meeting. Fuck. Do you know how much it sucks having your off time scheduled by an idiot? I'm so sorry to cut this short. I know I said that this would be lunch, but is it cool if I get back to you another time?"

"Uh, yeah, totally man. No problem."

"Alright, I'll text you, later, man. We'll be in touch."

Adam chugged down the rest of his beer, wiped off his mouth and walked away smiling at me.

That kid has some balls. He might have the stuff to really stand out later on.

As soon as he was out of earshot, my mind immediately shifted gears.

Okay, regarding Lindsay, what the hell do I do from now until at 4:00 pm. Do I look okay, do I smell okay? Let me head to a bathroom. Well, not any bathroom, I'm going to head back to my bathroom and uh, brush my teeth? What the hell else should I do to prepare myself? Hold up, let's slow down a bit. Let's go to the bar and order a shot to help calm my nerves.

But wait, what type of shot should it be? I would normally go for whiskey but, I have heard many sad stories revolving around whiskey dick. Maybe, I'll do a shot of vodka? Yeah, let's do that instead.

Vodka, bathroom, then I'll check if I smell/look okay, then I'll go from there.

I rushed to the bar and order a double shot of vodka. As soon as I got it, I kicked it back and dropped a $10 for the drink and tip, then rushed back to my room. My mind was racing this whole time.

Is there anything I need to bring? Should I grab some condoms, or something? Well, she would probably have some. Yeah, she's got it covered.

I was pulled out of those thoughts when I realized that I was dripping in sweat. It wasn't too hot of a day, but damn was I nervous as hell. While walking I decided to take a peek down and sure enough, there they were: the monstrously over-sized pit-stains. I've had them before, sure, but it the light gray colored button down I was wearing, I noticed that they weren't so much pit stains, as they were shoulder tracers. These fuckers were huge!

I scrambled my way through the lobby and rushed up to the elevator bay whilst fumbling through my pockets looking for my room keys. To anyone else, I probably looked like a goddamn mess. I wasn't entirely sure, considering my mind was operating at a million miles an hour. I wasn't focusing on what anyone else was thinking.

I ran to my room and scrambled with my key again; I finally unlocked the door and looked at the clock. It was 3:45. I only have fifteen minutes to make myself look fuckable.

Or is it fuckworthy?

What do I do? I've never appeared that way in my past, so how the hell do I do this now?

I took a deep breath and resolved to change and use my deodorant again. I decided against brushing my teeth, but checked them out in the mirror to see that they were passable at least. I took another deep breath and looked at myself in the mirror.

Stop freaking out, just go in there, relax, and stop thinking, just do.

I casually walked out of my room, and walked two doors down the hall to Lindsay's room.

I knocked on the door.

* * *

ALRIGHT, *before she opens up the door, just remember to not be a fucking idiot and listen to exactly what she wants. Remember dumb ass, you have the upper-hand!*

Linds threw the door open with vigor.

"God, finally you're here! I was getting so fucking horny I couldn't take it anymore"

How the hell should I respond to that?

"Hey Linds, I'm sorry to keep you waiting. You ready for this?"

She smirked and dove in.

"Fuck yeah, I'm ready. The real question is, can you handle me?"

Let's see what I have to do for him to get him ready.

She pushed me down on the bed, and started to pull my pants down hard. I opted for, and attempted to take off my pants in a more reasonable manner, like taking my belt off first. But she had no interest in that. Finally succeeding, she threw my pants across the room and immediately ripped through my boxers as well.

She let out a gasp when she looked back at me naked lower half.

Oh shit. What is this? Is, oh yeah, I remember this. It's his prosthetic. Do I do anything different? Or, you know what, probably best to just ignore it.

I was already starting to sweat. I reached that point where you get so nervous you freeze up and get clammy. Would she not have sex with me just because of my leg, was it too weird for her?

She sexily arched her back, and ended up resting her head on my hips, looking at me straight in the eye and smiled.

Lindsey got down on her knees at the edge of the bed, looked up at me and laughed.

"Oh! You're totally a virgin, aren't you? You look so uncomfortable."

I paused and let out a breath.

"Listen, you have nothing to worry about."

She smiled and giggled before she started up again.

"Just relax."

She said the exact opposite of what I wanted to hear at that moment. Never tell a person freaking out to calm down, it's only going to make them freak out more. Naturally, that is exactly what I did. She gave me a more gentle push, and now I was lying down on the bed, half naked, staring at the ceiling. I still couldn't relax.

While I was trying to talk myself down from a panic attack, before she grabbed me and started sucking me off, I heard her think: *I should have known he was a virgin! I probably shouldn't have started out so strong. Time to show him how good this can feel, and that'll fucking make him relax.*

At first, it was extremely awkward. I didn't know how to react while this was happening. I resolved to groan a bit. It did feel amazing. I thought I should grasp at the sheets on the bed, or something. I wasn't too sure of what to do.

Should I tell her what I like? Hell, I don't even know what I like, so what's the point of doing that?

There we go, he took long enough.

I was finally really hard. I didn't expect her to be impressed with my size or anything, but she certainly played it up. For her, I think she was doing exactly what she has learned to do. She eagerly smiled and said, "Mmmmmm."

That was really fucking hot, and that worked. I was able to get out of my own head long enough to enjoy that. I desperately tried to get out of my head and shut off my "gift." It felt like more of a curse right now more than ever. I tried to preoccupy my thoughts with the actual fantasy of mine that was unfolding right before me.

What the hell is wrong with me? Why can't I enjoy this amazing thing that's happening to me right now?

I started to feel myself getting harder and harder. She was groaning.

Fucking hot. This finally helped me get away from those fucking thoughts.

As if she were in a rush, she stood up and took off her shirt and pants. All of a sudden, I was now in the room, with a naked gorgeous woman. Holy shit.

She raised her eyebrows and smirked.

"Well, it looks like you're ready for me. Just tell me when you're about to cum, okay?"

I was a thrown off by this.

"Should I uh, take my shirt off?"

"No, don't worry about that. It's all good."

Okay, weird. Wait a second. Fuck my shirt. I need to ask the much more important questions.

"Wait, do you have a condom or something?"

She rolled her eyes and looked at me.

"Well, your balls are pretty big, but I didn't know they were THAT big!"

Realizing I was not laughing at her joke at all, she decided to add to that and actually respond to my question.

"Phil, come on. You know you can trust me."

She smiled at me, spit on her hand, rubbed my hard dick up and down, and slid me into her.

Fuck, that felt amazing.

"Yeah, you fucking love my pussy, don't you?"

She was biting her lap after she said that, which made it really sexy. Otherwise, I haven't experienced dirty talk before and it was pretty hilarious. It took me a hell of a lot of effort to not erupt in laughter at that comment by itself.

This looked like merely an act of dominance to her. She didn't look like she was enjoying it. This was like she was merely playing a part. I let my body undulate naturally, and hopefully that was showing her how good I felt; I had no idea what the hell to do or say right now.

Linds grabbed my hands. She started screaming at me.

"Scratch me, slap me! Take some fucking control of me!"

Her eyes rolled back as I started scratching her midsection. I couldn't get past how confusing this was in spite of how hot this was or how good it felt.

Is something wrong with me?

Is this asshole ready to cum yet?

This remark pissed me off. What the fuck does she think she is doing? I got incensed at this moment, sat up, and I started to bite her.

Finally! It's like he just now realized what he was doing.

I bit her neck, then kissed her down until I was at her breasts, then bit her right nipple. Hard. Probably too hard, considering she followed up with:

"Ahhh, FUCK! Too hard, asshole! Jesus, try it gently. Do you want to kill me, or do you want to fuck me? Or, if you want to hate fuck me, we can work with that too."

I wasn't going to put up with that shit anymore.

I finally took control of my circumstance.

"Shut up!"

I screamed at her as I bit her lower lip and started kissing her. I started to fuck her back, as opposed to merely get fucked. I took some control, and it felt really fucking good. So much of my life has been as passive one. It is well overdue me taking on an active role in it. She was really getting into it too. I rode her harder than I was before, while biting her lightly all over her body, and grabbing her ass and working myself into her as deep as I could.

We were both breathing very heavily, completely into the moment, when I realized I was about to have an orgasm.

"I, uh."

That was the best I could do, as I tried to hold off.

Linds fortunately got the idea of what was happening, got off of me, and finished me with her hand into her mouth. Lying down next to me, we were both trying to catch our breath. Linds patted me on the chest and looked at me in disbelief.

"Where did that come from? You were like a totally different person."

I smiled, knowing full well what happened, and decided to play into her game a bit.

"Yeah, well, I picked up on certain ticks you had, and what felt good to you. Then kept going with that."

She ran her hand through her unfurled, brunette hair, still breathing heavily.

"Huh. You might surprise me yet, Phil. Next time, we will work on me a bit more, alright? Not too shabby, kid. "

Linds pushed herself up and headed into the bathroom. While she was doing that, I was collecting my thoughts.

Holy shit! I think I did pretty well! She was a little dominant, and a little weird, but I could get used to that. But what the hell does this mean for us? She has been so casual about this whole thing. Is there any potential for a relationship there? Do I want that, or does she for that matter?

* * *

LINDS FINALLY came out of the bathroom and pulled up her pony tail. She looked at me with confusion, and disbelief in her eyes.

"You're still here? What are you doing?"

I quickly stood up and put on my pants. I always do that stupid thing where I try to put my foot in the pant leg, but I manage to put it crotch first. Even with my actual leg, I am completely inelegant, clumsy and do not utilize it correctly most of the time.

Damn, Phil's just sweet and stupid enough to be a clinger. I need to nip this in the bud.

"I, uh, was just gathering my thoughts. I'm gonna head out."

With that, she let her guard down a bit more.

"Oh, well, okay. I'll see you for our family dinner tonight, but, let's meet up again tomorrow sometime and we'll go for another round. I'll teach you how to eat me out like a champ."

I was finally dressed and now trying to regain some semblance of being calm.

"Alright, cool, I'll talk to you later, Linds."

I knew I shouldn't rush out, but I also knew I shouldn't strut out; I would look ridiculous. I ended up taking up a bit longer than I probably should have, but whatever.

What the hell just happened? Are people's first times normally just a casual, non event? Why was that so easy for her to do that?

This was as nonchalant to her as if I were a total stranger asking her for the time. But this was huge! How does one person so easily lose their virginity?

Or how does one person so easily take it for that matter? It's so fucking cliché, but is she a man-eater, or something like that? Maybe she was hoping me to be one of those mindless ants that are born to fuck and then die right after orgasm. Maybe I'm a potential casualty to her and that's it.

All of these thoughts—with slight variations on them (albeit all bug related)—were repeating ad nauseum in my head while I was gathering my composure and leaving the room. My room was two hallways away, but it was split with Brad. I needed to not look weird.

How does someone not have an I just fucked your sister *look?*

I need to be relaxed and as casual as possible. With my back up against the wall aside from the door, I closed my eyes and played cool. I walked in the room, and sure enough, there was Brad. That naive, happy idiot had the biggest smile on my face when I walked in.

"Hey, man! How's it been so far? What did you see earlier?"

"Hey Brad, it's uh. It's good but a little weird."

"Oh?"

He looked genuinely interested, which is something that I really liked about this guy. If you are having a talk with Brad, he is always completely engrossed and totally engaged in it. He is not a guy who is capable of passive interest, you have is full attention when you have him.

"Why's that?"

"Well, I saw Jeff Franklin's feature, and during the Q&A he was kind of a dick to people for no reason at all."

"Man. I hate that shit."

Brad sat down on the bed, but it looked like he was getting ready to head out.

"Hey man, were you just about to go somewhere? I don't want to hold you up."

"Oh no no, man, it's cool. I have a little bit of time."

He pulled out his sleek, gold iPhone to check the clock.

"Yeah, I'm good."

I've never met a man with a gold iPhone, but who am I to judge?

"Listen man, I was hoping to talk to you about this exact topic before it happened, but I knew it was inevitable."

He looked concerned and put his hand on my shoulder, and gently forced me to sit down on the corner of the opposite bed with him. I was extremely uncomfortable with him touching me, considering where my dick just was.

"First off, Phil, that sucks and I'm sorry. This shit was bound to happen though. Early on in a filmmaker's career, they need to have unwavering confidence about their work. If they come across as weak or anything like that, the press will devour them whole. They need to be as boisterous and as cocky as possible. It's this shitty learned culture that pushes people into this. Maybe somewhere down the road, they can become a little more humbled as time progresses, but initially, they all put on this ridiculous show."

There was some logic to what Brad was saying, but I didn't agree with this assumption that every filmmaker has to be a prick. He continued on with his illogical compartmentalization of filmmakers.

Not everyone in this business is an egomaniac. That can't be true, but maybe that's exactly what Brad's experienced, he would know more than I would I guess.

"That's why every time I've come down to this festival, I've done my best to completely remove myself from being around those creators, and have intentionally sought to hang out with the behind the camera industry people. They are much more down to earth."

I begrudgingly accepted his position on this.

"Well, I guess I can see your point. But, why do you keep coming back to these then, if you know how crappy the people can be? Do you have some good friends that return here over and over?"

Brad's smile started to deteriorate.

"Yeah, I do. I'm gonna head to see them tonight. I don't really know if I would call them my friends exactly. We don't talk too much outside of this, just through social media actually. But, we always have a good time when we get together. I'd like to hang out with them more. It doesn't really happen though, we never can connect."

He shrugged it off, and went on with his prevailing opinion.

"It's sort of like, you've heard of peacocking right?" It's how a male peacock shows off his feathers to impress a woman. Well, it's like the same kind of thing with attitude for these directors and creators. Put yourself in their position Phil, they are nervous as hell, trying to impress all these insanely influential people around them, and the last thing they want to do is talk to some schmuck about the minutiae of their movie."

Ah, it's like those god damned Africanized bees that look exactly like bumblebees. They look passive, but when they think someone is threatening them or getting in their way, it's over.

"Got it, man. Well, hopefully I'll find someone that will disprove your theory. Adam was saying he'd try to drag me to a premier and meet a director after the Q&A. Maybe he will be the guy that proves this whole thing wrong."

He has so much to learn. He's naive and excitable, but I don't want to be around when that blows up in his face.

I tried to not immediately grimace at his overheard, internal response, but didn't do the best job at hiding it. I desperately tried to change the subject.

"Well, thanks for the insight, man. I hear exactly what you're saying, but I'm not going to ascribe to that belief until I see it firsthand."

Brad smiled and patted me on the shoulder. He looked like he was about to respond, but before he could say anything, he got a message notification.

He brought his hands up in a "there's nothing I can do" fashion.

"Sorry, man, I have to go. I'll see ya"

"Alright, later, man."

He was off with a new energy in him that I didn't see before. Clearly, he was excited about going to hang out, but he is always extremely vague and elusive about who he hangs out with.

I wonder who the hell they are, and what they are up to?

* * *

I HAD that weird feeling that I was being watched. Have you ever been in that scenario where you can just feel yourself under someone else's microscope? That's essentially what was happening during the screening that I watched with Adam. He was studying my studying. It was very off putting and extremely distracting. I couldn't focus on the movie.

This kid needs to have a cinematic eye, but also needs to be practical, or else he's a lost cause. I wonder what's sticking out to him during this screening. Is he dissecting the carefully composed mise en scene, or is he barely picking up on this extremely heavy symbolism by this amateur?

I couldn't help but shift uncomfortably and refrain from my normal "Hmmm"-ing that happens when I watch a film. If I did that at the wrong place, he could potentially get the wrong impression and then whatever he was judging me on would be all for not. It felt like I was in a film class, without that really shitty kid who would wear the same outfit every day and be the token contrarian. What the fuck do those people end up doing with their lives aside from judging everything around them all that time, and be incapable of loving anything?

What's that saying? It's better to remain silent and wise, than open your mouth and be an idiot? Well, whatever that saying is, that's the approach I am taking with this film as opposed to any other film I'd watch in my free time. In addition to being aware of my verbal idiosyncrasies, I limited my amount of chin-rubbing, which I am unfortunately guilty of as well.

Adam had promised that after the screening, we would have some one-on-one time with the director. I was extremely excited by the prospect of this, but again, was painfully aware of the impression that I could potentially make; for better and for worse. I've never been in this scenario before and was very curious to see how it would occur. I've been here for about an hour twenty, and the denouement is just about wrapped up. Adam told me beforehand that immediately after the movie we would "regroup" whatever the hell that means, while Duncan, the director, would go through the initial q&a with the press. That was the standard for the festival circuit.

The credits started to roll, and with that came the applause. Some people started standing up, others were a little reluctant at first, but then stood up. I always wondered how sincere standing ovations were. If I was truly blown away by a performance or a film, then maybe. But more often than not, I think standing ovations are 15% sincere, and 85% peer pressure. Duncan's *Loveless* was great, but it didn't cast a new perspective on anything or rock me to the core, so I did not think it was worthy of a standing ovation. My ass stayed planted.

Adam nudged me with his elbow, and motioned me with his head to follow him outside of the theater.

He looked giddy with excitement for my response.

"Well, what did you think? I can't wait to hear what you thought about all this!"

Obviously.

"There was some very interesting, and very innovative techniques in use in this picture. But it wasn't mind blowing. I think that was an uncomfortably forced standing ovation."

Adam wanted to interject, but I cut him off with some other tangential thoughts.

"He was pretty derivative, and a little too heavy handed at times. Otherwise, though, I liked it a lot and I would happily watch more of his work. What did you think about it?"

This is great! Sam was completely right, this kid can do this!

Adam quickly responded, he was clearly waiting for his time to talk.

"I completely agree. This will work out just as well as Sam hoped."

I furled my eyebrows and gave him a completely unintentional, confused puppy dog look.

"Sam, like, Brad's dad? I don't understand."

Adam did not buy into my confusion. Instead, he addressed me bluntly, as if I were stupid not to know what was happening.

"Come on, Phil. Did you really have no idea that this whole thing has been one very informal interview? We've been grooming you, man! After hearing from Brad and talking to you a bit more on the trip up here, Sam is really impressed with you! He wants me to mentor you into a junior position at our firm!"

I was flattered, but beyond thrown off. I am pretty sure you need a degree in law, if not multiple other things to practice anywhere.

"Adam, I'd love to take an offer, " I whispered to him in confidence, "but I don't have a degree at all! Much less a degree in law. How could I do anything with your firm?"

Adam immediately snapped back, with a laugh.

"Oh, is that what you're worried about? Ever heard of this little thing called doc review? It's a foot in the door type of position that is just on its last legs, until it becomes completely automated. However, that has not happened as of yet, so we are all good."

He patted me on the back, hard. Harder than I was used to being patted.

"So what do you think? Would you be in to come to California with us? Brad also mentioned your home was in transition. Is that right? We can help with any unforeseen moving costs as well."

I would take time to think about this more, but fuck it. I can get the hell out of fucking Aurora. My starry-eyed gaze came crashing down to an immediate halt. Wait! I do have one concern about this.

"I do have one question. Why me? Why not Brad? He's Sam's son, after all. "

Quickly changing from excited, to a state of serious concern, Adam repositioned himself and spoke to me very sternly.

"Really good question, Phil. Brad has never really proved himself. First off, he wasn't interested in this and he is not capable of a lot of work. Finally, you have proven yourself as someone with enough insight to do what we do. Anytime we've talked to Brad, he gives us some half-assed response that clearly registers as a lack of interest, or passion for this field. Whereas you, well, you are brimming with both of those aspects."

Out of nowhere, we heard aloud "taxi hail" of a whistle. Adam took notice of this, and held his finger up at me.

"Hold on to that thought. We are getting signaled over for a brief meeting with the director."

"Oh."

I straightened up and adjusted my hair. Not that adjusting it would ever do anything to my ridiculously unruly curly head. I'm sure it always made me look like an unkempt jackass. But nonetheless, I would be remiss if I didn't try to fix it.

Adam nodded me over to the exit just to the left of the stage, which is where Duncan walked out.

I followed close behind. Immediately through the door, there was a narrow hallway; which lead to a green room that Duncan just collapsed into. He looked like he was exhausted, no doubt from the nerves of debuting at a festival like this. I didn't want to overwhelm him with my energy, so I tried to pass off as unexcited and casual.

I hope that doesn't come off as uninterested.

Adam was giving me the eye, and pushing his hands down to the ground as if he were non-verbally saying *relax*. He held has hand out to me, with an "after you" type of motion. I was petrified. I slowly walked through the threshold and meekly introduced myself.

"Hey, umm Duncan? My name's Phil, my friend Adam over here arranged this brief meeting. Is now still a good time?"

Ugh. May as well get the fanboy out of the way. I hope he doesn't eat up too much of my time. I have a lot more important things to do with a lot more alcohol to help deal with this shit.

Just suck it up. This is the last round of them.

"Hey! Yeah, Phil and Adam, was it? Yeah, come on in!"

Initially, I was worried about how I would come off to Duncan, but it looks like I'll have to worry about Adam. He was about to fangirl out in the corner. Moreso over the situation of me meeting the director and opposed to the director himself.

Man, this is so great! I think Phil would be a great asset to the company and then maybe, I'll have time to breathe over there!

Duncan patted the seat next to him.

"So, before we dive in and get too formal with this, did you have any questions you were thinking about asking in there?"

I abandoned being shy and opted to be more direct and casual with Duncan.

"There was one thing I wanted to know."

"Sure, go ahead!" Duncan responded enthusiastically.

"Okay, well, I wanted to know something about your blocking in one scene that really stood out to me."

I paused for a breath.

"During the scene where you had Ed's coworkers standing in line, I noticed you utilized a very desaturated color pallet that was reminiscent of a world that John Steinbeck would have created. My question to you in regards to the body positions and the stances employed in that shot is; were you trying intentionally to comment on the state of the manufacturing industry in the early 1920's and more specifically how the assembly line mentality led to the steadfast, unwavering individualism utilized by the self-proclaimed greatest generation? I thought it was a little subtle, but just wanted to be clear."

Duncan shook his head incredulously and only responded by saying, "Wowie! We got a live one."

* * *

DUNCAN was taken aback, and initially wrote me off like some idiot kid.

I might in fact be an idiot kid, but show some respect for someone who admires you.

"Kid, listen, I admire the things you were searching for, but sometime they are not there. Sometimes a cigar is just a cigar and nothing more, right?"

Maybe I was being naive, but I didn't believe him. If I had an honest feeling about it, how the hell was I wrong?

"So, just to be clear, you're saying that you put things without any deeper meaning in your films? Intentionally? Or, is that merely your interpretation versus mine?"

I didn't want to sound too combative, but I wanted to come off as confident, and press him for a significant answer.

"Well, your interpretation can very well be one thing, and you are entitled to that. But, sometimes things are just things. I am impressed that you pulled that much meaning out of a scene and I'm flattered, but there was no added intent with that scene."

I opened my mouth to quickly, but rather than my usual verbal diarrhea of whatever my immediate reaction was, I weighed my options of how to respond.

Before I could, Duncan cut me off.

"Listen, some dialogue and some visuals are necessary only to advance the plot. If I had a movie of nothing but deep symbolism and no plot forwarding device, well, I may as well start the credits crawl with *go ahead and fuck off, investors.* You will alienate your audience if you do something like that, especially today's audience."

He continued after a brief pause to collect himself. The more he talked, the more I hated this pseudo-intellectual looking fuckwad. He looked dumb enough with his typical blazer/graphic t-shirt and jeans bullshit that every other director copied, he didn't need to doing anything to add to my disapproval.

"Phil, right now. You are speaking directly with me, because you want to get to the point right?"

"Yes."

That was, however, the most direct thing I've said today.

"Okay, so imagine if you wanted this same answer, but instead, you spoke in nothing but flowery, and overly hyperbolic language that danced around the topic and gave you a connotation of my response as opposed to a by the book, quick, yes or no answer. Wouldn't that drive you insane?"

"I guess. So you are saying that there is a time and a place for symbolism?"

"Exactly."

I wanted to disagree with his smug, punchable face, but I couldn't. Adam jumped in and seized the opportunity of the silence. He offered a handshake to Duncan.

"Duncan, thank you so so much for your time, and congratulations again for a stunning debut. We'll be in touch."

Duncan shook his hand and smiled, then shifted gears, looked at me and curtly nodded. I think I left a shitty impression. I nodded back to him while Adam dragged me out by the arm. We got outside of the green room back to the screening area, where people were still decompressing from the film. Adam burst out in laughter.

"Well done, kid! He never saw that coming. Don't feel too bad about it, that guy's an idiot and you were right to question him. His opinion and interpretation doesn't matter nearly as much as yours. Remember Phil, the author's dead. Anything goes."

I took a second to skim the recesses of my mind to see if anything Adam was saying made any sense to me. It didn't.

"The author's dead? I'm confused. Duncan was right there. Oh, was this based on a book or something?"

"Yikes."

I'm assuming Adam wasn't too happy with my initial reaction.

"No, Phil. You know, like Barthes? It doesn't matter what the creator of art says. The only thing that matters is your interpretation. The scholar Roland Barthes said famously that in regards to interpretation, the author is dead. It doesn't matter what he thinks."

Huh. Okay, well that invalidates a ridiculous amount of my time spent watching/reading/listening to interviews about creators endlessly talking about their work.

"Anyway man, I'm impressed with how you handled yourself back there regardless of his awkward response. You can keep your cool in front of some people you admire. That was really all we were looking at seeing."

"Cool man, glad to hear!"

"So what do you think? Does that guy have a future, or would he just stay in the festival circuit, endlessly hoping for a future of greater things that he'll never get?"

I carefully considered the question, I understood that a lot was riding on my response, but should I just succumb to going with my gut here? That has failed me on multiple occasions before. My gut is saying no, and even without the aid of Adam's internal thoughts helping out he was emphatically shaking his head no.

"No, he will just stay in festivals, but I feel like he could get lucky. Some idiot might pick him up and see what he is capable of, but down the way, he'll do nothing but fail them."

Adam smirked.

"Wow. True and heartless, good work, man. I feel like you really nailed it too."

I have nothing else to say, I think we just found our guy. This is great!

"I couldn't be happier with how you did today, Phil! I'll let Sam know and whenever you are ready we will work out all the details. Until then, here's my card and call me with any other questions. "

"Thanks so much, Adam!"

I stood there, silently in disbelief. I put the card in my pocket, smiling like an idiot.

"Well, go! Go enjoy the rest of the festival!"

"Oh, right, yeah. Of course."

As I turned away from Adam to head back into the fray, I noticed he stepped back into the green room with Duncan.

I thought he was done with him? He gave me one last reassuring look and while he entered the other room he had a thought.

"Now, things can finally get interesting. Duncan—"

The strange thing was, as he closed the door behind him, I couldn't finish his thought, I had no idea how he was going to finish that thought.

I never noticed a physical boundary hindering my abilities before, weird.

Eh. I'll just keep that in mind for the future.

I paused, and collected my thoughts for the rest of the day going forward.

Maybe I'll head back to the hotel room, check the program, and see what else is up for the rest of the night.

While I walked back, I decided to check my phone and did a quick google search on Telluride festival, just to see what—if anything—had been posted so far.

Wow. There's already a couple posts about Duncan's movie? Cinematico.net? What the hell is that?

Clicking on the link and reading the article was a bad decision. This random jackass was already touting Duncan's film as "Virtuosic, and a one of a kind point of view!"

Really, man, that movie? That'll be the takeaway blurb for that film? That's disgusting. All this guy was doing was a rehash of his influences, it was all painfully obvious.

Before I even considered finishing the article and getting the total perspective of the work I had seen and how this "critic" attempted to dissect it, I realized I was right outside of my hotel. This was really good timing, considering I got the incredible need to go take a shit. I pushed through the lobby, and as I was waiting for the elevator, I grew extremely self-conscious of how much I looked like I was clenching it back. While I was waiting I couldn't help but think, that this was a completely humanizing experience.

All my dreams are potentially about to come true and the only thing I could think about is how badly I need to take a shit. Some things don't change at all apparently.

I was distracting myself to the best of my abilities while I waited in the elevator, but then rushed in the room and went for it. It was a completely fulfilling shit.

This was more virtuosic then that fucking movie.

After I was finally able to breathe again, I washed up and crashed on to the bed and took a second to collect myself. I reached for my phone again and accidentally swiped my messaging app, which revealed Lindsey's sext from before; full screen.

Thank god I waited to open that in private.

Seeing as I had all this free time now, rather than look at the program, I thought I may as well rub one out to help relax. I took my dick out and thought about how fucking good she felt when I was inside of her. I didn't even realize when I first looked at this text, how fucking sexy this shot really was. She had lifted her shirt and her bra up, she was on her knees spreading her pussy apart with her fingers with the other hand, and she was biting her lip.

This girl knew exactly what she was doing.

As soon as I became rock hard, someone pushed the door open and slammed it against the wall.

* * *

I **LAID** there in bed, with my rock hard dick in my hands and all Brad could do was stare at me.

This was embarrassing because of a multitude of reasons. Specifically, because from his point of view, he had a clear perspective of my taint. My knees were up on the bed and my legs were spread eagle.

I can only speak for myself, but out of all the surprise nudity I could ever anticipate or hope for; I don't care who you are, chances are I do not want to see your taint unless we are having sex. It is the least sexy place I can imagine. Especially speaking as a dude. There is some horrific shit going down there—literally and figuratively.

I quickly changed my position, but we both knew that any hope I had of decency was completely lost. There was no hope for me casually carrying on a conversation with him ever again without either of us thinking of that moment.

Personally, I subscribe to the "Boy Scouts Rule of D" theorem as so eloquently outlined in *Workaholics*. Essentially, if you see someone else's dick, there is an imbalance in the universe until you see the other person's. The only logical fallacy in that theory, is how do you clear that up without seeming over-eager to see someone else's dick? Therein lies the problem.

I've always maintained that Ders, Blake and Adam are philosophers first and foremost, gentlemen second, and comedians third. Brad was still staring at me as I shifted myself into a less vulnerable position.

"Fucking hell, dude! No one knocks anymore, I guess. It's cool. I am so so sorry."

I paused briefly, then continued to express my concern.

"I don't really know what to do from here, man."

I was about to continue to ramble insincere apologies, but then I started to hear his thoughts.

Holy shit, Phil has a nice dick, I wouldn't mind having that pulsating in my mouth.

I attempted to look unsurprised by that thought, but the truth of it was I never would have seen that coming. I guess that means he's been interested in me all along? I didn't even think he was gay.

Is he gay? Or am I some weird anomaly to his hetero life? I swore he was flirting with girls at that party.

He finally cut off the unnerving silence.

"It's okay, man, it's alright. Shit happens. We all need some 'alone time' after all. To be honest with you, I'm more impressed with it than anything else. And, I haven't really seen a prosthetic this close up and in such detail before."

Where the hell do I go from that comment?

"Uh, thanks. I never thought it was anything to write home about frankly."

Write home about? What the hell did was I talking about? I'm going to go ahead and ignore the prosthetic comment. The last thing I want to do is unveil any weird ass fetishes.

"Don't be so modest, Phil. I wouldn't say you're crazy hung or anything. You just have a nice dick."

Alright, let's cut the bullshit and get to the meat of this conversation here. I edged up to the backboard of the bed, further away from Brad, now in my flaccid glory fidgeting to pull up what sheets I could from the cripplingly tight hospital bed.

"Brad, I don't really know what to say here. Don't take this the wrong way or anything, but are you... are you interested in guys? Are... you gay?"

No turning back from that question. There is never a delicate way to put that, but I think it warranted being said. Brad sat on the opposing edge of the bed and looked vulnerable.

Shit. Maybe I was too harsh and pointed in my delivery of that.

"Well Phil, I haven't told this to a lot of people. I'm not gay, but I am bi-sexual."

I was ashamed of being so direct with him, but now more than anything, I was curious in talking to him about it.

"Oh. Okay. I'm sorry if I came off as crass earlier. I didn't mean to offend, I just wanted to understand."

Brad smirked at that comment, but it was a smirk that was welcoming and warming.

Wait is that even a smirk? What the hell are you even thinking Phil? There's another word for that. Was it grimace? Was it a chagrin? Can you have a chagrin, or are you chagrined? God after speaking this language all of my life, you'd think you'd know more of it instead of just being an idiot.

Before I could burrow an even larger shame pit, Brad meekly uttered a response to my last concern.

"It's okay, man, I appreciate how you are handling this so well. Don't be so hard on yourself. A lot of people don't understand, so I know what you are going through. It's difficult. It's weird."

I immediately shot back with a defensive response.

"No, it's not. Not at all, Brad, don't be so hard on yourself. It's not a weird, or difficult thing. It's what you are and always have been. It's no big deal man. You have nothing to worry about from me. And, furthermore, if you have someone in your life telling you that it *is* a difficult or weird thing, then it's not worth talking to them."

Brad was smiling now.

"Thanks, man, I really appreciate your response. I always am more defensive of that fact about myself. You just never know what or who you'll encounter in the world. I've always taken the approach of better safe than sorry."

"Well, you have nothing to worry about with me, man. Please, just relax. You're in good company here"

Brad inched closer to me on the bed.

"Thanks, man. So, in lighter news. Which pornstar do you deem worthy enough for jacking off? I know you were looking at something while I walked in. You want to look at it together and we can compare porn notes?"

Fuck. Brad can't know I was jerking off to his sister. I can't even stall for too long without him getting suspicious. Also, who the fuck compares porn notes? There is more than enough crazy fetishes out there and I don't know of one person that would want to air their dirty laundry of that.

I ended up rattling off the first names that came to my mind.

"Okay. I have a couple I love, but let me first tell you that I don't really openly talk to people about my fantasies or favorite porn stars, so forgive me if I'm a little weird during this conversation."

I was stalling to think of a couple and then I had a fairly easy outpouring of them.

"Well, I really love Joanna Angel, any of the Suicide Girls, or ridiculously tattooed and pierced porn stars really. Except Bonnie Rotten, she's a little much for my taste."

Taste? What the fuck am I talking about? I'm not comparing notes on fine cheeses or that shit, we are talking about hardcore porn stars. Sure there's a spectrum of what I like, but Jesus. Do I always come off as this pretentious? We're talking porn stars after all.

"Ah. Good choices."

Clearly I wasn't totally out of line, seeing as Brad immediately jumped in with his opinions.

"I'm a little surprised at you, Phil. A little more hardcore than I expected of you, but that's cool. I'm more the girl next door type. So, anyone on the Mofos circuit really."

Maybe if I discuss this at length with him, I could stop thinking about Phil's beautiful dick. I need some more distractions though.

"I really hate all the abuse fetish sites out there. They are horrifically misogynistic and disgusting overall."

I was floored by both the comment and the thought. First off, was he really interested in me? And secondly, misogynistic? He knows we are talking about porn right? There is no such thing as non-misogynistic porn, but, I guess there is a spectrum of tolerance for all of that stuff.

Maybe this was all an elaborate plan of his to watch porn together so he can jerk off at me jerking off? Oh my god. Would that be a meta jerk off? A circle-circle jerk?

As I had that thought, Brad was inching closer and closer to me. My pants weren't even fully pulled up, I was halfway under the covers.

I desperately need to get my pants on or this will get really weird.

He decided to stop dancing around the topic and got more to the point.

"Who were you looking at right now?"

He got closer and closer to me.

"I'm sorry, man, this is getting a little weird for me. Can you give me some space?"

"Oh, okay, sure man. I'm sorry."

Before he could finish his thought, I got another text from Linds.

Brad was now close enough that he could see this on my phone.

"Lindsey's texting you? I didn't think she had your number. What's she up to?"

It was at that moment that he decided to unlock the phone and check the message. Very uncool and wildly inappropriate in any regard. Unfortunately for him, my text conversation with her was already open; seeing as I was staring at that picture. As soon as he unlocked the phone, he saw—on a micro-scale—a picture of his naked sister spread eagle at me.

That poor bastard just saw two unwanted taints in one day. That had to be rough.

* * *

BRAD QUICKLY backed away to the other side of the bed.

"Fuck. She's got you too? She's unbelievable."

The look of pure horror in his face was something I would never forget.

And what the hell exactly did he mean that "She's got me too?"

I looked at him quizzically, but he quickly backed away and started rubbing the bridge of his nose.

"I need a drink. I'm sorry, Phil. We'll pick up on this later."

That was it. That was all he needed to hear. He was fed up and walked away. I looked down at her text. It was a declarative order.

"Come over at six."

That did not feel as good as I would have anticipated it too. She's telling me to come over so she can get fucked. I should be ecstatic about this, but I'm not. I'm more ashamed than anything. It was apparent that I was merely being used. Especially after Brad's comment, it sounds like I am not unique to that circumstance, at least in regards to his sister.

This was only amplified by the fact of him wanting to fuck me.

Wow, has there ever been someone in my same circumstance? This is way beyond ridiculous. I needed a fucking drink too.

I got out of the bed, finally pulled my damn pants up, and walked over to the mini fridge. I've never raided a mini-bar before, and now is as good as a fucking time as any. I checked out my options and as per my previous experience, I stick to any brown liquor and stay away from the clear ones.

Well, unless it's Everclear.

Out of all the possibilities I was expecting to see (Dewaar's, Jack Daniels, Glen Livet), I saw the highly unlikely Wild Turkey. Without any further hesitation I grabbed it and tore open the cap. I haven't had this cringe-worthy bastard since, well, drinking with Methhead Dan and Kaycee.

After drinking all of the Wild Turkey shooter, I decided I may as well continue with what I was up to before I was rudely interrupted. Plus, I hate that hedging shit anyway. I whipped my dick out again and pulled up Lindsey's picture. It was a little weird that I was completely into jerking off to her picture consider she was the "girl next door" type that Brad was just talking about. Ew.

I can't fucking do this.

I sighed and put my dick away. I was just too weirded out to be standing there in the middle of the room anyway. I opened the fridge again and grabbed the other bottle of Jamesons and drank that too.

I sat down at the table by the window in the room to think it all over.

What the fuck do I do with the rest of this trip? I'm unintentionally alienating myself from this family. I know I could head over and fuck Lindsey again, or rather, have her fuck me. I could try to patch things up with Brad, or I could hang out and do something myself. Who am I kidding? I never want to be by myself. That's when I'm the most miserable.

I took a couple of breaths and tried to get my head on straight. I knew what would be best to do, I needed to get on the mend with Brad. Given how he described—and wrote off—Lindsey as someone who can easily deal with me blowing her off, and considering my future is literally depending on my good relationship with this family. It was the best course of action.

Without giving it a second thought, I texted Brad begging his forgiveness.

"Hey, man, I don't know really where to start other than to say I'm sorry. I don't want to fuck up anything with us. I shouldn't have betrayed your trust, and I really should have told you about Linds and I, but it was so rushed and unexpected that I really did not know how to do that. I know the way you figured it out is the exact opposite way of how I wanted you to learn about this. I'm sorry, man."

After hitting send, I felt like I could breathe again. I attempted to delay my anxiety for a few minutes by pacing across the room, but that didn't do shit.

Maybe a nap would help?

I jumped off the floor and crashed on the bed. It was not as comfortable as I had expected, or hoped it to be. I took some deep, deep breaths and tried to get myself into a napping mood. I did this in spite of the fact I haven't successfully napped since I was eight or nine, but I thought it would be worth it to try.

Before I could even get into a calmer breathing cycle I got a text back from Brad.

"Thanks for saying that, man. It's okay. I'm sorry for not warning you about her ways."

Okay, good. It doesn't sound like anything is fubared but, I should still go out of my way to make sure that everything is still on the up and up with Brad.

"Cool, man. Listen, though, I still feel terrible. What are you up to tonight? Can I buy you those drinks that you needed to have?" I wrote him back immediately.

While I waited for his response, I thought it would be best to at least let Linds know that I would not be coming over tonight. I tried to write this as delicately as possible.

"Hey, Linds. Listen, I can't come by tonight. And I don't know if we should continue this, Brad knows about *us.* I thought it would be best if we didn't keep our relationship a secret. Sorry."

As I was still waiting for both of their responses, I decided to skim through the program again and think of all the awesome things, and the not so awesome things I experienced so far. I got to see a few pretty good movies, but in my meet and greet the Duncan guy was a condescending prick. Do I really want to surround myself in a world of that? Shortly after thinking that over for a bit, I received the two responses.

First, Lindsey's was extremely casual. It didn't even read like she gave a shit about any of this.

"Whatever, pussy, your loss."

Oh. Well, that's really fucking nice of her. Good to know she cares so deeply and passionately about me.

Then, Brad's was warm and inviting.

"That's so nice of you to offer! However, tonight I had plans with some of the guys, but let me check with them first to make sure it's cool of you to come down."

Everything seems on the up and up here, however, I think I shouldn't lead him on at all. If we continue this friendship, and it is extremely likely that we will, considering I will be now professionally linked to his dad's business at least; I shouldn't keep him wondering about anything and I should be upfront with him going forward.

"Cool, man. Keep me posted. Also, I don't think this was discussed earlier today, but just to be completely upfront with you: I am flattered of your compliments earlier, but I am not interested in you like that. You are a very valuable friend to me and I plan on continuing that aspect of our relationship."

He immediately shot back with a short—and kind of terse—response back:

"Yeah. I sort of figured that. Whatever, man. It's all good, just relax, okay?"

Well shit. That was easy.

I was finally able to stretch out on the bed and breathe. I smiled in relief. Come to think of it, I might actually be able to take a brief nap. As I began to close my eyes, I received one last, unsettling text from Brad.

"Hey, Phil, just checked in with the guys and they are fine with you coming over. We'll go at about eight o'clock tonight As a heads up thought, things can get a little weird with them. But beyond that they're all good people. I'll text you where to meet."

I shrugged it off. I'm sure Brad's *guys* were fine, he was just a little shy about bringing outsiders in or something. I snuggled into the bed, and completely disregarded Brad's "warning." What did he think he needed to protect me from anyway? I'm sure after our last conversation, all of our cards must have been on the table anyway. Brad texted me the location of where to meet. To my surprise, it was the location of an older, local gym, a little further down the road from the main strip of Telluride.

Maybe he plays basketball, or something with these guys? If that were the case, he would have probably told me to wear different clothes. More than likely this is just a meet up spot to go somewhere else after that.

After finally looking upon the gym, 8750 Alt (yes, it was really called that), I noticed that it was almost completely empty with only one dude running on a treadmill. Like most gyms I've seen, they have a completely open floor to ceiling see through window. That always struck me as the stupidest idea. If I were to go to a gym, I would much rather have it in a totally anonymous, windowless black box so no one could see or judge me as I sweat like an idiot and look like a human hamster trapped on a perpetual motion machine. I never saw the appeal of gym culture, but then again, for most of my life, I was a lumpy piece of shit.

I guess it balances out.

I got another text from Brad to come around to the back of the property, and after doing so, it finally clicked that this location was a mere meet up. Along the back of the gym was a caravan of Lincoln Towncars and Mercedes. Brad peaked his head out of one of the Mercedes.

"Hey, man! Come on over here!"

Brad looked a lot more jovial than when I saw him last. *Maybe he was fucked up on something? It's pretty early still, but I wouldn't discount him on that.*

"So glad you can come out, dude!"

He welcomed me into the back of the extremely sleek car. This looked as clean as if it were an Uber, but I saw no equipment or sign that I could use to confirm my assumptions.

"Yeah, no problem, man."

I looked around in the car, there were two other entitled looking—clearly from Westminster—guys. Taking the cue of my inquisitive and skeptical look, Brad introduced me with no hesitation.

"Guys, this is my friend Phil that I was telling you about. Phil, this is Devin and over there in the white is Tommy."

"Nice to meet you guys!"

That came across way too enthusiastically.

I put out my hand to shake theirs, but I was not received well.

Ugh, he just looks so desperate. It's like everything is depending on our approval of him. It's so sad.

Who is this again? Is this the guy with the really nice cock that Brad was talking about? Maybe we'll see some of it later.

They meekly waved at me and I briefly waved back.

Good to know stories of my dick are already making rounds. I never thought it was anything special but, to each his own I guess.

"So uh, Brad, where exactly are we going? And why the hell did you tell me to meet you here?"

Brad brushed it off with a quick laugh.

"Yeah sorry about that, tonight we are off to a house party. I thought it would be better to get people off of your trail as a preventative thing for certain people who might arrive later."

"Oh. Alright, cool by me."

Apparently, that comment was enough to warrant an eye roll from Tommy. Also, that was an extremely ominous comment, people who might arrive later. Is this going to be ludicrously VIP? Doubtful, but who really knows?

Maybe I was coming off as too eager, and I should roll with the punches? Or, that Tommy kid is a real fucking diva. I'm not too sure which.

For the rest of the ride, everyone for the most part stayed pretty silent. I rolled with it, for fear of being ostracized further. No one was really thinking of anything either. If anything, it wasn't about the immediacy of what was about to happen, but it was about innocuous sort of things for tomorrow or the following days.

Devin was mulling over his schedule for the final day of the event, and Tommy was having a dilemma about firing one of his family's inherited drivers. Really petty, shallow bullshit was all that was in their minds. Nonetheless, it was bullshit that did not give me any idea of what to expect for the rest of the night.

Speaking of driver, I never got this dude's name. I am still going to assume that this was a driver, and not a friend leading us to god knows where. As I took in the scenery around us, we were getting more and more isolated in a direction and location that was still unknown to me. There were no streetlights anymore. Traffic lights were extremely few and far between, and there were no real mile-markers or anything of the sort.

I was getting really anxious and decided to quell the silence in the car with some music.

Thank god for satellite radio.

My default is the grunge or metal stations, but I thought these guys would not be into that, so I settled on the modern alternative rock station. No one audibly complained, but I sure as hell heard a lot of their inaudible complaints.

Ugh, alternative rock? This guy is such a fucking cliché, what does Phil see in him again?

Devin at least took a slightly higher road.

Well, if we listen to music along the way it'll all help us relax and I won't have to deal with any small talk.

Brad didn't think of anything. At all. Not anything snarky, not anything defensive of me, or any type of an explanation of what the hell we were about to be doing; or, who the hell these douchebags were and why he chose to hang out with them. I was growing extremely weary of my company, and very suspicious of what the reason was for everyone being so quiet. It was as if their defense was intentionally up.

The driver was looking straight forward as well. No small talk, although, maybe he was paid for that, and nothing that could ever be interpreted as slightly amicable. With drivers, either you get the extremely talkative ones, or the extremely reclusive ones. I always found it was best to let them lead the conversation if they wanted to have it.

Out of nowhere, Devin, had a completely out of context thought.

Man, are we there yet? I'm getting hard just thinking about this.

What the fuck did that mean? It seems like we are going to be driving to an extremely isolated house, maybe there will be some strippers there or something? Maybe we would stumble on the set on those extremely elaborate, over the top, over-sexualized porn shoots/rap videos of the early nineties? Where the hell could we be going that would be leading to his dick getting hard? Was it a metaphor of excitement? Given the context of the entire week, maybe we'd actually go to an off the schedule off the records screening of a unreleased movie? I've heard of places like Quentin Tarantino's movie room, where he would invite people over and curate specific movie themes for the night/guest. Could this be something like that?

Now, I'm really excited at that prospect. My dick wasn't literally getting hard over it, but I could now understand the excitement of Devin's statement. But who the hell lives out here? Or, I guess this could be a rental, but who knows for sure? This really could be any-one's place that we are walking into, with *anything* being screened. I'm really glad I blew off Linds for this now.

If only I had known I would be walking amongst the private circles of film elite during this festival.

I was so excited, I was not able to finish that last thought. Right then, we took a hard right turn to an unlisted driveway. We went up quite a steep hill, to finally come upon an extremely elegant house with a four car garage, and a dried out fountain up front. This house was an ultra-sleek modern styled cabin. I only know that because you could see into one extremely modern, empty living room.

Just at that moment, Brad blurted out, "Gentlemen, we have ar-rived. Remember, just be cool, and everyone will have their fun to-night."

As soon as I opened the car door, I noticed a heart-pounding *THUMP-THUMP-THUMP-THUMP* of muffled techno music com-ing from the house. I could actually feel it from the ground.

Brad grabbed onto my shoulder, as well as Devin's and said, "This is the stuff of hedonist's dreams."

He said that with the biggest, shit-eating grin I have ever seen in my life. Brad followed up by shouting.

"Are you ready?"

Little did I know upon taking those first steps into the cabin, that I was walking into a scene that was probably edited out of Todd Solondz's *Happiness* (1998) mashed up with *Requiem for a Dream* (2000). It was not pretty.

The cabin was too dimly lit to notice anything good or bad about it. Any pictures on the wall came across as blurry, and the cabin itself lacked any "well-worn" charm of many other homes of the area. It was sickeningly modern. A grotesque, sobering cleanli-ness that you feel in any hospital hallway or any other place that carries a lot of dead people and has to do a lot of cleaning up after biohazards.

Brad attempted to be reassuring, with coy smiling and mild nods that came across as, everything's fine, just check out this next room. Devin was greedily rubbing his hands together and licking his lips, while Tommy's focused eyes and demented smile said it all.

My heart was pounding through my chest.

What the hell did I sign myself up for? Something about this feels really wrong.

I haven't seen anything but I knew something was off-kilter.

Brad then led us all to the basement door and opened it for us. We proceeded as if we were all gentlemen wearing the finest tuxedos entering some fine dining place like *Le Cirque* or, some other bullshit hoity-toity place that I would never willingly attend. I walked down the extremely sturdy staircase—it's always rickety and shit to spook people out, but this was top-notch craftsmanship all around—and entered a room that looked like a carbon copy of the vampire rave scene from the first *Blade* (1998) movie. The difference, much to my dismay, was rather than overly-sexualized vampires preying upon, well, their prey; it looked to be under-sexualized pudgy white dudes gathering around a circle.

I pushed away to see what the main attraction was, and I immediately regretted that decision.

What the hell did I just walk into?

In the center of the group of hideous looking investment bankers, corrupt politicians and other generic evil white people were waifish, naked, and crying barely pubescent teenage boys giving each other what appeared to be the saddest, most grotesque handjobs I have ever seen. This all was taking place whilst they were being cheered on by these horrific pederasts.

Brad did the Vanna White reveal motions with his hand and simply said,

"Welcome to the buffet. The only rule is to not disrupt, or acknowledge anyone at Mr. Singer's soiree. Anonymity is mandatory. Here are your masks."

Hold on, did I just stumble upon some underground fuck dungeon? Why didn't Brad give me any kind of notice whatsoever? Did he really think I would be okay with this?

I stumbled around mostly alone, Devin and Tommy slid right into place in the circle of crygasming boys, and I did not see where Brad went.

The thoughts that I overheard were mostly monosyllabic grunting with the occasional *"Fuck that's hot!"* interspersed throughout. Additionally, the lip-smacking and creepy old man ogling were unfortunately extremely audible. Everyone was wearing those masks a la *Eyes Wide Shut* (1999), but they were all a considerably older crowd. Mostly over the hill, waspy, and all wearing extremely formal suits, with the exception of two black guys whom I swore were Al Sharpton and Charlie Rangel, although I couldn't be too sure. Either way, they were grinding and mashing their dicks through their slacks hoping to get any sort of activity or a response. Their lip smacking cut through the drab party music and stood out like a disgusting, gangrenous thumb.

Maybe only this main room was completely debauched and I can find something not as horrifying with a little bit more exploring.

I took it upon myself to get the hell out of there and try to avoid the hellscape I just encountered. By doing this, maybe I could find Brad and confront him for bringing me to this sick fucking party. I slinked through the hallways while feeling the walls the entire time. This was done because I could not see anything except a stray ray of light derived from the black light, and god knows if anything was happening in the hallways I would not want to be involved in it.

I blindly groped for an object that was jutting out from the wall, hoping it was a doorknob and not some gloryhole with an extremity pointing out, and turned it to head into the next room. Thankfully, it was a doorknob. I would have turned on that light to see what was happening but even before doing so, I received multiple horrific warning signs that I should immediately leave.

First, the room was pungent of taint sweat and cum. Secondly, I audibly heard muffled "NNNNGH- nnngh- nng" noises, which sounded as if they were coming through a gag ball, followed by a series of whip cracking noises. Finally, the thoughts I was hearing were more than enough to drive me the hell away from that room. In addition to a *"Fuck, he's so tight,"* and *"His ass is so smooth and taut, I could fuck him all night with a couple more Cialis pills,"* the thing that really pushed me over the edge of further exploring that room was the follow up thought of, *"Is this guy done yet? I can only jerk off by myself for so long, and there are four more of us ready to go."*

I tried to close the door as gently as possible, without making any unnecessary sounds. I did not want any of those sick assholes to notice me. I went back to groping the wall moving on to the next room, but the further I lurked down this hallway, the hotter and hotter it got.

Was there an actual rise in temperature, or was this an unwanted side effect of a mild panic attack that I was having?

The next room had very little activity in it. I couldn't discern anything from my senses at first, and sure enough, when I snuck in and turned on the light it was an empty bedroom. This looked like any other mild-mannered bedroom, but I took it as my own personal haven. I sat down on the bed and convinced myself that as soon as this trip is over, I wouldn't talk to Brad anymore, but I would move to California and take Adam's suggestion.

How could he fucking do this to me? Is he really that clueless? In what fucking world would I, or anyone outside of this disgusting group of people be interested in casually coming to a rape dungeon for pederasts and underage twinks?

As these thoughts of leaving Brad behind were running through my mind at a mile a minute, I heard the sound of glass breaking in the bathroom adjacent to this room. I knew that what would be on the other side of that door would be something that would surely horrify me, and sure, call me a glutton for punishment or whatever, but I *needed* to know what was behind that door.

I snuck up to the door, put my ear on it, and heard nothing. No voices, no sounds, silence. I was about to convince myself that maybe I had *thought* I heard a crash, I started to hear the sound of—*what I'm assuming was piss*—hitting the interior of a toilet bowl.

I opened the door and immediately flipped on the light switch to find yet another room filled of horrors. There was a very old man with a shard of glass, digging into the surface of a young boy's neck, as blood was pooling up around the gash, forcing his shriveled dick and balls into this boy's mouth; and in the shower, there were two liver-spotted, mothball reeking men, pissing on a kneeling boy in the shower who was muffling his sounds of crying with a pale, shaking hand over his mouth.

They all looked at me completely devoid of any emotion, and one of them men in the shower said in an extremely grizzled—and obviously self-camouflaged voice—"Get in here and join, or shut the light and leave." None of them had any speck of emotion on their masked, sweaty faces. They all remained stoic and silent, until the boy with the old guy's junk in his mouth began to wince.

Another one of the men in the shower, without attempting to mask his natural voice finally uttered:

"You in, or what?"

How could someone doing something so horrific, say something so casually to me, while being so heartless to so many other people?

That's what pushed me over the edge.

* * *

THERE WAS a palpable disgust in the air. A quease-inducing sensation that I knew had to be undone. The only way I knew how to get rid of this disgusting situation, was to put an end to it. I sucker-punched the man forcing his limp, pathetic cock into the mouth of the pale waif on the floor, and as he fell—almost in slow motion—his head went crashing down into the corner of the lid of the now shattered toilet tank. There was a shard of porcelain that was a little longer than my clenched fist stuck in his temple.

Water spurted everywhere and helped disperse the blood flowing out from the skull of the old man, which was not as viscous as it was when it was pooling in the recesses of the white and cornflower blue bathroom tile. The pale waif was awestruck and didn't know what to do. He gawked at me, looking for direction.

I motioned at him to get out of the room, but where else in this rape dungeon could it have been any better? I inevitably pushed him out of the way and went towards the pederasts in the shower. I pried the shard of glass from the fist of the guy on the floor, and lunged towards the shower. The men didn't flinch. One of them even had the audacity to spit on me.

He stared coldly at me.

"Kill me if you want, but if you're here, you're no better than any of us."

I responded casually.

"Yeah, I know I'll probably see you in hell, but it might be hard to see you in the lower circles."

I slowly, deliberately sliced the shard of glass across his throat and I saw him gritting his teeth the whole time. The other guy in the shower cowered in fear.

Fuck. Don't do this, there's so much that you don't know about me. I know I've went down a horrible path, but, I can change!

I snarled my lip and stared at him.

"Give me one good fucking reason not to—"

Before I could finish my sentence, I heard Brad's shrill voice behind me.

"What the fuck, man!"

He sounded incredulous.

"You? You did this?"

I looked at him without any regret in my face, I still held that bloody shard, so I had no way out of this whatsoever.

What should I do? I have a witness now. and I could easily go to jail. My brief glimpse of a non-shitty life would forever be destroyed.

I owned up.

"Brad, I uh… I was just so disgusted, and angered by all of this that..."

Brad cut me off while rolling his eyes at me.

"Yeah, I'm not a fucking idiot. I know exactly what happened here. I'm more impressed and surprised than anything else."

"You, you what?"

"Yeah, man. This kind of shit happens all the time, someone freaks out. It's not that big of a deal."

Have I gone completely insane? It's not that big of a deal?

I took a breath and collected my thoughts.

"Brad, take a look around. There are two dead bodies at my hands. I'm a killer. As for you, well, I don't know what the fuck you are, but you're not exactly out of the shit here either."

"Yeah, yeah. This isn't anything new. This wasn't exactly the VIP room either. I'm not too worried."

I was still shocked, and my adrenaline was flowing through me. I was quickly getting exasperated.

"You're not too worried about this? Wait, before you even answer that question, answer me this: why the fuck did you even drag me here in the first place? What kind of sick asshole are you with these people, or, better yet, what kind of sick asshole do you think I am?"

Phil looked slightly regretful, and semi-embarrassed.

"I don't know. I thought you would be a person who is interested in new things and new adventures. I haven't really shown this part of me to a lot of people, and we were getting along so well. I thought you would understand and be accepting of—"

I finished the sentence for him.

"Of rape and child pornography? How shitty of a person do you think I am?"

The old naked man in the shower finally cut us off.

"While you two princesses discuss ethics, I'm going to go into the other room and finish up what I started. Come on, Billy."

The naked, whimpering, waif gave me a dead stare and followed out his escort? His client? As this happened, Brad turned to the old man, put on a standard shit-eating grin and coyly waved at the old guy.

"Sounds good, Mr. Peterson! We'll be in touch!"

"We'll be in touch?" I slapped away his waving hand. "What the hell is wrong with you?"

Brad put his hand down by his side, rubbed his chin for a second, and then asked me a question.

"Phil, do you smoke?"

"Do I what? What the hell does that have to do with anything that's happening right now!"

I was getting more agitated with each passing second.

"Well, come upstairs and smoke with me. Do you want some cigarettes or something a little more adventurous?"

He said that last part with a knowing smile.

"I don't want any more adventures tonight, asshole! I just want some answers, some closure, and to get the fuck out of here!"

"That sounds like cigarettes to me. Come on."

Brad dragged me by the wrist upstairs away from the ridiculous scene out in the main room in the basement, and we ended up right outside of the front door. He took out a pack of Red's from his pocket, lit up the first one and offered it to me. I inhaled hard. I never smoked before, so I was that idiot who was hacking up a lung because I didn't know how hard tobacco would hit me. However, I was the idiot who was naive enough to not know how to smoke, yet somehow able to kill three men with relative ease.

Brad lit one up and deeply inhaled.

He sounded much more casual and relaxed compared to how I must have come across.

"Phil, be honest with me. How do you think I'm so well off?"

I didn't understand the obvious line of questioning at first, so I easily dismissed it.

"Uh, it's because of your dad and his business? What does this have to do with anything?"

Brad took another drag and started to chuckle.

"That greedy son of a bitch? No way. He is keeping it all for himself. There won't be a trust fund for me or Lindsey. Sure, he has provided for us well but that doesn't necessarily have anything to do with my business."

"You mean, your high-wage, salary positioned at the Lazy Armadillo?"

Brad smirked.

"No, asshole. That's a front. I make quite a bit of my money, hosting parties and get togethers for the sexually deviant people that can afford my services. "

He paused knowing that last statement took some time to digest.

"I'm an entrepreneur, man! I take the largest cut of the overhead to secure location, the talent, and hush money for everyone else. I've been doing this for a couple of years now. The best part of it is, my parents think I'm great with saving. And the money I do make at the Lazy Armadillo is all just the cherry on top. They don't need to know about my other bank accounts, or the fact that the right clientele in this line of work could tip me tens of thousands of dollars."

I didn't know I was dealing with this much of a manipulative sociopath. Jesus.

"Okay, so, why did you think I would want to be a part of this at all?"

Brad rolled his eyes again.

"Man, I already told you that. I thought you would be interested in seeing what I was up to and being part of this grand adventure with me."

Okay.

"Uh, going forward, I would recommend a brief explanation of what the fuck to expect before walking into your specially curated rape dungeon. How could anyone be okay with that, if that is not their taste?"

Brad lit up another cigarette and blew out a ring into the crisp night sky.

"That's a fair point. I'll keep that in mind for later. Sorry about that, man."

Now that my heart was not beating out of my chest cavity anymore, I could approach things logically.

"So, what the hell do we do about the bodies in the basement?"

"Oh. Right. Listen, bud. Don't worry about that. Remember those hush money people that I told you about? That's one of the things that falls under their job description. We will clean up the scene and make sure that the appropriate coroners and cops are paid in full. It's all good, man."

It's all good? What the fuck kind of evil genius was in the presence of right now?

"Listen, Phil. This is obviously not your scene, I'm sorry I didn't let you know of what to expect earlier. Let's both of us get out of here, and just let those sleeping dogs lie. Everything will go right back to normal after this, okay?"

While he said that, he gave me a confident pat on the back. He didn't seem to care at all about the lives that I took, or for the relatives of the people's lives I ruined. He said everything after this would go back to normal, but I knew that shortly after this. I would be escaping all of this filth once and for all.

That was a silent, painful ride home which I would never forget.

* * *

I WAS SWEATING bullets in the passenger seat as time went on. Knowing what the night had previously consisted of, who the hell could drive at a time like this? As we were consistently listening to the static, muffled audio of the distant radio stations, I did everything in my power to appear as though I was relaxed.

In spite of my disposition though, I was nothing close to relaxed. I was so nervous that I felt exhausted. My mind was not slowing down. It was in overdrive as thoughts flew past me at what felt like 90 miles per hour.

New friends. I need new friends and a new life. If I surround myself in trash then chances are, I'll feel like trash, and that's not a way I want to keep on feeling. Feeling ill, how can I surround myself in this type of a lifestyle at all? How did I get to where I am in the first place? This is not somewhere I want to be and these are not people that I want to be with. After that interaction, all I want to do is take fifteen boiling hot showers one after another. Maybe then I'll feel good enough about myself and start to value who I am and who I'm surrounded by. Because until that happens, not one fucking thing is going to change. This is beyond ridiculous. Can I really continue to wake up with myself like this? How could I just on the drop of a dime change everything though? Is any of this realistic, or do I have my head caught in the clouds again? Is this some impossible dream? Escaping everything I ever have known? What the fuck have I done to get here and what can I do to get out?

I don't even have the money to do anything different. So what can I do? There's no safety net. No one can help me out with this. There's no money at home to be had, and I've done a great job at isolating myself away from any other kind of contact that could potentially help. What the hell can I really do right now?

I did everything I could to make myself seem calm. I put my arm on the edge of the window, just like I always did. I fucked with the radio, like usual. I even made sure that I stretched my leg out onto the dashboard.

How is this always comfortable to me? It's so ridiculous. Eh, whatever. If I can relax this way, I'll fucking do it.

I made sure his eyes were always on the road and he wasn't fading in and out, but I kept him entertained with simple, light-hearted conversation. Or at least, put the facade on like I could.

"What do you think, methhead, do you think I'd earnestly have a shot with Kaycee? At all?"

I thought playing desperate would be a good foil to his current *altered state*. If he was awake enough to roll his eyes at me and tell me to shut the fuck up, or judge me at all, then he'd still be awake enough to drive.

"Dude. Give it the fuck up!"

I was less than thrilled with his response. He was still cognizant, so he wouldn't black out, but by brushing me off in the way he did, he clearly did not want to engage in any type of a conversation whatsoever. He was being very closed with his responses. This was not conducive as a way to try and keep him awake and alert.

I saw that he was fading behind the wheel and I know I was too fucked up to take his place; it was just a bad situation to be a part of, and the only thing that would be my salvation in it, was looking forward to when it would be over. I started to fiddle around with the radio again, and seeing as we were normally on the rap station or alternative-rock, I thought it would do us both some good if I put some extremely irritating, twangy bullshit bluegrass. This was definitely something that would rile him up.

"What the fuck, man? Are you kidding me?"

He took a swipe at the radio and I felt the car drift into the next lane.

"Christ, man! Can you pay attention to the road like you should actually be doing? You're going to get us killed, asshole!"

I reached over and turned it down. I was fed up with his reckless approach and his fake too cool to care approach.

"Dan! Fucking park this car, man! I don't want to die tonight. I don't want to die with you, and I do not want to die a pathetic, drunk, virgin. Park the car."

"God, will you shut up with your whining? We are almost at your place and then we'll just crash there okay? Everything will be fine, just shut the hell—"

Before he could even finish that sentence, both of our lives changed within milliseconds. Dan ran a red light and got us T-Boned by some other asshole behind the wheel. As it was told to me by the attending nurse, when I woke up in the ER, that I blacked out instantly from the pain of my freshly amputated leg. They attempted to reassure me, but to no avail. They also said that there was no chance of saving what was left of my leg and reconstructing it.

"How's my friend who was driving?"

"Oh, he's getting his license suspended or something, but he's fine."

I always wondered why I bothered to ask that question. Out of all the things to fucking think about. Not what my life would be like without a leg; not if I could I ever walk again; not about what else happened, or I don't know, where everyone was?

I'll never forget that sheer terror I felt when I realized I was alone in the world. No one came to see me. I don't know how long I was out, but I knew I was alone for a day and a half before any visitors came. Even after the waiting, the first person to see me was Dan. He slinked in the room trying to be as casual as possible.

He probably did that because he could feel me fuming from a mile away.

"Hey Phil. How ya doin', bud?"

I wanted to do everything I possibly could at that moment to make sure he knew how miserable I was. Somehow, though, I couldn't muster up anything to indicate that. It hurt to yell, or even get frustrated at all. I wasn't crying, or furious, but I was devastated. I wish I could communicate it. I think he was able to tell, I mean, he was an idiot for getting as drunk as he did in the first place, but I think he still was capable of some common sense.

"Phil. Listen, you probably don't want to see me right now. I know I wouldn't. But you're at least entitled to an explanation."

This got me seething with rage.

"An explanation of what? You being a fucking irresponsible asshole and being able to carry on as normal, while I'm the only person shit out of luck because of your recklessness?"

Dan couldn't even look at me. He looked at the floor when he was talking. Good. He should be ashamed and feel horrible for what the hell he did.

"Well, I thought that would come up eventually, and I completely deserve it. But no, an explanation for something else."

"What could you possibly have an explanation of that I would be interested in hearing?"

I didn't give him any space to finish. I was so angry I steamrolled over the end of his sentence.

"It's a good thing you're sitting down, bud. I need to tell you why neither of your parents are here."

I was taken aback by this. What the hell would he know that would explain anything? More importantly, why weren't they here to see their only son after he was just involved in such a horrific incident?

"Listen, Phil. Your Dad, well, he died in the accident that night as well."

My eyes immediately welled up with tears, and my voice became strained with confusion.

"What? Are you—? You better not be fucking joking with me right now."

He finally looked up at me and I could see that he was crying as well.

"I wish I was, man. I really, really wish I was. I've been checking in with your mom and she's been devastated. She's definitely not in a good place to drive. That's why she hasn't come to visit you."

He took a pause to regain his composure and wipe away some stray tears.

"Listen, man, long story short, I think the nurse may have mentioned to you that I'm getting my license revoked, but I wasn't who the cops listed as at fault for the accident. The dude who slammed into me, well, that was a Denver County bus. He was drunk too. This started a pile up and your dad was at the tail end of it."

"Essentially, when I got to the center of the intersection it was red, but when I got to the end of the crosswalk it was yellow, so I was legal in that regard, but definitely not legal in the drunken regard."

"Also, this is super important. From your perspective, everything can go on as normal. You don't need to like drop-out of high school and immediately start working. Because this was a bus, there was a federal settlement that went out to everyone involved. That means you're covered for this hospital time, and there will be a lump sum given to your family because of your dad."

Dan rattled off an explanation for a while, but I never looked back into what all the messy details were that night.

* * *

WITH A head shake and a deep breath, I quickly came back to the reality I was in. I looked over to my left and there was one of the drivers Brad hired. He gave me a brief, courteous smile. It comes back to me in flashes sometimes, and I normally just have to wait it out. I looked back behind me and there was Brad, calm and collected in spite of the horrific things we just saw.

Weirdly enough, anytime I was in a car, in spite of the amputa-
tion, I still had a longing for putting my leg up on the dash like I did
in Dan's car.

Phil looked at me with concern.

"You okay, man? You just like, blacked out for a bit there."

"Yeah, I'm fine I guess."

I sulked back in the seat. I couldn't help but wonder why all of those
thoughts rushed back to my head whenever I was in the passenger's
seat. I definitely understood some, but, not all. I started to think about
what that all meant, and why I never took my inclination to leave everything behind after the night with the car accident. It would have been
hard to do at that time, sure, but nonetheless it could have happened.

Instead, I picked up everything just like I was supposed to do. It all
fell right back into place.

I looked back at Brad and smiled for a second. I thought that I was
extremely grateful to have yet another chance to start it all over and
move onward and upward. It was because of him that I met Adam, and
now I have this amazing, potential escape ahead of me. I could head to
California, and claim a brand new life for myself.

As I turned my head from the back, to the front. I noticed that
as we passed through the intersection where the light had just turned
red. I saw a flash of someone's bright headlines take over my entire
field of vision.

Family

COULD YOU leave it all behind if you had the opportunity? A complete disconnect from everything and everyone you knew, or thought you knew?

I still can't believe I'm here, but I did it; I'm finally feel free. It's all gone. No more methhead, no more mom, no more Kaycee, no more Brad or Linds even. Just me and Adam here in California. It was a much simpler kind life—I could easily get used to having no worries—but it was pretty boring. My day to day consisted of wake up, have some shitty Cheerios, head into the office, and read about 9 million pages highlighting key phrases. After that, I head home, jerk off, try to watch a movie and then go to sleep. I don't know anyone out here and these *fucks* can't even get me into any screenings much less one on ones with any directors.

Such is the glamorous life of someone who does doc review.

I was lied to, essentially. Adam talked me up here by promising me watching movies and talking to directors, but that has yet to happen here. At all. I sometimes bring it up and get brushed off.

"Yeah, about that. As soon as we find an appropriate movie/director for us to do that we will. But until then, you're doing an awesome job! I'll keep you posted."

It's normally at this point that he turns around and walks away. Every time he does this however, his immediate afterthought is:

Yeah, we'll keep you posted asshole. Does he think I owe him something? This smug little fuck. I got him this amazing opportunity. I got home away from that shit hole he called a life in Colorado and took him out here to the land of opportunity.

Who would ever have thought that I would grow to miss killing bugs? Mostly, I miss the fact that bugs don't have the capacity to be duplicitous. They normally want one of three things; food, shelter, and life. Any of their motives can be traced back to one of those functions. That's it. They don't use people, they all serve an independent function of one of the three needs they have. They are very methodical. Granted, they don't have to deal with our overly-complex emotions like grief; failure or anxiety. They just exist.

I'd love to just be without having any of these damn thoughts, wants, or wishes.

Of all the highlighting for this job, the most infuriating thing in all of it is that all of the work I'm doing is to defend these horrible, disgusting people. More often than not, I'm discovering, and identifying alibis for these monsters disguised as people doing irredeemable actions to people. One of these guys, is a serial rapist. The work I do essentially is justify his insatiable—deeply troubled—sexual hungers, to make sure he can go on to make overly-wrought movies with a ludicrous amount of over the top symbolism that's pounding you with the main themes and leitmotifs in his work.

If so much effort is going in to remove all doubt in your public records, and make it so that vox populi can understand your bullshit mystique, then why fucking bother?

Another one's a pedophile, whose movies are nothing but childish fantasies realized. Fast cars, big explosions, beautiful women with no agency somehow falling in love with these droll nerds who make no effort to woo them.

How could people not connect those dots?

Was this a stupid decision? Did I make the right move by getting out here? All it's done is make me more angry and disillusioned.

I did not sign up for all of this crap, and I wouldn't have if I had known exactly what the workload entailed. But I did, so here I am, whittling away at this never ending pile of paper to continue to help these extremely harmful, disgusting men. The takeaway for me, through all of this, has been that everyone in this industry is a liar. Nothing pans out exactly the way it should.

I'm currently pouring over these case documents looking to exonerate a known pederast from his fifth accusation; while he continues on the auditioning process of his next kids movie. It's pretty fucking disgusting of me to do this for a living. But the pay is a lot better than it ever has been before. (Even if it's still not great.)

This repetitive nonsense drives me insane.

Well, actually, maybe it helps me stay sane.

The more I do this mindless crap, the more distracted from how pathetic and pointless my life has become.

I guess it balances out then?

I know work is supposed to be, well, work and you aren't really supposed to enjoy it; but I am too brain dead by the end of the day to go out and enjoy my life and my new found independence. Even true freedom from anything that could possibly restrain me isn't that free. Well, okay, it's freeing considering I don't have to worry about anyone else but me. But who wants that kind of a life? Even the most narcissistic person can't truly be alone all the time. Interaction is a necessary evil.

Maybe I should abandon any and all hopes of true independence and get myself a pet. Would that help my loneliness? Or will that make me only think about how I'm making this animal depend on me and they'll have to love me because I'm their meal ticket?

All these thoughts perpetually ran through my head on a day-to-day basis. I finished up, and refiled the documents and headed to the parking lot.

One of the last encounters I had with Brad, on the ride home from that horrific night where I figured out his side business, he offered to incentivize my silence on my discovery by getting me a car. I begrudgingly agreed, considering I had no money saved up, and I was ready to get the hell out of that state.

After that, however, no one in his family talked to me. I'm not entirely sure why, seeing as I was nothing but grateful and kind during the trip to Telluride, but no one. No more texts from Lindsay, no more texts or calls from Brad—his mom was still too busy fighting random people on Facebook or reading her shitty magazines to acknowledge my existence—and anytime Samuel came into the office (about twice a month), he awkwardly waved to me and that was it.

What could I have done to ostracize myself from an entire family? What the hell could it have possibly been?

I walked out of the glass house style hallways and got to the lobby of my building. I thought about turning around and waving to the security guard of front, but considering I didn't give a shit before, why do it now? I stepped outside and it was another boring day in California. 80 degrees, no clouds, and enough sunshine to keep every vapid asshole happy as they indulge themselves along Sunset Boulevard. No, my office wasn't close to Sunset, but it was still true.

On the rides home I don't listen to music anymore. I don't listen to the radio, podcasts, or anything else. I merely drive and focus. I really don't know when I became so boring. I don't huff anymore, I rarely drink. I'm for the most part in my shell. I don't have a need to put myself out there. I'm pretty comfortable now. I've begun to accept my more quiet life here. While getting through the notoriously ridiculous traffic, I barely let it get to me.

Sure, after a specific amount of time, I could very well put myself out there and get a new job and then really start to enjoy this life out here. But then again, I knew that however tenuous the connection to the film industry they have, it is more of a connection then I did so I need to milk this for whatever it's worth.

I was sadly too naive to realize that this industry is about all these connections and the knowing a guy who knows a guy style of nepotism that I detested, but you did need to truly put yourself out there and market yourself. This, of course, involved self-esteem; of which I have very little. Certainly, I do not have enough self-esteem to really put myself on a limb and laugh at some dumbasses jokes even if I did not think they were amusing at all.

I finally pulled into the parking complex in my apartment and found a spot pretty close to my level. I turned off the car, pulled the keys out of the ignition, and rested my head on the steering wheel.

Who am I kidding? I'm not the only one in this position. There are millions of people in my shoes that need some extra confidence to really kickstart their career. And, like a lot of Californians, revert back to drugs. I think I know what I need to do next.

* * *

SO THIS is it? This is what I decided to sacrifice my former life for? Another shitty one bedroom life of total isolation, self-doubt, and deprecation? I was under the impression that my life would radically change when I moved.

But could I change?

Does change happen from external, or internal factors? I turned out to be the same self-obsessed asshole in a different zip code. That's really the only difference.

I can't think about this shit again, I need to get myself a drink and relax.

I walked across the living room/bedroom of my white-walled studio with no personality over to what my landlord called a "half-kitchen," and grabbed myself a beer. It was definitely a bachelor's fridge: beer, leftover fast food and condiments. That was all.

My landlord, Kris, was fine. She left me the hell alone most of the time and only made sure my rent was paid on time. That was easy enough. Our complete interactions consisted of mini-awkward runs ins and "hellos" in the hallway. Adam recommended her and sure enough, I was happy with her and the spot. I didn't need much, because I didn't bring much.

Covina was nice enough. Another nondescript suburb of Los Angeles, there were a million towns just like this. Plain enough, nondescript enough, they have a couple malls and other shit like that. It was nice, but I haven't bothered to look too much into it. I only have done the minimum requirements of the quotidian: shopping, laundry, booze. All that stuff.

Could I even relax anymore? I didn't have anything to worry about, but I still am as wound up as ever.

I used to be able to sit down with a drink, watch a movie, and get totally absorbed by it. Unfortunately, most of the movies I watch I know can tangentially affiliate with work because of all the bullshit I wade through every day at work to make sure these sick fucks don't get convicted for any of the horrific actions they partake in.

I feel like an old cop at times—I've seen it all. I've seen people charged with murder, rape, incest, pedophilia. I've even had to deal with finding an alibi for a fecophiliac. I'm not too sexually experienced but for the life of me, I will never understand the people who are into those ridiculous, extreme fetishes.

Who are these horrific people anyway? If I had known that my livelihood would exist out here only to exonerate the most disgusting people, committing the most disgusting acts I could ever fathom; I would have absolutely not taken it on. I would have much rather continued my lower echelon, bullshit life if I had known the power players would be as disgusting and reprehensible as they are.

All of the cinematic voices that have made themselves into household names; turn out to be full-time monsters and part time directors. Except for Steven Spielberg and Ridley Scott, those guys are as pristine and wholesome as their movies. They are unfortunately, the anomalies compared to the rest of the disgusting creatures that inhabit this ridiculous place called Hollywood.

Every time I go home and shift gears from work, I immediately think of Roy Batty's speech from *Blade Runner* (1982):

"I've seen things you wouldn't believe."

I can only relax when I'm watching a completely obscure director, or really, anything that is not pushed out by a major backer.

I know I'm generalizing, and I'm probably being a smug fuck, but there is definitely some truth to what I've seen and experienced. The more money you have, and if you can afford great representation you can really get away with some horrific shit in this country.

I've often thought about what I *should* be doing.

Oh, maybe I should go to some concerts, or premieres, or, anything for that matter.

I think it all over until I'm sick of thinking about it. Then I just become totally complacent, and resort to doing the same shit, over and over again. Like right now. Again.

What the hell is it about companionship? I know I'd love to be with a girl again, but I'd also just like to not be alone all the time. Why couldn't I be completely self-sufficient AND satisfied with that? What's so problematic about that? Is there something wrong with me for think-

ing that way and wanting to live that way? Does true self-sufficiency exist at all? People idealize Henry David Thoreau, but in actuality he was just a cranky, nihilistic squatter who didn't want to pay taxes and hung out at his friend's estate.

Come to think of it, I can't even say I got this job or this new life of mine on my own. I had to know somebody who knew somebody to get a recommendation in.

This life I've created for myself felt a lot like the beginning of that stupid movie *Fight Club* (1999). I am going through the motions and waiting for my Marla, or whomever my catalyst might be. Then again, that's still hoping for an external agent of change, not relying on my internal resources (assuming there are any resources to be utilized).

Fuck this. I can't keep doing this. I'm an hour into this weird documentary about a random musician from the 80's that I won't talk to anyone about and it's a subject I'll never need to know about, so why am I wasting my time doing this?

I turned off Netflix and checked some of the local listings to see what the hell was happening tonight and where it was happening.

Hmm, there's a gallery opening about 20 minutes out and it's a mixed media piece, or there's a re-enactment of Troll 2 (1990) *at the Hough Center! Fuck, but that's like a 45 minute drive and parking over there sucks plus I already have a drink in my hand. It starts in an hour. I'd be cutting it way too close. Maybe tomorrow I'd head on out. Yeah, that's a much better idea. I can deal with one more night of weird ass movies and killing time.*

The one redeeming quality of living out here now is the money. I don't worry about money anymore. All that means, though, is that I have a lot of other things to worry about; just more to scrutinize and be hyper aware of. I don't think that it will get any better.

I haven't gone out, or done anything since I first got here. It's almost like I've forgotten what going out is like.

Maybe if I go back to exterminating, it will bring back some equilibrium in my life and let me go forward by going back; like the whole Ra's al Ghul's pit thing.

The first couple weeks in my apartment were rough. I *really* started missing everything at home. I still don't know why. Everything at home was shit. I did speak once with my mom. She is liking Steamboat Springs, everything with her boyfriend is good. When I talked to her, she sounded completely distracted and not at all interested in what I was doing with my life.

Maybe she didn't care. Why should she? She is free of me anyway.

Nonetheless, I ended up not missing my family, my friends or anyone else. But for the most part I started missing my interaction with bugs. I took it upon myself to start luring them out. I made sure that certain areas of my cabinetry were wet around the pipes, and I started planting cotton swabs on paper towels that were covered in peanut butter, and I also went as far as making sure of leaving crumbs along that crack in the walls and by outlets as well.

I tried out something new to lure insects to my place. Desperate times call for desperate measures. I cooked up some simple syrup and brushed on a thin coat around the entire perimeter of my studio. Sure enough, after four days, I did see some ants, but not nearly as much as I would have liked to see.

How pathetic am I? No new friends out here, no old friends/family that care about you enough to check in on you or see how you are doing. Am I a complete pariah? Brad hasn't tried to get a hold of me, neither has anyone in his family. This cannot stand. I'm taking my first sick day tomorrow, and I'm going out and exploring this damn city.

* * *

SLEEPWALKING. *I'm sleepwalking through life now. This whole damn thing has reduced me to merely going through the motions. I don't even know why I bother at all anymore? What's the point? I don't have any goals, I don't have anyone to share my goals and successes with, I just have this weird ability, a fake leg, and a relationship between my dick and my hand that's gotten way too familiar over this time. It's like they're fucking inseparable.*

I've been saying for a while to get out and do something, anything; but what would that even be? Would I pick back up exactly where I left off in Colorado? A scummy, chubby, introverted, pariah? Am I capable of anything else? There's a whole world out there that I can take complete advantage of, but why am I sitting here watching it all pass by while I highlight a fucking paper making sure that another celebrity pederast director walks away clean?

These were one of the many rants that ran through my head on a day to day, hell, even hour to hourly basis. I couldn't shake them until something was done. Between these thoughts, the incessant ticking of that fucking second hand on the huge clock above the doorway, I truthfully was not getting a lot of work done. I still couldn't get past the fact that the easier and less physically demanding your work was, the higher it pays. What kind of sense does that make?

I've been up to my knees in literal shit before dealing with extermi-nations while I was getting paid garbage, but sitting my ass down on a desk and being able to zone out, finally affords me a comfortable life? What the fuck is that about?

That one day, would be the last day I would ever go under a deck looking for a mound with my street clothes on; it would be my bio-hazard suit only. But then again, why are there so many septic tanks built under fucking decks? That seems like the construction crew just wanted to fuck with the future home-owners.

Anyway, given the furious pace of these negative thoughts that take up all of my energy, I determined that I needed more distrac-tions. So, I decided to take myself to the land of purchasable, time-consuming attractions: Amoeba Music. It's about 30-35 minutes away, but I determined that I needed to go out and buy a fuck ton of movies and music in order to further distract myself from everything else. Including my idle mind.

Hell, mainly my idle mind.

I had a frenetic, childlike excitement at the prospect of going to this place. Everything I've ever heard of, and watched of this place, was that it was very much like a mecca for culture-vultures. I can find some incredibly hard to come by movies and music. This is a place where you could find those white-whale collector's items you were looking for. I didn't think I was that, but, why the hell couldn't I be that? I mainly wanted to go there, wander, and get out of my comfort zone.

In Denver, I used to love going to this record store called Twist & Shout. That was one of few places in my life, where I felt comfortable in my own skin. I was like the rest of the music junkies in there. We were all wanderers. Lost, and looking for something new. That was a place where getting out of your comfort zone was the collective experience. Inevitably, there would be some music on that would either attract or repel you. Or, you would bump into someone who gave you a recommendation that led you to a radically different genre of music or film that you would have never considered previously. I used to go there anytime I felt like I was reverting back to my old ways, and needed to change things up.

Maybe I'm giving that place too much credence. After all, I started going there when I was fifteen and at that age, everyone is exploring, wandering, and trying to figure themselves out. Also, maybe I should just shut the fuck down and stop thinking so much about all of this nonsense and just cut out early and leave.

Without that place, I would have never known about Tarsem Singh, *Litmus Green,* or any other one off oddity of a specific genre I ended up loving. Amoeba, I'd imagine, would be infinitely more nuanced and have an endless selection of new movies or songs to wrap my head around. I was about 45 minutes before my shift was over, but I decided to head out.

I screamed down the hallway at Adam.

"I got to go a little early, Adam! I have an appointment that I forgot about. I'll see you tomorrow!"

Without giving him any time to respond, I got the hell out of there.

That felt really good. I should do that more.

I rushed out to the parking lot and turned on my car. For some reason, this felt like an exciting, mini road trip unto itself. I probably spend more time driving in and out of work then the total amount of time for this, but nonetheless, it was the feeling of excitement and the unknown; which is something I have missed quite a bit. I'll take that and run with it.

Where would I end up? What would I end up being turned on to today? This is the first time I've been to one of these places and never had to really factor in price at all. Does that mean I'll go insane for the ridiculous collector's editions of anything? Or, will I remain conser-

vative for whatever reason and look for the bargain? For that matter, would I ever have to look for a bargain again?

I started thinking of what I was familiar with that I wanted.

Should I opt for a bunch of box sets and limited b-side releases of some of the established artists I love, or should I go in a completely different direction and feel out what I'd like to get and see where the day takes me? Or, if I start browsing and someone asks me if they could help with anything, do I take the bait? Can I do that without being extremely pessimistic? When was the last time I was able to have an open mind on anything without being extremely cynical and judgmental. Is that possible anymore, or has all the other crap of my life got in the way of that capability?

I've read or heard somewhere that the closer you get to thirty, the less ambitious you get with seeking out new music and art. That was a completely terrifying prospect. If you aren't pursuing new things and remain stagnant then what's the point of any of this life? Not to get too existential, but, what the fuck else is there to do? Get lazy and comfy in your own ways and stay that way forever? That's something I could not fathom at all.

Any successful piece of art should challenge you. Film, music, visual art, books, or whatever else can (and should) make you question and challenge all of your conventions. I still think the majority of people get into any type of movies or anything for a distraction. Or maybe, like a young—not as controversial or corrupt (yet) Woody Allen, maybe people just want to be in a place that has air conditioning on a hot day. But is that really it? I cannot understand the directors, or authors out there that don't take their captive audience and shake them to their bones with new, inspiring, or troubling perspectives that challenge their system of beliefs.

Okay, that's not entirely true. I can understand people that only want to make something extremely profitable and get fatter, comfier and lazier. But then again, most of the time it's these so-called troubled artists that I really love; are they all corrupt assholes, or are there not horrible people out there making some challenging work? Those are the ones I need to find.

I was so wrapped in my own thoughts that I barely noticed that I had just finished parallel parking on Sunset. Sadly, that's not the first time that's happened, and I'm not on any heavy medication any more. I parked and looked up at the sign. I fucking loved this logo. We're all these little pathetic organisms out there in the world, looking for food, and reaching out for anything to help us grow and change. As I was looking up at this sign and thinking of all it meant to me, I realized the problem in my assessment and the smile shifted into a grimace. I was at first, completely enthralled and excited; but now I was disgusted and disappointed.

If our sole purpose is to acquire new things that can help us grow or change, like an amoeba, then we are all selfish creatures at heart. Are we able to sustain on our own without acquiring, and using things only for selfish purposes? Do we do that with our everyday people and interactions as well?

As I thought about it more and more, I compared it to the Shel Silverstein book *The Giving Tree*. I grew up loving that book because I saw it as a symbol of unconditional love. That fucking tree was giving everything it had to that boy. Only later in my life, did I realize that the boy was a selfish prick who did nothing but use and abuse that goddamn tree for his own comfort, wants and desires. That tree sacrificed everything, and what did it get in return? Dismembered, crippled, and burdened with that boy for the tree's whole life.

That's what everyone does, though. We all use each other for all we can, and then completely discard whoever we aren't gaining anything from and move on to the next person or thing we want to devour.

I couldn't be inspired by this anymore, I could only continue to be disgusted; like a true curmudgeon. I felt a hard hit and pressure in my shoulder. As I turned to my right where I noticed that some dumbass leather clad euro-trash kid walked straight into me.

This is fucking California, land of open spaces, and you walk into me? How fucking dumb does this kid have to be to walk in to me while I'm standing here, the only person here, and I'm not even blocking the entrance.

I heard a distant, and muffled, "Sorry bro!" as he walked in.

Let's see if the inside can surpass my experience out front.

As soon as I stepped inside, I felt like a fucking kid in Disneyland. It's stupid, but it's very true. I could not believe where I was. This was a place like Twist and Shout, that people loved so much. To be in their favorite place was a truly surreal experience.

I'll think I'll dive into the used rock CDs first. There was always something so exciting about the prospect of finding the diamond in the rough when it came to music. Who fucking knows what will turn up or where it's been? Or better yet, who knows what kind of tangents will my mind wander to while I'm looking for something? It's happened time and time again. I'll be looking for the side project of—say—Superjoint Ritual, and start thinking about all of the other side projects those guys were involved with, then I'll end up chasing down solo work of certain musicians I've loved in those bands.

The only thing for sure I'm going to pass on is stuff in a radically different vein. Sure, I'll get the Rebel Meets Rebel *album, but I don't need to pick up all of David Allan Coe's back catalog.*

In addition to the joy of finding artists and albums I have long forgotten about, I really do love people watching in a place like this. Everyone here is into their own weird thing. I found that extremely refreshing. New perspectives are always good, it's just a goddamn shame that I can't shake my skepticism at all. You'd think I'd be able to, but that is sadly not the case.

Let's start at the beginning and see what I can find. Oh sweet some AC4! I heard about them after International Noise Conspiracy and The Refused but I never checked them out. Man I miss that band, and that shirt I had. I remember everyone thinking that was a fucking weird Dallas Cowboys shirt because they saw that star and neglected to read the rest of it.

As I continued to flip through the racks of CDs, I started to listen to the overhead music. It was a really low-key, string quartet version of, wait, what is this?

Huh.

I was focusing in on the name of this song, when serendipitously, a store clerk asked if I needed help.

"Yeah man, *who* is this?"

"Oh, this is Apocalyptica doing a cover of Metallica's *One*. What do you think?"

"Uh, it's alright. It was on the tip on my tongue and I couldn't figure it out. Thanks, though."

"Okay, well, can I help you look for anything else? Or recommend something for you?"

I smirked because this was exactly what I was hoping would happen. I didn't want to impose, but then again it's his fucking job.

"Yeah, I'm not too sure what I'm in the mood for. I definitely feel like I need to get out of my comfort zone. Can you help me?"

I eyed his name tag, let's see what this Tim character is capable of.

"Alright, well, what kind of stuff are you listening to now?"

"Uh, well, I'll always love Stiff Little Fingers, The Refused, Big Black, stuff along those lines."

Tim started doing that chin-scratching shit which drives me crazy, but he was trying to be nice, so I decided to put up with it.

"Okay, so you've heard, Buzzcocks, U.K Subs and those guys?"

"Yeah."

"Hold on one sec. Let me grab our more punk/friendly guy, Curt."

I figured I may as well stay and see what they recommend for me and not be my normal, dismissive self. But instead of walking away, he just screamed across the sales floor.

"Yo! Curt! I got a live one here for ya, man!"

"One sec, Tim!"

Then, out of the blue, I see this really tall and emaciated nerdy dude, who looked like if Steve Albini and an R.Crumb character had a love child.

Shit. Come to think of it, that's a pretty good description for me too. Whereas he looks more like Crumb's "Keep on Truckin'" guy, and I look more like one of his neurotic, extremely sweaty self-portraits. Come to think of it, in most of his work he talks about how much joy he gets in record collecting and browsing through the shops. Holy shit.

The more I thought about it, the more it rang true, and the further my sadness sunk in.

"Hey man, I hear you dig some punk? Let me show you a couple of things over here, we just got 'em and you let me know what you think."

"Cool, thanks, man."

I followed without question, and tried to push out the thoughts of me essentially being a younger, more pathetic version of that extremely neurotic man.

"You ever hear, like, Black Pus, or Hella? I just got some in things in that you can take to a listening booth upstairs and check them out."

We got back to the buying booth, and Curt handed me two albums. *There's No 666 in Outer Space* and *Metamorpus*.

"Take a peek at these and get back to me. Black Pus has a side project called Lightning Bolt, I think we have that in the used aisle, too."

"Cool, thanks so much."

Considering this CD was four bucks, I decided to load it on and just buy it anyway. I may as well head over to the "L" aisle and check that out as well.

Maybe they had more of the Refused singer's other stuff as well. What the fuck was it? Invasion? Something like that.

While I walked over to the "L" aisle, I started Googling that band to see what it actually was.

Invasionen. Right, I remember hearing briefly about that.

But before I could finish my thought, I bumped into someone who, even before I could look up from my phone, blurted out at me.

"Do we have a fucking problem, man?"

I looked up and it was the same euro-trash piece of shit from before.

Oh fuck, it's this guy again.

"Listen man, I said I'm sorry, can we just move on?"

"Huh?"

I didn't realize what he was mentioning before but then, the appropriate response finally clicked in my mind.

"Yeah, man, we're cool. I wasn't, I just wasn't looking where I was going. It's kind of funny if you think about it. Some weird ass coincidence I guess. I'm sorry"

He immediately calmed down.

"Cool man. Cool."

Weird fucking coincidence, maybe this dude is trying to not so subtly get my attention because he wants to hook up with me or something? How pathetic and desperate do you have to be though?

He walked away. It was about fucking time too. He gawked at me for what seemed like ages after I apologized.

Some people, I guess. Eh, whatever.

I shook it off and got distracted again. Out of the corner of my eye, I saw the used movie section.

Shit, I may as well get comfortable.

I turned and walked straight ahead and thought about what I'd always wanted.

I'd love to have the audacious, ridiculous movies. All of Fellini's work, maybe Chan-wook Park's vengeance trilogy.. What do they even have? They probably don't have any of that used; who am I kidding? All of that would immediately be sold. It's probably just like a little better version of one of those crappy Wal-Mart bin features. Maybe I could get myself a three-pack of Sean William Scott's greatest films.

I shuddered at the mere thought of that.

As I fingered through the selection, I had a thought that brought me back to my real world for a second.

So I'm just going to go home and watch all these movies alone? Like always? It shouldn't have to be like this. I know there are people out there that love these kind of movies too, so why I have relegated myself to watching them this way?

I audibly sighed and tried to rush that off.

Who fucking cares. If I enjoy it, why not?

I knew I was settling for that thought process, but either way. I wanted to come here for the sake of a distraction. This wasn't meant to be a therapy session, this was meant to be a completely selfish splurge.

If I can eventually watch these with someone, cool. If not, then that's still cool.

I need stop thinking these ways. I need some more distractions. Then something came to me. And like a swift kick in the ass, I knew what I needed to do. I turned around again and walked close by the euro-trash kid.

"Hey man, sorry to bother you again but I have a question, and I think you could potentially help me out with it."

He looked skeptical, but still willing to play ball.

"Alright, fine man. What's up?"

*   *   *

HE GAVE me the profile up and down, he definitely looked concerned and confused.

What could this kid possibly want? The way he's looking at me is really creeping me out.

I was very nervous, I didn't know how exactly to start this conversation.

"Hey, um, first off, what's your name, man?"

He looked even more confused.

Who is this rigid fuck, and what does he want from me?

"My name is Piotr, but just call me Pete."

"Alright Pete, cool. So listen man, I just moved over here from Colorado and I'm still getting to know people. It seems like, with our interactions so far outside, and in this store, that fate has brought me to you. And I think I know why."

I took a pause, and wanted to think about the best possible way of stating what I was going to ask him.

"There's no good way to do this, so I'll dive in. Pete, I'm at a place in my life where I need some *distractions,* if you know what I mean. Are you the person I can buy some distractions from?"

As soon as he heard that, Pete stopped slouching, and immediately stood straight up. This guy towered over me. He looked down at me and pulled me closer to him.

"Are you seriously doing this right now?" He stared me down and puffed out his chest.

"What the fuck is wrong with you, man? Just because I dress like I'm at a dancing club, and because I'm here looking for A *KMFDM* album, you *assume* that I can sell you some drugs?"

"Is this really happening?"

I choose my words carefully.

"Alright Pete, calm down. Clearly I assumed, and I assumed incorrectly. I apologize, man. I never meant to offend you. I'll just go now, okay?"

At that moment Pete started cracking up. He was laughing so hard, it was almost as if he was doing an impression of someone laughing really hard. He was earnestly wiping tears from his eyes, and slapping his knee.

"I joke with you! Of course I have drugs, my friend!"

I breathed a sigh of relief.

"Oh, thank god. I felt so horrible!"

I was finally able to start laughing as well, but I wasn't as into it as he was.

"So my new friend, what would you like? Would you like some weed, some crack, some meth, heroin? You kind of look like your classic downer guy, am I right?"

"Well, yeah. Good guess."

I felt like I was blushing while I was saying this. Why the fuck would I be blushing? What's wrong with me? I may as well be gently kicking up dust and saying, "Aww shucks." Am I totally incapable of having a normal person to person interaction? What is my problem?

Piotr rubbed his chin and looked at the ground for a millisecond, then it looked like he'd had an epiphany.

"Tell you what, my new friend, after we are done browsing around for whatever we would like to buy, why don't you come over to my apartment and we can get you set up for a while."

"Okay, sounds good, man."

"Oh, yes. Also my friend, what is your name?"

Of course I'm too awkward to introduce myself.

"I'm sorry, my name is Phil."

"Very good, Phil, nice to meet you. So, let me tell you my immediate plans. I wanted to take some time and browse here for a while. I don't have an exact amount of time plotted out for this, but I think I shall spend a couple of hours here. What was your timeline like?"

"Pete, that's perfect! I was thinking of spending a lot of time here as well. This is my first time at this store and I heard they had some amazing things if you are willing to look for them. And that's exactly what I wanted to do."

"Okay, that's great! I am so glad to hear this! Let me get your number, and I'll text you when I'm ready to go, and we will go forward from there with our plans. Does that sound good to you?"

"Sure, Pete, that sounds great. My number is 303-432-7463. Just let me know whenever you are ready."

"Sounds good, my new friend. I will speak with you shortly, and I look forward to our future business relationship."

As he said that, he gave me the most obvious wink I have seen since one Monty Python sketch from ...*And Now For Something Completely Different* (1971) , that I had in my distant memory. He may as well have been gently giving me with a nudge as well. I started to move in a different direction and while I moved on, he stood there waving like a happy idiot.

Come on Phil, don't be hard on the guy. He seems nice, and by first sight of him, you knew exactly what you were getting into by engaging him in any kind of a conversation. You saw that coming from a mile away. He's an awkward, euro-trashy kind of guy, and that's fine. Just let him be, and he doesn't need to know that you are using him. Who knows? He might turn out to be a great friend, and you'll think back to this moment and realize how much of a judgmental fucking prick you are.

As I walked around, aimlessly in the store, I started to think about Pete's comments.

What did he mean I looked like classic downer guy? Did that mean he could tell I had low self-esteem? Did he think that because I was an ugly, fat fuck? What did that mean, and how dare he so casually say that. Who the hell does he think he is to tell me that I'm a "classic downer guy?" He's a classic euro-trash asshole, and I should tell him that. What a fucking prick.

Maybe I'm over thinking this.

Eh. Either way, I found my hookup to get me further away from this new life. Maybe I should try some uppers for once, what could that be like? Does that mean that I'd carry myself with more confidence? Or I'd be more outgoing? I think uppers might be exactly what I need. And you know what? At the very least, I'd give it a shot.

My mind continued to wonder about my what specific upper I should try out with Pete later tonight.

As usual, my mind was racing with what the possibilities later tonight, but as I was doing this, I was scanning all the aisles and seeing what I could grab. I heard this place had a listening station as well, but with most of these, I knew that I needed to buy a lot of these albums without listening to them at all. Additionally, I knew exactly which movies I was going to buy as well.

By the end of my shopping spree, I had found the vinyl of The Smashing Pumpkins' *Machina II,* (which I always wanted to listen to). I still had the *Hella* and *Black Pus* CDs that Curt found for me, I grabbed some more Sonic Youth, I got the one Angelfish album, some Naplam Death, Celtic Frost, Venom, and Tom Wait's *Swordfish and Trombones.*

For movies, I was able to pick up *The Enigma of Kasper Hauser* (1974), Sam Fuller's *Street of No Return* (1989), a box set of Ingmar Bergman that had the faith trilogy, Peter Jackson's *Bad Taste* (1987), *and Babyface* (1933).

God, pre-code movie are so ridiculous!

I think that was more than enough to get me started. Also, my budget wasn't an issue in this rare scenario, but nonetheless, the quantity alone made me feel like I should stop. I took a quick break while I was browsing and, realized how this store, in spite of its employees and customers, didn't really feel as much of a *High Fidelity* (2000) type of feel as I imagined it would be.

It was at that exact moment that I got a text.

"Hey, this is Pete. Are you ready to head out?"

I texted him back that, "I'm heading into the line now, and I'll meet you outside."

After ringing everything up at around $300, I headed outside and there was Pete, leaning up against the wall, chain smoking.

"Ah! Are you ready, my friend? Come with me and I will drive you over."

I gave him a concerned look.

"Oh, uh, I was planning on driving myself over and following you."

Pete looked at me for a second.

"Fine. If that is what you would like to do."

He seemed a little offended with my response.

"Are you okay with that, do you mind?"

He responded meekly.

"No, it's no problem. That's fine. Come on over then. Follow me."

Fucking prick, I'm offering him a nice gesture, and he is being nothing but rude to me. Who does he think he is? I'm doing him a favor after all? You know what? I'll ride with you, if that's still cool.

* * *

PETE WAS nice enough. But I couldn't get it out of my head that he looked like a more emaciated version of the classic eastern-European (with no obvious place of origin) *Die Hard* villain.

If his hair was a little bit longer, and he ate nothing but protein shakes for 8 months, the guy would probably be a dead ringer for the sub-boss of Hans Gruber.

Or, maybe if that guy watched *The Big Lebowski* (1998) in his free time, and was inspired by those really dry, funny nihilists. and decided to live his life in that style. Yeah, I could see it. In spite of his very specific looks, he was a nice enough guy and I unfortunately typecast into what I normally would assume him and other *KMDFM* fans to be; a burnout.

I must have been staring at him for an uncomfortably long time without talking. He was starting to look very uncomfortable.

I need to remember to get out of my own head and talk to people, ask them about themselves and not come off across as a total sociopath.

"So, Pete, was that your first time at Amoeba?"

As soon as I said that, I could see him relax a bit in his own seat, instead of driving like your average grandma with a white-knuckle grip on ten-and-two with no distractions, he eased up, stretched out in the seat and became instantly comfortable.

"No, my friend."

He smiled at me and looked as though he was about to start off a long story.

"When I first came to Amoeba, I remember it as if it were yesterday. You see, I come from a country where our selection of imports are extremely limited. Well, it was limited until the Singing Revolution in '89 in Estonia, but then we still got samples of music all of the world. Certainly, it was not everything that we experienced just now. Anyway, before I moved to California for school three years ago, I had just gotten to a point where I really felt a connection to the music, and its fans. That's why I love industrial music so much."

He took pause, smiled, and threw one of his hands up in the air.

"I know it sounds crazy, but I can finally relax after I listen to these guys, or Ministry, or things like that."

"Anyway, where was I?"

As he remembered exactly where he left off in this extremely long rambling session, he had the most animated face I had ever seen when his train of thought got back on track.

He looked so happy during this story. More happy than I have ever been. But what does he remember so fondly? It sounds like growing up in Estonia was rough, and he's away from all of his friends and family that he grew up knowing. Wait a sec. I'm in this exact same boat and miserable. What happened? Did he truly find a circle of friends through this piss poor excuse of a genre of music? Could that really be it? Or was it something else?

"And that was why I'll never forget my first time at that store. Quite an amazing story, isn't it?"

Holy shit. Did I really just blackout that entire story and get lost in my own thoughts? Wow. Am I that self-involved? Hurry up and say something before you come across like a completely narcissistic asshole.

"Wow, man, that's incredible. Thank you so much for sharing that with me."

He smiled, and clearly did not anticipate that response.

Nice! He bought it!

"You know, Pete, you're a great storyteller. I was basically right there with you, because of your descriptions. They were so vivid."

His smile grew even larger.

"You mean it, my friend? That is very, very kind of you to say."

"Ah! We are already here! Would you look at that?"

Pete pulled into the driveway over a shitty, concrete grey building with green trim and graffiti everywhere. In addition to that, there was that one ambient fluorescent light, endlessly flickering, swaying back and forth on a chain hanging down from the ceiling. This place only needed a sign posted that said, "Welcome to the shithole" to be even more inviting.

But who am I to judge? It is what it is. I've become a selfish, materialistic asshole.

"This may sound a bit strange of a request to you, but my spot is on the far right over there, so would you mind getting out first? If not, you'll have to climb over my side and get out."

I was kind of shocked by his polite nature, but then I remembered he's eastern European. It really is second nature for him to act this way.

"Of course. No, that's fine."

He parked and offered to get out and get the door for me, but I declined.

Maybe he's not so weird after all.

As he parked, I took in more of the scenery.

This place was not great. However, I am not in any kind of position to judge anyone especially if he is happy.

Almost as instantly as I had that thought, I caught the strong, scent of vinegar and urine coming from somewhere down here. It was so potent that it very well could have been everywhere around me. I don't think I made any indication of my distaste for that smell seeing as after he parked, he was all smiles again.

"So, here we are. Now we need to walk up a couple flights of stairs and do then I will be able to show you my home."

"Sounds good, Pete."

He gestured that I should walk to the right, as if he were a waiter, desperately trying to leave a good impression to acquire a bigger tip.

Who is this person? He might just be the kindest, most polite fan of some truly fucking atrocious music. It's like if a Juggalo invited me for high tea. What the hell is happening right now?

I did my best not to get too distracted by the fanciful thought of fine china with *Faygo* poured into it, but I still was pretty distracted as Pete was attempting to have a conversation with me again. We had to walk around one whole side of the complex before we could get to the stairwell, that seemed like a really odd construction choice, but, oh well.

As I finally saw a mini-staircase to a concrete walkway, Pete chimed in and pointed down to the third step.

"My friend, please do not think that this is an impression of the quality of my building, but currently this step has been known to fall away. I would recommend stepping over it entirely. My landlord knows about it, and is getting everything he needs to fix it."

I'm already getting annoyed and bored with his formalities.

"Oh! Sure man, no worries, please. It's all good Pete."

"Good, thanks."

As I stepped over the one, loose step onto the one directly above it, the next step cracked, and fell immediately to the ground. My shin caught the receiving end of the concrete. It hurt like hell.

It almost distracted me enough not to hear the gunshots.

* * *

"**I SWEAR** to you Phil, I am normally not the one to speak in such a crass manner, but fuck these fucking crackheads! They know that they need to keep the guns away or I'll call the cops!"

I inhaled deeply.

"It's, it's fine, whatever. Can we just go inside and I can lay down a little bit?"

"Of course, come. You'll be fine soon. Right this way, my friend. Please disregard these current unpleasantries and I will be sure that you are comfortable soon."

Pete grabbed my arm and put it around his shoulders. He helped me up the rest of the stairs until we got to the end of the concrete walkway. He reached in his pocket and tried to grab his keys.

"One second and we will be inside. Ah! Here we are!"

He put in his keys, twisted the lock and kicked open the door.

"Come on in, lay down on the couch on the left. I'll go to the bathroom and grab everything I need to tend to your wound. Roll up your pant legs, please."

I threw myself onto the couch and stretched out. While wincing in pain, I rolled up the pant leg and saw the wound. I didn't see any bone thankfully, but it didn't look good. It was a light purple and yellow, with one thin red line of blood protruding from my kneecap. I tried to ignore the pain while waiting for Pete by taking in the scenery of his apartment. The inside was not as nearly as bad as the outside led it to be.

It wasn't exactly a refined bachelor pad that you sometimes see on Bravo and that shit, but it was nice. He was clearly a gamer, he had a ridiculous three monitor setup that even had led backlights.

I didn't even know people did that. I thought that was for the sake of nerdy bragging rights only. No one really plays like that, do they? That's ridiculous.

Pete came rushing back into the room with gauze, cotton swabs band-aids of all sizes, and some topical cream thing.

Fuck fuck fuck. Hopefully it's not that bad. I can't believe this. I'm gonna kill my landlord, that bastard.

"Okay, my friend. Let's do this."

He grabbed the swabs and put the cream on them and started cleaning up my knee. It stung like hell. Actually, it stung like a million little demons poking at me with pitchforks on a microcosmic level, but, you know, hell would also summarize how it felt. He looked at my knee and saw the damage and stared blankly.

"Ah. Okay, sorry, let me help. It's, uh, not too pretty, my friend. It could be a lot worse though."

He took pause and pulled back, checking out the situation.

"I think we've done just about as much as I could and it doesn't look like anything is broken. I'll get you some painkillers in a little bit. But for now, let's check out the other leg."

Before I could stop him or say anything, he pulled up the cuff on my other leg. He was clearly surprised. He slowly backed away and raised his hand to his mouth. I tried to play it off and make a joke of it. People always get so weird when they hear about this.

"No blood on that one, right?"

I gained a chuckle out of him, but it didn't look like it would do any good in this scenario.

"Oh, I see. You're a cri—… You're handicapped."

He had cut himself off before he said the word cripple. That was the first word people wanted to say whenever they figured out my condition.

Why is that?

"Yeah, that's one way to put it. Don't worry about it, man, everything's cool."

He had no idea what to say, and he was clearly dumbfounded by this. I guess I'll play into it this time.

"Do you have any questions about it?"

"A lot, but I'm trying not to be rude."

"It's okay, you want to know how it happened?"

He sat back and nodded silently.

I took a deep, resigned breath, and gave him the entire story of that one shitty night and the car crash. I tried to be a little more nonchalant about it, but didn't want to come across as bored or annoyed because I was telling it. While I was doing this, he was on the edge of his seat. It's bizarre, I never really told this story to someone before like this—or at all—but I've relived it so many times in my mind that it was old hat to me. I did live through it after all. I never really thought about how it would affect another person before. Pete's face was stern throughout me retelling it, but he was clearly mortified and trying to hide it. I finally stopped and he laid back into his couch, he looked exhausted by me merely talking to him.

"My god, I am so sorry. No one should have to have gone through all of that."

I didn't really know how to react to that.

"It's fine. I survived and everything's going fine now, really. Don't worry about it, okay?"

"Okay, my friend. Well, I'm going to get a drink after hearing a story like that, what can I get you?"

"Uh. Whatever you're having is fine."

He stepped away to the kitchen part of his studio apartment. It wasn't a lot of space, but it was more than enough for one person, and he made his best with it. He had his desk, a living room, and he had a murphy bed on the wall furthest from the TV. It didn't look like much, but it was clean and felt homey. Pete came back with a light blue drink. I couldn't hide my judgmental look.

"I know how it must look, but trust me, just try it."

He held it up the glass eagerly and smiled.

"Ziveli!"

"I mean, uh, cheers! Sorry!"

"No, I like the other one more. Ziveli!"

I took a swig and realized it was one of those new versions of Mountain Dew and a really well-blended vodka. I actually liked it a lot.

"Huh, that's great Pete. Thanks!"

"Of course! Now, that you are relaxing, let's get down to what we were originally talking about. What do you really want to try?"

"Well, like you said. I am a downer guy, but right now, I would love to stop thinking about this pain and I'd like to go on a trip."

"My apologies, I'll go and get you the painkillers, and a couple other things. I'll be right back."

I didn't want something too hardcore, I still had to get home, but I definitely wanted a diversion from the pain, and I wanted something to help me. Pete came back into the room with a shoe box he must have pulled out of the tiny, narrow closet by the hallway. He came back and sat down next to me.

"Okay, Phil, what would you like? I think you need something to distract you from the pain you are in, would you agree?"

"Absolutely, man."

As I mentioned this I tried to re-adjust on the couch and got a sharp, shooting pain in my knee.

Seeing me in that pain made him grimace.

"God, I am so sorry, again I fucking can't stand my landlord. He's the worst, I'd kill him if it wasn't hugely mega-illegal. He's a waste of space and a neglectful piece of shit."

Maybe there's still hope for this night yet. Let's see if I can help call Pete's bluff.

* * *

I COULDN'T HELP but smirk at the possibilities of what I was hearing.

"Pete, I think I'm actually going to take it easy tonight and just grab some weed from you if you don't mind. But, don't mind me you do whatever you want. I think you need to do more relaxing than I do."

Pete looked a little deflated, but I knew he agreed.

"You're right my friend. I do. I don't know what I want to do. Anyway, is it cool if I roll some joints for us?"

"Yeah man, that sounds great. I don't really do that bong shit or anything else for weed. But, tell me while you're rolling, why do you dislike your landlord so much?"

He was quickly straying from the subject. I needed to rein him in.

I could tell that upset him, because he lost his focus as he was rolling the joint.

"Well, he's just the type of guy who never finishes anything you know? It's a lot of empty promises and no follow through."

"So you mean he's like any other landlord, then?"

He chuckled, but then got very serious again.

Either he doesn't understand me, or he doesn't take me seriously.

"No. It's not like that. I've been living in this shit for a while and am to the point of harassing him to follow up on things and it just doesn't happen. It's very upsetting to me. I'm sorry, I do not enjoy speaking in this manner."

He handed me the joint, finally rolled and prepped with a lighter. I took it, gave him a nod and put the joint in my mouth

"Well," I started as I was trying to slyly light up and speak at the same time, "it sounds like you have some potential legal recourse then, don't you?"

As I spoke, I kept dropping the joint out of my mouth, while simultaneously being inaudible because I was focusing so hard on inhaling and lighting up at the same time. I took a moment for what I thought was some composure and then finally lit this joint.

In the middle of my coughing fit, Pete very nicely decided to get me a glass of water to help.

"Thank you."

I said this meekly, it barely squeaked out of my throat as I continued to furiously cough. My eyes started to water and I took another sip.

I haven't smoked weed in an embarrassingly long time. The least I can do is not look like it. As usual though, I manage to look like an idiot. I always do this shit.

While I was recovering, Pete excused himself from the room and came back in pajamas. He was also holding what looked to be an old photo box. It was very floral and ornate. He placed the box in his lap, and cracked all of his knuckles at once. This was immediately followed by a jarringly quick cracking of his neck, which was something I could never get used to seeing or hearing. He very methodically, and delicately opened the box. He started unraveling an old tattered tie with a tiny, rolled up white bag followed by a really weirdly shaped and heavily tarnished spoon and finally, he pulled out a syringe.

Holy shit, Pete's going for some heroin.

I've never really been around heroin, nor have I ever been interested in it. I didn't really know how I'd deal with it.

Okay Phil, just be as casual as possible; don't stare, and don't lead him on like you're worried. Just be casual, how many times have you not cared about anything else?

After all, this dude listens to KMFDM. What did I expect?

Pete - rightfully—gave me a confused look.

"I'm sorry, I'm not too comfortable talking about my finances. It is still something I'm working on. Give me a second, will you?"

"Yeah, sure."

I laid back as I saw him cook up the heroin in the spoon with the same lighter we used for the joint. He balanced the spoon on an errant glass cup that was on a folding table As that melted, he started to wrap the tie around his arm, and bite down on the shorter end. It was very interesting to watch. I was fascinated by his every action. He then took the syringe and absorbed the liquified heroin. Then, like a really magnificent crescendo, he injected into his arm.

It all was a very quick process. He started to slightly spasm; and from what very little I know about heroin—all by hearing and reading Nikki Sixx from Motley Crue talk about it—I'm pretty sure that was normal. I let this slide.

His eyes started to roll back into his head, and the he slumped down and looked like his body started to mold into the chair. That's how much he sunk into it.

He bellowed out,

"Holy fuck!"

He then mumbled something completely inaudible. Intermittently with his shooting up. I had yet another coughing fit. I completely lost any kind of credibility I've gained at this point. Pete regained his composure and started laughing at me. Then, I was very surprised to see he dove right back into the conversation we were having. As if nothing has changed. Everything was exactly how it was a second ago, with the exception of a little slower paced diction.

"I feel so helpless in the big scheme of things. For example, I know I'm always going to have a landlord, but why am I putting up with his shit more than anyone else's? First it was the break-in, and the three months—and two other break-ins before he fixed the door and windows. Then it was the plumbing problem that lasted for two months. Then the exterminator crap which I'm still going through as well. And the one time I brought Jess over, when he started hitting on her right in front of me. I mean, who fucking does that to another guy's girlfriend? In any other circumstance, none of this would be okay. So why am I tolerating this?"

My ears perked up when I heard exterminator, and I wanted to ask more and figure out how to help. But, why? I don't have the time, or the equipment and I didn't even truly know if I wanted to do this anymore. Moreover, what the hell do I have to gain by helping out at all?

Also, why did I not give a shit at all about his landlord hitting on some girl Pete was hooking up with? That's pretty reprehensible, but here I am thinking about bugs again. What the hell is wrong with me?

I kept this all in mind as I attempted to console him by patting him on the shoulder, and took one last hit and passed it over.

"So what the hell are you thinking of doing about this?"

"I don't know."

He paused and looked down. Staring at the floor and weighing out his options.

My lease is up in two months, maybe I should look at moving out? In addition to not having any money to have some sort of legal representation needed to get out of the lease early, I definitely don't have the money saved up to get a new place. Could I possibly make him more accountable for his future actions with the next lease signing? What the hell kind of power do I have right now to do this?

This is where I decided to interject. I could tell he was racking his brain for any kind of solution, but there was nothing there.

"You feel completely helpless, don't you? Like there's no way out and you are stuck in this hellhole forever, right?"

"Yes. You are exactly correct. But then what the hell can I do? There truly is no option and no way out."

I unintentionally developed a sly smile. Pete called me out on it.

"What are you thinking, man, you look like you're developing a scheme?"

I decided to ignore all apprehensions and dive into my initial response.

"What if we kill him?"

* * *

IT MUST have been the length of time that I spent enunciating the phrase "Kill him," but as soon as I looked to see Pete's reaction, I noticed he had already dozed off.

It was only a matter of time. I should have seen it coming.

So what was my plan? How could I take someone mild-mannered (and currently out of his mind on heroin) and take him to the next level of violence and get him on board with killing a man? Better yet, why did I want to kill him? I don't know this dude. I don't know anything about his life, or his family, but did any of that matter?

I think I missed feeling anything much less something as grand as the feeling you get from killing someone. It truly is a divine satisfaction. It's the same high I got from killing all those bugs, but exponentially longer lasting and more fulfilling. I didn't think it had that effect on me previously, but it did profoundly impact me more so than I realized.

Maybe that's why I've felt the need to be so introverted recently.

On top of all of that, It sounded like this dude was a dickhole. So why not get rid of him and make the world a slightly better place. I realized at that moment, that I should take a step back from my machinations, and make sure that Pete was okay. He looked like his neck was on the cusp of falling off, that's how slouched he was in his chair. His head looked like it was dangling by the most delicate of threads.

I decided that I should check on him.

I walked over to him and tried to wake him up. I gave him a nudge on his shoulder and whispered his name.

"Pete. Pete!"

I shook him harder and said his name louder.

I paused for a second, then realized maybe I should try to incept his dreams with this idea.

"Wake up so we can go kill your landlord, Pete!"

This is stupid. How could I be so naive to think that would ever work? Also, is that the right verb, incept? Am I using that correctly? Either way, how the hell do I do that? I don't know this guy's name? Do I just maniacally whisper "kill your landlord" over and over again until I leave an impression?

The truly ironic thing about wanting to incept him was that I could see and hear what he was dreaming about. He was having a weird nightmare. He was in some type of hellish game show that was structured like a seventies show with a smarmy host. The torturous part was how the host interspersed wrong answers to random geographical questions with either a fire raid alarm, or an appearance of someone in his past that he definitely did not want to see.

There were no right answers. Just a lot of air raid sirens and what I'd imagined to be ex-girlfriends, shitty substitute teachers, or possibly bullies.

How the hell do I know that this would stick with him? This is absurd. What am I even talking about? I am painfully disconnected with reality if I think something like this can happen.

How did I even end up here? I've completely isolated myself from everything and everyone by moving out here, and now the first person I meet, I decide to egg him on to kill someone with me?

Why did I start there and not something a lot less committal, like, I don't know, watching a movie that one of us just bought and having some beer? That would be normal, right? How did I ever think I could get away with acting like this?

Then it all hit me at once.

Why don't I call Brad? I haven't spoken with him since that one ridiculous night, but that dude deals with unsavory people all the time. I'm sure he has dealt with—or knows how to deal with stuff like this or worse. He would probably know what to do in my situation.

As I thought about it, I realized that he was my liaison to the seedy, sketchy core lying at the black, rotten heart of the commercial film industry. More specifically, if he deals with those people, he's probably dealt with the worst stuff I could ever imagine and beyond.

I realized that, as I normally do when I'm thinking, I was pacing around Pete's apartment. I decided to take advantage of the situation and snoop around at the usual stuff: medicine cabinet, bedroom, the usual stuff. It's pretty reprehensible behavior to do something like this, but then again, I imagined it was less reprehensible than asking someone new in your life to straight up kill someone you haven't met. It was a pretty boring place, but surely the only scandalous thing in his apartment couldn't have been his weirdly floral and "formal occasions only" looking drug box.

The first thing I did was endlessly stare at his shelf of DVDs. He had a couple books mixed in; mostly classics. There was a bunch of those holier than thou looking classic faux-leather bound prints of classics, even if they're still in print. He had *War and Peace*, the complete works of Hemingway, Homer, and ew, shit, is that *Atlas Shrugged*? Really?

Why was he giving me these drugs then? He probably thinks I'm one of those fucking parasites that's weighing him down. God, that shit is sad.

I truly think Ayn Rand started a generation of self-absorbed and painfully unaware megalomaniacs that have done nothing but stifle this country's progress if not completely revert it to a worse form.

Regarding movies, his taste was pretty scattered and all over the place. His collection ranged from; *10 Things I Hate About You* (1999) to *Zombi 2* (1972) from Fulci.

Actually, looking at it a little closer, he had a lot of zombie movies, He had all the Romero's, the now mandatory *Shaun of the Dead* (2004), *House of 1000 Corpses* (2003) and all the slasher movies that I was truly aware of; every *Friday the 13th*, every *Nightmare on Elm Street*, *Hellraiser* (1987), *Candyman* (1992), *Children of the Corn* (1984), and even the abysmal *Ginger Snaps* (2000)? Those aren't exactly zombie movies, but they are in that ilk, I guess.

After investing even the slightest amount of time into thinking about the god awful *Ginger Snaps* series of films, I decided I needed to quickly distract myself. I wandered into his kitchen to check out his fridge. It was the stereotypical bachelor's fridge: more condiments than solid foods.

What was Pete's story? Was he a forever alone hardcore gamer, with his only friends being whatever dumbass pseudonyms people thought up on Steam?

I am a forever alone culture junkie?

There is a part of me that felt bad for him, but then again, he might have been doing the same exact thing I have attempted to do: reinvent his entire life.

Long story short, this dude needs to wake the hell up soon so I can figure out who exactly he is and what he's all about.

I dug into his cabinets and finally found some semblance of food, albeit they were the most childish cereals I can find.

After first investigation, I can conclude that there was no official sign of any "adulting" going on.

I started walking to his bathroom, but as soon as I took a step in that direction, I heard the most blood-curdling scream I have encountered in my life.

* * *

"FUCK!"

Pete shot up from his laid back position in the chair, and white-knuckled the armrest. He was doused in sweat. He took a quick survey of the area, looked at me, slapped his hand to his forehead and ran his fingers through his hair.

"Damn, dude. I'm so sorry."

In spite of his apology, the tenor in his voice changed now to the "classic seventies stoner" type of voice. Whenever he talked, I may as well have been talking to Jim Breuer from *Half Baked* (1998).

"I just, like, should have laid back with you and smoked some weed. Instead, I went all in and made myself look like an asshole. No one wants to see that man. I barely met you, and now totally embarrassed myself. It's not cool, not okay."

"Don't beat yourself up about it, man. It's all good, I know what to expect when someone pulls out a needle."

I can't fucking believe I did this again. I always do this, why can't I just meet someone and not completely freak them out? I really need to kick this shit, man. I need to pull myself together and beat this once and for all.

"Pete, take a breath, man. Don't worry so much. Listen, let's just chill out, we'll crash here tonight—I think I'm way too high to drive as it is—and then we'll restart everything for tomorrow. Do you have anything to do then, or are you free?"

Pete, still clearly ashamed and not looking at me, nodded in agreement. He began to speak, still into his chest with his hand covering his face.

"That sounds good, man. I feel horrible, but that sounds really nice. I think I might go crash a little early. I know it's only 10:00, but I feel like I need to sleep this out of my system, you know?"

"Yeah, man. That sounds fine. No sweat, and please do not worry about thing for tomorrow, okay? Tonight was a casual accident, and it was definitely not a big deal. Just relax!"

He silently nodded, and struggled to get himself up out of the chair. I grabbed his arm to help him up.

"Thanks again for being understanding, man. I appreciate it."

He brushed my arm away and walked to his bedroom, where he quickly returned with another sheet and a pillow.

"Here ya go, man. Just crash on the couch if you don't mind. Let me know if you need anything, alright? Tomorrow, I'll take you out as an apology for me being a selfish prick tonight."

He flashed a peace sign behind him as he walked away.

"Night! See ya tomorrow, man".

And with that, I was alone with my thoughts; again, as always. It was surprisingly quiet given the not so great introduction to the apartment that I got earlier. As Pete went to sleep, I thought it would be a good time to give Brad a call and weigh out my options. I couldn't help but think that this was a poor decision, but then again I figured out of all the people that I've known he might be the only person to understand where I'm coming from given his business endeavors.

I took pause, then filtered through my contacts to find him, and gave him a call. He picked up after the second ring.

So he was skeptical at first, but then decided to get a hold of me? Maybe I think too much about these things.

"Hello, Phil? Is that you?"

I faked my enthusiasm, I was calling him on a mission to understand something, not casually enjoy his bullshit banter.

"Hey man! Yeah, it's me how've you been?"

"Uh. Good, man, pretty good. Can't complain. I'm just very surprised that you called. We haven't spoken since, well, that night."

"Yeah. I'm sorry, man, I didn't know how to react to that at the time."

He took a deep breath.

"Yeah, yeah, I completely understand what you mean. That's the normal response I get. Well, truthfully after a night like that, I mostly don't get any responses. It's pretty much a once and done kind of deal. Ya know what I mean?"

"For sure, man, don't worry about that. It's fine."

"Well, great to hear man! How the hell is California treating you? Matter of fact, how is Adam and the new job treating you?"

I grimaced at the mere mention of that.

"To be honest with you, Brad, I feel like I was lied to regarding the job. Adam led me to believe that we go to a lot more screenings than we have. Actually, we haven't gone to any at all. I've done nothing but paperwork this entire time."

"Shit, man, I'm sorry to hear that. I'll see if I can talk to him for you. Aside from that though, what's been up?"

"Well, in addition to wanting to check up with you, I did want to ask you something specifically. Do you have a little bit of time to talk?"

Alright, that part was a slight lie. I didn't care about checking up on him. I didn't really care about him any further than I could throw him especially after putting me in that fucked up situation as he did. It couldn't hurt to butter him up though, right?

"Sure, sure. Let me just step into another room real quick, gimmie one second. Okay. What's up?"

"Well. I don't really know how to say this, but what happened that night, it, uh, it changed me. You probably expected that, but maybe not in this way. I miss the feeling I got. Specifically, I miss the high I got from killing that guy. The power that washed over me, after I knew I was doing something right by killing off that pedophile. It was something I'll never forget."

I didn't give him a chance to respond, I continued on.

"I don't really know what to do about it. I feel this craving again, but I know how horrible that makes me sound. I was wondering if, maybe you've dealt with something like this before and what you—or whomever—did to deal with these feelings in that circumstance."

At this point, I got a lot more emotional than I ever expected to get on the phone. The pain and confusion in my thoughts became audible at this very moment. I went from strong-headed and confident to emotional pulp.

"I don't know what to do. Can you, can you help me at all?"

That last sentence was said with all the strength I could muster. I started to sob, but held it back as best as I could. It was painfully obvious to Brad I'm sure, but it was uncontrollable.

"Oh boy. Okay, Phil. Just sit down and take some deep breaths first, alright?"

I sat there, corrected my posture and took four deep breaths. He was right, I was able to stop sobbing and regain what little composure I had left.

"Alright, that's better. Phil, listen hard and listen good. Yes, I've dealt with some weird crap in my life—and sure, I brought it onto myself—but I've never sought it out aside from these parties I've hosted. This is, as I'm sure you know, very unhealthy behavior that I will not condone unless it is justified and you feel threatened and it's an act of self-defense. "

He briefly cleared his throat.

"That being said, this feeling you have is sadly not uncommon after someone who's gone through what you have. I've been able to direct some people that I've encountered with your same problem to a place for some help. Ultimately, you are the one that needs to decide if you want to use that help and take it seriously. Does that make sense?"

"Yeah, of course it does."

"Good. Now that my official recommendation is out of the way, what would you actually like to do with this feeling that you have? If it is what I think it is, then you need some advice on either what do next, what to do with a body, or would like some advice on how to kill again. Right?"

I laughed at that line, but that suave, smarmy motherfucker was right.

"Well. Sort of. I wanted to ask you if I wanted to do this again. How would I get someone else to join me?"

Brad had a burst of laughter.

"That's what I fucking thought."

Genus

7

AS I AWOKE, I violently shot up from reclining to sitting up on the couch. I was breathing in and out very heavily.

I don't think I had a bad dream, but I keep doing this and it really fucks up my back. This couch helps, that's for damn sure.

For a brief moment, I forgot where I was. I forgot I was in Pete's apartment. I missed my old room in my old house. I'm not too sure why I did, considering that place was definitely a shit hole. Before I could start to wonder why I was missing what *was* home, Pete emerged from the door stoic and rigid like he was a boss from *Shadows of the Colossus* .

"Hey, man. Not too rush ya, but I'm brain dead in the morning until I have coffee, and I'm out of coffee. You cool to just get going? I know this diner up the way."

"Oh, uh, yeah, man. Sure. Let me just put my shoes back on."

"Cool. Let's do this."

He said this as he was already out the door.

Pete was a decisive guy, I guess. Not too wishy washy. I wonder what the hell that's like. I'd love to have that quality if only for a day.

He gave me a nudge and after sounding like a whiny partner, "I'm coming, I'm coming, hold your horses jeez!" we were out the door.

Pete gave me a wild look, and then, with a sudden burst of energy, he proudly proclaimed, "We're going to Norm's, motherfucker!"

I had absolutely no idea what he was talking about.

On the way there, he was his normal, sluggish self that I encountered less than ten minutes ago. But not talkative at all. He was eerily silent.

Can't lead him on, can't lead him on, just be normal.

Over and over and over again.

I attempted to start some conversation, but he was not having it. To be fair, he told me he was not a morning person, but I was still very surprised with his abrupt, and passive-aggressive acts to avoid conversation. He didn't *need* to turn the music up as I was talking to him, but whatever. After what felt like entirety of our journey, because of that silence. We took our first sips of coffee. He finally spoke to me like a human again.

"I had a very weird dream last night. Whenever this happens, in the morning, every morning, I try to remember what exactly all of the details of it. I also try to interpret what this could mean for me at this stage in my life. "

I looked at him incredulously.

"Every morning?"

He smiled back arrogantly.

"Yup."

"Man, that shit must be exhausting. What the hell were you dreaming about last night?"

"Well, this one was weird. I was in what looked to be like a seventies game—"

At this point I completely zoned out. I knew where he was going, and I didn't care. The only possible resolution is that he thought some bullshit along the lines of *"Oh man, maybe I shouldn't repress all those memorable confrontations and maybe I should speak to someone about that"* or some other easy and flimsy interpretation of that ilk.

Was it mean of me not to care? Whatever. I need a lot more coffee and energy to deal with this nonsense.

The vivid dream description got cut short when we got our plates that we had ordered not five minutes ago.

The grizzled waitress came up to both of us and said in her lackluster, chain-smoking addled voice.

"Chicken fried steak, and French toast with sausage and scrambled eggs. I'll get ya some more coffee in a sec, hon."

In spite of her terse manner, that's kind of how I always want my waitresses to be.

"I don't know what it is about her, Pete, but I wish all my waitresses ever were like Barb."

Pete narrowed his eyes and thought about it for a second.

"I don't know why either, but I agree. Let's, if you don't mind, let's finish my dream breakdown on the ride home. Are you okay with that? It goes in a very different direction that is not really suited for public."

I hope he doesn't think less of me as I tell him. It was so unlike me normally that I think it would be fine.

"Of course, man. No worries. So, to uh, to change the subject. What did you have on the agenda for the rest of the day?"

"Mmhm!"

He exclaimed with a mouthful of food.

"Yes! Good question. Well I thought we could head back to my place and watch one of my old, long-lost favorites. I propose we watch *Riki-Oh: The Story of Ricky* (1991). Then we could watch whatever else you'd like."

"Okay. Sure man, sounds good."

"Have you ever seen it before?" He finally was at the same level of energy that I saw last night.

"No. I can't say that I have."

"It's a fucking trip, that's all I can really say. Ah! This is perfect, I'm so excited to watch it with you! It'll be great, trust me!"

This sounds ridiculous.

As Barb came back to pour our coffee, it felt as though my cottonmouth hit me instantaneously. My throat dried up, and before I could even mention how desperately I wanted a glass of water, she read my mind.

"I'll get ya's some waters, too."

I shrugged in a way that implied she's amazing. It must have made sense because Pete was there nodding the whole time.

"She is fucking incredible."

We ate as if we have not eaten in weeks.

Must have been all the drugs.

We chugged both of our waters after they arrived ridiculously quickly and I was again encouraged to hurry up and eat. I scarfed my food and Pete threw down a twenty. The drive over here was longer than our stay at Norm's. Hopefully that French toast wouldn't haunt me later on in the day.

Pete got back in the car and took a deep breath.

"Phil, I'm sorry to have rushed you back there, but the more I remembered my dream from last night, the more I wanted to discuss it with you in private. I promise you, that this dream I am about to tell you is not indicative of the type of person I am, or anything of my character."

"Okay. Go for it, I won't judge you, Phil. I promise."

He took another breath and deeply looked into my eyes.

"I promise you I am normally not a man who is like this."

After I finally wrapped my head around what he meant, I noticed that normally he doesn't speak like that.

Sure, he had a pretty thick accent, and you can tell English was his second language, but it never really became *undone*. This dream must have profoundly impacted him.

"Okay, Phil. So I guess last night, somewhere along the way of me complaining about my apartment and landlord. After the game show dream, I had a dream that Keith—my landlord—and I met up in a dark alley. I don't remember what it was about, but he was yelling at me. A lot. Spit was flying out of his mouth, he was violently pointing his finger at me, and I could see the veins popping on his neck with the amount of screaming he was doing."

He took a moment to swallow the spit that was building up in his mouth. This was building tension for the story, sure, but then he anticlimactically swallowed quite a bit of phlegm. I must have shown on my face how disgusted I was, because he reacted to my disgust.

"Sorry. I had to do it."

Did you, though?

"Anyways. He was getting closer and closer to me in this alley and I was screaming right back at him. I turned to my side to get an idea of my immediate surroundings, and noticed there was a two-by-four behind a trash can."

He slumped down in his seat.

"It shames me to say it, but I quickly took the two-by-four, and smashed it into his throat with as much power as I could. I ended up swinging and hitting his Adam's apple. Then, after the wind was taken out of him, I continued to hit him as hard as I could with the two-by-four, until he was writhing on the ground I'd successfully hit his throat so much, that it burst with bits of blood and bone all over me. I was covered in it."

"Holy shit, man."

Apparently, I sold my surprise to Pete as well, he could do nothing but hang his head.

"Phil, sadly, it was not over at that point. As I was covered in his blood, I took one long, last look at his decapitated head; and mustered up all the strength left in me to smash his head to a fine pulp."

He was clearly upset, and he was now visually shaken.

"It was at this time that I woke up in a cold sweat. Please, do not think that I am some monster of a man. As I mentioned, this is very uncharacteristic of me. I'm far from it in fact, I am a law-abiding former Christian. I hope you don't judge me.

"However, if you feel the need to go home, I completely understand."

I couldn't believe how well I'd kept myself together until now. The only thing I could think was:

Holy shit! I've incepted him! I don't even care how dumb that sounds! Looks like I didn't need to call Brad at all!

As much as I wanted to hone in on what Pete just said, I thought it would be best to subside this feeling and the urges, and ultimately try to enjoy the day like we planned out. We ended up watching a bunch of stupid, magnificent movies and zoning out. It was a really nice day that I ended up needing. You need to trust yourself when your brain tells you to fuck around. Procrastinating is fine as long as it's not towards your detriment. It's cool to relax sometimes and I need to remind myself of that.

I was driving home thinking it all through. All the movies, all the potential with Pete, and California in general. I wanted to let his thoughts linger in that air for a while and not jump on the opportunity; that would have made me seem pretty fucking desperate. Regardless of me not taking the initiative right in front of me, Pete was thinking about it all throughout the day. It seemed that whenever there was a lull in the conversation, he would immediately return to think.

"I am still so mad at him. He's done some pretty shitty things, but normally I've been able to brush it off and roll with it. This time, something is different. That dream affected me. Maybe it's some sort of sign. Keith's always been an asshole, but does he really deserve that?"

I didn't outwardly seek the opportunity to egg him on, but if it presented itself, I absolutely took advantage of it. In between the movies, Pete asked what I was up to before moving out here.

"I didn't really have anything in mind aside from keeping my father's extermination business running."

He asked what it was like, and you better believe I took the opportunity to embellish my past.

"It was pretty great, man. Think about it this way. You know that feeling you get of accomplishment and power when you've been seeking out a pest that's been driving you crazy and you finally get rid of it? A spider, a wasp, some ants or whatever? Well, when you do that for a living it's a pretty easy, and a great way to measure out all your accomplishments. Additionally, you know that feeling you get when you kill the bug in question? It only gets bigger and better. Think of how great it feels to kill 1,000 termites in a nest, or a spider's eggs. Man, it's definitely an adrenaline high. The bigger the thing you kill, the more of an adrenaline high you'd get. It's totally empowering."

"Sorry. When I get passionate about something I get a little rambly."

The look on Pete's face after my rant was everything I hoped to accomplish. He was completely intrigued, and excited by that description. He went on to smile and even rub his chin about it. He was curious, but showed no signs of fear or trepidation.

Should I feel guilty taking advantage of this guy? This was way too easy. I shouldn't have any remorse I guess, nothing happened after all. If and when something does occur, and I do completely take advantage of this circumstance, maybe I'll feel bad. Probably not, though.

I pulled up to my driveway after what seemed like a never-ending night away. It didn't feel like that in the way of a horrendously long, and drawn out *thank god it's over* type of way, but more so in the *I'm finally home and can get in my own bed* kind of way. As soon as I got in the door I did the usual routine; take off my pants and shoes and throw them wherever, then sit on the couch and completely zone out.

I took an extremely deep breath, and then realized that I had a ton of movies and things that I got that I can unwrap! This was one of few occasions where I was extremely excited to do something. Albeit, an extremely nerdy thing that I should not love as much as I do, but nonetheless, this was my "kid on Christmas morning feeling". I got up, went back to the door where I dropped my bag of stuff from Amoeba, and started to take them all out and place them neatly in order with how I should open them.

I arranged them in the way that I knew best, or the only way I arranged anything: chronologically. I placed my Bergman films earliest, and my Shane Carruth films towards the end. From afar, this would have looked extremely pathetic. A chubby loser, unwrapping box sets and Blu-rays with the utmost joy. I could not care less about how dumb I looked. This was akin to me going to church. This moment was my sacred space.

Unfortunately, it got interrupted with a call.

Again, I got up and headed over to the crinkled ball on the floor that was my pants, reached into the pocket and noticed that Adam was calling me.

This motherfucker leaves me all alone in the office without so much as a word of instruction, or casual conversation, and he has the audacity to call me on the weekend? What the hell is this shit?

"Hello?"

I started this conversation in the most begrudging, shitty tone that I could to make it known that he was not welcome to call me on the weekends.

"Hey, Phil! How ya doin', bud? Hey man, sorry to bother you when you're off the clock, but I wanted to apologize to you and let you know of some upcoming good news."

"Okay. That's fine, man, no worries. What's up?"

I didn't know what to expect, but I was definitely intrigued.

"So listen. I talked to Brad this morning and I understand that you are a bit upset about the job so far. You feel like I sold this position and everything to you incorrectly. Is that right? That's at least the impression I got from him."

I felt the need to tread lightly, so I responded meekly.

"Well, Adam. Yeah. I felt like some of the stuff we talked about from the film festival that was promised has not come to fruition yet, and that's really frustrating. The job is monotonous. It's fine, but it's extremely monotonous. I didn't feel really comfortable speaking up about it beforehand, but now that it's out in the open; yes, I do feel like this position was misrepresented to me."

Adam sighed uncomfortably.

"I understand your concern. You were under the impression that you would be taken out to all these premieres and meeting all these people. I'm sorry I haven't delivered what I've promised yet."

Before I could accept his apology and move on, he rambled on.

"But, I do have some things on the horizon that might interest you greatly! I promise you with my heart and soul, man. I'll tell you more about it when you are on the clock, but please keep your head up! Great things will be happening soon!"

"Okay, man. That sounds awesome! Thanks for the call, and I appreciate you reaching out and talking to me about this."

"Of course, man! You got it. Have the rest of a good weekend and I will see you Monday in the A.M., sir!"

What the hell could he have been talking about?

* * *

WHY DO I *always do this?*

I have so much free time on my hands, but I end up wasting it. I waste it on movies I've seen before, or endless runs and reruns of garbage pseudo-reality television. And yet as much as it drives me crazy that I do this to myself, I always go back to it. I end up watching the same things that make me feel completely disgusted with the world around me. I could be challenging myself, or cultivating a new hobby or skill or something, but I revert back to killing off whatever active brain cells are left of my mind and completely waste my time.

After all the adventures with Pete this weekend, which only really consisted of watching movies while we were high, I convinced myself that today was going to be my fuck around day. I truly believe that everyone, once a week, should have at least one day where they can unwind and do whatever they damn well please.

I continue to stifle myself, chastise myself, and then do nothing to change. I could watch another movie, or something else that would challenge me and make me grow, or; I could order in a burger and watch people getting screamed at about having cockroaches in their bar. When I look at it like that, the choice is simple.

I resigned myself to the plan I just created, but still felt like I should be ceasing the day and all of that crap.

Here I am in California with this brand new life that I should be making the most of, but I am the same lazy person I was back home. I grabbed my phone. My knee jerk reaction was to sift through some more porn, but I thought I'd pull myself away from that and see what the hell was new in the world.

During many various points in my life, I have earnestly tried to dutifully watch the news and be aware of what was happening in the world on a day to day basis. Ultimately, every time I try to watch, I end up abandoning that notion entirely. There are not a lot of things that make me furious, but watching network syndicated news programming, is reliably one of those infuriating things.

After 9/11, news media has dramatically shifted in tone and has intentionally tried to cripple us with fear of the outside world. I don't think I'm the biggest conspiracy theorist or whatever, but that much is definitely certain to me. It really is like that episode of *South Park*, where Stan's mom starts watching the news and becomes couch-ridden for weeks because she is to terrified to move.

It's because of all that garbage that I mainly got my news from a variety of social media—and yes, I know it's rife with error and bias, but I try as much as I can to double check my sources. I don't know why I felt compelled to vigilantly pursue the stories and articles that I did, but nonetheless I'd never blindly believe them.

I ended up reading a lot of crap online. I think we all do now. Anything from the latest narrative on an African war monger, to what the result of the most recent wrestling pay-per-view, I felt compelled to read it all.

That really drives me crazy, I read everything I can about wrestling but I haven't actually watched a match since I was 6.

What the hell was wrong with me?

I started to browse through my Twitter feed, seeing the usual split-second teaser crap that happens all the time now, when something big caught my attention.

I studied the tweet, and re-read it three times.

"CEO's of WB, Fox, Disney, Universal, Paramount. and Columbia announce parent org. 'FRAME' to unify cinema under an umbrella corp. "

I eagerly linked through to see the whole story.

Ugh, there's the adware blocker removal plea. Yeah, I'm sure you really need my fucking support; you're owned by Hearst media. Shut the fuck up.

That shit drives me crazy.

Anyway, the article went on to describe that the FRAME will consist of multiple CEO's and like-minded artrepreneurs who seek out new "talent, material, and technology" that will further the landscape of cinema in relationship to its ever changing world. One of the CEO's went on to say:

"FRAME is, of course, an acronym. It stands for, Friends for the Reinvigoration of Arts, Movies, and Entertainment. FRAME will own all entities associated with it, but rest assured that the association will still have every aspect of their respective industries run independently, with no interference."

I immediately got very anxious. This hit closest to home for me. I identify with art and cultural elements more than I have ever identified with a person. Without these movies, my life is even sadder than I imagined.

Fuck. What the hell does this mean? I don't believe a word of this. How can this even happen? What happened to monopolies being disbanded in this country? How could this not be detrimental to the arts, and how the fuck do they not see this at all?

I was starting to get physically invested in my paranoia. I began to feel the blood rushing to my head and became slightly nauseous.

This can't be happening. Everything I've ever loved will shutter and cease to exist! They'll devour all the smaller indie filmmakers, and then there won't be any independent voices left! There won't be any other Cannibal Holocaust *(1980) or,* Repo the Genetic Opera *(2008), or anything worthy of being watched!*

Of course, I know that there was nothing I could do. I'd never been in a scenario where I'd consort with this kabal of the super-wealthy, elitist assholes that are doing everything they can to ruin culture in this country. Nor would I want to be. But what the hell could be next?

Maybe I'm being too pessimistic, but I associate all of this news as a signifier of the end of times.

Alright, maybe just check out their website. It can't be that bad after all. Right?

After some quick, nervous searching, I landed on their site and was horrified to find the results.

Nothing. It says nothing at all. It was some extremely vague, peaceful pictures. This is worse than I could have imagined. Or, maybe their site is brand new and they haven't had time to update it right? That's a possibility.

After some more searching, I discovered the truth.

It was registered over three years ago. We're all doomed.

It was at that moment that I knew I had to retaliate, but I didn't know how or when. The only thing I knew was that my retaliation wouldn't be soon enough, and it would be so insignificant that it would probably barely register to them.

I had to do something though.

* * *

I WAS on edge all last night, and I could barely pay attention as I was working. I scanned and filtered every document I could, but at the back of my mind there was nothing but trepidation of what's to come.

What could happen here? What does FRAME plan on doing? Whatever they end up fucking up, could it ever be un-fucked? That's a word right? Unfucked?

I kept checking on their feed and website to see about any up-dates, but as a parent corporation, you don't end up seeing most of the evil behind the scenes action. After a while I started to think about why they even decided to get together in the first place? They said it was more about presenting a unified front of what mainstream film could be, but does that mean consolidating their ideas and making one amalgamous, homogenized piece of garbage again and again forever? Instead of one crappy romantic pseudo-comedy about holidays there will be nothing but them?

Will we see Arbor Day next? With a treasure trove of cash-hungry actors clamoring for attention as their star power fades off into oblivion? Wait a second, it just occurred to me that if it's the one parent company that's bringing everything together, that means that as it pertains to my work, this could potentially mean that FRAME would be representing—or covering for—the entirety of one group.

Actually, if it's one company presenting a unified front, they could develop their own favorites or preferred vendors for everything and do a lot of economic damage. Rather than have up to ten law firms representing their studios, maybe they would consolidate it. Who's stopping them from consolidating everything?

During my lingering on that thought, Adam arrived at my desk. I was surprised to see him there. He hasn't done this once in my three and half months here.

"Hey, bud! How are you doing? Well, I hope."

Before I even had the option to respond, Adam led the conversation. He's always struck me as one of those dudes that doesn't listen. He's like a cocked-shotgun, waiting for his opportunity to unload. Our desks are within earshot, and I've heard him do this to his other co-workers time and time again.

"So, I was wondering if I could take you out to lunch today. Would that be cool?"

As if I had a choice in any of this, I feigned my surprise, and ultimately accepted.

"Sure! That sounds great, man. Let me just finish up this section and we'll go."

"Awesome man, sounds good."

I pretended to studiously get back to work, but I was actually only staring at the paper and moving my hand back and forth.

What could he want, and why the hell has this taken so long to happen? What should I say to him during this time? Should I tell him how unhappy I am here, and how I feel like he misrepresented this position to me? Wait, he said that to me last night on the phone.

Before I finish up, I try to clear my mind of all that bullshit and I wrote some spare notes on a Post-It. Over time, I've noticed that has helped me collect my thoughts and regain my composure. My mind generally runs and runs on a steady diet of unhealthy, belittling and depressing thoughts. This was one way to drown them all out. Rather than have these poisonous thoughts at the forefront of my mind, I get them out so I can be more perceptive to whatever incoming ideas I may have, as opposed to pushing them all away. I closed the report on my desk and knocked on the frame of Adam's door.

"Alright, sorry about that. I'm ready to head out now."

"No need to apologize for hard working, my good man! Now let's get the hell out of here."

"Sounds good."

Adam made an awkward attempt to put his arm around my shoulder; I resigned, smiled at him, and dealt with it. I really do not like to be touched.

He's going to be so excited! I can't wait to tell him what we have in store for him, he is going to freak out! Where should I take him? Some place celebratory, or someplace extremely casual? Wait, what I am thinking, why don't I check in and see what he wants?

I couldn't help but think:

Yeah asshole, what a novel concept. Try asking someone what they want!

"So Phil, do you care of any place where you'd like to go? Or better yet, do you have any allergies or anything that I don't know about?"

Anticipating some good news, I defaulted my selection to my normal, trashy good news place.

"Well, it's nothing special, but would you be alright to head over to La Cienega & Cadillac? I can't say no to a Western burger."

Adam seemed slightly surprised, but happy with my response.

"Yeah, man! That sounds awesome! Thank god you're not one of those organic, green-juicing motherfuckers that run rampant in these streets!"

"Cool, man."

I'll never forget the first time I got into someone's car to get some burgers.

The more I think about exact phrasing, the more that it sounds like a kidnapping story. Maybe I should reconsider how I say that the next time I tell that story out loud.

When I was really young, I remember winning some contest in pre-school. I don't remember what the contest was, but I remember that reward was an extremely greasy, ridiculously sized burger and chili-cheese fries. That probably fucked me up for life. The reward center in my mind was now only associated with garbage food. Nothing that made me feel good or anything like that—and actually, now that I think about it, it makes me feel terrible.

"You seem a little distracted, Phil. You okay?"

I failed to realize that I was reliving a scene from my past all while completely ignoring someone in my present, who is in a very confined space with me.

"Yeah, yeah, I'm sorry. Just a little sleepy from last night."

"Alright, well while we're out I'll grab you a coffee too, if you'd like. Either way, we are right here."

"Oh. So we are."

Don't let this weirdness get you down. Phil is just a little confused by everything that's happening and doesn't know what you're about to tell him.

As we got out of the car, he held open the door in a very formal manner. It was way too formal given the fast food joint we are in. I thought I'd over-exaggerate my response, just to fuck with him a bit.

"Why, thank you so much, sir!"

That probably weirded him out, but whatever.

As we stood there in line, waiting to figure out what we'd order, I could tell Adam was getting increasingly antsy. I decided to be blunt about it, as opposed to dancing around the subject.

"So what's going on, man? Are you going to tease me forever about this, and not deliver? Or what?"

That was a little rude of me, but, oh well.

"Well, fine."

He looked slightly annoyed, but he quickly got over it.

"So listen. I'm not too sure if you were aware of it or not, but this weekend was a pretty unprecedented one for our industry."

I curiously raised my brows.

"Really, how so?"

I played a little dumb, but I'm pretty sure I knew exactly what he was talking about.

"Well, on Sunday, it was announced that all of the studios will be operating under an umbrella corporation called FRAME."

He looked at me skeptically.

"Come on, Phil, you know damn well that you heard about this merger. Or could I have been completely wrong about you?"

"No. You're right, I heard about that. I thought you were specifically talking about something pertaining to entertainment law, and this is correlated, but right outside of it."

"Yeah. You're right. It's tangentially related, but nonetheless we have not really seen the impact of this merger as it pertains to our industry."

He briefly paused.

"What the hell was I about to say? Oh! Of course, the big reveal. So, I know you feel like I haven't been honest with you about this position and all the screenings I mentioned. But I do have something that I'm very excited to mention to you. FRAME will be hosting a conference and I was able to get us an invite!"

Again, before I could react, he steamrolled right over me and continued on with his upselling of this event.

"Phil, this will be the elite of the Hollywood industry elite and I got YOU an invitation! Isn't that exciting?"

And just like that, what I thought was going to be a victory Western burger, turned into a sad, defeated crunchy, spicy chicken sandwich.

* * *

SO THIS would be it. I'd be standing by these mythical figures in the film industry. What the hell do you say to a person like that? They have everything. I'm sure their problems are completely unrelatable to mine. Do I say anything at all to them, or just slink along in the background, like some weirdo at a party?

As I sat there scarfing down my chicken sandwich, I was miles away. Adam was there, still trying to talk at me (not to me or with me, that's for damn sure), and I was completely zoned out. I couldn't think about anything else then this truly bizarre realization that I'd be in the same room as the people that have brought such joy, and such agony into my life. Adam was still speaking, but I heard it as if he were underwater; muffled, distant and non-distinguishable.

He finally resorted to waving his hand in front of my face. I felt like that was a move straight out of a nineties movie, but I digress. I may as well start listening to whatever the hell this guy is saying.

"Uh, hello?"

That felt like it was lifted directly out of the Amy Heckerling catalog.

I shook my head and held it in shame. I was embarrassed about my non-stop thoughts and I was being a dick for not even acknowledging this poor guy. I didn't care, but I should still at least acknowledge that I was being a dick. Right?

"Shit. Adam, I am so sorry. I got carried away in thinking about all of the exciting possibilities of attending this conference and—well, I just got lost for a second there."

"It's okay, Phil. I know it's big news, but you need to handle yourself much better than the way you just did. Not only with me, but I'm talking about every interaction going forward. Your first impression is all you have. You need to make it, and you need to make it good."

I nodded in total agreement.

"Absolutely."

"So Adam, what exactly is this event of FRAME going to be? They just had a kickoff party, so it's not that, but do you have any info on what's happening?"

Adam clearly looked annoyed.

This fucking kid better not make me regret my decision of inviting him.

"Well, if you listened to anything I was saying, you could have heard all the finer points of the agenda that I have received for the day."

"Shit. I'm sorry, man."

It took Adam about a half-second to break his disappointed routine.

"Don't sweat it, Phil. I was totally fucking with you. I have no idea what the hell this could be, and as you can imagine, everything with these guys is very hush-hush."

He paused for a second, hunched down at the table, and conspicuously shifted his eyes before he began to whisper.

"If my gut feeling is right, they will be announcing some pretty big shit that's going to change the game for better or for worse."

"Why are you whispering?"

"Phil, with a company this big and nondescript, don't you think they could be listening? Who knows what they are capable of, you know what I mean?"

I gave him an annoyed look.

"Well, yeah, but they're not the fucking Illuminati or some other secret society."

Adam shot a knowing look right back at me.

"They're not? Phil, if anyone is likely to be in a secret society, wouldn't it be them?

"Fair point."

It was a lot easier to begrudgingly accept anything that Adam said, as opposed to fighting him on it. Adam's proven himself to be one of those never wrong type of people. *The world sure needs more assholes like that, doesn't it?* My curiosity piqued, seemingly out of nowhere, and I grew extremely curious and skeptical.

"Wait a second, how did we even get an invitation to this type of thing? Are any of our clients a part of FRAME? How the hell are we affiliated to them?"

Adam suddenly looked very uncomfortable. Naturally, I decided to pry more and make him sweat.

"Don't I know all of our clientele, or are you holding back something from me?"

He looked as if the air had been knocked out of him.

"Well, I knew I shouldn't have held anything back with you. But yes, we are. Some of our top partners represent clients that you are not aware of, and you didn't need to be. I can't tell you whom exactly, but I can tell you that we represent some very powerful, yet very deplorable people. They've created an extremely impressive body of work behind them, and some of them still create—but they've also left a trail of bodies and victims in their wake."

I didn't need to hear names. I knew exactly who they were talking about.

Fuck, I work for the company that has let pederast after pederast and murderer run free, while they continue to torture only god knows how many more people. I feel like I need to take a long, cold shower.

Adam saw how contorted and disgusted my face has become, and offered a meek apology.

"Phil, I'm so sorry I lied to you about this, but I have to protect our clients. Additionally, I have to protect our firm's best interests. You understand, right?"

Whether I believed him or not it didn't matter. He was right, and I was just a sucker who took the bait of a dead end—sort of well paying—job, that no one else wanted to do. Especially when they heard about the moral ramifications of it. I exaggeratedly sighed just to irk Adam, but I took umbrage with the fact that I have to accept this and have no say in the matter whatsoever.

But then again, what the hell could I do about any of it? What could I do about all the predatory rapists and murderers in both my company and beyond in my industry? This was horrific behavior that so many people have let go on unpunished for god only knows.

Then it all hit me at once.

Wait a goddamn second. I have one night in a room concentrated with these rapist fucks. I could do a whole hell of a lot of damage.

* * *

I ABSOLUTELY couldn't focus after that lunch meeting, so I decided to reach out and call Pete. Just to try to get my mind off the subject. I eagerly dialed his number. After the second ring, he picked up.

"Hello?"

"Hey man, sorry to bother you. I'm pretty sure you're at work, but would you be free to sneak out early and grab some drinks or something?"

He was kind of surprised at this call, but picked up the fact that I was anxious and needed to talk to someone.

"Hey Phil! Sure man, I can't get off early like, right now, but I actually get off in an hour. Where do you want to go?"

"Well, there's this divey place by me off of Grand Avenue if you are okay with that?"

"Sounds good, sure. Are, are you okay, Phil? Is something wrong, you're talking awfully fast and you sound stressed out."

I was annoyed by his comment. I didn't think I was that easy to read, but I guess I was wrong.

"Yeah... Well, I'll tell you when I see you, but I'll text you the address. It's really close to me."

"Okay. You got it, Phil. See in you in a bit."

"Sweet, talk to you then."

"Alright, later."

As soon as I hung up the phone, I thought about how much of a lunatic I would sound like if I were to show up, ranting and raving about this umbrella company. He would think I'm ridiculous, he'd probably expect some other conspiracy theories to spew from my mouth. First FRAME, then, how the ancient aliens created all of the unexplainable, natural phenomena.

I closed my eyes and took a deep breath. My eyelids felt heavy. Ever since I moved over here I have not been sleeping well. This news from Adam wouldn't help with my insomnia. I would be up all night not sleeping and thinking about this garbage now. I started to shut down everything I had on my computer. This consisted of tabs that had nothing to do with my work, it was movie review and film industry gossip sites. I doubt that anyone else in the office ever noticed, or cared either. I yelled down the hallway, and didn't wait for a response.

"Adam? I have to run out early, so I will see you tomorrow! Thanks again for lunch! See ya, man!"

After waiting another second or two for my computer to shut down, I grabbed my keys, cell phone, and bolted outside. I knew if I would have waited for a response I would have been trapped there with someone ridiculously time-consuming, tedious bullshit busy-work. I managed to make a pretty clean escape.

I sat down in my car, and as I was buckling in, I felt a nerve pop in the side of my head. It stung like a motherfucker. Unfortunately, I was used to this happening. From everything I've gleaned from my brief readings online, it's a blood pressure related thing. I took another moment, did some neck and shoulder stretches, and started to drive.

Should I be worried about this? That's been happening more and more.

Rather than be proactive and think about a solution to that, I synced my phone with my car's sound system and put on my old 90's playlist again. As much as I love seeking out new music and art, I've strongly felt the urge to regress to what I was listening to back in middle school and high school.

Is that indicative of something larger that I should be paying attention to? Or, again, am I thinking way too much?

I got lost in the music, it was some seriously embarrassing stuff.

Who the hell still listens to Lit and Rufio? And should I be sad or happy that I know all of the words to these songs?

Seeing as I got out of work really early, I didn't get swamped with the normal amount of infuriating traffic. The second time I sang the chorus to Rufio's "Angel Above Me," I noticed I was almost home. This made me happy, but it was a short-lived happiness. My heart was pounding at a ferocious pace. I quickly found a spot in my building's parking garage, and b-lined to the bar. I think I should definitely have a cool down drink before I see Pete, or he might see how exasperated I am and think I'm insane.

As soon as I spent enough time to get out of my own head to pay attention to what I was doing and where I was going, I noticed that I was basically speed walking. The only people that did this were fifty years my senior and wore neon and shit.

Yeah, I definitely need to cool down some.

I halved my walking speed, but still was thinking at a mile per minute rate. Here was this insane opportunity I had, to be in the same room with these amazing, mythic figures I have heard about for all of my life, and the only thing I can think about it is how I could stand myself for being in a room with these people I loathed.

These people are some of the most vile in the industry, if not the world, because they have enough money to buy their way out of any scandal they encounter. Additionally, they are the people that are making the decisions to stifle the hopes and dreams of so many independent people I admire. Do I feign interest in them? Just grin and bear it? Or what? Should I follow Adam's lead and succumb to his smarmy bullshit and be led by example? Fuck that.

After finally getting to the bar, I was greeted by the bartender, Jules.

"Hey Phil, haven't seen ya in a bit, how ya been?"

I reluctantly smiled, and ignored her question.

"Can I get a double whiskey ginger? Oh, and sorry, I sort of have a one-track mind right now and I'm meeting a friend in a little bit. I'm okay I guess."

She didn't need to respond with words, or thoughts to clearly communicate with me. Her contorted expression said enough. Jules retracted her neck, slightly pursed her lips and squinted her eyes at me. This clearly meant: Okay, well fuck you too. You better tip me well today.

"I promise you, Jules, you'll get a bigger tip for me being a prick today. Sorry."

She smiled again.

"Fine. When you want to talk to me, you always can, but whatever. Here's your drink."

I took my guard down a bit.

"Thanks. I'm gonna open a tab and wait for my friend over in that booth."

I gave her my card, and she sarcastically smiled and flipped me off. I smiled back.

I thought my regular communication skills were bad, my non-verbal communication is horrible! I don't know what else to do aside from smile and nod.

I finally sat down in the booth and took that sweet, first sip of relief. This was my standard cocktail that I ordered ever since watching *The Long Goodbye* (1973). Elliott Gould orders seven or eight of these drinks during the movie, and every time he does so he looks effortlessly cool. I always wished I could be like that. But maybe that just wasn't for me. I took out my phone again to kill some time and wait for Pete. I immediately started playing some video games.

What was it with me and escapism? I never wanted to be present in my circumstance. I always wanted to break away from it.

At about half way through the drink, Pete rushed in and sat down with me. However I was too enthralled in the game to even notice he sat down.

"So what's going on, man?"

I jumped in my seat. Again and again, I find myself too caught up in my own world to notice anything or anyone around me.

Pete looked harried, but concerned. He knew something was up by how I sounded on the phone. He sidled up next to me and immediately dove into conversation.

"Hey bud, what the hell is going on? You look like shit. Are you sick or something?"

"No. Not sick no. I'm worried and I'm kind of freaking out about something I have coming up."

"Oh? What's that"

I paused, trying to brace myself for the fact that although this is a very big deal for me. He might not give a shit at all.

"Yesterday, or maybe the day before or something, did you hear about that coalition of CEO's of the movie studios & the Hollywood elite merging together and forming FRAME?"

Pete was reluctant and looked confused.

"I'm sorry, but I have no idea what you are talking about."

I couldn't help but roll my eyes at him.

"FRAME? It's an acronym for something, I forgot what. Hold on a sec."

I began searching through my phone and finding out what that definition was. In the meantime, I thought I'd try to spell it out for him in a different way.

"Let's put it this way. Did you watch Power Rangers growing up at all?"

Pete nodded and spoke a barely audible but inquisitive, "Mmhm?"

"Well, think of it this way. FRAME is like the Megazord of evil companies merging together as one."

"Ah! Found it, Friends for the Reinvigoration of Arts, Movies, and Entertainment. God, doesn't that just sound horrible?"

Pete attempted to looked concerned for my behalf, but in actuality he had no idea what I was talking about, or how this as relevant at all.

"I'm sorry, Phil, I'm having a hard time understanding what exactly is happening. Why are you making such a big deal of this?"

It took all of my restraint not to grab him, and shake him in that moment.

"Pete, there will be one company overseeing and distributing all of the content in the film industry. Basically, that means every little company that we love, will have a hell of a lot harder time getting their own creations out to the public, especially if they own a large chunk of the box office distribution channels."

I took a breath and collected my thoughts. I grabbed Pete by the shoulders and looked at the whites of his eyes.

"Pete, everything we love about movies and art will cease to exist because of these fucks. Do you understand why this is a huge problem!"

I took a sip of my whiskey ginger. It had that nice, long bite, of a really horrible whiskey. But then, it mellowed out over time with the ginger ale. Realistically, I think this was not having any effect on me calming down. Pete's eyes finally started to widen with fear and trepidation, however he retained his composure and did not get all worked up about it like I did.

"I see. This could be very bad indeed. I am not looking forward to what they will do."

He paused and scratched his pathetic excuse for a beard.

Wait.

"Wait a second. This may all very well be happening and yes, of course, I understand how awful this could be, but what could be done about this? These people are million—er, I mean, billionaires, right? What are you freaking out about? It's not like you would ever run into any of them."

I slyly smiled.

"Well, funny that you should mention that. I just got an invite from my boss. His firm, well, my firm I guess, represents a few people within FRAME that I didn't know about. They invited us to an event next week!"

Pete smiled, nodded genuinely, but then his face quickly contorted to one of extreme concern.

"Ah. I start to see your predicament now. So you could potentially have an interaction with someone within this, collective? What should I call these people?"

"I don't know."

I took pause, and thought about it for a second.

They announced themselves as a group, but group of what? What do they refer to themselves individually within that group?

"Uhhh. I guess, collective works, but I like calling them a cabal."

Pete looked confused.

"Like, the Mortal Kombat character?"

Before he could attempt to finish that thought I cut him off.

"Sort of, but with a different spelling. It's a word for an evil, secret organization. Regardless, you're right. I have some potential interaction time with them and I don't know what to do. Can I be amongst them and lie through my teeth about how excited I am about their company? Am I capable of that? Could I say to them I love your work , but under my breath think that they are some of the most horrific lecherous monsters I've ever heard about? All I really want to do when I think of them, is relive the last moments of *Inglourious Basterds* (2009) and torch the fucking place to the ground and watch them burn to death."

I took a moment to calm myself down from my rant and let that last idea linger.

Would anything like that be possible? They'd all be in the same place at once. But, who the hell am I to pull off something that cool?

As I stared off into space, thinking about my potential future scenarios with this event, I started to map it all out. I could go back and dig around in my old stash of pesticides in my storage unit, bring some back and do some damage. Pete, without any prompting, finally chimed in.

"That's pretty dark stuff, man. You zoned out a little bit after that too. Are you okay?"

I was sort of surprised by his comment. I thought he would just roll with the punches and fantasize along with me, but apparently not.

"Yeah. I'm alright, man. I'm just so sick and tired of these people constantly, literally and figuratively getting away with murder and god only knows what else. If they make a fuck ton of money, and some well-regarded movies, does that make it ok for these people to be monsters? Where do you stand on this?"

Pete took a short, heavy breath.

"It sucks. But you're right. At what point do we hold them accountable? And, I'm sorry, I need to just say this, it's a bit of a digression but man, how brilliant was *Inglourious Basterds* (2009)? He literally kills history's most notorious monsters with film. That's still one of the coolest things I've ever seen."

He took a second, had an epiphany and was apparently really proud of it.

"He wants to kill the Nazi regime with art, and you want to kill off the current Nazi regime—of art!"

I smiled, nodded and sipped my whiskey ginger again.

"Yeah, I guess so. They aren't exactly Nazis. Or, maybe they are, who knows what these sick fucks are into?"

He quickly got deflated from his previous thought.

"That shit would never work in real life. Especially now with all the security and surveillance techniques out there. You know this event will be covered like crazy."

He started shaking his head in disbelief.

"But then again, we aren't the bastards and you are not the bear Jew. Neither am I. Who the hell are we to think that shit could happen. Or even that we would be capable of killing anyone, much less a mass amount of people. We just have to deal with it like all other broke idiots in the world."

I coyly smiled at him.

"Are you sure about that? You don't know me as well as you think you do. You just met me, man, you don't know what I can or can't do."

Pete immediately laughed that off. It was clear to me that he wouldn't believe a word I said, in spite of how I said it or sold it to him. I needed to prove it to him. I needed to show him what I could do. I then knew what needed to happen for us to move on with this—or any idea about what to do regarding FRAME.

"You're right, man. I'm just playing around. Anyway. I'm sorry I've been sitting here being rude this whole time. How the hell have you been? How was work? Also, have you been able to speak with your landlord at all and resolve any of the issues that we talked about?"

Game on.

* * *

IT WAS CLEAR he didn't believe me. He still looked as skeptical as the first time I mentioned it, except this time he looked a lot more concerned. He tried to write it off and pretend like he was interested in what I was asking, or even heard what I said.

"Uh. I don't know what you're talking about. What did you say again?"

I chugged the rest of the drink and slammed it down back on the bar. I apparently slammed it way too hard because it cracked and broke in my hands. I tried to resist looking at my hand, but had to open it anyway to assess the damage.

Fuck. What is wrong with this dude?

Pete was clearly disgusted and looked away with his hands in front of this eyes to not see the damage I had done to myself. My hand was shaking furiously while some shards of glass were embedded in my palm. Blood was getting everywhere. I bit my lip hard and desperately grabbed for napkins. I took a short, stilted breath and tried to continue on with my conversation.

"Listen, man, do you want your landlord to keep being a prick for the rest of your life, or are you going to stand up and do something about it?"

Now annoyed, Pete responded quickly and pointedly.

"Well what the hell do you want me to do about it, man? There are assholes everywhere in the world and he is just one of them, ya know?"

"Yeah. I got that."

I was short with Pete only because I was in so much pain.

"Jules?"

I shrieked. Desperately trying to get her attention.

"Could I get a pain killer and some paper towels please?"

Knowing she'd ask why, I held up my hands to show her the blood.

"Oh shit! Give me just a second."

As I waited on her response, I focused my attention on Pete.

"Listen, man, are you really okay with him being a total dick to you and you not doing anything about it? What kind of shit is that?"

Pete gave me the biggest eye roll I've ever seen.

"Listen. You can talk all you want to, but I have no recourse. My rights as a tenant are really limited. He holds the lease, he holds the power."

I fixated on his "rights as a tenant" sentence.

"Uh. I'm pretty sure that you are entirely wrong here. But regardless, I'm not talking about your rights, I'm talking about the principal of him being a dick and you doing nothing about it. I'm talking to you as a man, not as a citizen with rights and all that shit."

Jules finally got here with paper towels, her bar's first aid kit, and some painkillers.

"Fuck, man, are you okay? Do you want some help with this?"

"No, I'm cool, I can take care of this. Thanks, though."

"Alright, well next drink is on me, and how about I bring it to you in a plastic cup?"

I couldn't help but chuckle.

"That'll be nice. Thanks."

She waited patiently while I dressed my wound. On the other hand, Pete was anything but patient, I could see and hear how upset he was.

Phil needs to mind his own fucking business, there is nothing he could do for me that I couldn't do for myself. I'll go back home and double check my lease and see if there is anything that explicitly details neglect from the landlord's part. I'll check it out and I'll go from there.

I finished up and smiled back at Jules. Making sure everything was cleaned up and I got up to take out the trash and broken glass to make sure she didn't have to touch anything.

"Thanks, Jules!"

"No problem. I'm getting you a beer right now."

As I walked back to the trash can, I noticed my beer was already there, and Pete looked like he was at his boiling point.

"You're being immature. I don't even want to hear about it anymore. I'm not going to give you Keith's info. This is absurd. We aren't in the third grade anymore. We are men and we deal with obstacles responsibly and with maturity."

"Fuck that. Let's kick his ass. Where is this son of a bitch?"

"You're unbelievable. You are a petulant ridiculous person."

I exploded back at him with that response.

"I'm unbelievable? Who of us here actively listens to KMFDM?"

I took a pause and thought about it for a second.

"Hey. I'm sorry about that. That was uncalled for. I'm upset at your landlord, not you. Sorry, man. But regardless, where the fuck is he? Let me talk to him. What's his name again? Kevin?"

Pete looked like I knocked the wind out of him.

"It's Keith."

He sighed, then continued.

"That's, that's okay, I accept your apology. Are you sure you want to do this? You don't exactly look like you're in fighting shape, and this guy is built. Listen man, I'll just look into my lease and see if I have any legal course I can take with him."

"That's all well and good, but lawyers are expensive and I'm offering myself to do this for free. You don't know what I'm capable of, Pete. Trust me."

Pete shrugged, and accepted my response.

"Well, it's 4:45 on Monday. He always goes to the gym and gets out at 6:30."

"Perfect! Do you know what gym he goes to?"

This was great! I could get him right outside of his gym and not have Pete associated with this at all.

Pete immediately killed my excitement.

"Yeah. He goes to Gold's Gym, if you want to take him on, have fun with that. You think you can just kick his ass in a random parking lot? Well, good fucking luck. He always goes with a lot of people and he is huge. Like, Sigma from *Mega Man X* in his final form huge. But, you know: real."

I could tell he was worried about me and my well-being. It was sweet.

"Alright, well, what the hell kind of car does he drive?"

I really should have seen this coming, given everything else I knew about this guy.

"He drives a dark blue Ford truck. You can't miss it, it has a bunch of shitty protein shake and CrossFit bumper stickers on it."

"Alright. Well, let's see what I can do."

* * *

I SAID my goodbyes to Jules and Pete, and hit the road. Pete gave me one last, look of concern.

That motherfucker really is skeptical, does he really think he won't see me again? That's ridiculous. I'll show him wrong.

Either way, this was for the greater good. This was yet again, one of those endless "abused underdog" stories and I was sick of hearing about them and just letting them fall by the wayside. I was determined. Something needed to be done about this travesty of a landlord and I was apparently the person to do it.

Do I have it what it takes though? If he is as huge and imposing as Pete says, what the hell could I do?

I got behind the wheel and drove with an unwavering purpose. I knew I had to do whatever it took to make sure this shit got done, if it was killing a man with my bare hands again, or beating him within an inch of his life. Something needed to happen. At the next stoplight, I put on some Terror to get me in the mood for whatever was about to happen. Something about their endlessly driving rhythms and ruthlessly tight drumming and guitar riffs always made me snarl my lip and nod my head to the beat.

Gold's was about 10 minutes away, but who knows if his truck would still be there at all? Maybe he finished his lessons early or something.

Maybe I shouldn't ambush him at the Gym, but I should follow him around a little bit, see where he ends up, and then hopefully take him on in someplace a little more isolated and off the beaten path. Yeah, I'll park across the street from him and wait until I see him pull out of the parking lot and follow him from there. That would work fine.

I parked across the street and waited it out and blasted my car's air conditioning. After exhausting the Terror selection on my phone, I moved on to Coliseum. Fuck I love those guys. I tapped a long in my car while thinking of all the potential scenarios that could unfold here.

Pete could be all wrong, and maybe Keith is this really puny dude. Could Pete be fucking with me for any specific reason? Or maybe this would be a really brutal, long and drawn out fight. I'd rather not end up in too bad of shape. I only have a week out to plan whatever is going to happen with the FRAME convention.

A smile from ear to ear just came across my face with the epiphany I had.

Maybe I wouldn't need to get physical, and I could blackmail him with some of the thoughts he has. Like maybe, I could pick up on him being a necrophiliac and threaten to tell everyone of his embarrassing truth and a fight wouldn't even be necessary!

I stopped my endlessly rambling mind for a second.

Necrophilia? Come on Phil, really? As remote as that is, in what part of a maximum ten minute conversation could you have that would expose the deepest of his depravity? You don't think of this as much, but it always helps to be grounded in reality, if only for a little bit of time. Necrophilia. Man, don't be so ridiculous.

I resigned to my stream-of-conscious. That was an extremely ridiculous notion. I can't continue on thinking these truly absurd thoughts out of nowhere. There are some indicators of things that could lead me to believe these notions, and that's okay.

Oh crap, I think that's him pulling out now.

Well, Pete appeared to be right. He had a huge blue truck, and he looked as if he were a long lost Wyatt brother from the WWE. Ridiculously unkempt black beard, with a sopping wet, slicked back hair to match.

Fuck, what the hell did I get myself into?

As Keith was looking around and oncoming traffic to pull out of the parking lot, he quickly turned his focus on me. It looked like his eyes were shooting mini-daggers through me. I could feel every muscle in my body tense up, the muscles in my neck were as taut as they've ever been. The worst part of it was, I couldn't look away. I was staring right back at him. Keith eventually shifted his focus back on the road, and finally pulled out of the lot. While he did that, I turned my car back on, and started to follow him—three cars behind, but his truck was lifted, so it was pretty hard to miss.

Additionally, he had (like Pete said) a bunch of dumbass Cross-Fit stickers:

"I'd rather being doing burpees." and "#Gainz".

There were a bunch of other nonsensical stickers as well.

What the hell does any of that even mean? And what kind of person feels the need to have that shit on their truck and advertise that all the time? This cross-fit nonsense must be some ridiculous kind of cult.

I kept on him, still at that sweet spot of three cars back, but I had a really upsetting thought during the drive.

Fuck. What if he is driving back to Pete's apartment. There are probably a ton of cameras there and other stuff that would make this a lot more difficult for me. What the hell will I do if we go back there?

It took me about 15 more minutes of tailing him to realize where I was, and that we were in fact going in the opposite direction of Pete's place.

So maybe we are going to his house then?

We got off the main drag and starting taking those windy roads of Laurel Canyon. I've never really been this way before, but it's pretty beautiful up here. My three car lead, quickly became one car, and then Keith suddenly turned into a driveway. Thankfully, there were no cars behind me, because I needed to slam on the brakes in order to pull in as well.

As I pulled into the driveway, Keith slowly got out of the car, leaned up against it and stared me down. I shifted to park, took a breath, and headed outside.

"Who are you, and what do you want? Why have you been following me?"

His brusque demeanor and deep tones should not have been as shocking as they were to me. If he looks the part, more than likely he is going to play that part. I stood up to him and inched closer and closer with the best impression of a menacing look as I could muster.

"You don't know me. I'm here for a friend who has beef with you that needs to be sorted out."

He folded his huge arms. Unfortunately for me, he was wearing a tank top and I could see all of his extremely well defined muscles.

"What's that?"

I stopped in my tracks just out of punch-throwing distance from him. I was hoping to gain some kind of leverage from the thoughts in his mind, but the only thing I could gather from that was:

Who the fuck does this dude think he is, and what does he want from me?

"You have to sort your shit out for your tenants. They are sick of you being a half-assed landlord. They're sick of you being a lazy piece of shit who doesn't take care of them, and this conversation, right now, is your last hope before more drastic measures need to be taken."

Then, it was as if he transformed into a meek, concerned weakling. His body language changed radically. What was an imposing, force to be reckoned with, suddenly became that of a confused, embarrassed teenager (who still happened to look like he could crush me with his pinky).

"Wait. What's going on?"

I realized I needed to be as short with him for me to communicate clearly.

"You need to fix shit in your apartment. Your tenants are fed up. If you don't fix this, you have to deal with me."

He looked completely astonished.

"Deal with you? I don't want to deal with anyone, and I don't have any idea what you're talking about."

I was dumbfounded.

"Your apartment, man! It's falling apart, you have to rebuild the steps! You can't just let this shit go on forever and not do anything about it. People are furious! They've been calling you non-stop and you just don't respond? What kind of asshole does that?"

He now looked as cowardly as I felt. Almost as if I already had beat his ass.

"I don't get it. I love my tenants and I'd do anything in the world for them. I haven't received any calls or complaints from them at all. I'm sorry, man, this is all brand new to me. I've been trying really hard to be a great landlord and they've been complaining and not telling me?"

I was astonished.

No, that word isn't quite good enough. this was, mind-boggling? Yeah, let's go with that.

"So, wait. You've never heard of these complaints before? At all?"

"No. I just don't get it, why would they send someone like you over here and not tell me first. Or at all, for that matter?"

He looked like he was about to completely unravel. He went from stern and commanding to now being extremely pathetic and pitiable.

"I really don't know why they, wait a second... are you crying right now?"

* * *

KEITH QUICKLY became discombobulated with my information. In what appeared as an overly dramatic audition for a part of a Shakespearean play, as he cried, he slowly sank to the ground. First on his knees, then to his hands and knees.

This tower of a man was completely unraveling before me.

"How, how could this have happened? I can't believe nobody would tell me this, and then send you out here to beat me up?"

I was stunned.

Do I comfort him? Better yet, can I comfort him?

While he sobbed at my feet, I begrudgingly patted him on the back and tried to motivate him.

"Listen, man, I don't know you, and this is really weird for me to shift from aggressor to comforter, but if you really want to make a difference for this people as much as I believe you do, then we can do something about it together."

He sniffled. That's right, he seriously sniffled.

"All I've ever wanted is for people to like me and get along with me. I've been ostracized my whole life for being so big and intimidating. No, *sniff* no one ever wanted to talk to me because of how I portray myself to be. But, there are gentle giants. Right? Am I doing something wrong?"

He straightened up back to his knees. What I said finally appeared to be registering.

"Wait, we could do something about this together? What are you talking about?"

I smiled at him but the only thing I could think was:

Jesus fucking Christ, man. Are you serious right now?

"Yes, Keith. Yes, we can. Let's go back there and fix it up together! It's just the one spot on the stairs that I'm aware of. There might be more, but wouldn't it make you look better if you went door to door and ASKED your tenants what they thought?"

Keith took to one knee to try to leverage himself back up, but extended out his hand as if he were some goddamn princess in need of salvation. I attempted to pull him up, fully knowing that I was incapable of such a herculean task, and he got up—he did most of the work, but I did help.

He wiped away the tears, and started to sniffle. Keith meekly asked:
"Do you have a tissue or a handkerchief?"

Ugh!

I rolled my eyes in the most exaggerated way possible, and tried to stifle my frustration.

"I might have one in the car. Hold on."

Is this dude fucking serious right now? Maybe I should just kill him out of pity for being that way in the first place. And what the fuck is wrong with Pete? I don't remember if he told me or not—or maybe he lied about it—but this is the first time Keith is hearing about this stuff? That's bullshit.

I begrudgingly carried a napkin back to Keith.

"Here ya go."

He graciously took it and blew his nose. This was getting out of hand and I just wanted this to be over.

I clapped my hands together to signify a change.

"Okay! So, let's get all the materials we need in order to fix everything at the apartment complex. I'm not too sure what exactly that all is, but I'm sure you have most of it. And if not, I'm sure you know where to find it right?"

Keith was still on the cusp of being empowered, as he masculinely blew away the last snotty, boogery bits from his nose. He crumpled up the tissue and threw it in the driveway. He violently shook his head and assumed his regular stance when I first encountered him. It seemed as if he was ready to go.

"You're right. Let's do this! I'll grab my things from the garage. Just follow me back over and you can help me with this. Thanks so much again for your help! Could you, uh, do me a favor and not tell anyone that you saw me like this?"

He paused briefly, ran his fingers through his beard like Pai Mei from *Kill Bill* (2003).

"Oh yeah, and uh, what's your name kid?"

I could help but smile at this ridiculous circumstance.

"It's Phil, man, my name is Phil. I don't know how much help I can be with everything that needs to be done for the apartment, but I'm happy to do it."

Keith finally smiled.

"Great. So, give me like five minutes, and then just tail me back over to the complex."

"Sounds good, man."

That five minutes time is perfect for me to call Pete and figure out what the fuck happened and why none of this was communicated correctly.

I pick up my phone, and dial the most recently dialed number—Pete's.

He responded quickly, anxiously awaiting my response.

"Hey, Phil! You're still alive! How are you doing? Is, uh, is Keith, still alive?

I wasted no time to be pissed off at him.

"Yeah, motherfucker. I'm still alive and so is Keith. When were you going to tell me that you never asked him about this in the first place, or did anyone for that matter talk to him about this stuff in the apartment? What the hell is wrong with you people?"

"Shit."

He took a long pause.

Maybe he was trying to figure out the best way to lie to me.

"Yeah, man. You're right and we should have tried that first. I definitely should have communicated that to you as well. I'm sorry, Phil."

"Yeah, well you better be fucking sorry! Keith is a really cool guy. He's a little overly sentimental, but I'm not going to hold that against him. He is a completely reasonable person! All you needed to do was ask and you could have saved my ass a lot of time and stress."

"You're completely right. I don't have an excuse for lying to you like that. I'm sorry."

"Whatever, man. You owe me a drink or something. Listen. I'm about to head back over to your apartment with Keith. We are going to fix the steps together, and then go door to door and ask everyone what any other issues they may have are. Can you do me a favor, and pretend you don't know me when we go to your door?"

"Sure, man. You got it. Thanks so much again for all of your help with this. I really appreciate it."

I disregarded that last compliment. I was still really annoyed at him.

"Uh huh, no problem. You got it. I'll see ya around."

In almost perfect timing, Keith came back outside.

"Alright!"

He approached me in the exact way that you would expect a huge, teddy bear of a person to approach you. Open arms, huge smiles, and rosy red cheeks.

"You ready to do this? Listen man, these steps shouldn't take too long, but the door to door stuff, I might have to cut short. I have a shift tonight starting at nine."

I was a bit disarmed at this response.

"Oh, yeah okay. Wait. You have a shift at nine, tonight? Do you have an overnight job?"

"Not really. I do some freelance security work and it's based on the hours of the club. It's not technically an overnight, but it's pretty damn close."

He clapped his hands together and did a brief neck crack.

"Alright. Let's go do this!"

I sat down in my car, and at the exact same time of me clumsily stuffing the key into the ignition switch, I mumbled the words Keith just said to me.

"Freelance Security."

It all occurred to me at that moment. I knew exactly what I was going to do for the upcoming FRAME meeting.

Species

8

FOR THE FIRST TIME in my life, I finally felt like I had a driven purpose. I knew exactly what needed to done, how to do it, and most importantly: why this needed to be accomplished. Fixing up the apartment complex was for the most part a waste of my time. Keith and I literally tightened some screws and replaced a couple slabs of pavement. He even had spares just in case. It's still beyond bewildering to me that out of all the time spent complaining and bitching about the state of disrepair of the complex, nothing was actually done about it and people were always too scared of Keith to mention it to him.

After he went door to door and profusely apologized and presented his case on why he's a nice guy not to be feared, I learned that he was a new landlord to that property. The prior owner had recently passed away, and Keith was bequeathed this property to manage. In spite of lots of uncomfortable silences, I managed to secure him, as a security guard for an upcoming event I am in the midst of planning.

As I sat here, thinking over every possible aspect and scenario of my plan, I couldn't help but grin. Considering I was here stuck on a plane, I decided it would be best to make a list of what still needed to be done. I began to search for a pen in my carry on bag, but then my mind began to wander.

Going back to Colorado wasn't as weird and off-putting as I thought it was going to be. I have a lot of bad memories there, but I have some really good ones as well. I was sure it was going to be a rehashing of all those old feelings, but it was a lot more than that. It was sort of good seeing some of my old vendors, the old places I liked to go to, ultimately it was still was very isolating.

Would I have had a better time if I tried to rekindle any older friendships? Should I have given Kaycee a call? I don't even know where she is anymore, or even if I have her current phone number. It could have maybe been better, but it could have definitely been worse I think. I probably should have reached out to my mom.

I finally started to come back to my original plan, which was outlining the plan.

God, I guess I'm not good at this stuff.

Anyway, I dug through the pouch in front of my seat, and decided to write down my plan on the white space of a cologne advertisement. I wrote "Plan" on the top center of the page.

This is ridiculous. How immature am I?

I shook of that notion of crippling doubt, and moved on. I feel so isolated, but at the same time, I know what needs to happen and I don't think I should spread myself too thin, with the same, never-ending worries about friends, family, finance, and all that crap. Stay focused, and follow-through. That's all that needs to be done. Not just right now, but in life as well.

I took my pen to the ad again and officially got started:

Materials
Venue
Invitations
Process, style, and who to invite?
Security
Bait
Lure
Funds
Transportation (or is that done on its own?)
Timeline
Brad
Resources to determine invitations
Escape Plan

I think this was a really good start, but let's circle back and get a little more detailed.

Alright, so for materials, I bought and recovered all of the pesticide and hazmat stuff I need to get the job done.

Let's go ahead and scratch that off then.

For the venue, I still have no idea. It should be somewhere a little more isolated, but where the fuck would that be? Southern California is nowhere as close to as remote as some spots in Colorado. Maybe it should be more north and out of LA? But it still needs to be kind of a swank atmosphere. Or does it? I think I should check in with Brad for all of this. I'm going to go ahead and underline this. This one is kind of a make or break.

Invitations. First off, the notion that something like this would even have invitations is beyond absurd. Or, better yet, maybe this is one big Facebook invite?

I couldn't help but chuckle. Yeah, sometimes I laugh at my own jokes. Whatever. Better defer that to Brad as well.

Process, style, and who to invite. Hmm.

It's best to tap into Brad's info to be sure of that, but I can do some digging on my own as well. I'll utilize the files and all the work I've done in helping stifle these cases and unearth some of the old files and that should be good.

The one x-factor to all of this is how the hell I'm going to get access to the stuff that Adam was talking about, like the clientele we have that I was previously unaware of.

How am I going to get him to fork over that information? Could he do that willingly, or would I have to tear apart the office and find it all?

I'm going to go ahead and double underline this as well.

Security.

I think Keith is on board. I told him this will be very confidential and he'll need to wear a suit. How the hell we he be on board with this and how do I make sure that he doesn't utilize all this knowledge against me?

Can I make this look like an extremely convincing accident? Is that a possibility? Or do I take him down with me? Shit, for that matter how do I convince Brad to help? Maybe I can just blackmail both of them and have them be guilty by proxy, and use that to my benefit. I'm going to circle and check this one off. Still some concerns to address, but not nearly as bad as the others.

Bait.

How will I convince people to come? How does Brad source his "talent?" I want to make sure I have the most sought after kids in the industry there. Or maybe, one of the weird parts of the fetish they have is like it's anonymous? They don't know who the victims are and vice versa; the kids don't know who the perpetrators are. Maybe it's like some really sleazy, much more illegal version of *Eyes Wide Shut (1999)* to them? Or if it's not that, maybe it's a good idea to make it like that? Either way I need to check in with Brad here as well.

That's another circle and underline.

Lure.

Hmm. This is kind of a redundant thing on the list with only the slightest difference. I want to make sure that I attract as many of the FRAME people as I can in addition to the most horrific abusers I can. I'm looking to do the most damage, with the biggest impact possible.

This is definitely another Brad question, so there is another underline.

Transportation.

More than likely they do that on their own, with their own drivers and everything, but still check that out with Brad. Maybe, in some bizarre universe people take party buses to these sex slave dungeons. Ugh. Why did I even think that? I just got more sad and disgusted by one of my own thoughts than ever before.

Either way, I think I can check that off. Or, no, you know what, I'll do another underline here too.

God, a lot of this working out does depend on Brad. I hope I can convince him/blackmail him of this if need be.

Timeline.

I'm nowhere close to this but I need this to be down to an exact science. I need to have it like I'm running a full-scale production, like a film shoot, for that matter. I need to make sure this is 100% accurate.

This motherfucker deserves a triple underline for sure.

Brad.

Wow. This list is poorly organized.

Brad is necessary in every aspect of this. Either way I need to make sure he's with me. I'll cross this off and write a subscript capital B on all of the Brad related plans. That way, when I talk to him, I can make sure that I cover all the aspects that I need to cover.

Resources.

Again, really poorly thought out list. This part has already been covered and I'll make sure it gets addressed earlier on.

I'm crossing this out, too. Do you even plan, bro? Come on, Phil.

Last thing here:

Escape plan.

This was a much bigger question. What the hell do I do after this? Do I just continue along with everything like nothing happened? Either way, my physical escape from the scene needs to be coupled with the timeline, but there are a million things that need to be done with the escape. I need to develop an alibi, and think about all the potential fallout and aftermath. How can someone do something like this and pull it off? There are so many aspects to consider. What the hell are all of my options. Or if I get caught, what the hell happens?

At that moment, my planning was interrupted.

"Excuse me, sir? May I ask what you are doing?"

* * *

I SMILED like a fucking idiot the whole way home that night. Yeah, it was a red eye, and yeah, I'm exhausted, but now at least I have a clear—if not very tentative plan of what the fuck to do. Everything's been right in front of me this whole time.

I was very trepidatious about this call with Brad. I didn't know what to expect when I told him what I was thinking of, or if I was even planning on telling him the full scope of my plan. Then again, he'd have to know that some people don't make it out alive depending on the circumstance.

He's dealt with this shit before, and god only knows how many deaths his parties have totalled. When I finally got back, I sat in the car and thought every aspect of it through and through before I gave him a call. I decided that he only needed to know the minimum of what was happening and we would go on from there.

As nervous as I was, I picked up the phone and started dialing.

"Hello?"

"Hey, man! What's been up? How have you been? Long time no talk."

Brad sounded distracted, or disinterested. I needed his full attention.

"Not much, man. What's up with you?"

"Cool, is, uh, now a good time to talk?"

"Yeah. I'm routing this from my car and I'm driving right now, but what's up? How did uh, everything work out for you with our last conversation? You remember?"

Fuck. I completely forgot about that.

"Yeah, man, sorry I never called you back."

"I was being overly dramatic. Nothing really ever came from that. Man, I should really be more aware of the things I say to whom and how it affects them, shouldn't I? Sorry about that, man."

"It's all good. I figured I would have heard something if anything had actually happened."

"Yeah. You definitely would have."

I took a breath to gain some composure before I presented my grand plan to him.

"Hey, I wanted to pitch something to you, and I wanted your opinion on it.

"So, as I'm sure you heard from your dad about this, but nonetheless, Adam invited me to that organization FRAME's kick-off party or whatever it is."

"Oh! I didn't hear that… That's awesome!"

"Yeah. "

Just fucking rip off the band-aid.

"So listen. I wanted to host a party in the same vein of what you did for Telluride, and I need your help."

"Uh, okay. And why would you want to do that?"

I feel like he's on to me a little bit.

"Well. For future reference of my career, I'd like to know who is into this kind of a thing, and frankly, who the hell I should avoid if I don't want to be around it."

"Okay. Well, what do I have to gain by setting you up with something like this?"

This is where I knew I needed to take the reins of this conversation.

"Well, it's not something to gain exactly, but it's more like something that I have to keep."

Did that sound menacing and maniacal enough? I hope so.

"Phil. I have no fucking idea what you are talking about. What do you mean?"

"Well, man, I could, I dunno, NOT tell the cops about your previous parties and all of that ridiculous shit that you are involved in."

"I'm sorry. You, what? Are you fucking kidding me, man? Why would you do this?"

"Listen. I know this sucks, but I know what I need to do and you're going to have to trust me on this. I'll make sure this isn't totally one sided. I'll get you back on this eventually, I don't know how or when."

There was an uncomfortably long pause.

"So, just to be clear. I didn't do anything for you to hate me, right? If that's the case, I'll just help you out with this."

He cleared his throat and followed up with me.

"Dude, you didn't have to threaten me. You should have just asked me for help with this to begin with."

I squinted hard, and thought about what I said.

"Dude, I literally just did ask you for help. You pulled the what do I have to gain card on me. Were we having the same conversation?"

"Huh. I think you're right. My bad, dude. Anyway, sure I'll help out."

I knew it was the wrong time, but it felt so, so right to do my best Ron Burgundy impression.

"Well, that escalated quickly."

"Yeah. Indeed it did."

"Sorry. I think we got off on the wrong foot here. Regardless of that, I need your help to make this party special. This needs to be the biggest and the best of the parties like the ones you've hosted. Have you ever held one of these in California?"

Brad burst out laughing. He was so loud I needed to move away from the speaker on the phone.

"Yeah, Phil. That's where I hold the lion share of my events. My clients eat that shit up over in Cali, literally and figuratively. Some of those sick-fucks actually request to have the sex slaves..."

I cut him off before he could finish.

"Okay, okay, I got that one. Loud and clear. You didn't have to keep running with that. You had me at literally and figuratively."

"Sorry. Most people don't believe me, man. I've told that to so many people, so many different times that I guess I've become accustomed to it and not fazed by it."

I silently shook my head.

"I'm just going to disregard that and quickly move on. I do have a bunch of questions for you, that I'll ask in a lightning round, style. Okay?"

"Sounds good, man. Shoot."

"Alright, so first of all, for these types of things, people organize their own travel, right?"

"Yup. We keep these things as incognito as possible."

"Good. So secondly, how do people hear about these things?"

"I've developed a list over time, and then people kind of tell other people from there. Chances are if they are into this weird fetish shit, they will find someone else who definitely is, and drag them along as well."

"Got it. So, uh, what do you do after all of this is done to make sure nothing is heard or seen about this? You mentioned that you've been around some other casualties are that still the case?"

"Yeah. Unfortunately these kind of things happens when you have a soiree like I do. Don't you worry about that. I'll take care of that too. I know some people."

His use of soiree really threw me off, but I admire how interesting, and lascivious that word choice made these parties out to be. Hearing that specific word made me want to take a shower.

"I'm going to quickly move on to my next question, what about a venue?"

"There are some spots in the more industrial zone of Santa Monica that I've used before. We can dress them up however we'd like. They look like shit on the outside, but we can stage a bunch of crap and make it really nice."

"Sounds good. Cool."

I searched the recesses of my brain for anything else.

I feel like there were a couple more questions I had for him, but what the hell were they?

"Okay, okay last thing. How do I (or we) make sure that this will be the best soiree like this, that you've ever thrown. I want it to be extremely elite, and extremely enticing for the elite, but how would we do this? I need to make sure they are getting some high-quality product. If you know what I'm talking about."

"Okay. I can do that for sure. I have one tiny question for you? Why are 'we' doing this? What's your endgame?"

"Well essentially, I want this to be the biggest and the best. I also wants this to be the LAST time this ever happens. I know this is some crazy profitable enterprise for you, but both you and I know that this is deplorable, disgusting behavior. I'll never forget the looks of horror on some of those kids faces."

I took pause. That was completely true. I really believe I saw the worst of humanity that night, and I never want to see that again.

"So, Brad, why do I want this to be the biggest and the best? Let's just say, I want to go out with a bang."

I was happy with how I wrapped that up, but, I knew I needed to add something.

"This goes without being said, Brad, but confidentiality is extremely important. If any of this leaks out, then I will blackmail you. And I don't want to do that. Do I make myself clear?"

* * *

THE FOLLOWING days were wrought with planning: checks, balances, and overall tedium. Everything must be in order for my night to take the power back from FRAME, and give it back to the creators. Everything must be executed flawlessly. I will not accept anything less than perfection.

I will not accept anything less than perfection? Shit, maybe I'm starting to turn into a robot or something. Who says that?

Seriously though, shit needs to go down 100% on point tomorrow night. It was now the night before, and I had everything laid out and already set. One more painfully boring day ahead, I'll make it through them, but it doesn't mean I won't be any less anxious or bored. For the first time since our lunch, Adam strolled by my desk with a smile on his face.

"Hey, bud! How ya feelin' about tomorrow night?"

I was appalled by him calling me bud.

What am I, a fucking puppy to him? I'm a person, dammit.

I made it clear to him that I was not okay with that because he pulled back and became less friendly.

What the fuck is wrong with this kid?

"You okay, man?"

Unbeknownst to me, I pursed my lips and scrunched my face up in disgust when he addressed me like that. I only felt it now, and quickly changed my contorted looks.

"Huh? Yeah, yeah. Sorry, I had a weird taste in my mouth."

"Do you want some water or something?"

"No, I'll be fine. Thanks, though."

There was a brief, awkward moment of silence.

"So what's going on, Adam?"

He smiled casually, and slipped back into his previous demeanor.

"Well, I started thinking about tomorrow night. Phil, this party will be unlike any party you've ever attended. And additionally, I'm starting to get invites to some very lucrative after and after-after parties as well."

I'm glad he doesn't know the types of parties I went to with Brad. Or maybe he does?

I played dumb to respond.

"Okay. What exactly do you mean?"

"Well, just the idea that it'll be an extremely high class affair with some of the most elite people in the world. I can't imagine you've ever been to a party like that."

Well that was unnecessarily shitty and condescending.

"Nope, I can't say that I have."

I lied through my shit-eating grin. Fuck him for thinking he's better than me. This elitism is the shit that I will be ending very soon.

For the time being, I'll let you have this. But it's all going to change.

"I thought so."

He smirked and continued.

"I thought it would also be nice to get a suit. And I thought it would be really nice, if I bought you a new suit for this as well. Are you cool with that?"

It was at these moments that I felt like an extreme prick. I thought about apologizing for my earlier shitty demeanor but then again, that shitty-ness was reciprocal.

Is shitty-ness a word? Oh well. Fuck it.

"Oh. That would be really cool of you! Thanks, man, did you have a place specifically in mind to head to?"

"Well, I know a guy so I was planning on going through him again. We're going to get custom-tailored suits, and I'm going to expense it so you don't have to worry about a thing."

"Whoa. Are you sure, man?"

"Yeah! It'll be great."

The smile on my face quickly diminished. Adam hasn't been that good of a guy to me. Sure, he did give me the initial chance to be out here at all, but during my time here I've often been ignored and mislead. So why would I accept from this act of charity? Wait a second, is he buttering me up for something? Why would he just out of the blue decide to buy me a suit?

"Hey, Adam, is there any reason you decided to buy me a suit? I mean, don't get me wrong, it just seems really out of the blue. Is, is there a catch or something? I hate to ask that, but this feels like the start of *She's All That* (1999) as opposed to something that would, and even could happen in my life. You know what I mean?"

Adam burst out laughing.

"Oh man, that's rich. Phil, I'm not taking you to prom. I just thought I'd do you a solid considering nothing was exactly as it was described to you out here. I wanted it to be an apology."

"Alright."

I was still uneasily suspicious.

"If it's all the same to you, I'll go out and grab a suit myself. I think I'll be fine. I've been saving a ton of money ever since I got here. Thank you very much for the offer, but I can't accept."

Adam look dumbfounded at first, but then accepted my statement.

"Okay, man, that's cool. You want to do your own thing. How could I not respect that?"

"Alright, so here is what I'm thinking of for tomorrow. Show up a little later; you'll be working more of a half day tomorrow. At about noonish is when you should come in. I'll grab some lunch for the office, and then we will make an agenda of who talks to whom for tomorrow night. There are certain key players at this party that we need to check in on, in order to make sure that they are happy with us. Additionally, there are some people we would like to seek out and represent. Phil, that's where you and your knowledge will come into play. This will be exactly what we were doing in Telluride, except this time you will be leading this ship for our company."

He took a pause and rubbed his chin feverishly. He then gently put his hand on my shoulder.

"Listen, man. I know that you normally keep to yourself, and that you have a propensity to be deeply, deeply cynical. You're going to need to move past that, and I need you to be excited and be magnetic tomorrow. I need people to believe that you are the element that they've been missing in their life. By doing that, it will make people want to sign up for our representation."

"Okay. So, what exactly does that mean?"

Adam looked slightly annoyed here.

Come on, kid, don't be that dense.

"That means I need to you to do anything you have to to get them on our team. Be the most gregarious version of you. I need you to be the most smarmy, ostentatious, ridiculous version of yourself that you could possibly imagine."

"In short, if someone says jump, you fucking say how high, sir or madam?"

"Do I make myself clear? This is a really big night for us, Phil. There is a lot of opportunity for us to gain on this, but there is also a lot of exposure for us. So if one person fucks up, we feel it and so does the rest of our company. This party is not a joke."

Adam took a quick, deep breath and collected himself.

"Hey man, I'm sorry for getting so caught up in this and I don't mean to put you or your actions under the microscope, but I just literally got this speech from my boss a couple of minutes ago. So, half of this is genuine, and the other half is just regurgitation for the sake of my memory."

"To be honest with you, Phil, I'm really nervous because I've never been in a scenario like this before either. So I don't really know what to expect."

"Just know that if someone asks you for something, or to do a favor for them so they'd consider being represented by our firm, I need you to do it without question, and I don't care what it is.

"Now. Do I make myself clear in that regard?"

I timidly responded.

"Yes, you do."

*   *   *

I WENT through my mantras endlessly as I got dressed. I was sweating like crazy and it wasn't anywhere close to being hot outside.

Do this for the artists. Think about how excited you get when you watch a wholly original creation. You are doing everything you can to preserve their legacy and their future.

Or better yet, think of the filth you'll be getting rid of in this god forsaken city. Do we need all these pederasts, rapists and criminals around? The world will be a much better place without all those perverts.

I took a quick, short breath and tried to focus on the greater good of this outcome. After this is all said and done, will I have to go into hiding? How long will I have to stay there? Will I ever be able to have some semblance of a normal life again, or is this all over for me? I took another breath and said out loud this time.

"It won't be all of over for you if you make this look like an accident. Just focus and stay determined. You got this."

Yeah, I look pretty trite doing the motivational speech in a mirror thing, but do I do it because it feels better, or do I do this because it's been absorbed into my head after watching god only knows how many movies and TV shows have with this trope?

I didn't know, or care at this point anymore. Maybe all my idiosyncrasies amount to nothing more than conditioned behavior because of all the bullshit I've watched over the years.

Oh well.

I straightened out my tie and moved on.

The suit I got looked great on me, but that didn't make me feel any less awful and disgusting. This was major shit I was dealing with today and the stakes are as high as they will ever be. I still didn't exactly know what Brad had in mind for today or how the venue looked as it was getting set up. I have to make sure I have a little bit of time later today to sneak over to see the place and figure out exactly what I'm working with and what Brad got me into.

My car was already packed up with everything I needed for tonight. I walked out of the bathroom and heard a faint notification sound from my phone in the bedroom. I took a peek at it and noticed 3 missed text messages.

One was from Brad:

"You ready for tonight, man? I have all my shit settled and have heard responses from everyone. This will be the biggest & best 4 sure."

Ugh, he really texts like that? 4 sure? It's only three more characters, man.

The next was from Adam. It was a selfie of him showing off his suit and pointing to his rented Mercedes Benz for the day.

"#Gooddaygoodlife! Can't wait for tonight, hope you're ready man! #1shot #donotmissyourchance #Eminem #jk.

I don't know which text I'm more disgusted by. The self-promo king, or the king of the underground sex dungeons.

I took pause, and thought about how absurd this moment was. How the hell did I end up here, on the cusp of doing something amazing like this? Then again, how did I ever get involved in all of this nonsense?

The last text was from Pete.

"Hey, man! Long time no talk. You want to grab a drink in a bit?"

The only one I thought about responding to was Pete, but decided I'd get to it later and start heading out for the day. I took a quick inventory of everything I needed.

Hazmat suit, two tanks of Endosulfan, matches, a really long fuse, and some small steel girders for the doors. Yep, I think I'm good. Thank god I stored Dad's old pesticides when I did. (And thank god for those damn Potato Beetles in Colorado in the early aught's.) It's not exactly street legal, but damn is it powerful! That's the only thing that really mattered.

I got in the car and pulled out of the driveway.

Already this day was giving me a lot of anxiety. That's why I'm a big advocate of a morning coffee and scotch. It definitely has helped ease me along these nerve-wracking times. My normal morning routine of waking up, watching porn, breakfast, and shower; had already been screwed because of my late start time today. However, all that really meant was more sleeping in and more porn.

The day has felt, and will continue to feel as if it were unraveling in slow-motion. At least until I was done with everything I needed to do. Who am I kidding? It would probably last long after this as well.

I attempted to zone out as best as I could during the drive by listening to a couple podcasts I wanted to check out, but when that didn't work I went back to some songs I've known and loved for a long time. I still couldn't shake this anxiety and how distracted I was.

The infuriating part of it was I really only had a couple things to do today. Work was going to be no stress, if not extremely boring, and then it was all about heading to the ceremony and bullshitting with god only knows how many Hollywood elite douchebags; and potentially douchey-women.

What's the word for douchey-women? Is there one?

But then again, whatever the word for those women, they are not the ones exploiting all these sex slaves like their male cohorts. It's these monsters that need to be stopped once and for all. Either way, my main function of the day was be a mass-murderer. Not the easiest of pills to swallow.

It won't be murder considering it will all be a "freak" accident. Plus, at the end of the day who knows if these people will actually be missed? Sure, they have their legacy and their films, but depending on who shows up, is it anyone who's reputation is truly worth a damn? Are these good people to anyone? The more and more I hear about these rapists the more and more I don't think anyone respects them at all. I couldn't help but chuckle.

That last sentence was the most ridiculously constructed sentence ever. Who would ever respect rapists? That's absurd.

After I finished laughing, I resolved to give up on the music. I turned it off and felt the slightest bit of relief of what I had to do. I'd be ridding the world of these horrific, shit stains of people. That's valiant! That's not something I should be ashamed by, or anguished about. I'm doing the world a favor.

In the middle of that brief moment of silence and calm. I heard a noise that immediately kick-started my anxiety again. Ever so faintly, I heard the muted "Hiss-s-s-s-s-s" of a pressurized container.

* * *

MY EYES widened at the prospect of what could have been, but then I remembered how much of an idiot I was. Last night I bought a soda and left it in the car. It was barely opened, and was not so quietly releasing the carbonization. Sometimes it is truly a miracle that I can function at all, much less excel at anything. I unscrewed the cap, and took a sip of the flat cherry cola. Sometimes I like it better when it's flat.

Man, I'm boring.

As I pulled into the office was Adam was outside, leaning on the hood of his car trying desperately to look as cool as humanly possible. Attempting to be discreet, I noticed I got a text message from Brad. I took a peek at the message as I walked over to Adam.

"You wanted this to be the biggest and the best tonight? Just you wait and see."

I had to fight off my natural instincts of giving a concerned look as I read this. I needed to be stone-faced and cool. Especially given the nature of everything regarding that text.

"Hey, man! How ya feelin? Big day baby. BIG DAY!"

He looked like the protégé of Hunter S. Thompson—a bespectacled monster with a white suit that reeked of Californian pseudo-cool. He was sweating like crazy, more so than I've ever noticed before. I couldn't help but chuckle, I played it off like a cough.

"Hey, man. Still waking up, but I'm doing good."

"Still walking up?"

I need this kid at 110% today and his first response is he's still waking up? Does he have any idea what today means for our company, or for me, or better yet, for him?

He clapped loudly and rubbed his hands together at a furious pace.

"Okay, no worries, man. We can fix this."

He slapped me on the back, hard.

"Alright man, what do we need to get you to wake up? Tea? Coffee? Energy drink? Cocaine? Whatever it is, I'll find a way to get it."

I was dumbfounded by his response.

"Uh, how 'bout we start with coffee?"

Adam livened up after that.

"Yeah, man! Sounds good."

Without giving time for any of that to sink in, he immediately shifted gears and steam-rolled ahead.

"So listen, we talked about a half day scenario beforehand, but ultimately, we're not doing that. We're gonna go grab lunch, then head straight into the pre-party."

"Wait. Pre-party? What the hell is that?"

Adam scratched his head.

"Oh yeah. I guess you haven't gone to those before either? Well, come on to lunch, kid. I have a short time to tell you a lot."

"Alright, sure. Where are we going?"

Adam, immediately responded.

"We're going to get some motherfuckin' steaks on me! I'll give ya a ride over. Let's go!"

"Okay, after that, could you bring me back here though? I don't know where I'll end up tonight and just want my car a little closer to the meeting. Is that cool?"

"Yeah, yeah, whatever, kid. No problem."

He motioned me in as he held the door open for me.

"Sorry to rush you like this, but this is one of those meals that I've been savoring for a while now. I've avoided eating in preparation."

"Oh. Okay, no worries I totally get it."

"Good, good."

He moved his sunglasses above his eyes and gave me a once over. This increasingly felt like a scene from an early Robert Downey Jr. movie, as opposed to my real life.

"You clean up well, kid. Good job. I doubted you, but you showed me wrong."

He took a beat, and immediately shifted gears into a much more serious tone.

"Listen, man, not to damper the mood when we have this steak, but I wanted to talk to you beforehand and make sure we are one hundred percent on the same page for the duration of the day."

"Okay. Go for it. What's up?"

"I know I already told you this before, but today you will see nothing like you have ever seen before, or will see again. Now, this includes the highest, greatest things about humanity, but this also might include the lowest, more grimy, disgusting aspects of it as well."

"Uh-huh, and?"

"And what you don't know is that everything you thought you knew about some of your favorite people might be either, completely wrong. Or completely misrepresented. You might see some repugnant shit today and even if it's your favorite, actor or whatever. You have to deal with it, and you have to be stone-faced about it."

He was ranting quite a bit for it being so early in the day.

"Let me be clear. No matter what happens, you can't have any kind of tell. Good or bad. Does that make sense to you?"

I nodded quickly. He grew increasingly stern and boorish as he continued on and on in what felt like a never-ending rant.

"Additionally, regardless of what type of morally comprising scenario that you may or may not end up in today, you cannot say no at all. You have to do everything, and you have to be completely chill about it. Don't play dumb, just play along. I'll be doing the same, so don't judge me. Alright?"

"Okay. I got it. Why are you yelling at me about this?"

"Because you have to get this, and there is a lot riding on tonight."

His eyes narrowed and he started focusing more on me and this conversation we were having, than the road he was driving on.

"Phil, do you think you're unique and special? Do you think you have a magnetic personality that everyone can get along with? Because I have a secret for you."

He motioned that I should come closer to him. I didn't.

"Listen, kid. You don't. We've done this before, and we've gotten burned before by people just like you, in your position. I'm not going to allow any room for any mistakes. All it takes is one naive kid with a moral compass to come into this industry to ruin it for all of the people around me that I work with and love."

He can't know about a lot of our activities, and I'll have to do a lot of steering with him, but there is a chance that this might work out extremely well.

"I'm sorry if I'm coming off as a huge dick right now, but the fact of the matter is I can't allow myself to be burned again. Every time it happens it takes so, so much work to rebuild all the damage that was done."

I finally snapped back at him.

"Yeah, man! I fucking get it. I'm not an idiot, okay? Have I ever done something where I've proven myself incapable? No? That's right, I haven't. So chill the hell out and treat me like a goddamn man."

He looked like he was about to apologize, but I cut him off before he could do that.

"I hear you, I understand you. And that's it. Move on."

He looked a lot more calm than at the start of this car ride.

"I'm sorry, Phil. I get worked up about this shit. I have one last thing that I wanted to stress to you, okay? I hope you don't mind too much, but this has been hard for me to say as well. I have this last tiny thing, then we'll go back to normal. Does that sound okay to you?"

I nodded, and he steamrolled ahead for the last time—so he said.

"If you fuck up today at all, consider yourself not only fired, but excommunicated from our office. We won't talk at all anymore, and I'll make sure you don't work in this city. But, depending on the scope of your potential mistakes tonight, more than likely they'd recognize you as a prude, and no one would want to work with you anyway."

As we drove on for about ten minutes, he relaxed more and more exponentially with each quarter mile traveled. He tried to make a point, I get it, but this was a side of him I never saw before, and hope to never see again.

* * *

WE SAT down and looked at the menu. I mentally prepared myself to be apathetic throughout the day. Normally, I would be visibly disgusted when I saw an egregious amount of excess. I took a deep breath. I looked over at Adam and smiled, then immediately buried my face in the menu. I looked at some of the prices and was mortified.

Adam seemingly read my mind when he said:

"Remember man, don't worry about any of the prices on the menu, this is all on me!"

"Yeah sure, man. Thank you in advance for this. It's really, really kind of you."

Meanwhile, I'm starting at the menu and it's $45.00 for a fucking side of spinach? How could this even exist?

It took me awhile to get my bearings, but after that happened, lunch was fairly boring and full of small talk. I thought keeping the general conversation light and irrelevant would be best, given how worked up he was beforehand. I was low key, but Adam was erratic, and very high strung. He seemed really nervous.

The only thing on Adam's mind was him repeating the same things over and over, as if he were trying to convince himself of them.

Everything's going to be cool today. Phil will be fine; and everything will be good. All we need is one more. Just one more and we'll be alright. Just one more. Phil will be fine, it's all good, Adam, it is all good.

I didn't have any idea what the hell he was talking about, but I also didn't know how much I cared. I quickly grew bored of this. Especially considering how much time Adam had spent hyping up the rest of the day to come. I hurriedly ate my meal in order to move on to these pre-parties. The saddest part of this entire meal was this it was only okay. As Adam and I waited for the check, he started talking about what our first responsibilities were for the day.

"So, first part of the day is checking into the hotel, and heading into the bar. We're going to binge drink, and see who turns up. Then we'll do some mild socializing, brag about our amazing gifts bags that we won't actually get, and we'll see who we could ride along with from there."

I was dumbfounded at his response.

"That sounds pretty pathetic, man. That doesn't even sound like a true strategy. That sounds like what we would do if we definitely did not belong here. Like if we crashed, or were just slumming it and they allowed us there."

Adam slammed his hand down on the table and pointed at me.

"Exactly! That's exactly what we want to do. We want to be as casual as possible. We need to appear as though we aren't impressed with any of the ridiculous opulence around us. By doing that, we can get these people comfortable enough to give us more info about the rest of the day."

"Alright. Sounds good, man, let's head on out then."

After I picked up my car, I followed him over. It was another really quick drive, but as soon as we parked, he invited me over to his car again. He rolled down the windows, then popped open the glove compartment in front of me and pulled out a brown paper bag. From that, he pulled out a smaller plastic bag filled up with cocaine.

"Son of a bitch, Adam! I thought you were acting ridiculous. Why wouldn't you have just told me about this?"

I felt like a total idiot. How could I not pick up on this, he's totally been coked up all day! He's been a sweaty, ridiculously antsy mess wearing a white suit and sunglasses.

"I should have told you. I'm sorry, man."

"It's cool, whatever."

"Listen, do you want some?"

"Adam, I've understood everything you've said about today, and based off of the significance you impressed upon me, I'm going to say no. Even though you don't want me to say no to anything today, I think you're really nervous and I don't know how I'd react to that. I've never done it before."

He looked reasonably upset.

"That being said, I know to not act like this for the rest of the day. Okay?"

"That's cool, I get that. Regardless of what you want to do, I'm taking another hit."

"That's fine, but hold on a second. Do we have anything to worry about if tonight doesn't work out like you think will?"

Adam went from 0-100 real quick after I said that.

"Fuck, man! Are you kidding me right now? How were you able to figure that out? Do I have a tell or something? Listen, you weren't supposed to know about any of this. This is my crap to deal with, and I haven't deal with it well. Everyone's really stressed out and I'm bearing the brunt of it. You were not supposed to know about any of this. I have the entire fate of the company riding on my back, and you're not making this any fucking easier on me. You're not giving me any hope that I can calm down in the immediate future. Man, we might be all fucked and lose our jobs."

I started to laugh, I couldn't help it.

"Your reaction to all this is you laughing? What the hell is wrong with you?"

I finally stopped laughing. I coughed a bit, but then I regained my composure.

"Dude, are you hearing yourself right now? You're ranting, raving, and repeating yourself. Are you sure you want to do another line? From my perspective, you can barely keep yourself together right now."

He sunk into his seat.

"Damn. You're totally right. I'll pass on this. Let's head into the bar and get some drinks that can even me out."

"Cool, man. Trust me, you'll be fine by the end of the night. I'll make sure everything is fine and we won't get fucked, alright?"

"Alright, cool. Let's fucking do this."

Adam put the coke back in his glove compartment, rolled up the window and we headed inside. After walking through the thresh hold of this restaurant, it was very clear to me, that I would never, ever go to this bar. I definitely felt like this was an out of body experience. This looked like a place that *The Bling Ring (2013)* would try to hang around for their next victim. This was definitely not a casual, easy going bar.

* * *

IT WAS ABUNDANTLY clear to me, from my first interactions with the people attending this FRAME event that I never would want to be earnestly associated with these people. They were all vapid, egotistical, and completely uninterested in anyone except themselves. But, I knew what game to play and I was playing it well.

Eleanor—yes, that's what she prefers to be called, and do not try to make up a cutesy nickname for her—was laughing hysterically. Like legitimately slapping her knee at a very gauche joke I just told her that I learned from Uncle Steve (wherever he is). I even said that it wasn't classy enough for her, she said she "didn't mind at all."

With not even 15 minutes into being here, Adam was grabbing her second drink from the bar, and I was left to my own defenses; which apparently include ridiculous jokes from my weird uncle.

"Oh man, what was your name again, kid? Paul? I'm sorry, I started pretty early today, if you know what I mean."

"It's uh, Phil, actually. No worries, though."

Eleanor was the wife of Greg, the CEO of one of the many companies that founded FRAME. Not one of the studios, but he led a CGI house.

"Sorry about that, kid. Oh! Lovely, thank you so much, Adam. Great timing!"

"Yeah, of course!"

Adam instructed me that this was a potential acquisition, and when he was around he was planning on leading the conversations. He would let me know when I should jump in or not. I hated it, but I understood where he was coming from. If I were in his position, I'd want to do the same.

As much as Eleanor went on like she liked us and she was excited to meet us, the only thoughts that were running through her mind were typical of the god only knows how many well-to-do housewives in this area.

"When I get home, if Ivelisse did not have all of those dishes done, and cleaned up the mess the Cale and Kallen made, I'll fire her on the spot. I'll simply tell Greg I saw her stealing some jewelry, and casually misplace some."

She truly was a nightmare of a person that I would otherwise have nothing to do with. Adam mindlessly trudged on in this pathetic excuse of a conversation.

"So, Eleanor, what are your plans for the rest of the day? How much time will you actually get to spend with Greg?"

She put her drink down as I smiled politely, and I proceeded to hang on to her every, stupid, word. I was clutching to my vodka and soda with a twist of lemon hoping that maybe, with the next sip it would taste better.

Why did Adam have to order me this horrible fucking drink? I couldn't even get buzzed on some shit I like? I get that it's all about keeping up appearances and what not, but come on, do I look like a guy who would enjoy this shit? Well, notwithstanding the suit, I normally look like a guy who would order well Tequila and the cheapest beer the house has. But that's not the point.

Eleanor rolled her eyes before she started to ramble on for god only knows how long.

"Well, unfortunately, I won't be seeing my dear Greg for quite some time today. You know how these things work of course. He had a shareholder's lunch, followed by car over to the meeting for some light socializing and drinks beforehand—which might be wrapping up soon come to think of it, then there's the keynote. I think I'll see him then, for a little bit at least. Then it's off to the after parties, and we'll be going to separate ones sadly. Me for pleasure and social with our friends, and him for more networking. It's truly a bore. Well, it'll be a bore for him. I'm going out with the girls tonight and drinking my weight in wine."

Yeah, you don't fucking say?

Adam chimed in, with feigned concern.

"It must be hard, but I'd imagine it's worth it in the end. Although, who can really say for sure."

Adam shifted in his seat. He clearly looked like he was trying to be poignant. He wanted to clearly change the conversation in his favor.

"So Eleanor, I must confess, I have some selfish reasons for asking this question. I wanted to check in with you regarding how everything wrapped up during the last issue Greg's company had this past fall?"

She exaggeratedly rolled her eyes and put her hand to her heart, as if she were a delicate lady. And responded despondently.

"Oh, you mean with those lazy animators who were saying they never got overtime pay?"

"Well. I think that's all water under the bridge and they finally agreed on some terms, but my poor Greg has been losing so much sleep over it."

I was impressed with what I thought was an endearing reaction to that touchy issue.

Oh good, maybe he had an ethical dilemma and maybe understood all the grievances they had.

"He had hired what he thought was the best legal team, that specializes in disbanding potential union uprisings, and was furious over how poorly they handled that matter."

Oh. Well there goes that. Stupid me, why would I think something positive were to come out of any of these people, or their ridiculous problems?

"I see. I see."

Adam was spending this time being overly emphatic and looking concerned about the welfare of their personal life. He isn't too bad at doing this. I have to give him credit where credit's due.

"Well, pending the status of that, I work for Weissberg & Associates. Have you heard of us before? We specialize in public relations, and have had quite an extensive history of success with our labor specialists. If you have any questions for us, or if you'd like to pass on this information to Greg, please take one of my cards. And regardless of any kind of a decision, or commitment, just keep in touch with me! I'd love to meet up again with you and Greg and just catch some drinks on more of a downtime for all of us."

Eleanor smiled and nodded.

"Sounds great! I'll definitely pass this on. I think we should be on the run though, look at the time! Can't wait to see what this FRAME thing is up to!"

Yeah, can't fucking wait.

* * *

ALTHOUGH it felt like an award show, the FRAME symposium looked like it would be a panel discussion. I was seated rather uncomfortably next to Adam, while the group collected themselves on stage.

Why is this even a public event? From everything I've seen so far it's been functioning as a shareholder's meeting.

The lights dimmed and over the microphone we heard a booming:

"Thank you for arriving. Please find your seats. It is with great pleasure that I introduce to you, David Barnes, CEO of FRAME."

The CEO of FRAME, which of itself is a group of CEO's and power players. Does that make him the CEO of CEO's?

He gawked and smiled as the lights shifted focus onto him.

"Thank you all for coming today. We have some exciting things to talk about, so let's just dive in."

I braced myself for what I believed was going to be a very long, and tedious presentation.

"In the seminal film, *Sullivan's Travels* Joel McCrea goes on a journey of self-discovery, and ends up realizing the power that comedy has on the masses, when he watches an old cartoon amidst laborers.

The message that conveys, and the power that cinema has, still rings true to this day. Here at FRAME, we want to do the best we can to make sure the most people are as entertained as they can possibly be."

Oh great, so broad comedies are coming back and every individual voice is going to get snuffed out of the public perception. What does that mean for dramas though? Does this mean the death of all those weirdos I love? No, Werner Herzog will still be making his shit, it might just be a lot harder to see now.

"We have our hands full to say the least. This doesn't necessarily mean we are going to make every decision based on majority, and committee rule. We're not being presented with a horse and churning out any camels if you know what I mean."

Ugh, is he really doing the fucking pause for laughter bit? Is he kidding me right now? Yeah, dude, we get it. Committee jokes, har har.

"That being said, we are going to homogenize some of the films to be distributed, that's for sure. But, our plan is to not ignore the independent voices at all. Our distribution will consist of: the lion-share going to broad comedy/dramas and big names, the next tier being horror/thriller/mystery, the next tier below that will documentaries, and finally, the bottom tier will consist of an 'independent spotlight' series, where we take a vast amount of independent submissions and determine what would be best. This will be determined by social engagement, in addition to ideas or scripts that intrigue us. I assure you, however, the majority share in these decisions will be left up to the people outside of this room."

Oh god. I can't wait for YouTubers or Vinestars to replace all of our actors with talent.

"This will also consist of reconsidering our distribution methods, seeing as we have the CEO's of multiple multiplexes on our board, we can create more engaging events and ensure that everyone gets a chance to see the movies we will distribute by holding them in a wider array of cinemas for a longer amount of time."

Fuck, independent movie theaters will die without housing FRAME productions.

He removed his head from staring down at his speech.

"Wow! Try saying multiple multiplexes five times fast, folks!"

He paused again for laughter.

Ugh.

"We call the aforementioned film development strategy our Pyramid Plan."

I feel like the entire room is simultaneously rolling their eyes. I wanted to jump up and shout:

"Just call it a pyramid scheme, asshole!"

But I didn't. I bit my tongue and sat there and clapped like every other idiot in the room.

"Thank you. Thank you, we are very excited about this too. Additionally, I wanted to speak briefly as it pertains to the rest of our work, outside of the film industry. We will take this crowdsourcing approach and use that to funnel submissions for our literature and fiction division, in addition to our art sector—public and private—and theater as well. We have a lot of great things to do, and we can't wait to do them!"

"Thank you all so much! Please, help yourselves to some refreshments and snacks outside in the lobby, where we can all meet and discuss what's to come and what to look forward to! Our official slogan going forward will be adapted from the great MGM films of the past, as we boldly look towards the future: *Ars Gratia Artis*! We will see you soon!"

This left me infuriated.

Ars Gratia Artis? *That sounds like the exact opposite of what you'd like to do. Art for art's sake? This is going to be more like Ars Gratia whatever the Latin word for cash is. Oh god, so basically they will be controlling and determining what art forms make the most money, and that's what will be the determining factor for all of this nonsense? This sounds horrific.*

I looked over at Adam who smiled with an idiot's glee.

"How great does all of this sound, man! So happy to be a part of this historic announcement!"

"Yeah, man… I'm going to need another drink. I'll see you in the lobby."

I shuffled over to through the self-congratulatory crowd and headed directly to the bar outside, where I ordered a double scotch and ice, and picked up one the prettiest fucking appetizers I've ever seen. It was a piece of salmon on a potato pancake with creme fraiche and micro dill. As pretty as it was, however; it definitely had no substance to it. Also, this was a very far cry from my days of eating pizza rolls and booze that only a homeless person would touch.

Adam nudged me on the shoulder from behind.

"Listen man, and I know why you're upset, but I'm not going to let you kill my vibe and this good time. We have to plow on to keep our goals in mind and... Megan! Is that you? I wanted to talk to you, come here! I have to introduce you to Phil. You'll *love* him!"

I was just tipsy enough to continue on with my bullshit pleasantries. But my nerves were starting to sink in, considering what the hell I had to do later tonight.

* * *

I HAD about an hour left of this nonsense until my starting time. I needed to head to the venue early and make sure that I start pumping the gas into the room and let it diffuse into the building. Additionally, I wanted to check and make sure everything was ready. I wanted to have about two hours lapse, then I would light it up and get the hell out of there.

There were multiple types of parties. Apparently there was pre, there was the main party, there was the after party, and let's not forget about the after-after party. God, how did these people even function. Did they do anything else but party?

I was smiling and putting on whatever bullshit conversation I needed to in order to get by. It was mainly filler, and it was mainly guided by Adam. I met people that I instantly forgot because that's how uninteresting they were to me. This was starting to get agonizing.

"So Phil here had some exciting plans for the rest of the night, didn't you, buddy?"

Adam elbowed me gently.

"Isn't that right, Phil?"

I suddenly remembered my script.

"Yeah, we're going to tour the after party scene and figure out see what's out there. You don't want to put all of your eggs in one basket, right?"

"Oh, that does sound fun!"

"So, did you hear of any that he should check out?"

God, what a stupid segue. He may as well be saying, "we're desperate, please help us and tell us what we need to know."

"Ummm. Let me check my phone, I've heard of a couple, but I haven't decided which one I'm going to myself."

His name was Marcus. He was an executive producer of three of the past year's top five grossing movies and one of six EP's within FRAME. He had a Jerry Bruckhemier level of fame, just without the ego (and hopefully the ludicrously troubled business partner). Marcus seemed fine, and supposedly Adam knew him through a friend of a friend? I don't know if I was truly buying that story, but it's what he was selling, so I played along.

"Yeah, so as I see here in my calendar there is one down in West Hollywood at Ink, then someone rented out the Magic Castle, then there is one in a warehouse in Santa Monica. I mean, with a night like this with so much to celebrate there's something going on everywhere. I don't know yet. Did you have any must go to places in mind?"

I had a minor twitch when I heard Santa Monica. Both Marcus and Adam looked at me and I wrote it off as a shooting pain.

"Sorry, must have slept weird."

"I heard about the Magic Castle one, I love that place. But what's going on in Santa Monica?"

I pressed him to see what exactly he knew.

"Oh, well, it's this warehouse thing, and it's probably like a rave or something. I'm not too sure."

He doesn't seem like he would be into anything that's offered up at that party, he's way too boring for it.

"Ah, okay. I'm not really big on the clubs, but maybe I'll swing by. Could be fun!"

I smiled like an idiot back at them. Rather than let it linger, I cut off the awkward silence.

"Hey Marcus, I'm gonna swing by the bar again. Would you like anything else?"

"That would be lovely, just a gin and tonic please."

"Got it. How 'bout you, Adam?"

"No, I'm okay, thanks."

"Okay, be right back."

It wasn't until I took that first step away from them that I finally felt like I could breathe again.

How the hell do people do this for a living? I'm exhausted of smiling like some fake asshole, I just want to go back to being me. Maybe I should get out of here a little earlier than I thought and make sure everything is ready.

Considering I didn't have a fake tan or a ridiculous amount of cleavage, or a perfectly quaffed haircut with a nine-to-five shadow, the bartender took his sweet ass time to notice me. I forcibly held up a twenty.

"Hey, just a gin and tonic for me. Thanks."

I grabbed the change after another two minutes and headed back to Marcus who looked like he was in a rush as well.

Maybe he doesn't want to be around us anymore either. Wouldn't that be nice?

"Here is your drink, sir."

"Thank you so much!"

He started to sip it down in big gulps.

"Listen, I think I need to head out, unfortunately. It was lovely speaking to you gentlemen, and Adam, I'll consider what we discussed. Do you have a card on you?"

"You bet I do."

"Great. We'll be in touch. Ciao."

God, he can't be fucking serious? Ciao? Where are we dude? You're from Tallahassee and you say Ciao now? Fuck that.

Adam looked at me as soon as Marcus was out of our eye line.

"Well, I think that went pretty well. How are you doing?"

"I'm pretty good. I'm actually a little sore. How are you feeling about everything?"

"I'm feeling like we did some good work. Listen, I wanted to talk to you about tonight. I think us splitting up would be the best move, we could cover more ground for us. As you've heard, there are a lot of parties going on and we can't possibly hit them all together. Does that make sense? Are you up for that?"

Shit, we weren't going to do that in the first place?

"You look concerned, is everything okay?"

I nodded my head slowly.

"Yeah, yeah, everything's fine, man. Splitting up sounds okay. I was going to say, I might recuperate for a tiny bit before everything really kicks off. Is that alright?"

"Yeah, of course! No problem. It's a little weird putting on this act all day."

He patted me on the back, and continued.

"Listen, I think we did a great job so far for us. Eleanor seems pretty interested, Michael and Angelica, I'm not too sure on from earlier, but Marcus, Thomas, and John sound like they're all on board as well."

"Oh. Really? I'm not too sure about Marcus, but I agree with you on everything else."

"Yeah, man, splitting up sounds fine. Did you have something specific in mind?"

He paused and scratched his chin.

"Yeah, I think I do. How about you head over to the Magic Castle then over to Ink? I think I might check out everything over in Santa Monica. That kind of sounds fun, even though I'm not a rave guy either."

Shit.

"Okay, that sounds great to me, man! We'll catch up tomorrow then?"

"Yeah, that sounds fine. Just text me if you have any questions throughout the night or anything."

"Sounds good, man. I'll talk to you later."

Or maybe never again. Fuck.

* * *

AS SOON as Adam and I said our goodbyes, I rushed back to my car. I needed to shake off everything that I felt from all the drinks. First, I need to drive over to a gas station and get me some coffee. As

I did that, I was multitasking and checking my texts while stopped. I saved Brad's message which had the address in it, and made sure that I told Keith to cancel—that was a stupid idea in the first place—and before I started any of this, I took a peek into my trunk to make sure everything was still there and intact.

I tried to slow myself down, right before taking a sip of that horrifically sludgy gas station coffee, but I was so nervous and excited that it was useless. *It's also useless to try to relax considering caffeine is an upper and you need to get yourself sober from earlier dumbass.* May as well caffeine up. I took a couple of deep breathes and got started on the trek to Santa Monica. It was about twenty minutes of a drive, and I attempted to mellow myself out by listening to some Jets to Brazil.

Fuck, I love this band.

I couldn't help but think about the significance of what I was about to do. I was for the first time in a long time, pretty happy about myself, where I am and what I stood for. By the mere fact of me contributing at all to this industry that I've loved for so long, it was really quite rewarding.

Granted, I know was just about to intentionally kill god only knows how many people, but they were all corrupted, and poisonous and beyond the point of any return. As I pulled up to the building I noticed it was already smoking and I was very confused. I pulled up and rushed inside.

Brad was right, he did a great job with the place. It looked swanky, low-lit and atmospheric. If I had to be standing in a rape dungeon, I would definitely say that this was classiest of all of the rape dungeons—that I've seen at least. I noticed the smoke was from a smoke machine in the corner.

That's fucking perfect. This would cover the gas that I'm pumping into the building, and theoretically, it would cover the minor scent too!

It really was a great place, there were eight separate rooms in here and one huge open space as well.

It's a pretty big shame that I'll be blowing it the fuck up, but eh, what can you do?

After moving the car a bit further away—and a lot less conspicuously parked right in front of it—I grabbed all of my supplies, I made my way to the roof from the fire escape. I unloaded everything right by the air conditioning system. I put on my supplies and dragged those horrendously heavy Bipyridilium tanks in place. It was that perfect time in the night where the stars didn't quite set yet, so it was still very, very dark on this rooftop.

I took out my fuse from my pocket, and started uncoiling it around the roof. I wrapped it around the entire perimeter twice, with about four feet of distance between each line.

At about this time, I heard a car pull around the corner. I quickly laid down flat on the roof. I didn't dare to look up. I heard the engine turn off, followed by the clop of wooden shoes walking around and opening a car door. Then I heard a bunch of kids.

"Why are we here?"

A pouty, precocious voice asked.

"Well, you're here for a party tonight! It's a really important one. Aren't you excited?"

"This doesn't look like a party kind of place."

"Just wait 'til you all get inside. We might be the first people here, but that's okay."

"What are we celebrating?"

Another voice asked, this one was very, very shy.

"Well, I didn't want to spoil this, but we're all celebrating you kids! Everyone inside is just going to be so happy to see you. It'll be great!"

I cringed hearing their responses.

"Really? Oh, wow! I can't wait to tell Dad!"

That felt like a punch in the kidney.

"Listen, go wait in there. There will be some really important people coming soon. Just head inside, and go play a game, okay?"

"Ooh, we get to play a game?"

Other kids echoed that same sentiment. They were all so excited to be there.

"Yeah! Let's go play hide and seek!"

He continued on with these horrific lies.

"So listen, you're gonna go inside, and you're going to close your eyes and take off all of your clothes. Then, in just a little bit, some older friends you haven't met yet will come and find you. Doesn't that sound fun?"

They responded almost simultaneously. There was probably ten or twelve of them.

"Yeah, wow! That sounds cool!"

"Okay, so remember when your new friends come, be really nice to them and do anything they say. They are people that will be figuring out if they want you in their next movie, okay!"

"Okay, cool!"

"Alright, so I'm gonna leave you here and you'll have a nice sleepover with your new friends and I'll be back in the morning."

"Okay, we'll see you soon!"

"Wait, Sam? It's a little smoky in here, is it okay?"

"Yeah no worries, kid, that's just a smoke machine for the party. You're going to have so much fun! I can't wait to hear about it tomorrow. Bye, kiddos!"

"Bye, Sam!"

Again, all in unison.

Well, if hearing all of that didn't make me dead fucking sober, then nothing will. Christ, that was tough to hear.

I'd say about twenty minutes after listening to kids cough and giggle through the air ducts is when the first car pulled up. I took a peek.

Holy shit. It was Duncan, that asshole from Telluride. I thought he would be above this shit but I guess not. I looked up for just long enough to see him lick his lips as he walked up the ramp to the entrance.

Ugh, god that was gross.

I didn't want to think about what the hell was happening inside, but as the party progressed and more people arrived, I heard a lot more screams and squeals from those kids than anyone should ever hear in a lifetime. As fucked up as it is to say, as people kept arriving to whatever den of iniquity was below me, I got bored and browsed the news.

I waited and waited, and until about two hours in—after 30 cars showed up. I decided to swiftly head back down the fire escape, and start to bolt all the doors and exits of the building with those girders.

While I was doing that, I noticed that not parked too far away, was Adam's car.

Fuck, that stings.

I shook my head in disgust and climbed back up the escape. I didn't dare peer into the windows. I got back on the roof and I thought I was ready to finally get this over with. As soon as I inspected it all once last time, there were some Jets to Brazil lyrics from the album I listened to that stuck out to me.

"I can't wake up… from this."

This was a pretty big step, and there was no "waking up" or going back from this, but it needed to happen. I know what I was about to do, and I was too far in to go back now. Plus, I had a rough idea of the horrors that were going on downstairs. I shook out my nerves and got to business.

I screwed on the nozzle, and sprayed all the Bipyridilium I had into the ventilation duct of the roof. I lit the fuse, watched it ignite; then quickly got down the fire escape and ran over to my car. I heard it ignite, and I quickly got down the fire escape and walked over to my car. I turned it on and pulled out as fast as I could in the opposite direction. I heard the huge explosion. I was about a block and a half away.

Then I watched the fucker burn in my rearview mirror. This was a very gratifying kill; a quick and heartless mass genocide of perverts. I imagined thousands of barely audible screams. I smiled with relief and pride. Flames can be very soothing and cleansing.

Maybe, just maybe, this could be the end of FRAME as we know it. I think there were enough people in there. But either way, I played my fucking part.

www.ingramcontent.com/pod-product-compliance
Lightning Source LLC
Chambersburg PA
CBHW070444030726
47503CB00004B/885